Best wqy·

J Ryan Fenzel

*J Ryan Fnzd
24 Nov-18*

EQUAL
MEASURE

A Novel

Ironcroft Publishing

This book is a work of fiction. Names, characters, places, and incidents are the product of the author's imagination or are used fictitiously. Any resemblance to actual events, locales, or persons, living or dead, is coincidental.

Equal Measure

Copyright © 2018 by J. Ryan Fenzel

Cover Artist: Damonza

Interior Design: Thomas Gideon

All rights reserved. No part of this book may be used or reproduced in any manner whatsoever without written permission except in the case of brief quotations embodied in critical articles or reviews. For information address Ironcroft Publishing, P.O. Box 630, Hartland, MI 48353

Printed in the United States of America

First Printing: June 2018

ISBN-10: 0-9771688-5-9
ISBN-13: 978-0-9771688-5-9
1. Fiction – Action & Adventure
2. Fiction – Thrillers

In memory of my father
Arthur Raymond Fenzel

BOOK I

BLACKBIRD AND THE PHOENIX

Dawn. Five thousand feet. Two Pratt & Whitney turboprop engines roared on the wings of a Viking Twin Otter Series 400 aircraft, filling the cockpit with a constant drone. In the pilot's seat, Kade Mitchell regarded the clamor as white noise, consigning it to the background like he would the rhythm of rainfall. He had logged a lot of hours in a lot of planes, and had learned to filter out the benign sounds an aircraft makes from the whines, whirs, and shudders that heralded trouble. Still, it surprised him how quickly he had tuned back into the Otter's voice. He had been away from her for a long time. Two years to be exact. And to Kade Mitchell, two years away from the yoke felt like two years away from home. He had missed flying, missed the sky, but it was all behind him now. At least that's what he kept telling himself.

In the copilot's seat, a portly young man with disheveled hair and a scruffy beard bobbed his head in a losing battle to fight off sleep. Kade pulled a folded twenty-dollar bill from his shirt pocket and tickled the man's beard with it. "Cody, got something for you."

Cody startled awake and sat up straight. He scratched at his whiskers and brushed the breast of his Hawaiian shirt as if checking to see if he had drooled. "You say something?"

Kade waved the bill in front of his eyes. "This is yours."

Cody focused on it and then snatched it up. "For what?"

"The hunters we flew to Copper Harbor tipped us for carrying their gear off the dock."

"Oh." Cody thought a moment. "We both carried their gear. We should share this."

"We could split it, but half a twenty-dollar bill doesn't go very far."

"Well, I'll buy you a couple beers at The Cellar. How does that sound?"

"Just one sounds good."

"Right. That's what I meant." Cody gazed at the glow of the warm July sunrise. "I'm glad we're running again. I didn't like working at the dealership."

"I didn't like doing what I was doing either, but it's over now."

Bright rays of sun pierced the cockpit windows, and placid ripples danced on the surface of Lake Michigan below. Cody smiled. "Every time I see sunup, you know what I think about?"

Kade had a pretty good guess, but he didn't want to go there. "What?"

"All those times you, Travis, and I stayed out all night drinkin' and gettin' in trouble." Cody smiled wide. "If we didn't get picked up by the county boys, we'd sit on your back porch and wait on the sun." His smile slowly faded. "You ever think about him, Kade?"

Kade's voice caught and he cleared his throat. "Every day, buddy. Every day."

Cody cocked his head. "Wasn't it right after the funeral that you and Rachel started going through your thing?"

Kade scanned the instrument panel. "Yeah. When it rains, it pours."

"Guess so." Cody dropped silent. "Hey, I didn't mean to bring you down."

"It's okay. The past is the past. I'd be a fool to let it keep bashing me upside the head."

Cody nodded and then unbuckled his seatbelt. "The coffee's coming back around. Time for a pee break." He climbed out of the seat and headed back into the nineteen-seat passenger cabin.

Kade waited for him to go, and then reached for a scheduling folder he kept in the door pocket beside him. He thumbed through the paperwork until he found the edge of a photograph. He began working it free, but something caught his eye through the cockpit window.

A tiny plume of black smoke rose from a point on the western horizon. Something was on fire, most likely a ship. Kade bumped the port and starboard engine throttle levers and maneuvered the yoke, banking the aircraft into a gradual turn. The column of smoke drifted to cockpit center. The distance closed. A ship was indeed ablaze. Kade called into the passenger cabin. "Cody, get up here."

The lavatory door in the rear of the cabin burst open and Cody walked out. "What's wrong?"

"Found some trouble."

Cody's eyes popped and he cocked his head, listening. "Engines sound right." He touched the cabin wall like a trauma doctor. "Feels right. Where's our trouble?"

"It's not our trouble," Kade said. "It's theirs."

Cody worked his way up to the cockpit and immediately saw the smoke. "That's not just an engine burning oil."

"She's too big to be a pleasure craft," Kade said. "I'd say she's three hundred feet end to end, give or take. Most likely a merchant vessel of some sort." He glanced at the Otter's instrument panel, keeping tabs on flight status. "Maybe something in her hold caught fire."

Cody scratched the side of his head. "Whatever it is, it's gettin' the better of them."

Kade tuned the VHF radio to channel 16 and spoke into the boom mic on his headset. "Mayday. Mayday. Mayday. This is commercial aircraft November-3-2-7-Delta-Bravo." He repeated the hail two more times while checking coordinates on the GPS display. "Heading 1-8-5 degrees at position 4-4-2-0 North and 8-6-6-0 West. Ship in distress. She appears to be a merchant vessel, three hundred feet LOA, on fire and listing." Kade reached up and eased the throttle levers back a touch, gradually dropping the Otter to a better observation altitude.

A woman's voice responded through the radio. "Aircraft November-3-2-7-Delta-Bravo, this is Coast Guard Station Frankfort, channel 1-6. Please confirm your location. Over."

Kade again read the coordinates from the GPS display.

"Roger. Good copy on position. Is distressed vessel under power?"

"Negative," Kade replied. "I don't see a wake behind her. I think she's drifting."

"Roger. Request status of persons on board distressed vessel. Over."

"Stand by."

The Otter had nearly reached the ship; Kade flew directly over her beam, five hundred feet off the water. "I see people topside, but no boats or floatation devices in the water. I count six, maybe seven souls."

"Roger that." The radio fell silent.

Kade banked the Otter into a wide turn to circle back.

"Aircraft November-3-2-7-Delta-Bravo, this is Coast Guard Station Frankfort. A boat and chopper are dispatched. Can you maintain position near distressed vessel? Over."

Kade eyed the fuel gauge. "Half a tank," he said to Cody. "That gives us ninety minutes of hang time before we have to break for home. You agree?"

Cody shrugged. "Sure, ninety minutes sounds about right."

Kade spoke into the mic. "Coast Guard Station Frankfurt, this is aircraft November-3-2-7-Delta-Bravo. Affirmative. We can hold position ninety minutes. Nine zero. Over."

"Roger that."

"How long on the response team?"

"ETA of response team is thirty minutes, Three zero. Over."

"Copy that." Kade put the Otter in a wide circular pattern above the ship. Far below, beneath a blanket of black smoke, the crew of the floundering vessel rushed back and forth, but something in their actions didn't seem right. "What the hell are they doing?" Kade said. "They're not fighting the fire and they're not abandoning ship either?"

"One of them just tossed something overboard. Maybe they're trying to save the boat by lightening the load."

Kade thought it through. "My mayday call was the first the Coast Guard had heard about this. That crew didn't get a message out. Whatever happened must have happened fast, and it took out their communication gear." Kade checked the turn-and-slip indicator on the instrument panel, confirming with the needle inside the gauge that he had the aircraft in a standard two-minute circle pattern, but the more he considered the unfolding scenario, the more discontent he became with just holding position above the ship. "That crew is in serious trouble," he said to Cody. "They may not have thirty minutes to wait for a cutter. Know what I mean?"

"Yeah," Cody said. "We have the floats installed. We could set down next to that ship, but the dispatcher said to just stay in the area, not to land and assist."

"She didn't know we're flying an amphibious airplane."

"Landing and taking on a bunch of passengers changes the fuel calculations. Getting back home could get dicey."

"I can do dicey."

"Kade, I want to help them too, but if we get ourselves into trouble by—"

A fiery plume suddenly burst from the vessel's starboard side. Cody's jaw fell open. "Okay, let's go."

"Roger that." Kade broke the Otter out of the circle pattern and headed downwind to set up his approach. "Cody, secure the cabin."

The ship listed hard to starboard. Still no lifeboats in the water. Still no life vests. Kade turned the Otter for final approach and pulled back the throttle levers to three-quarters. Airspeed bled off. He lowered the flaps and pitched the nose down. The Otter passed through a hazy patch of smoke. Altitude decreased. Kade finessed the yoke, kept the plane level. Twenty feet off the water he pitched the nose up, just past the horizon, and then chopped the throttle to zero. Waves grabbed onto the floats and plumes of water shot into the air. The plane decelerated. Kade braced himself against the lurching motion until the ride smoothed to a gentle rolling pitch. He had hit the mark dead on. The Otter taxied fifty yards abeam of the burning ship.

"Cody, break open the first-aid kit and pull my hiking pack from rear baggage. I've got a kit in there too. No telling how many people are injured."

Cody unbuckled and pulled out of his seat. "I'm on it."

Kade steered the Otter closer to the sinking vessel. Smoke obscured the aft section of the boat, but a breeze thinned the haze long enough to reveal a crewman tossing a container over the side. It sank as soon as it hit the water. On the bow, another crewman waved toward the plane, but he seemed to be signaling, *Get out of here.*

Kade didn't quite believe his eyes. *Doesn't this guy know he's on a sinking ship?*

On the vessel's aft quarter, a third crewman threw a dirty, white cube overboard. About a foot square on each side, it splashed into the water and sank, taking with it a line that was fixed to one of its faces. A small buoy with a red marker flag was tied to the other end of the line, and it too disappeared below the surface into the lake.

And then it clicked—and the hairs pricked on the back of Kade's neck. He twisted in his seat and called into the cabin. "Cody, forget the first-aid kit."

Cody had his hands on a large hiking pack and was pulling it free from the rear baggage compartment. He shouted over his shoulder. "What?"

"These guys don't want help."

A crewman with a pistol in his hand emerged from the ship's wheelhouse and staggered across the angled deck to a bow handrail. He steadied himself to take aim … at the Otter.

"You've got to be kidding." Kade powered up the engines. "Cody, get down."

The crewman fired and the pistol muzzle flashed against a patch of black smoke. A ray of sun blazed through a bullet hole in the cockpit side wall, just behind the pilot's seat. Kade pulled back the starboard throttle to prompt a clockwise turn away from the ship. "Cody!"

"I'm all right. What's going on?"

"They're smugglers, and they're dumping their cargo."

Kade peered through the cockpit window. The nose of the plane had turned clear of the ship. He throttled up the starboard engine to cancel the spin. Another series of gunshots sounded and the port engine sputtered. Propeller RPMs dropped off. The Otter heeled back toward the ship. "Cody, port engine took a hit." Kade cut power to both engines and then called into the boom mic. "Coast Guard Station Frankfort, this is aircraft November-3-2-7-Delta-Bravo. Be advised, the crew of the distressed vessel is armed and dangerous."

After a pause, the dispatcher responded. "Did not copy last transmission. Say again. Over."

Kade cursed and transmitted again. "It's a smuggling ship. The crew is dumping cargo. They have fired on my plane. Tell the response team they're walking into a hornets' nest."

"Roger that. Is your aircraft damaged?"

"My port engine took a hit. It's winding down."

"Can you maintain altitude?"

Kade hesitated. "I'm not in the air. I'm down on the lake. I have floats on the plane and I landed to offer assistance."

Another pause. "Response team is nearly there. Keep clear of distressed vessel."

"Roger that." Kade stopped transmitting. "Brilliant advice," he muttered.

Another cluster of reports sounded. Two more crewmen had joined the first in firing at the Otter. A bullet blew through a passenger window in the main cabin and cobwebbed the glass with cracks. Kade's anger flared. "We can't just sit here like a rubber duck in a shooting gallery. Cody, can you reach my gear in rear baggage?"

"Hold on." Cody shoved the hiking pack aside and reached into the compartment. "I'm guessing you want the Scoutmaster."

"You got it." Kade crawled from the pilot's seat and crouched in the center of the cockpit. "Slide it to me."

Cody extracted a black case from the compartment and slid it down the center aisle between the two rows of passenger seats. Kade stopped it with both hands and popped a pair of clasps along the seam. He lifted the lid. A Marlin lever action 45/70 rifle lay nestled in a bed of black foam. Customized with a shortened barrel and ammo tube, the weapon was a compact piece of iron Kade used as an insurance policy against bear and wolves on the northern trails that he sometimes guided charter groups through. Today, however, he faced a different kind of predator. He lifted the rifle from the case and frowned. "Sorry I got you into this, Cody."

"You didn't know these guys were psycho smugglers."

"No, but you didn't want to come down in the first place." Kade grabbed a handful of shells from a box in the case and began feeding them into the rifle's loading gate. "If I'd listened to you, this wouldn't have happened."

Cody gave him a nervous smile. "Okay, when we get back to Sparta, you owe *me* a beer."

"Deal." The Otter's engines rumbled at idle, with the port side belching and stammering. Kade wondered how bad it was damaged. He filled the Marlin's magazine to capacity with four shells, and then stuck his hand through the lever and worked the action, chambering a round with a click. He engaged the safety and made eye contact with Cody. "Stay down."

"What are you going to do?"

"I'm going to make these guys think twice about popping holes in my airplane." Kade worked his way to the port hatch in the passenger cabin, keeping out of sight below the windows. "Take cover in the baggage compartment."

Cody raised a finger. "They've stopped shooting," he said. "Maybe they decided saving themselves is more important than killing us."

"Maybe." Kade clicked off the rifle's safety. He unlatched the passenger hatch and, as usual, it did not lift open on its hydraulic assist like it was supposed to, but he had counted on that. He took the Marlin into both hands, set the butt against his shoulder, and then positioned his foot to kick open the hatch. "Let's find out what they're up to."

"Wait." Cody lifted his gaze to the cabin ceiling. "You hear that?"

Kade listened. A thumping sound wrapped in mechanical thunder swelled in the sky.

"They're here." Kade kicked open the hatch as a Coast Guard helicopter roared overhead. She was an MH-65C Dolphin, and she came in low, so low that Kade felt he could reach up and touch her red body. She soared into position off the ship's starboard quarter, and a guardsman behind a door-mounted machine gun fired a volley of shots. A line of impact geysers erupted in the lake alongside the vessel.

Crewmen on the listing, smoke-choked deck threw up their hands in surrender.

"They're giving up to the Guard," Cody said.

"I think they call that the 'nick of time.'" Kade clicked on the rifle's safety with a sigh of relief, but something in his head told him this little adventure was not over. No, something was telling him it had just begun.

TWO

Kade sat with his feet dangling over the forward edge of the port wing, watching an oil slick spread over the spot where the cargo ship had gone down. He was listening to a Coast Guard lieutenant speak to him from a rigid-hull inflatable bobbing ten yards away. Cody crouched beside Kade with his hands inside an open access panel on the damaged engine. Kade squinted in the mid-morning sun, second-guessing his decision to land. Would he do it again? Probably. In his estimate, big stakes required bold decisions.

"Mr. Mitchell?"

Kade snapped out of his thoughts. "Yes, Lieutenant?"

"I asked if there was anything else you recall from your encounter with the crew."

"Nothing else," Kade said. "I landed. They waved me off, started shooting. You know as well as I do they're smugglers of some sort."

The lieutenant nodded. "That may well be true, but we didn't find any contraband on their ship before it went under. We'll detain them for the assault on your plane. If you can ID the shooters, they'll get charged with attempted murder. Think you can do that?"

"It happened fast. There was a lot of smoke. I doubt I could pick them out in a lineup. Maybe the first guy." Kade handed Cody a wrench from a tool bag on the wing. "Tell you what, Lieutenant, send a diver down underneath that oil slick and he'll find the crates that the crew dumped overboard. That'll give you something else to hold them on."

"You're that sure they're smugglers?"

Kade nodded. "Better yet, wait a few days. I saw them toss in a buoy marker tethered to a salt block. Once the salt dissolves, that buoy will shoot to the surface right above their precious cargo. That's how they intend to find it later for recovery."

The lieutenant thought about that a moment and smiled. "How'd you figure that out?"

Kade stood on the wing and brushed off his hands. "The History Channel did a show about smugglers a while back. They're creative criminals. Fascinating stuff." Not completely candid, but Kade thought it best not to go into detail about his knowledge.

"Guess I missed that one," the lieutenant said. "I'm sure we'll be following up with you for a statement about the incident, probably another interview during the investigation. Is the contact information you provided the best way to reach you?"

"Yes. Unless I'm flying through a dead zone."

"That shouldn't be a problem."

"What I want to know," Kade said, "is how the chopper got here so quick. The dispatcher estimated a thirty-minute ETA, but it got here in about half that."

"Different chopper," the lieutenant said through a wind gust. "A Dolphin from Tactical Squadron was in the vicinity on an interdiction drill and intercepted the dispatch."

"This must be my lucky day."

The lieutenant smiled. "Lucky would have been staying airborne."

Kade forced a laugh. "Can't argue that."

"Can we be of any further assistance to you, Mr. Mitchell?"

Kade checked with Cody. The mechanic shook his head. "I think we're good," Kade said. "Fortunately, the bullet just punctured a fuel line to the injector. Cody's splicing in a patch that will get us back home. If we come across any more trouble, I'll be calling you back."

"Channel one six." The lieutenant smiled. "Semper paratus."

Kade waved farewell and then walked down the centerline of the Otter's topside, careful to not step on an antenna in the avionics array. He slid through the open passenger door in the main cabin and started forward. The shattered port window gave him pause, and he remembered the bullet that had punched through the cockpit door. He continued forward and sat in the pilot's seat. A warm breeze blew in through the jagged hole in the door. Kade assessed the damage and found that the bullet had ripped through the side pocket too, where he kept the scheduling folder. He pulled out the folder and rifled through its contents, extracting the photograph he had searched for earlier.

No damage. Kade exhaled and settled back to gaze at the image. It was Rachel, his wife, or rather, his ex-wife, taken four years ago while she stood beneath the Otter's port wing, looking off beyond the camera. She wasn't smiling, but Kade knew she was happy. It was right after he had purchased the dilapidated plane from a graveyard of decommissioned government aircraft, back when their charter business had great promise. It was before Rachel had lost her faith in him, before her sister Leah had died, before dark days and bad decisions. It was a time before her smile disappeared.

Kade knew all her expressions well. Every line of her face and her moods and her quirks. That she liked coconut milk in her coffee. Put Post-It notes on the floor to remind herself of things. And that she cherished her family and respected her father. The only thing he did not know, for certain, is why she gave up on their marriage so quickly.

Kade considered the picture. In the age of digital photography, a black-and-white photograph was about as cutting-edge as a handwritten letter, but to him it was a tangible reminder that at one time, for a little while, he had everything he had ever wanted.

"I think that should do it," Cody said from the port wing, directing his voice through the open cockpit window. "Fire it up. Let's see what happens."

Kade slid the photograph into the folder and returned it to the side pocket. He glanced out the window to make sure the lieutenant had moved off in the rigid-hull inflatable. He had. He was headed toward his cutter stationed fifty yards west. Kade scanned the instrument panel and flicked the fuel switches to normal position. "Clear?"

"Clear," Cody replied. "Let her rip."

Kade engaged the start switch and the propeller began to turn on battery power. Indicators showed oil pressure rising and the rotor spin stabilizing. Kade hit the fuel switch. Light off. The engine kicked and sputtered. RPMs rose nice and steady. "Good job, Cody."

Cody pumped his fist. "Let's go home. You owe me two beers."

"Two beers?" Kade stepped through the start-up procedure for the starboard engine. "I only owe you one."

Cody slithered into the main cabin through the passenger door, buttoned it shut, and took the copilot's seat. "One beer for getting us into trouble, and one for fixing the engine." He laughed, and then noticed the bullet hole in the pilot side door. "Did Rachel survive?"

Kade nodded. "Yeah, she's fine."

"You going to call and tell her about this?"

Kade maneuvered the Otter into the wind. "I stopped calling when she stopped answering."

Cody put on a dopey smile. "If at first you don't succeed ..."

Kade didn't bother to respond.

"You know," Cody said, "you used to be more positive."

"A lot has gone down in the last few years." Kade slid the throttle levers forward for takeoff. "Some things are hard to get around."

Cody's face fell. "Yeah, I know."

Kade felt Travis's ghost pass through the cockpit, and he laughed aloud to lighten the mood. "Smugglers," he said. "Who would have guessed?"

Cody cracked a half smile. "Kind of leftfield, wasn't it?"

The Otter bounced over wave crests and began to gain altitude. Kade eased back the yoke, angling the nose of the plane skyward. The Otter climbed. At cruising altitude, he leveled her out and then settled back in his seat.

Smugglers, he thought, *who would have guessed?*

THREE

Michigan Intelligence Operational Center (MIOC)
Lansing, Michigan

"Why?"

Department of Homeland Security Agent Ely Edwards rested his arm on the half wall of Lieutenant Gabriel Walker's cubicle, waiting for Walker to look up from his desk. He didn't. Instead, the Coast Guard officer continued to peruse a mess of paperwork in front of him. Ely wrapped his knuckles on the wall. "Lieutenant Walker."

Walker glanced up. "What?"

Ely leaned forward just a touch. "Why?"

"Why what?"

"Why did the chopper from Tactical Squadron get redirected this morning?"

Walker's jaw hung open as if he did not understand the question. "Ely, I told you why ten minutes ago at your desk, and you didn't even acknowledge I was there."

"I was on the phone with my daughter."

"I thought you two weren't on speaking terms."

"We're not."

Walker leaned back. "Not being on speaking terms usually means no speaking."

"She's making an effort to connect, so I was connecting."

Walker nodded his understanding. "Did she ask you for money? My daughters usually want to connect with me when they need cash."

Ely frowned. "Rachel's twenty-nine, and she holds a corporate position at an international company where she makes more money than I do. She's past asking dad for a loan."

"Lucky you. My girls haven't gotten past it yet. They're in college."

"Gabriel," Ely said, a bit agitated, "why did you tell me about the chopper?"

Walker looked at Ely as if it was a silly question. "Because of the cargo ship."

Ely just stared at him.

Walker straightened his back. "At six fifteen this morning, Coast Guard Station Frankfort received a mayday call from a Good Samaritan reporting a merchant vessel in distress. They dispatched a cutter and a rescue chopper to the site. A few minutes later, they received word that the crew of the merchant vessel was shooting at the Good Sam, who was trying to help them out. Meanwhile, a chopper from Tactical Squadron, flying an interdiction circuit in the area, intercepts the chatter, contacts the dispatcher, and redirects to the sinking vessel to intervene. And, guess what?"

"What?"

"The merchant vessel turns out to be a smuggling ship." Lieutenant Walker paused, and then added, "I guess I should say a *suspected* smuggling ship."

Ely perked up. "Smugglers?"

"Yeah." Walker glanced at a sheet of paper on his desk. "Suspected. See, the interdiction team boarded the ship, but it was sinking too fast and they had to abandon their search before they actually found any illicit cargo. All they have is the eyewitness account of the Good Samaritan, who says he saw the crew dumping cargo while he was being shot at."

"That's all they've got?"

"Yeah, but it's a good bet the crew didn't open fire on the guy to protect a load of limestone. They must have been carrying something else."

"No kidding."

Walker shrugged. "I figured this might fit into that trafficking database you're building."

"Thanks. It'll help me arrange the bones of a theory I'm piecing together."

"Show me the carcass," Walker said. "I'm interested."

"I haven't collected enough bones to share yet. It still looks like the remains of a KFC chicken dinner, and I don't want you to think of me as the wacky DHS guy at MIOC."

"Too late, Ely."

"Thanks. Did the interdiction team get the cargo ship's name and registration documents?"

Walker spun the sheet of paper he had been reading from so Ely could read it. "She was the *Olympia*, enrolled out of Buffalo, bound for Chicago. Vessel documents say she was owned and operated by a small shipping company headquartered in New York."

Olympia. The name sparked in Ely's head. He lifted the paper from the desk and scanned through the incident report. While reading it, his cell phone buzzed with a text notification. He checked and found a message from his daughter, Rachel.

Sorry, Dad, can't meet today. Something came up at work.

Of course.

Ely gestured to Lieutenant Walker with the sheet of paper. "Can I have this?"

"Sure. Let me know if it helps."

"Will do." Ely stepped from the cubicle. "Thanks for the information." He headed back to his desk through the operations area, glancing at the large video monitors displaying newsfeeds as he passed. He typed a reply to Rachel's message.

That's ok. We'll get together some other time. Good to finally hear from you.

He sat at his desk and opened a spreadsheet on his laptop titled *Discord* and clicked through the tabs. He settled on the one labeled "Suspect Vessels." A long list of names and corresponding registration data popped up. They were all names of ships suspected of participating in trafficking activity. Ely had been collecting the information for over a year, some of it coming from documents seized during raids conducted by the Coast Guard and the Customs and Border Protection Agency, some of it gleaned through interviews of individuals detained in said raids, but all of it tying a ship to either a known drug trafficking player or a port of call known to be used by a bona fide trafficking organization. After a year of collecting bits and pieces, he had compiled quite a list of suspect vessels, and all of them were potentially plying their illicit trade on the Great Lakes. Ely scrolled down the alphabetized list of vessel names, through the Ls, into the Ms. Another text pinged in.

Why say "finally" hear from you? Comms is a two-way street, right?

Ely frowned. Apparently poor word choice. He replied.

Did not mean anything by "finally." Don't read into it.

He scrolled a little farther down the list on the laptop screen, and then grabbed his phone and sent a follow-up message.

But it HAS been two months.

He took a moment to consider the wisdom of sending that follow-up text, but then went back to the monitor. He found the *Olympia* among the few vessels beginning with the letter O. Ely's information corroborated the Coast Guard report. A small New York shipping company owned the vessel: Adams Bros. Marine. Ely clicked the name *Olympia*, and it linked him to a navigation chart of the Great Lakes with an overlay of a shipping route from Buffalo, New York, to Chicago, Illinois, the exact route the cargo ship had been on when she sank in Lake Michigan. He checked the Coast Guard report for the coordinates of the sinking and dropped an icon resembling a tall ship with a broken keel at the corresponding coordinates on the chart. "That makes thirteen this year," Ely said to himself.

His phone buzzed again.

Maybe I didn't want to hear preaching, Pastor Edwards.

Ely exhaled. Why did it always lead to this? He typed a reply.

I wanted dinner with my daughter, that's all. No preaching.

He tossed the phone on his desk and returned to the laptop, calling up a composite view of the navigation chart. Twelve more shipping routes appeared, as well as twelve more broken ship icons, each denoting a location that a trafficking vessel had sunk, or the general area where it had disappeared.

"What's going on, fellas?"

Ely focused on the icon he added for the *Olympia*. "Can't confirm you yet. You're still just a suspect." He changed the color of the icon from red to blue and got up from his chair. On the way out of the cubicle, he heard his phone buzz. He picked it up.

If you say so. We'll talk later. Gotta run.

If I say so? Ely shook his head and crossed the operations area to Lieutenant Walker's desk. The Coast Guard officer had his head buried in paperwork again. Ely wrapped his knuckles on the half wall. Walker slowly lifted his chin.

"The Good Samaritan who witnessed the crew dumping cargo …" Ely said. "I didn't see his name in the report. Think you can find that out for me? I want to talk with him."

Lieutenant Walker frowned. "Would you mind terribly if my Coast Guard brethren take his official statement first, before you grill him?"

"Sort of," Ely said. "I'm not good with the patience thing."

They stared at each other a long moment.

"Okay," Walker said. "I'll get you his name. Give me a few minutes."

Ely waited.

Walker shooed him away like he would a fly. "I said a few minutes. Maybe longer."

"Fine. I'll be at my desk." Ely started away, talking absently to himself. "Poor guy. That Good Samaritan was probably out fishing and ended up getting a gun stuck in his face."

"He wasn't fishing," Walker said. "He's a pilot. Has a seaplane or something."

Ely stopped. "What did you say?"

"I said he's a pilot." Walker sorted through the mess on his desk.

An improbable notion popped into Ely's head and he chuckled. *Not likely.* He took two more steps. Stopped again. He couldn't shake it. "Gabriel, you got that name yet?"

"Damn it, Ely!"

Ely raised his hands in defense. "All right, I'm going." He started for his desk again. "I half expect you to say his name is Kade—"

"Mitchell." Lieutenant Walker said.

Ely spun around.

Walker stood and spoke over the cubicle. "That Good Sam's name is Kade Mitchell."

"For real?"

"Yeah. What's the matter, you know him?"

"You bet I do. He was my son-in-law."

"No kidding?" Walker looked surprised. "What are the odds of that?"

"Apparently better than I thought." Ely chewed on it a bit. "Guess I'm going to catch up with my daughter's ex."

Ely walked through the operations area digesting the news. Indeed, what were the odds that Kade would turn up at the site of a suspected smuggler's ship sinking?

In retrospect, they were actually pretty good.

– FOUR –

Sparta Airport, Sparta, Michigan

Kade confirmed his order for the glass he would need to repair the Otter's cabin window, reiterated an overnight delivery, and ended his call with the sales rep. He downed the last of a cold coffee and shoved the empty mug next to another empty mug on his desk. The old swivel chair squeaked when he stood, as it always did. Kicking a box of paperwork out of the way, he pushed open the office door into the hangar bay, just in time to catch an eyeful of flash. White spots filled his vision. He blinked and called across the floor toward a MIG welding setup in the corner. "Danny, could you please put up the damned flash curtain?"

A welder, clad in a black flame-resistant coat and flash helmet, looked up from a steel worktable and feigned deafness. Kade realized the buzz of a small engine was filling the air. Cody had the Otter hooked up to a motorized tug and was repositioning the plane for repair work. Kade gestured to him with a cutting motion across the throat. Cody switched off the tug's motor.

"The flash curtain," Kade said to the welder. "Put it up before you burn out my retinas."

Danny peeled off the helmet, unveiling a blonde ponytail and silver hoop earrings. She set her gaze on Kade. "Sorry, sweetheart. Didn't see you come out."

"If the curtain was up, it wouldn't have mattered if you saw me or not."

Danny gave him a playful smile and slowly pulled a red, opaque curtain closed across the front of the worktable.

"I got the glass coming overnight," Kade said to Cody. "How'd you do with the fuel line?"

"I'm picking it up this afternoon. Why the big rush?"

"I booked a run to Minneapolis. Wheels up in three days."

"Three days? When were you going to tell me? Two days from now?"

"Sorry. It slipped my mind."

"Sometimes you make it hard to be your mechanic." Cody went back to work, disconnecting a pair of towing lugs from the Otter's forward spreader bar.

Danny pulled back the red flash curtain. "Oh, before *I* forget. Some guy came looking for you about an hour ago. You and Cody were out scrounging for the patch kit."

Kade faced her. "Who was it?"

She shrugged. "Ed something. I don't remember his name, but he reminded me of my dad. Carried himself like ex-military, you know, always at attention." She shook her head. "Wonder if he's a prick like my old man."

"Ed something? That doesn't help. Why didn't you write down his name?"

"I'm not your secretary, Kade."

"I didn't say you were."

"Sounded that way to me." She loaded a bracket into a jig on the worktable, positioned her MIG torch, and flipped down the helmet.

"Danny, I didn't mean—"

"Eyes," she snapped, and struck an arc.

Kade turned his head, avoiding the flash this time. *Touchy.* He approached the Otter, thinking about his mystery visitor. *Ed somebody. Ex-military. Possibly a prick. Wonder who.*

"How are things, Kade?"

A tall, lanky form stood silhouetted by the afternoon sun in the open hangar door. Kade recognized the man's stance right away. Relaxed confidence. Yes, the guy was ex-military, a Navy officer to be precise, and then a Coast Guard officer, and then a Homeland Security agent.

A prick? Frequently.

Ed somebody. Edwards. Ely Edwards.

Shit.

"Ely," Kade said. "Why are you here?"

Ely didn't answer, but silently stepped into the hangar. Kade's mind raced through all the possible reasons for the unannounced visit. One struck him with concern. "Is she okay?"

Ely stood a good ten feet from Kade, giving the Otter a once over. "Rachel's fine. This has nothing to do with her."

Kade relaxed a bit. "It's not my birthday, and I don't see a beer in your hand, so you must be here on business."

Ely raised an eyebrow. "Business? Are you expecting someone from a federal agency?"

"Hardly." Kade felt his heart beat a little faster. The ex-father-in-law was pushing buttons.

Ely smiled and strolled around the airplane. "I heard you were humping the line in Flat Rock, building Mustangs for Ford ever since … you know."

"Don't believe everything you hear." Kade concealed how close Ely had come to hitting the mark.

"I don't believe everything," Ely chuckled. "Just some things." He continued strolling around the Otter, studying it carefully. It didn't take him long to spot the shattered passenger window. "What happened there?"

It then fell into place. The cargo ship. The crew of smugglers. The Coast Guard's incident report. It would all funnel through MIOC and right onto Ely's desk. "You know what happened," Kade said. "That's why you're here."

"I know facts from a sheet of paper. You know the story behind them. I want to hear it."

A twinge of anger surged in Kade's chest. "I'm not involved with those guys."

"I never said you were."

"Just showing up here tells me you think I am."

"You witnessed an incident involving suspected traffickers and a Coast Guard interdiction team. Witness interviews are SOP."

"You're not with the Coast Guard anymore. This isn't your playground."

"I'm with Homeland Security. *Everything* is my playground."

"Damn it, Ely. If you've got something to say, then say it."

"Why are you so defensive?"

"Because you're being offensive."

Ely smiled. "If your hands are clean, you've got nothing to worry about."

"If you were impartial I'd have nothing to worry about."

Cody and Danny began paying attention to the elevated conversation.

Kade realized he had his fist clenched.

Ely thought a moment or two, and then relaxed the hard expression on his face and dialed back his tone half a degree. "Just tell me what you saw, what you know, and I'll be on my way."

"It's in the Coast Guard's incident report."

Ely did not reply.

"Fine." Kade took a breath. "I'm dead heading back from Copper Harbor. I see a ship burning. I radio in a mayday on behalf of the vessel, and then, for some stupid reason, I decide to go down and offer assistance. Instead of thanking me, they shoot at me. The Coast Guard arrives to save the day. End of story."

"That's it?"

"That's it."

Ely stared at him a long while. "Was it your intention to be at those coordinates at that time?"

"No."

"Did you know or are you acquainted with anyone aboard that vessel?"

"Absolutely not."

"Are you sure?"

"I didn't actually meet the crew. They were too busy shooting at me. But if you're asking if it's possible one of them might know me, sure, that's possible." Kade added, "And tomorrow I might win the Mega Millions jackpot."

Ely frowned. "You were dead heading from Copper Harbor. Who chartered your plane there?"

"A group of hunters from Monroe."

"Any of them friends or past acquaintances?"

"No."

"Did you pick up any items or packages in Copper Harbor?"

"No."

"Did you make any unscheduled stops between Copper Harbor and the site of the sinking?"

"No."

Ely recited from memory the dates and locations that the twelve trafficking vessels sank. "Were you at any of those locations on those dates?"

"No." Kade set his jaw. "This feels like an interrogation."

"We call them interviews," Ely said. "And I'm just asking questions."

"Are you through?"

"Almost. Just one more."

Kade wanted this to be over. "Shoot."

"Why did you fly for them?"

Kade stared hard at him. "You're not talking about this morning, are you?"

"No."

"Go to hell, Ely." Kade turned his back and stormed off. "We're done."

Ely watched him go. "I doubt that."

Kade marched into his small office and slammed the door. Danny stood back from the worktable and flipped up her welding helmet. She and Cody exchanged a glance. Ely focused on the office door, as if contemplating whether to follow him in or not, but his cell phone distracted him with a text notification. He read the message and then gestured to Cody. "Tell Kade I may be back later with a few more questions."

Cody nodded. "Yeah, sure, Ely."

"Take care of yourself, Cody." Ely walked out of the hangar.

Danny set her helmet on the worktable. "What was all that about?"

Cody watched Ely disappear around the corner. "Ely and Kade never really got along. I mean, Kade's not even married to Rachel anymore, and Ely still gives him crap about it." Cody shrugged. "Guess it takes a long time for hard feelings to go away."

Danny pulled off the welding jacket and hung it on a hook near the worktable. "What happened between them to get Ely so pissed?"

Cody thought it over. "You'll have to ask Kade."

Danny glanced at the closed office door. "I think I will."

FIVE

Ely dropped into the driver's seat of his Chevy Tahoe and re-read the text message.

The Blackbird is cooking. You want it?

It was from a man named Daryl Cobb, a crime boss underling whom Ely had been trying to turn informant for months. The message seemed to indicate he was ready to flip. Looking into Kade's potential misdealing would have to wait. Ely sent a response to Cobb's message.

Yes. Where and when?

He started the engine and pulled out of the gravel parking lot. Before turning onto Vinton Avenue, his phone chimed with a text notification.

Lake Huron. Off Port Austin. Numbers and time to follow.

"All right, Cobb, it's about time." Ely set course for the MIOC office in Lansing, and then called Lieutenant Walker. The Coast Guard officer answered with an unenthusiastic hello.

"Gabriel, I need you to pull together Gerard, Anders, and Decosta for a meeting."

"All those names are above my pay grade, Ely. What's up?"

"I think I've got an interdiction opportunity."

"Think?" Walker said. "You want me to call together the State Intelligence Officer, the Ninth District Interdiction Tactical Commander, and the FBI Liaison Officer because you *think* you have an interdiction opportunity?"

"Confidence is high," Ely said. "Just got tipped off to a meth ship operation."

"Who's the source?"

"I'll tell you when I get there. About an hour. Thanks, Gabriel." Ely disconnected.

On the drive down Interstate 96, Cobb sent a text message comprising geo coordinates and a time. Ely rolled into Lansing with a smile on his face. He walked into the MIOC offices on the third floor of the State Police Headquarters building and met up with Lieutenant Walker.

"Did you get the players I asked for?" Ely said.

"You're welcome," Walker said. "Yes, I got all but Special Agent Decosta, who's in Detroit and can't make it back in time, so the FBI won't be represented."

"That'll have to do." Ely checked the time on his phone. "How soon until they get here?"

"About fifteen minutes."

"Perfect. Thanks, Gabriel."

Ely walked to his cubicle and reviewed the *Discord* spreadsheet on his computer. All that data and he still could not determine what had thrown the Great Lakes trafficking underworld into upheaval. Did Cobb have the answer? Ely certainly hoped so, because he did not have the evidence to support the theories he had concocted. And if he didn't know what was happening, he couldn't stop it; and if the violence kept escalating, innocent people we're sure to get caught up in it, maybe even Rachel. Her job with a freight company might put her aboard a merchant ship at some point, potentially in the crossfire. Ely could not bear if something happened to her, not after what happened to Leah.

He printed off the incident chart and the enrollment sheet and made his way to one of MIOC's vacant meeting rooms. Along the way, he met Coast Guard Commander Robert Gerard. The barrel-chested officer with a regulation brush cut gave him a half smile. "Walker told me you wanted to meet about an interdiction. Did you finally gain some insight into the surge of drug activity on the Lakes?"

"It's not quite that, Bob, but it is good. Trust me."

A tall, lanky man in a white shirt and black tie caught up with them as they filed into the meeting room. A badge dangling from his shirt pocket identified him as State Intelligence Officer Gary Anders, from the Department of Homeland Security. He scrutinized Ely a moment. "Walker says you have a hot tip on a potential interdiction target, but he didn't give any details."

Ely stood near a whiteboard at the head of the conference table. "That's all I told him."

"It's not much to call us together," Anders said.

"You'll understand shortly."

Commander Gerard sat down at the pressed-wood table and looked at his watch. Gary Anders seated himself across from Gerard. "Okay, Ely, what've you got?"

"I've got Daryl Cobb."

"For real?"

Commander Gerard glanced between them. "Who's Cobb?"

"Cobb is a well-placed lackey in the Ricco Perry organization," Ely said.

"You mean Great Lakes drug runner Ricco Perry?" Gerard said.

"Alleged drug runner," Anders corrected. "Perry's good at isolating himself from his operations. The DEA hasn't been able to stick him with any solid charges yet."

Gerard shifted in his chair. "We intercepted four of Mr. Perry's go-fast boats this year, all loaded down with heroin. I don't mean to allege anything, but the guy is dirty as they come."

"And he's slippery," Anders said.

"That just changed," Ely said. "Daryl Cobb is turning on him."

Anders crinkled his eyebrows. "How did you finally get Cobb to turn?"

"I don't know. I kept him out of jail after that Port Huron raid a few months back. Been working him ever since, trying to get him to break. For some reason, today he did."

"Why is DHS so interested in Ricco Perry?" Gerard said. "He's a regional drug thug. I figure you guys would be more interested in international terrorists and leave Perry to the DEA."

"We suspect Perry is involved in something bigger," Anders said.

"Like what?"

"It's still not clear." Ely sat in a chair at the head of the table. "One theory suggests Perry and his Great Lakes counterparts are being targeted by those international terrorists you mentioned." Ely set the printouts from his spreadsheet on the table. "I've documented a series of ships that have sunk or gone missing over the past year." He tapped a finger on the incident chart. "There are twelve ships. Three of them are Perry's, but they're all confirmed trafficking vessels. Each one made port in a facility known to have ties with Taliban or Al Qaeda operatives before their demise or disappearance."

"How did the ships sink?" Gerard said.

"I don't know. Some went down in flames like yesterday, but in each incident weather conditions were fair, no other vessels were involved, and no calls for help were heard."

"If they were drug smugglers, maybe they didn't call for help because they didn't want the Coast Guard to find them with a hold full of narcotics."

"Perhaps," Ely said. "Or something took them out so fast they didn't have time to send a message."

"Six of one, half a dozen of another." Gerard pondered a moment. "Now, don't judge me, but if terrorists are wiping out drug traffickers, so what? Isn't that a good thing for us?"

"Nothing Islamic militant terrorists do is good for us," Ely said. "If they're killing drug traffickers, we don't know why, or what comes next. This might be the first step in establishing a new order in the drug-running world, one designed to flood our border with cheap narcotics, and make the drug problem in this country a hell of a lot worse."

Gerard's face soured. "I see your point."

"This is all speculation," Anders reminded them. "Given what we know, the drug traffickers could just as easily be engaged in a regional turf war. We need solid answers."

"Agreed," Gerard said. "So, find out from Cobb what the hell Perry has gotten himself into."

"That's why you're here, Bob." Ely set his cell phone on the table. "You've heard about the *Blackbird*, haven't you?"

"Just stories," Gerard said. "It's supposedly a floating meth lab. Rumor has it churning out more product than any cookhouse in Michigan. My teams have never seen it though. It's more like a ghost ship than a real thing, an urban legend, really."

Ely slid his phone over to Gerard. "Take a look."

Gerard read a text message on the screen. "These are coordinates in Lake Huron."

"The *Blackbird* will be at those numbers at one a.m. day after next, fully crewed and cooking meth. Cobb will be on board. That's our interdiction target."

Anders sat forward. "Do you trust Cobb is giving us authentic intel?"

"I wouldn't call it trust, but I think we should roll the dice with him. The potential windfall of information on Perry and the traffickers is too valuable to pass up. Cobb may be a lackey, but he moves in Perry's inner circle. He knows what's going on in that organization."

"Wonder why he flipped all of a sudden."

Ely shrugged. "Don't know, but he's giving us the *Blackbird* to show us he's not playing games. My guess is something spooked him, pushed him off the fence. He wants me to take him into custody after the ship is captured. Says he'll tell me everything he knows about Perry."

Anders straightened his tie. "What does Cobb want in exchange for turning?"

"He wants out. That's all he's asked. Just get him out of there."

Gerard slapped the table. "Sounds like a win-win to me. We take a meth lab out of operation, and you two nab a high-value snitch. I say we move on this. Gary, are you with me?"

"Yeah. Let's take down the *Blackbird* and snatch up Cobb."

Gerard stood. "I'll mobilize the HITRON team, have them at those coordinates at one a.m. day after next. You want a front row seat, Ely?"

"Absolutely. I don't want to disappoint Cobb."

Anders nodded. "I just hope Cobb doesn't disappoint us."

SIX

Sparta, Michigan

Kade ran his thumb across the patch that Cody had placed over the bullet hole in the Otter's sheet metal skin. Topnotch work. Between beer binges, the guy really was a meticulous craftsman and brilliant mechanic. Kade wouldn't want anyone else servicing his plane. It kept the charter business running smoothly, it kept Cody employed, and it kept the promise.

Kade picked up a socket set off the floor and put it away in a toolbox. He and Cody had arrived at the hangar early that morning to knock out their to-do list on the Otter before the forecasted heat and humidity rolled in. In addition to fixing the bullet hole in the fuselage, they replaced the shattered passenger window and performed scheduled maintenance on the engines. They also changed out the amphibious floats with fixed-wheel landing gear. Even though the Otter's amphib floats allowed Kade to land on water as well as land, he preferred the plane's performance with the fixed wheels in place. Now the aircraft was ready for the Minneapolis run.

Kade wiped beads of sweat from his forehead. It was a steamy July day. Even the Otter looked hot and tired. The wheel on the front landing gear assembly rested in a recess in the oil-stained concrete floor, dipping the nose slightly downward and giving the plane the appearance of a bird searching for a puddle of water to drink from. Kade smiled at the image.

Outside the hangar, a lawn mower buzzed over the grounds, spewing the scent of fresh-cut grass into the air. Kade lifted his chin to take in the smell. That's when he saw the two guys in suits walking into the shade of the hangar through the open bay door. They were clean-shaven, with car salesmen smiles and elite postures. Kade read them to be either corporate executives or government officials. The cut of their suits made him lean toward the latter. *Great. Ely yesterday and these guys today.*

"Kade Mitchell?" one of them said.

"Who's asking?" Kade replied.

The tall suit with an irritating smirk nodded toward the Otter. "You glad to be flying again?"

Definitely government. Joe Executive wouldn't know about his pilot license suspension. *Probably a federal agency of some stripe. Hell, Ely probably sent them.* "I said, who's asking?"

The guy widened his smirk into a smile and pulled his credentials from an inner suit pocket. He held them out for Kade to read as he strolled casually around the nose of the plane: Intelligence Research Specialist Nystrom with U.S. Customs and Border Protection. Nystrom jabbed a thumb at his partner. "That's Agent Rifkin, same agency."

Agent Rifkin stepped forward, perspiration glistening on his narrow cheekbones and a manila folder in his hand. He glanced around the inside of the hangar. "Are you alone, Mr. Mitchell?"

"Yeah, for the moment. My associate went out to pick up some lunch."

Rifkin nodded toward the door in the back. "May we speak with you in your office?"

Kade didn't bother asking how the guy knew he had an office in the hangar. "Do I have a choice?"

"You can refuse to talk with us now," Nystrom said, "but we will end up having a conversation sooner or later." He smiled. "I'd bet sooner."

Kade fumed. These guys had to be working with Ely. Customs and Border Protection fell under the DHS umbrella. They had to have come because of that cargo ship. Kade turned his back on Agents Nystrom and Rifkin and headed for his office. "What's this all about?" he said over his shoulder.

Rifkin wiped sweat from his cheek. "It's about a customs and border issue."

"No kidding."

"And your part in it," Nystrom added.

Kade stopped at the door and faced them. "I'm clean. You're wasting your time here."

Nystrom smirked. "Let's talk first, and then I'll decide how clean you are."

The smug federal agent stood silent, cool as a slate of marble. It didn't seem the guy was capable of sweating. The thought of popping him with a quick right flashed through Kade's thoughts, but instead he opened the door and walked into the office. "Shut the door behind you. I've got an air conditioner in here that's barely keeping up." Agents Nystrom and Rifkin followed him in and studied the messy room.

Kade plopped down in the old swivel chair behind a cheap Ikea desk. A pile of charts and empty coffee mugs covered the desktop. "Take a seat, gentlemen, and tell me what's on your mind." He glanced about as if just realizing he had only one visitor's chair. "Sorry, guys. One of you will have to stand. I think that should be Agent Nystrom."

Nystrom gave a crooked smile and considered the clutter of aircraft components, cardboard boxes, and empty fast-food bags littering the room. "You didn't color inside the lines when you were a kid, did you, Mitchell?"

Kade let out a genuine laugh. "No, I did not. And I'll bet a hundred bucks, you did."

Nystrom's smirk returned, but he did not reply.

Rifkin found a clear spot on the desk and set down the manila folder. "Two years ago, on the night of June 16, you were involved in a drug-smuggling operation that the DEA broke up."

Any levity Kade had felt a moment ago vanished. These guys were getting right to it.

Rifkin paused as if waiting for a reaction.

Kade didn't give him one. Kade didn't give him anything.

Agent Rifkin glanced at Agent Nystrom, and then cleared his throat. "One DEA agent was shot and killed in the takedown. Travis Bennet. You were taken into custody, Mr. Mitchell, and somehow managed to get off with probation and a two-year suspension of your pilot's license for your role in the affair." Rifkin paused again.

Kade's stomach knotted at the mention of Travis's name. "That's history, gentlemen. My probation is over. What's your point in bringing all this up now?"

"The man you were flying for that night was a drug trafficker named Raymond Firth," Rifkin said. "That DEA raid hobbled his operation, but it didn't put him out of business. He's recovered quite well over the last two years."

"That's your problem, not mine." Kade kicked his legs up on the desk. *Keep cool,* he told himself, but inside his blood boiled. He still didn't know what these knuckleheads were after.

Nystrom regarded his casual demeanor. "Yesterday morning, you went to the aid of a sinking cargo vessel in Lake Michigan."

And there you have it, that damned cargo ship. Kade paused to take a breath. "Did Ely send you here?"

"Nobody sent us," Nystrom said. "This is our investigation."

"But you heard about the incident with the cargo ship from the Coast Guard, right?"

"The Coast Guard merely confirmed what we already knew." Rifkin opened the manila folder and slid a photograph toward Kade.

Kade studied the image. It was an aerial shot of the Otter floating in the lake next to the cargo ship moments before it sank. The picture had been taken from a high altitude, much higher than the Coast Guard chopper had flown that day. "Who took this picture?"

"We did," Rifkin said.

Kade picked up the photo and studied it again. "From where?"

"The sky," Nystrom said.

Kade shot an annoyed glance at him and then dropped his feet to the floor. "I offered assistance to a vessel in distress. Not a crime as far as I know."

Nystrom's smirk crossed over to a smile again. "We believe that vessel was owned and operated by Raymond Firth."

Kade felt the bottom drop out of his stomach. *Stay calm.* "You *believe* Firth owned it?"

"Our confidence is high," Rifkin said.

"High enough," Nystrom added, "that we thought it a good idea to speak with you about your appearance at the site of the sinking."

Kade fought to keep a level head. "Like I told you before, you're wasting your time. I haven't been in contact with Firth or any of his men since the night of the raid."

Rifkin raised an eyebrow. "Are you saying you just happened to land next to a sinking cargo ship owned by the very drug smuggler who once employed you? Did I hear you correctly?"

"Firth did not employ me. I took a short-term air-freight contract job to pay the bills."

"You're splitting hairs, Mitchell," Nystrom said.

"I'm clarifying the facts. There's a difference."

"Back to my question," Rifkin said. "Are you telling us your presence at the scene of Firth's sinking cargo ship was a coincidence?"

"That's exactly what I'm telling you."

Nystrom let out a discontented sigh, which in Fed-speak, Kade read to mean *bullshit.*

"Do you have a problem believing that?" Kade said.

"Yes, I have a big problem believing that."

Kade leaned forward. "In all your research, Agent Numbnuts, did you come across the fact that I'm the one who tipped off the DEA to the time and location of the shipment on the night of the raid?"

Nystrom retained his marble façade. If he had known that tidbit, he wasn't letting on. Or he didn't care. Rifkin, on the other hand, did not have a good poker face. His eyebrow dipped. "That might explain how you got off so light for your part in the incident."

Kade feigned surprise. "You think?"

"Why?" Rifkin said. "Why take the job only to tip the authorities and go down in the raid?"

Kade settled back in his chair and considered the question, like he had a thousand times before. "I had a crisis of conscience at the last minute." He pondered the grim fallout of the raid. "You know what, Agent Rifkin, sometimes it's not a good idea to listen to your conscience."

Rifkin began to respond, but Nystrom interrupted. "Have you had any recent contact with Rachel Edwards?"

The question came so fast out of leftfield it hit Kade like a fastball to the temple and derailed his thought process. "Have I what?"

Nystrom spoke as if annoyed he had to repeat. "Have you had any recent contact with Rachel Edwards?" He added, "Your ex-wife."

"I know who she is, Numbnuts." It irked Kade that Rachel went back to her maiden name.

"Mr. Mitchell, I'm a representative of the federal government, and I'd appreciate a little respect," Nystrom said. "At least address me as Agent Numbnuts."

Kade almost laughed at that, but the question had thrown him off balance. "I haven't talked to Rachel in months. Why do you want to know?"

Nystrom deferred to Rifkin, who rambled into an answer. "Rachel Edwards is employed by a marine freight company that conducts a great deal of business on the Great Lakes. Smugglers operating in the same arena could conceivably share some synergies with that type of legitimate maritime entity." Rifkin let that sink in a moment. "Obviously, Mr. Mitchell, you could be a bridge between two such entities."

Kade found a laugh in that. "I'm not a damned bridge to anything, especially with her. Apparently, your investigation missed the fact that our separation wasn't all that amicable."

"There's a fine line between love and hate," Nystrom said, "and a lucrative business deal has a way of crossing that line, for better or worse." He smiled at his own pun.

Kade didn't smile back. "Rachel and I are not talking. We're not working together. And we're not sleeping together. There is no *together* when it comes to us." He leaned back and put his feet up on the desk again. "No synergies are being realized by anyone."

"Wow, Mitchell, you sound like a real Romeo," Nystrom said.

Rifkin considered Kade a long while.

Kade stared back, calm, unshaken.

"Okay, Mr. Mitchell," Rifkin said, sliding the photograph back inside the manila folder. "I think we're finished for today. We may, however, need to speak with you again."

"Don't go on any extended trips to faraway places," Nystrom warned.

"Duly noted," Kade said, "but I do hear Cabo is nice this time of year."

Nystrom stopped with a hand on the doorknob. "I advise against it."

Kade crossed his arms. "That's bold talk for a Customs and Border research specialist."

Nystrom smiled one last time. "We're not your father's CBP."

The federal agents exited the office, leaving the door wide open behind them. Kade grumbled and got up from the desk. *Come on, guys, the air conditioning.* He swung the door closed and watched through the glass window as the feds left the hangar.

Something didn't feel right about those two. Kade didn't like it. And he definitely didn't like that they brought Rachel into the conversation. Things weren't making sense. Kade began to wonder just what he had stumbled into when he landed next to that cargo ship.

- SEVEN -

US Coast Guard Station, Port Huron, Michigan

Ely Edwards walked the dock just east of Coast Guard Station Port Huron, where USCGC *Defiant* was moored. A breeze off Lake Huron made the afternoon heat bearable, and it felt good to stretch his legs after the two-hour drive from Lansing. He had tried to call Rachel in route to smooth over their last text exchange but got no answer. That girl was as headstrong as her mother.

Ely shielded his eyes from the glare off the cutter's white hull and stopped to consider the vessel a moment. The *Defiant* was a modified Reliance Class cutter that stretched more than two hundred feet from bow to stern and displaced over a thousand tons of water. She topped out at twenty knots and sported a sophisticated suite of electronic equipment that provided the ship with state-of-the-art GPS, radar, fathometers, and communication gear. She had a Mark 38 auto cannon on her bow, and a stern launch that gave her the capability to easily deploy Rigid Hull Inflatable Boats (RHIB) for boarding operations, as was the plan for the *Blackbird*. A helipad built across her aft deck allowed her to count an MH-65C Dolphin helicopter as one of her assets, officially making her part of the HITRON initiative.

"What do you think?"

Ely had heard the steps approaching before he heard the voice. The tone had timber and the words were spoken with authority. The owner of the voice was a man in a standard tropical-blue operational dress uniform with commander's insignia. He had a square jaw and a brush cut like he had come fresh from the Academy in New London. "You must be Ely Edwards." The Guard officer extended a hand. "I'm Commander Adams. *Defiant* is my vessel. Commander Gerard told me you'd be riding along tonight."

"He told you right," Ely said. "*Blackbird* is a big catch. I want to be there for the takedown."

"I've heard stories about that ship," Commander Adams said with a smile. "It's not every day you get a shot at the *Flying Dutchman*."

Ely gestured to the helicopter on the cutter's helipad. "Helicopter

Interdiction Tactical Squadron. HITRON. It started in Jacksonville, knocking out go-fast boats with Marine Corps tactics. Isn't that right?"

"It is. We had a lot of success in district seven. As a matter of fact, drug running activity has cooled off significantly down south, so the decision was made to introduce a HITRON team to the Great Lakes to help with the growing problems here."

Ely chuckled. "The Canadians don't much like bigger deck guns or tactical choppers in the region, but the world is getting more dangerous every day."

"A lot of our problems come across their border," Adams said. "But Canadians aren't the only ones resisting HITRON. I'm told some senators in Washington are against expanding the HITRON force into the Great Lakes too, citing the non-militarization treaty with Canada."

"I'll bet those senators don't represent states on the border," Ely said. "I, for one, welcome your presence here. It puts the advantage back in the good guys' hands."

Ely and Commander Adams walked to the gangway to board the cutter.

"Gerard told me you served in the Coast Guard."

Ely smiled. "I did. Right here in district nine for almost a decade. Ended my active duty skippering a patrol boat. I'm at home here, Commander."

Adams laughed. "Don't get any ideas about stealing my chair. I want this feather in *my* cap."

"You can have the feather," Ely said. "All I want is Cobb."

"Who's Cobb?"

"He's the guy who told me where and when to capture the *Blackbird*. He's got more to share, but I have to get him off that ship first."

A shade of concern crossed Commander Adams's face. "Are you certain he's not jerking your chain with the whereabouts of *Blackbird*?"

"Certain enough. Hell, I convinced Gerard to get you involved, didn't I?"

Adams thought about that a moment and nodded. "Fair enough." He continued walking. "Regardless, we'll be on station and ready at the designated time. If *Blackbird* doesn't show up, well, I guess it will be her lucky day."

"She'll be there," Ely said. "And you'll get that feather."

They walked a few steps in silence.

"Have you been monitoring Great Lakes activity the past few

months?" Ely said.

"I've kept an eye on things. I knew HITRON would eventually get here, and thought I'd better get a sense for the ebb and flow of Lakes' activity before that happened. Why do you ask?"

Ely thought about his theory that terrorists were targeting drug traffickers. Without evidence to support it, he figured he shouldn't ring the alarm bell. Not yet. Best to keep it simple, stay away from the sensational. "There's something going on," Ely said. "Ships suspected of trafficking activity are sinking, too many to chalk up to happenstance, coincidence, or good fortune."

Commander Adams regarded him. "You think they're fighting over territory?"

Ely shrugged. "Maybe. At this point, I can't be certain. It could be that smugglers are just stupid when it comes to maritime transportation. My biggest concern is that innocent people are getting caught up in whatever it is that's going on."

"Is our mission tonight part of that scenario?"

"Not directly," Ely said. "The *Blackbird* is a floating meth lab and needs to be taken down. Consider my informant aboard her as a separate but related item."

Commander Adams stepped up to the gangway. "Cobb notwithstanding, one less drug ship is a good thing in my book. If we secure your pigeon along the way, and he helps you sort things out, well, that's just icing on the cake."

"I think we're on the same page," Ely said.

Adams took an admiring look at the *Defiant* and her tactical chopper. "Whatever the drug smugglers are up to, it's about to get a lot more difficult for them to keep doing it. HITRON just moved into the neighborhood."

EIGHT

Sparta, Michigan

Kade squared up disheveled paperwork inside a box on the floor, and then shoved the box into a corner. He glanced around the office at the clutter of aircraft parts and empty coffee mugs. "Color inside the lines," he said to himself. "Piss off, Agent Numbnuts."

He plopped into his swivel chair and adjusted a flat-screen monitor. His business e-mail account had been collecting dust for a week; he figured it was time to check it. While waiting for his antiquated computer to chug and hum its way to displaying the messages, Kade pondered Agents Nystrom and Rifkin's visit. They were certainly quick to connect him to Firth and that cargo ship. If the feds had had that kind of dot-connecting prowess in 2001, maybe the Twin Towers wouldn't have fallen.

His e-mail inbox flickered onto the screen. A hundred and fifty unread messages. Kade groaned and started skimming subject lines, deleting the ones from reverse mortgage bankers, Nigerian royalty, and blue-pill pharmacies. A couple creditors had dropped him a note as well, just to let him know they were getting nervous. He reviewed and responded to a couple of inquiries into charter flights, and then he saw the message from The Bluewater Foundation. The group was a Great Lakes historical preservation organization; they had sent a note to promote an aerial poker run they were holding to raise money for their cause. Although flying to various airports collecting palying cards to build a poker hand sparked Kade's interest, it was the name of the group that grabbed his attention. Rachel had been involved with The Bluewater Foundation, and had even forged a philanthropic partnership between the foundation and her current employer, Teague Global Associated Freight.

Kade read about the poker run. It had actually kicked off that day and was scheduled to conclude tomorrow. He skimmed through the particulars, the destination airports, the routes, the entry fee, which was rather steep, and the prize money, which was generous. He scanned for names of event officials, hoping to see Rachel mentioned somewhere, but she was not.

He sat looking at the screen, and thought about Nystrom, and Rifkin. *Have you had any recent contact with Rachel Edwards?* He pulled his phone from his pocket and swiped open the speed-dial list, poising his thumb over Rachel's name. He had not talked to her in months, just like he had told the agents. Their last conversation had ended with an abrupt hang-up. *What good would it do to call her now? She probably wouldn't even pick up. Besides, Rifkin's bridge theory was pure fantasy, why even tell her about it?*

Why? Because you want to talk to her, dumbass.

He hovered his thumb above the glass, debating whether to call, but he got too close and actually touched the call button. *Crap. Now she had an incoming from Kade Mitchell. What to do?* He actually got nervous. *Screw it. Just hang up.*

Before he could cancel the call, the speaker clicked. "Kade?"

He nearly fell out of the chair trying to put the phone to his ear. "Rachel, hey." His mind went blank. "How've you been?"

A pause. "I'm fine." Silence. "And you?"

"Not bad," he said. "Staying busy."

"You got your pilot license reinstated a few months ago, didn't you?"

Kade bristled at the mention of the suspension. "Yeah, that's right."

"Do you have the Otter flying yet?"

"Yeah, Cody and I have the charter service back up."

"That's great," Rachel said, "because I heard you were flying puddle jumpers out of Bishop for Southwest."

"Where did you hear—?"

"How's the business going?"

"Okay. We're getting some good word-of-mouth referrals. The schedule is picking up."

Rachel stayed silent a few awkward moments. "Why the call, Kade?"

He stammered. "I, uh, I had an interesting conversation today and your name came up."

"A conversation with whom?"

"That's the interesting thing," Kade said. "I was talking with a couple of Customs and Border agents, and they asked about you. How crazy is that?"

"Very," she said. "Did they know me from someplace?"

"No. They wanted to know if I had spoken to you recently."

"Why were you talking to Customs and Border agents?"

Kade toyed with the phone. "Long story."

"I've got some time," she said. "You called, so you obviously want to tell me."

"Solid logic, as usual."

"That was our marriage. Heavy on logic, light on everything else."

Kade took the bait. "Are you really going back to the I-wasn't-there argument?"

"You weren't, especially at the end. Impeccable timing, I might add."

"The business was failing, we were both dealing with issues."

"We were both dealing with issues, but you decided to go it alone."

"I was trying to save us. You were too wrapped up in yourself to see it."

"Really?" She laughed. "All you cared about was keeping the Otter in the air."

"Bullshit. What happened to Leah blinded you—"

"Blinded? I'm the only one who saw things clearly. I saw my husband's delusion of greatness strip away his soul, until all that was left was a pilot and a plane. And what did you get for it?" she said. "A dead end on a dark runway."

Kade kicked the desk. "You know where to hit me, and you always take the shot."

Rachel stayed silent a long while. "I'm sorry."

"Are you? You apologized last time. Why is it you can't resist drilling into the nerve?"

"I said I'm sorry."

Kade watched a fly buzz around the office. "We always do this. We can't get past it."

"There's no point digging up our dirt any longer. We both know it."

Kade did not reply.

"Long story," she said, as if trying to reset the conversation. "Tell me about the CBP agents."

Kade took a breath and pulled his thoughts back to the present. "I made a mistake," he said. "I tried to do a good deed, and it's coming back to bite me."

"What happened?"

"I stumbled across a sinking ship and offered to help the crew." Kade paused. "Turns out, Raymond Firth owned the ship. Now the feds think it was no coincidence I showed up there."

"How did I figure into the conversation?"

"The agents I spoke with think I might be leveraging my relationship with you to connect Firth to your employer for some type of illicit partnership. He called it *synergy*."

"Those agents have obviously never been through a divorce."

"Obviously."

"And, after you told them their theory was ridiculous, what did they say?"

"Not much, other than they might want to speak with me again."

Rachel didn't say anything for a long while. "On the surface, that does seem odd."

"On the surface?"

"Think about it. Those guys are trained to dig in every direction their little minds lead them. On one level, their suspicion makes sense. They're dead wrong, but I can see why they asked."

"I can't see it," Kade said. "They're trying to find fire without smoke."

"Look, if the feds question me about this, I'll make clear to them how it is between us."

Kade lifted his chin a bit. "And how is it between us?"

"Not at all like the CBP thinks."

"Right."

"Kade …"

"What?"

"Nothing." A voice in the background distracted her. "Hey, I've got something I need to take care of, so I've got to let you go. A big T-GAF charity event has got me crazy busy."

"T-GAF? Oh, right, Teague Global. I just read they're sponsoring the Bluewater Foundation's aerial poker run." Kade's phone beeped with an incoming call. He checked the ID. It was Danny.

"Yes. You would have liked flying in it." Rachel added, "The final leg is amazing."

"Why is that?" Kade's phone beeped again, and he remembered he was supposed to be meeting Danny and Cody at a roadhouse in town.

"Rachel, I've got a call coming in that I've got to take."

"All right," she said. The background voice distracted her again. "It was good to hear from you, Kade. Really. I'll let you know if the feds contact me. Bye."

Kade lingered on her closing remarks before switching to Danny's incoming call. "Hey, I didn't forget. I'm on my way."

"You better hurry up," Danny said.

"Why, what's happening?"

"Cody's getting hammered."

NINE

The wheels on Kade's Jeep squealed as he pulled into the Cellar Brewing Company parking lot. He jerked to a stop in the first parking space he saw and threw open the door. Danny met him in front of the building. He noticed she did not look like a welder. Dressed in tight Rock Revival jeans, high-heel boots, and a silky sleeveless top, she was a knockout. She had her blonde hair up in a clip and teased out, which Kade thought was sporty-sexy. He almost forgot why he had raced from the airport to get there.

"Is Cody still on his feet?" he asked.

"Yeah," Danny said. "But not for long." She pulled a cigarette from the little black purse slung across her shoulder. "He's ten feet tall and bulletproof."

"Sounds like tequila." Kade headed for the front door. "Cody knows that stuff goes right to his head. Damn it, why does he mix like that?"

Danny followed after him, trying to light the cigarette. "You weren't there to stop him."

"Has he turned into bad Cody yet?"

"Yeah, he started into some guys at the bar, told them they were disrespecting me."

Kade pulled open the door and glanced back at her. "Were they?"

"They're guys in a bar."

"Got it." He felt adrenaline begin to flow. "How many?"

"Two," she said. "Maybe three."

Kade cursed under his breath and went inside.

She gave up lighting the cigarette and followed him in.

A commotion in the back corner of the bar held everyone's attention, below a flat-screen TV and behind a long, crowded table. Cody was jabbing his finger at a man who had at least a foot height advantage over him. The guy had bulky arms, like he spent his days carrying heavy things around a construction site, but his belly looked as if he spent his overtime checks at the tavern. He had a flame tattoo twisting up his arm from his wrist to his bicep, and he clenched his fist open and closed as Cody egged him on. Fueled by liquid courage, Cody staggered into a square-up position in front of him. Near the bar, a skinny guy with a beard and an earring watched with intensity, like he had a stake in the matter. Kade figured him to be Bob the Builder's buddy. Number two.

Kade waded into the crowd, pushing past curious patrons and obnoxious drunks to get to the hardwood dance floor where Cody had decided to make his stand. He emerged next to a table of white collars. Ahead, Cody slurred something about manners, and shoved Bob the Builder. The guy absorbed the assault with barely a stagger, and then shoved Cody back a full five feet. Cody righted himself with a clumsy, intoxicated effort. Bob cocked back his flaming arm to strike. Kade stepped between them and held up a hand like a traffic cop. "Hold up, buddy. You really want to hit a guy with a traumatic brain injury?"

Bob held back, shifting his gaze to Kade.

Cody dropped his arms. "Kade!" He paused. "I don't have a … whatever you just said."

Kade rolled his eyes.

Bob re-clenched his fist. "Nice try, douchebag."

Danny stepped from the crowd. Bob glanced at her, and then at Kade, calculating the situation. Kade guessed his math did not go much beyond one plus one.

"She's with you?" Bob chuckled. "Figures a bitch like that would have a pin-dick boyfriend."

Kade's nostrils flared. "Is that the beer talkin' or are you really that big an asshole?"

Bob snarled and threw a powerful right cross, stepping in to leverage his weight. Kade ducked under and landed a sharp jackhammer into Bob's gut. The big guy gasped for air. Kade sidestepped, keeping Bob just out of reach, waiting to see how far he wanted to take this. The bearded guy with the shiny earring at the bar decided it was a good time to get into the brawl. He came off his stool and charged.

Kade kicked an empty chair from the table of white collars into his path, tangling up his legs and bringing him down. Drunken spectators cheered. Kade smiled, but Bob took advantage of his distraction. A rocky set of knuckles cracked Kade's chin and rattled his skull. Bar lights dimmed and flashed back on. Or that's what it seemed. Kade didn't want to take another punch like that. He shook it off and pivoted left, jabbing Bob in the nose. *Keep moving*, Kade thought, *float like a butterfly*. He circled, making Bob track with him to stay engaged.

The crowd cheered with each move they made. Kade couldn't tell who they were rooting for, but he didn't care. He wanted to end this fiasco as quickly as possible. Bob took another drunken swing. Kade dodged, weaved, jabbed. Hit. Bob's head snapped back.

"Kade, behind you!" Danny shouted.

The bearded guy had kicked the chair clear and was pulling himself off the floor.

Great. Kade pivoted to keep both men in view, but Cody came out of nowhere and tackled the bearded guy. *Thank the Lord for high school football.* Kade sharpened his focus and squared up with Bob again, but the big oaf had decided to change tactics. Bob stopped throwing punches, and turned into a kamikaze bulldozer, charging head on and hitting Kade in the chest. The impact drove Kade back into the table behind him, scattering the white collars and knocking over their beers. Bob straightened his back and cocked his big paw for a knockout blow. Kade felt around the table for something to defend himself, grabbing a pitcher of beer wobbling next to his ear. He expected a nice solid glass anvil to wallop Bob with, but it was made out of plastic. It nearly flew out of his hand it was so light. Irish Stout splashed everywhere. Kade tossed the remaining beer into Bob's face, and then bounced the pitcher off his head.

Bob wiped his eyes and staggered around an overturned chair. Kade rolled clear of the table and reared back to deliver the biggest roundhouse he could muster. Bob's vision seemed to clear just as Kade's fist blasted him between the eyes, and he fell over like a redwood on the dance floor. The crowd whooped and hollered. Kade spun around, looking for anyone else who might want to rush him. A pudge-faced guy at the bar stood. Number three. Kade made eye contact with him. "Don't just stand there. Come on."

The guy considered Bob wallowing on the floor and decided to sit back down.

Three burly bouncers in Cellar Brewing polo shirts suddenly came out of the woodwork, pushing their way through the crowd to get to the scene of the fight. Kade pulled Cody to his drunken feet. "Come on. Those guys aren't coming to show us to our table."

Danny grabbed Kade's arm. "This way."

She led them through a hole in the crowd and out a side exit door. Kade made a beeline for his Jeep, keeping Cody moving, and then rolling him into the backseat. Kade and Danny hopped in the front.

"What about my car?" she said.

Kade fired up the engine. "We'll come back for it later."

He squealed out of the parking lot and gunned it down Division Street as the bouncers burst through the front door. Danny laughed so hard she couldn't breathe. Kade kept barreling down the road, but after a couple miles with no one on their tail, he relaxed and slowed to the speed limit. They were all jacked up and decided to drive to Lake Michigan to unwind. Not long into the trip, Cody passed out. Kade stopped at a party store and bought a six-pack of beer. Within a half hour, they rolled onto Lakeshore Drive and found a scenic section of road to watch the sunset. A cool breeze blew in off the lake and pushed back the heat of the day.

Kade opened a Pale Ale and handed it to Danny. "Sorry I was late to The Cellar."

She sipped the beer and smiled. "It's okay, sweetheart. It made for an exciting evening."

Kade felt a throb of pain where Bob's knuckles had hit his chin. "I can do without that kind of excitement." He opened another beer and took a swig, and then glanced back at Cody sleeping in the back. "This guy is a handful to keep out of trouble."

She gave him a puzzled look. "Why do you watch after Cody like you do?"

Kade considered the question. It was a can of worms. "He's like family, and no matter how much trouble family can be, you watch after each other."

"That's not true in every family." Danny smiled like she knew the truth in her comment firsthand. "How did you and Cody get so close?"

"We grew up together." Kade felt himself cracking open that can. "We lived in Allegan County—me, Cody, and his brother, Travis. It's a tough place for rambunctious teens to hang. Not much to do between the blueberry and cornfields, so we found ways to entertain ourselves." He laughed. "We rode home in the back of a squad car so many times our dads became friends with the county sheriff."

Danny pointed at Kade with her bottle. "So you spent the first half of your life getting Cody into trouble, and now you're making amends by trying to keep him out of it?"

"Not exactly, but I was there when the drinking started. Every Friday after the game, we'd all go to Curtis's field. Tailgate down and the radio up. Sounds like a damned country song."

Danny grinned. "I think it is."

"Cody took to beer a little more than the rest of us. But right about then, his skill as a mechanic blossomed, and in a town where people drive on dirt roads more than asphalt, that kind of thing gets noticed. Every auto shop in the county wanted to hire him. Ironic, isn't it? Cody's greatest strength and greatest weakness popped out at the same time."

"I think that happens a lot," she said.

"He always had spending money," Kade continued, "and it fell on Travis to keep an eye on him, to make sure he didn't drink it all away."

Danny reclined her seat a couple notches. "Why doesn't big brother Travis watch over him now?"

Kade took a while to answer. "Travis is dead."

Danny sat up. "Oh, God, Kade. I'm sorry."

"It's okay, you didn't know."

"How did he die?"

"He was a DEA agent. Killed in the line of duty." Kade noticed his palms were wet; it wasn't condensation from the beer bottle. He dried them on his jeans. "I promised …" His voice caught, but he cleared it and started over. "Travis knew he had a dangerous job. We had talked at one point about Cody, and I promised Travis I would look after him if anything ever happened."

Danny regarded him a long while. "Amazing. A real, live man of his word." She grabbed a cigarette from her purse. "My ex-husband promised he'd love, honor, and cherish me 'til death and all that. Guess what?" She traced a circle in the air with her finger. "O for three."

"Every time something like this happens to Cody, it feels like I'm letting him down."

"You said it yourself, sweetheart, Cody is a handful. No one else could do better. You're keeping him on track and out of jail. You should get the big brother of the year award."

"Travis deserved it, not me. I wish he was still here, watching over Cody … I wish I had stopped him from going on the raid that day."

"Baby, that wasn't your fault."

Kade did not reply.

She searched his eyes. "What are you thinking? What's the matter?"

He could not begin to tell her. "I'm thinking about mistakes," he finally said.

"We all make mistakes. I should know. I've been with some big-time assholes in my life. They were all mistakes." She touched Kade's cheek and looked into his eyes. "You're nothing like them. The way you are with me, the way you take care of Cody ... you're amazing."

"Danny, I'm not amazing."

"You care for me and respect me more than anyone else has. You're one of a kind."

"My ex-wife wouldn't agree with you." Kade wanted to pull the words back, but he couldn't. He took a swig of beer.

"Wow, baby. You don't mention Rachel very often. I think we're reaching a new level of intimacy here." She lit the cigarette but held it to the side so the smoke did not drift into his face.

Kade smiled at the gesture. "I didn't actually bring up her name. And yes, there are other topics I'd rather discuss, like the time I threw up at the Bow Tie after rattlesnakes last month."

She laughed and took a drag off her cigarette. "Why do you hate talking about her so much?"

"Do you enjoy discussing your mistakes?"

"I do discuss my mistakes. It's therapeutic. You know, there's a saying about learning from the past, right?"

"Yes. Those who do not learn from history's mistakes are doomed to repeat them."

She blew a stream of smoke. "That's the one. Do you really look at Rachel as a mistake?"

"The way it ended, yeah."

"That's not what I asked."

Kade tipped his bottle toward hers. "Your beer is getting warm."

"Do you still love her?"

"Danny, come on."

"Why is this so hard for you?"

"It's not hard." He took another drink. "Hey, strange thing. A couple of agents from the Customs and Border Protection Agency visited me this afternoon. That's why I was late to the Cellar."

"Nice change of topic." She flicked ash out the window. "What did they want?"

Kade filtered the conversation he had with Nystrom and Rifkin. "They wanted to know why I stopped to help out that cargo ship. Turns out it was a smuggling vessel. Who knew?"

"Did they think you were smuggling with them?" She laughed and snuffed the cigarette in the console ashtray.

"Maybe. They weren't real clear about that. I think my ex-father-in-law sent them. He works for Homeland Security now and can do things like that. He never really liked me."

"You haven't been married to Rachel for over two years, right? Why would he hold a grudge that long?"

"He's a prick, that's why." Kade considered telling her that the feds asked him about Rachel, but decided against it. "Then again, maybe Ely has nothing to do with them. Those agents were probably just covering all the bases, making sure they're not missing anything." He didn't really believe that, but it sounded good.

She took a sip of beer. "As long as they didn't accuse you of something you didn't do."

"No, they didn't do that." He smiled. "At least, not yet."

"Funny."

Kade finished his beer and set the bottle in the carton. "I'll say one thing. It's been quite an eventful couple of days."

"Yeah, ending in a brawl at the The Cellar," she said.

"Which, by the way, was your fault." He smiled and took her hand. "I mean, I was defending your honor back there."

She pulled her hand away and slugged his arm. "Oh, no. Don't make me your escape goat."

He laughed. "My escape goat?"

"Yeah."

"I think it's called a scapegoat."

"Whatever."

"Hey, Danny." He squeezed her hand and made sure he had her full attention. "The past few months with you have been great. You changed my outlook on a lot of things, helped me get back into the light. I want you to know how much that means to me."

"You did the same for me. My divorce had me down lower than I'd ever been." She wiped away a tear. "I gave up trusting anyone. Guys say anything, you know? But not you."

They sat together in silence as the orange sun melted into the lake's blue horizon. Kade leaned forward and gently kissed her lips. She leaned in, deepening their embrace.

Cody snored in the backseat.

"I think we need to get Cody home," Kade said, "so he can sleep off that tequila."

Danny caressed Kade's cheek. "Good idea. Let's get him home."

TEN

Bridge of USCGC *Defiant*, Lake Huron

Ely stared at the contact blip in *Defiant*'s darkened wheel room, comparing its relative location on the surface radar display to the coordinates Cobb had given him. They were nearly a perfect match. Commander Adams stood beside him, staring at the same display. "Is it the *Blackbird*?"

Ely caressed his chin. "If Cobb's numbers are good, it has to be."

"How certain are you he coughed up good numbers?"

"Not a hundred percent, but what the hell? In for a penny, in for a pound."

"I concur." Commander Adams nodded to his XO. "Mr. Choi, launch the HITRON team."

Lieutenant Commander (LCDR) Choi acknowledged the order and picked up the 1MC mic. "HITRON team, you are go for launch."

Aft on the helipad, crewmen released the Dolphin's tie-down cables, and the HITRON team rushed into the aircraft. The pilot spooled up the rotors for takeoff and the gunner checked the door-mounted M240 machinegun for action.

Ely peered into the night. A sliver of moon tucked behind thin cloud cover offered little light, and he could barely make out the horizon on the dark lake surrounding the cutter, but he felt confident the *Blackbird* was out there, and Cobb was aboard her. If the intercept went as planned, Ely would soon be getting answers to many burning questions.

On the chart table in the aft section of the wheel room, the ship's quartermaster marked *Blackbird*'s location in relation to the *Defiant*. Commander Adams approached the table. The soft glow from nearby navigation screens illuminated his face as he read the field before him. "Mr. Choi," he said, "get the boarding team on deck."

LCDR Choi relayed the order over the 1MC.

Dressed in full tactical gear, the Coast Guard boarding team swarmed the Over-The-Horizon (OTH) boat in the stern launch, prepping the craft for the coming interdiction.

Commander Adams joined Ely near the bridge windows. "We're about to find out if your friend Cobb is jerking your chain."

"He's not my friend," Ely said, "but my gut believes him."

"Then I guess we can call this a gut check."

"I guess we can."

The rumble of the chopper's engine and the thumping of her rotor blades bled in through the wheel room windows. She flew past *Defiant's* bridge and vectored in toward the *Blackbird*, settling into an easterly glide path.

"Here we go." Ely unlatched the nearest bulkhead door and stepped onto the starboard wing outside the bridge. A cool wind brushed across his cheek, and he strained to see through the darkness and distance. Still no visible sign of the fabled meth ship. As the buzz of the helicopter's engine faded, Ely considered the danger of the approaching confrontation. In and of itself, a meth lab is an unstable place. The combustible chemicals and toxins used to cook methamphetamine; and the crude, sloppy nature in which most meth labs were operated, made them powder kegs ready to go up in flames. The *Blackbird* compounded that volatility by cramming such a lab inside the belly of a ship; adding to the mix unwelcome variables such as fuel-oil fumes, the spark potential from the vessel's electrical system, and the general stupidity of individuals who would put themselves aboard a floating stick of dynamite with a lit fuse. Without a doubt, the Coast Guard had a dicey mission on its hands.

Ely sniffed the air. A subtle scent stung his nostrils, and in that instant, he knew they were closing in on the *Blackbird.*

Commander Adams stepped outside. "The HITRON team is a minute from intercept."

"You smell that?" Ely said.

"Smell what?"

"Cat piss."

Adams looked at Ely like he was crazy but took a whiff of air anyway. "I don't smell anything but lake water. Why would I smell cat piss?"

"We're downwind of that ship. If she's cooking meth, she's putting out a lot of fumes, and those fumes typically smell like ammonia."

"Cat piss. I get it." Adams added, "I've never been near a meth lab before."

"That'll change tonight," Ely said. "Cobb gave me good intel."

In the distance, near the horizon, a bright light flashed on. It swept over the waves and landed on the broadside of a vessel. A garbled voice through a loudspeaker rolled back across the surf.

"They're engaging." Commander Adams returned to the bridge. Ely followed him inside and sensed the crew's intensity had ratcheted up several notches. Radio transmissions from the HITRON team filled *Defiant's* wheel room. The team leader was ordering the *Blackbird* to come to a full stop. After several hails, Petty Officer Bowman, Operations Specialist on deck, turned to Commander Adams. "No reply from the vessel, sir."

Adams set his hands on his hips. "Is she flying colors?"

"No, sir. She has no nation status."

"They're criminals," Ely said. "The only flag they'd be flying is the skull and crossbones."

Commander Adams nodded. "Helm, plot intercept course and increase speed to eighteen knots. Mr. Choi, get the boarding team in the notch."

Defiant closed in and the helicopter's cone of light crawled over *Blackbird's* deck. The ship came into focus. She was an old merchant coaster, maybe a hundred fifty feet long, with her superstructure set back on the aft quarter. A series of rectangular windows ringed her pilothouse, and the forward angle of the structure gave the impression that the vessel was fighting the wind. Her bow deck was devoid of any structure, save for a makeshift stack that rose nearly twenty feet and belched out a stream of gray smoke. The hull appeared battered and seemed to have been splashed with an incomplete coat of black paint. Mostly likely to aid her concealment during night cruises. Alas, the *Blackbird.*

"She's running dark," Ely said, noting the black pilothouse windows. "And that stack isn't kicking out steam-engine vapor. She's cooking meth. We're catching her in the act."

Commander Adams cracked a hint of a smile. "That feather's going to look good in my cap."

"Don't celebrate yet," Ely said. "She's still kicking up a wake."

"Not for long." Commander Adams faced his Operations Specialist. "Mr. Bowman, inform HITRON team leader he is clear to lay down warning shots across *Blackbird's* bow."

"Yes, sir," Bowman replied.

"Mr. Choi, target the 38 on *Blackbird's* aft quarter. If she doesn't heed the warning shots, I want her drive shafts in pieces on my mark."

"Aye, sir."

"It's a floating meth lab," Ely said. "If you put a 25mm round in the wrong place, that whole ship will go up."

"My gunner's mates are well trained. We won't hit her in the wrong place."

Bowman cleared the chopper to fire, and Choi ordered the Mark 38 auto cannon in the forward turret trained on *Blackbird's* aft.

Defiant closed to within two hundred yards.

The HITRON chopper took up a firing position alongside the meth ship.

Ely had not smoked in ten years, but he had the sudden urge for a cigarette.

The HITRON team leader ordered *Blackbird* to stop one last time.

"Light up the field," Commander Adams said.

Crewmen on *Defiant's* superstructure and bow activated her searchlights. Brilliant beams flicked on, flooding the darkened drug-making vessel with illumination. Ely watched the tactical helicopter. She had been cleared to fire. And she did. A staccato muzzle flash from her open door lit up the night sky like a strobe; 7.62mm rounds peppered the water ahead of the drug ship, kicking up dozens of impact geysers—but *Blackbird* kept moving forward.

"Bow gun," Commander Adams said, "stand by to fire."

Ely tensed. "She's a meth lab."

Adams frowned at him. "Mr. Choi, confirm the gun crew is targeting aft quarter only."

"Aye, sir."

The helicopter cut loose another barrage across *Blackbird's* bow. She kept moving.

Silence fell over *Defiant's* bridge. Commander Adams drew a pensive breath. "Bow gun, open—"

An unfamiliar voice burst into bridge through the comm speakers. "We're stopping. Do you hear me, Coast Guard? We are stopping."

Adams spun about. "Bow gun, hold!"

A breath away from speaking the fire command, Choi released the mic switch. "Yes, sir."

"She's not stirring a wake anymore," Ely said. "Looks like her engines are idle."

"I want the HITRON team to confirm that."

Petty Officer Bowman hailed the chopper and relayed the order. The HITRON pilot maneuvered in a wide loop around the *Blackbird.* "Suspect vessel is no longer under power," the pilot reported. "She's drifting."

"Helm, all stop. Mr. Bowman, inform *Blackbird* crew to prepare to be boarded."

"Yes, sir."

Ely scrutinized the meth ship as she wallowed in the lake a hundred yards out. She was still dark, but the smokestack on her bow no longer belched out fumes. "They're shutting down the lab, probably trying to destroy as much evidence as possible before you get there."

"They can't toss the equipment overboard with us sitting on top of them," Commander Adams said. "Whatever they try to do, it won't be enough to make that boat look innocent."

Ely shrugged. "We won't know what they're trying to do until your men get over there."

"Mr. Choi," Commander Adams said, "launch boarding team."

"Aye, sir." Choi keyed the 1MC. "Boarding team, launch. Boarding team, launch."

Deckhands in the stern launch released the main catch, and the OTH boat containing the five-man boarding team slid down a ramp into the lake. The boat's pilot revved the outboard motor, and the rigid-hulled inflatable craft veered toward the *Blackbird.*

Ely watched their advance. "Your men do understand there's an informant aboard that ship expecting to be taken into my custody, right?"

Commander Adams nodded. "I briefed them myself."

"Cobb will be asking for me."

"You're covered," Commander Adams said. "You'll get your man, and I'll get my feather."

"Provided we have a good night."

"We will. I have confidence in my men."

"I don't doubt your men," Ely said, "but it's been my experience that things out here don't always go as planned."

"Lieutenant Rhodes is leading the team. He's my best. The operation will be textbook."

The HITRON chopper circled around *Blackbird,* and its searchlight flashed across *Defiant's* bridge, blinding Ely. He closed his eyes, and then set his gaze back on the boarding team in the OTH boat. They had reached the meth ship and were climbing aboard. A man emerged from the *Blackbird*'s pilothouse with his hands in the air. Three of the team breached the gunwale and trained their M14 tactical rifles on him. They ordered him down and secured him with flex restraints. The rest of the guardsmen arrived on deck, and the team entered the ship through the pilothouse.

"Show me the feed from Rhodes's body cam," Commander Adams said.

Bowman routed the incoming signal to a nearby monitor, and a black-and-white image of a narrow corridor inside *Blackbird* appeared on the screen. The boarding team had begun clearing the vessel. Ely watched their progress, from the ship's bridge to the decrepit lower decks, getting an occasional glimpse of the rifle in Rhodes's hands and the other team members around him.

On the third deck below the pilothouse, they came upon a trio of crewmen in what appeared to be a section of cabins. Two of the men looked shabby and disheveled. The third seemed to have some notion of personal hygiene. None of them offered any resistance. They raised their hands immediately. Rhodes ordered them face down on deck, and his men secured them with flex restraints. Rhodes and two guardsmen began searching the cabins, while two other team members lifted the crewmen to their feet to escort them topside. The body cam image swung left and right, catching brief shots of the crewmen's faces as they were led away. Ely locked his eyes on the screen, trying to find Cobb among them. No luck. "Damn it, Cobb, show yourself."

Rhodes quickly searched the dirty cabins. Apart from empty beer cans, whiskey bottles, cigarette butts, and tins of Spam, he didn't find anything of value or interest. He continued forward, leading the team through a bulkhead door into a corridor in the bow section of the ship. The body cam picture jerked and jumped, freezing for an instant, and then resuming. Ely thought about the location of the smokestack, and figured the boarding team was nearing the lab compartment. "They're about to walk into hell's kitchen."

"Mr. Bowman," Adams said. "Tell the team to put on their respirators."

Rhodes received the warning, and the guardsmen donned respirators from their equipment packs. They moved to the next bulkhead door. One of them tried to push through it, but something blocked it on the other side. He stepped back and kicked it open with his boot heel. Rhodes shouted into the compartment, "U.S. Coast Guard! Stand back with hands raised!"

Stark overhead lights washed out the body cam picture, but the camera compensated for the brightness and the image returned. Rhodes entered the compartment with two of his men, sweeping left to right, reading the situation. His body cam broadcast pictures of a laboratory somewhere between Dr. Frankenstein and the Nutty Professor. Two long tables were pushed against the port bulkhead, both cluttered with chemistry flasks and mason jars. Pie tins filled with crystals, chemical bottles, and low-grade burners took up the rest of the table space. A similarly cluttered table sat in the center of the compartment, and a row of tall steel tanks stood between them, feeding propane to the various burners through a tangle of rubber hoses. Dark-brown moonshine jars were stacked under the tables.

Voices shouted, "Don't shoot! Don't shoot!"

Four men, two wearing army surplus gas masks and working near the tables, and two standing in the back of the compartment near a stack of wooden crates, froze in place when Rhodes and his men burst in.

"Everyone on the deck," Rhodes shouted. "Face down, hands behind your head. Now!"

The two guys in gas masks dropped right down. The other two did not move so quickly. One of Rhodes' men stepped forward and trained his rifle on them. "Get down! Now!"

Ely stared hard at the jerky, black-and-white video, focusing on the men without masks. "That's Cobb!" he shouted. "Back left."

Eyes wide and hands up, Cobb seemed to be searching the guardsmen's faces.

"I said down!" the guardsman ordered.

Rhodes moved to secure the men in the gas masks. His camera angled away from Cobb, sweeping over the drug-cooking table.

"Pull Cobb out of there," Ely said to Adams.

"After we secure the ship."

Rhodes crouched and cinched a pair of flex restraints on the guys in gas masks.

Someone shouted, "Gun!"

Rhodes spun and lifted his rifle. His camera whirled to the crewmen in back. The guy near the crates had grabbed a shotgun from somewhere. The approaching guardsman fired a burst of rounds, peppering the man's chest. The guy shuddered and triggered his weapon. A blast of twelve-gauge shot shattered a group of flasks on the center table and hit the guardsman's body armor. Cobb panicked and jumped away.

Rhodes targeted him.

Ely's heart pounded. "No! Tell Rhodes that's Cobb."

A muzzle flash burst from Rhodes's rifle barrel.

Bowman transmitted. "Lieutenant Rhodes, hold fire on that crewman."

He ceased fire, pulling his barrel away after just two rounds.

Ely focused on the screen, trying to see if Cobb had been hit, but a flash of light shined through *Defiant*'s wheel room windows and into his peripheral vision, like the helicopter searchlight had done earlier. He lifted his head to see what was going on.

For a split second, all seemed calm. The *Blackbird* drifted quietly in the glow of the cutter's searchlights as the HITRON chopper hovered over her starboard side. Then the seams along her hull plates came apart, ripped open by a blast of fire and smoke. An explosion mushroomed and consumed the bow. Pieces of steel sizzled into the air, twisting and spiraling, leaving corkscrew trails of smoke behind. A shard of shrapnel rocketed into *Defiant's* wheel room through a window, striking Commander Adams in the chest. He reeled about, sliced open from shoulder to sternum. Ely caught him as he toppled over. Bowman and Choi rushed to assist, setting Adams on the edge of the chart table to check his wound. Ely faced the fiery scene.

The helicopter pitched fore and aft in the dissipating explosion. Her rotors were still turning and she didn't seem to be damaged, just buffeted by the shockwave. Below her, *Blackbird's* burning shell listed to starboard. A handful of bodies floated in the water in the glow of *Defiant's* searchlights, some fighting against the waves and debris, others not moving. Ely stared at the flames and billowing smoke. "Damned meth lab," he said under his breath.

In shock, Commander Adams sat bleeding on the chart table, trying to get his bearings, unaware of the injury that Choi and Bowman were attempting to treat. "Rhodes and the team," Adams said. "Where are they?"

Ely and Choi exchanged a glance.

"Don't know yet," Ely said.

Adams seemed confused, and then slumped over and lost consciousness. Ely caught him and lowered him to the deck.

"Med techs are on the way," Bowman said.

"Choi," Ely said. "You're in command now. I'll look after Adams."

Choi nodded. He stood and issued commands to the bridge crew to begin a search-and-rescue operation, and to find out what was left of the boarding team.

The ship's med techs arrived and dressed the commander's wound. They moved him onto a stretcher to carry him below deck. Ely helped them get Adams off the bridge, and then walked onto the port wing to watch the helicopter hoist a survivor from the lake. He thought about Cobb and the boarding team being at the probable epicenter of the explosion.

Chances of survival: almost none.

Such a waste. The guardsmen had dedicated their lives to protecting and rescuing others, and ended up dying because a despicable drug lord had packed a deadly meth lab into the belly of a ship. Regarding Cobb, it seemed a tragic irony that he perished in the very moment he thought he would find salvation. From a selfish perspective, Ely realized he was back at square one. Without Cobb, he wouldn't be getting any answers.

It wasn't a good night for anyone.

ELEVEN

Walker, Michigan

In the hour before dawn, Kade did not have much light to use to reach the bathroom, just his knowledge of the bedroom's layout. He moved cautiously through the dark, trying to be silent and trying to remember where on the floor Danny had left her tall, leather boots. Their dark shapes came into focus on his third step and he maneuvered around them.

"Why are you up so early?" Danny's voice, almost a whisper. The flick of a lighter sounded, and a small yellow flame illuminated the room.

Kade did not particularly like it when Danny smoked in the apartment, but that's not why his shoulders slumped. He turned around. She was sitting up in bed, lighting a cigarette. "I didn't mean to wake you," he said.

"I know." She reached for the nightstand and switched on the lamp.

"I'm meeting with Baldy this morning, about next year's hangar-rental agreement."

"It's a little early for a meeting with Baldy, isn't it?"

"It's a maintenance day for the plane too. Cody and I are getting coffee before heading to the hangar." Kade picked up a T-shirt from the floor beside the bed and pulled it on.

"Sweetheart, Cody tied one on last night, remember?" She puffed on the cigarette. "He's not getting up this early either."

Kade had run out of pre-planned excuses. "Danny, listen—"

"Why are you trying to sneak away without talking to me?"

"I'm not. I've got things to do and I didn't want to disturb you."

She gazed at a stream of smoke rising from her cigarette. "You still love her."

"I what?"

"You still love Rachel, and you don't know how to tell me."

"I thought we put this question to bed last night."

"You never answered that question last night."

Kade walked into the bathroom and switched on the light. "We're not discussing it now."

"Sweetheart, you can't keep doing this. Every time her name comes up, you brush it off, change subjects, take a piss—anything to avoid the topic."

Kade closed the bathroom door and lifted the toilet seat. "That's not true."

She laughed. "Damn it, Kade. Quit being funny. We have to talk about this."

He finished his business and opened the door. "You weren't so interested in having this discussion when we got home last night, if I remember correctly."

She gestured with the cigarette. "I know you hate these things, baby. I'm trying to quit." She stabbed it out in a nightstand ashtray and pulled up a spaghetti strap that had slipped from her shoulder. She patted the bed next to her. "Sit."

Kade's stomach tightened. He walked over and sat beside her. The lamp glowed softly on her face. "Are you going to tell me you're starting the nicotine patch today?"

"You're still doing it," she said. "Avoiding the issue."

He opened his mouth to reply but conceded her point and didn't speak.

"Kade, our relationship can't be a series of distractions to avoid talking about Rachel."

"Why is it so important we discuss my ex-wife?"

"Because you never let her go." Danny gently tapped the top of his head. "She's in there whether we talk about her or not, and that's not okay with me."

"I can't just erase memories."

She squeezed his hand. "I don't want you to forget her, but you shouldn't still grieve over your relationship with her. It's like a wall between us."

"I'm not grieving." He stood and searched for something in the room to focus on instead of Danny. "I don't obsess on Rachel," he said. "My memories of her don't get in our way."

"They do, sweetheart. She's always with you."

"I'm with you," he said, "not her."

Danny smiled. "We have a great time together, but some days it seems like you wake up and remember a time when you were truly happy and realize that I wasn't part of it."

"That's not true."

"You keep her picture in the plane," she said. "I've seen you open your desk drawer just to look at your wedding ring. And that day you got drunk at the Bow Tie was on your anniversary."

Kade did not reply.

"I can't go on feeling like the other woman when I'm the only woman."

"Danny, I love—"

She placed a hand over his lips. "Don't say it to me while you're thinking about her. Say it to me when you're thinking about us." She wrapped her arms tight around him.

Kade hugged her and closed his eyes. "It isn't the way you think." As he spoke, he felt a twinge in his gut, like maybe she was right. "I don't know how to explain it."

"If you can't tell me what you're feeling, then she's still got a grip." Danny pulled away from him. She picked up the cigarette pack from the nightstand, thought about it, threw it back down. "You need time to figure this out. I'm going to give it to you."

"You don't have to do that."

"Yes, sweetheart, I do." She picked up her robe from a chair. "You need distance right now. I'll take my things out of here, and I'll clear out my gear from the hangar too."

"Come on, Rach—" Kade stopped midsentence, but it was too late.

Danny just stared at him. "You better get going if you want to make your appointments."

"We were just talking about her … It doesn't prove your point."

She walked past him into the bathroom.

"You're making this a bigger issue than it is. It's no reason to leave."

She leaned against the doorframe with arms crossed. "I'm giving you a chance to clear your head, so you can decide whether you want to keep living in the past or move forward."

"I don't need to clear my head."

She disappeared into the bathroom and closed the door.

Kade waited for her to come back out. She didn't. He tried to talk to her, but no response. She had made up her mind and it wasn't going to change. He felt empty inside. He had gotten close to Danny, but he had to admit the truth. Rachel's ghost had stepped between them.

He finished dressing, deciding he would shower at Cody's place. He went into the kitchen and found a Post-It pad and a pen and wrote Danny a note.

Danny, you're right. I have to get my head together. I promise you I will. Love you. Kade.

He left the apartment and hopped into his Jeep. Fortunately, they had picked up Danny's car on the way back from Lake Michigan, so he wasn't stranding her there. He pulled out of the lot and headed for Cody's place. The scent of Danny's perfume was still on his shirt. He had to get his mind off it. He had to get his mind off everything.

He switched on a local radio station and listened to a top-of-the-hour news break. Wedged between a political scandal and the Tigers latest loss, a story about a disaster on Lake Huron caught his attention. A suspected drug ship had gone up in flames, and the Coast Guard was on the scene conducting a search-and-rescue operation. The report reminded Kade of the cargo ship he had tried to help a few days ago, and his visit from Agents Nystrom and Rifkin, which inevitably led his thoughts back to Rachel.

All roads seemed to be leading to her. Why?

He had to find out. He had to resolve that part of his life, one way or the other.

TWELVE

Michigan Intelligence Operational Center (MIOC)
Lansing, Michigan

Ely warmed his hands on a steaming cup of black coffee while watching a Channel 6 news broadcast on the central screen in the Ops Area. After helping with the search-and-rescue effort aboard the *Defiant*, flying back to Port Huron on a chopper at sunrise, and driving back to Lansing, he had not slept all night and exhaustion draped over him like a lead jacket. Now, having arrived at the MIOC office only a half hour ago, it seemed surreal to watch live video from a news helicopter circling the *Defiant* as she operated amid the doomed meth ship's debris field.

State Intelligence Officer Gary Anders walked up beside him. "You look tired, Ely."

"I am tired, Gary."

"What's the latest?"

"Nothing new in the last hour. When I left the site, we had fished out four of the *Blackbird's* crew and two of our boarding team."

"Any word on Commander Adams?"

"They say he's going to pull through."

"He got lucky," Anders said.

"If any part of getting hit in the chest with shrapnel is lucky, I guess surviving would be it."

"Are you absolutely certain about Cobb?"

"*Blackbird* went up in a blaze of glory. Anyone who survived was pulled from the water hours ago. *Defiant's* just covering all the bases right now."

Commander Gerard approached from his office across the floor. "I just spoke with Choi. Search and rescue is over. They're transition-ing to recovery operations."

"There's our confirmation," Ely said.

Anders' face fell. "Meth labs are volatile. The takedown was risky. We knew that going in."

"Yeah, we knew that going in ... still."

"Still what?" Commander Gerard said.

Ely shook his head. "Nothing."

"What's on your mind?" Anders said.

Ely hesitated. "Cobb was going to spill his guts, but he can't talk now, can he?"

Anders and Gerard stared at him.

"Are you suggesting someone blew the ship to silence Cobb?" Gerard said.

Ely shrugged. "It's possible."

"Perry wouldn't destroy his own ship to kill a snitch," Anders said.

"No, he'd take him into a back room and double tap him in the head," Gerard added.

"That would be more logical," Ely conceded.

"It's more likely the firefight in the meth lab triggered the explosion," Anders said.

"I know, but I have a suspicious mind. I suppose that's why I'm not married anymore."

"Suspicion without evidence doesn't get us very far."

Commander Gerard frowned. "Regardless how it happened, taking down the *Blackbird* cost us three good men, and I'm having a hard time convincing myself it was worth the price."

"So am I, Bob." Ely's phone buzzed with an incoming call from Rachel. "Excuse me, gentlemen." He stepped away and answered. "Hello?"

"Dad, I just heard on the news that a ship blew up during a Coast Guard boarding operation."

"Yeah, I know," Ely said. "I was aboard the cutter at the scene."

"Oh my God, are you okay?"

"I'm fine. Our boarding team wasn't so lucky."

"You're not with the Coast Guard anymore. Why were you out there?"

Ely glanced around the Ops Area. "I'd rather not get into that right now."

"You've done your thing for king and country, Dad. Leave the dangerous stuff alone."

"I'll do my best." Ely's thoughts jumped tracks. "Hey, this might sound like an off-the-wall question, but has T-GAF experienced any incidents involving their ships on the Lakes?"

"Incidents?"

"Incidents, like a vessel sinking under mysterious circumstances, perhaps a fire or a mechanical failure, anything that might be considered out of the ordinary."

Rachel paused. "Not that I am aware of. Why do you ask?"

"I'm investigating some events on the Great Lakes. I don't know the scope of it yet, but there's a chance T-GAF shipping could get tangled up in it."

Silence. "Well, if something peculiar comes up, I'll let you know. Okay?"

"Sure. One more thing. Does your job ever put you aboard a ship on the lakes?"

She paused again. "Sometimes, but not very often."

"Then, do me a favor," Ely said. "If T-GAF asks you to ship out, say no."

"You're making me nervous. What's going on?"

"Just do as I ask. I'll explain when I can." Ely noticed Anders and Gerard had been joined by Lieutenant Walker. They were calling him back. "Listen, honey, I've got to go."

"Okay, but you promise me something," she said. "Stop volunteering for Coast Guard duty."

Ely smiled. "Don't worry about me. Talk with you later. Love you."

"Love you too." She disconnected.

Ely pocketed the phone and joined Walker and the others. "What's going on?"

"I just got a call from the DEA," Walker said. "They want you to come to Detroit."

Ely looked at him funny. "Why do they want me?"

"The Coast Guard transferred the *Blackbird* survivors to the DEA's downtown office for questioning," Walker explained. "Apparently, one of the survivors is asking for you."

Ely's tired eyes opened wide. "Is it Cobb? Did he survive somehow?"

Anders shook his head and read from a scrap of paper in his palm. "No, we just confirmed that it's somebody else. Someone named Lester."

"The guy started asking for Agent Edwards," Walker said, "but the DEA agents didn't know who that was, until an officer from the *Defiant* told them the DHS observer aboard the cutter last night was named Edwards. DEA did some checking and found an Elias J. Edwards stationed at MIOC. Since the *Blackbird* takedown was a Coast Guard op, my phone rings."

Ely felt three steps behind everyone. "Now, hold on. What's the guy's name?"

Anders read from the paper again. "Reno Lester."

"Never heard of him."

"Well, he's heard of you, and you're the only one he says he'll talk with."

"I'd be happy to oblige. Just tell me where."

Anders handed him the paper. "You can be there in an hour and a half."

Ely took the paper and read the DEA's Detroit office address, and the lead investigator's name from it. "Gary, your handwriting is impeccably neat. Do you practice?"

Anders ignored him. "Go talk to this guy. Find out what he wants."

"He must have known Cobb." Ely tucked the paper into his pocket. "Maybe they were both going to turn. Maybe he knows what Cobb knew. We may not be at square one after all."

"That would be fortunate."

"You better believe it." Ely glanced at the Channel 6 news report. "After a night like last night, we can use a little good luck."

THIRTEEN

Sparta, Michigan

Kade listened to the Otter's engines idling outside the cockpit windows, making sure they sounded healthy and in tune. Satisfied that they did, he checked off the last box of the After Start check procedure on his clipboard and tucked it into the side pocket beside the pilot's seat. Out on the tarmac, Cody inspected the aircraft's brakes and nose gear while nursing a hangover. Kade watched him a moment, recalling the incident at the bar. *You're definitely a handful, buddy.*

Cody climbed into the plane's passenger cabin and secured the door behind him. He struggled into the cockpit and plopped down in the copilot seat, head back and eyes closed. "Taxi checks complete."

"Looks like you drank a little too much last night." Kade set the aircraft's brakes and feathered the engines.

"Why didn't you stop me?"

"You didn't wait for me. By the time I got there, you were too far gone."

Cody wiped his eyes with his palms. "Some kind of friend you are."

"I did stop you from getting your ass kicked."

"Don't remember that." Cody searched the cockpit. "Do we have any Tylenol in here?"

Kade laughed. "Check your front left pocket. You put some in there this morning."

"Oh, yeah." Cody found a small package, ripped it open, and swallowed the pills dry. "Tell me one more time. Where are we going?"

Kade released the brakes and began taxing toward the runway. "Cherry Capital Airport."

"And, why are we going there?"

"It's the next stop in an aerial poker run happening today. Teague Global is the sponsor, so the prize purse is sweet. A lot of pilots signed up, and I want to check out their planes."

"Teague Global? Isn't that where Rachel works?"

Kade made like he had to think about it. "You know, I think

you're right."

"Mind like a steel trap." Cody put his head back. "Think she'll be there?"

Kade shrugged. "Haven't given it much thought." White lie.

He radioed their departure to Grand Rapids, and then throttled up for takeoff. The Otter accelerated down the runway. Once airborne, Kade banked into a flight path toward Northern Michigan. Cruising at a hundred and fifty knots, the trip to Cherry Capital Airport in Traverse City took about an hour. Cody slept the entire way. Kade received clearance to land and set down on runway 10-28. The thud of touchdown jostled Cody awake.

They taxied off the runway and rolled toward a group of airplanes clustered on the general aviation ramp. Kade figured they belonged to the poker-run participants. It was a nice cross-section of aircraft, from Cessna Skycatchers and TTxs to Beechcraft Bonanzas and King Airs. Throw in a Pilatus PC-12 and a Cirrus SR22T and you had quite an array of private craft. It seemed Teague's sponsorship and prize money had drawn a top-tier crowd.

Kade rolled the Otter to a stop on the fringe of the ramp. He and Cody shut down the engines, secured the plane, and then disembarked. The General Aviation Terminal was busy with people coming and going, pilots and support teams Kade figured; some studied playing cards as they walked. This being the fourth stop in the poker run, they would be looking at the penultimate card of their hand. Kade started to wish he had signed up for the run.

Two men walking by seemed worked up about something. Kade eavesdropped on them. "I was forty-five seconds past check-in deadline," one of them said, "and she almost didn't give me my card. I just about hit the ceiling. I paid good money to get into this thing."

"Yeah," the other man said. "Class-A bitch."

Kade smirked. *Maybe Rachel was here.*

"Hey, Mitchell. Kade Mitchell."

A guy beside a Cessna with a five-day beard and ratted blond hair waved to him.

Kade recognized the man. "Is that who I think it is?"

Cody took a moment to focus. "Yeah, I think it's Jesse?"

They walked over to the guy, and noticed he had an access panel to the Cessna's engine propped open. He had a grease stain on his half-buttoned khaki shirt, but he gave Kade a hug anyway. "Kade

Mitchell," he said again. "I didn't know you were in the poker run."

"I'm not in it," Kade said. "I'm just a spectator."

"Well, it's good to see ya. Where have you been hidin' out?"

"I haven't been hiding anywhere."

"I heard you were in California flying movie directors back and forth to Lake Tahoe."

Kade laughed. "Where did you hear that?"

"Don't remember. Just around. When a guy drops off the radar like you did, people tend to talk. Mostly BS I suppose."

"Mostly," Kade said. "What about you? Still dusting blueberries?"

"Yeah, blueberries, blackberries, any berry I can find. Doing a little courier work too. Not nearly enough of anything to get by though. That's why I joined this poker run. The prize money will fix me. It cost some coin to get in, but the payoff will be worth my while." Jesse slapped the Cessna's fuselage near the exposed engine. "Well, that was the plan until this happened."

Kade considered the cables and tubes on the engine block. "What's your trouble?"

Jesse frowned. "She started making a racket on approach. Lost some power." He smiled at Cody and slapped his shoulder. "Hey, Cody, think you can take a quick look under the hood while I'm picking up my card?"

"Yeah, sure, Jesse." Cody's eyes brightened.

Jesse kissed his cheek. "Thanks, amigo." He tapped Kade's shoulder. "Let's go get my card."

"Let me see your hand so far," Kade said as they started off for the terminal doors. Jesse dug into his pocket and pulled out three playing cards. He fanned them out in his hand and showed Kade. "Not bad, right?"

Kade studied them. Two aces—a spade and a club. One jack of diamonds. "Lots of good possibilities. Not bad at all."

They pushed into the GA terminal and found the check-in station for the poker-run participants across the floor near the FBO's office. A banner emblazoned with the Teague Global Associated Freight logo hung over a table draped in black cloth. A cluster of pilots milled around the table. Jesse headed that way. Kade hesitated, trying to get a look at the workers at the table, wondering if Rachel was with them.

Jesse noticed his buddy had fallen behind. "What are you doing?"

Kade looked up at the vinyl banner. "Reading." To back up his story, he actually read it. *The Blue Water Foundation Aerial Poker Run: Celebrating the Great Lakes Aviation Heritage.* Something clicked in Kade's head, and he pondered the tagline a moment.

"Come on, Kade-O," Jesse said.

"Did you just call me Kato?"

"No, I said … Hell, just come on already."

They walked up to the table. Kade tried to get a look at the workers handing envelopes to the waiting pilots. Too many heads in the way. He searched for people wearing the ID badges that organizers of the run had pinned to their shirt. A nervous twinge tightened his stomach. *Why the hell did I come here?* Before he knew it, he and Jesse were at the front of the line.

"Name?"

The voice spun Kade's head around.

Jesse opened his mouth to answer but stopped when he recognized her. "Rachel?"

She smiled. "Jesse Granger. It's been a long time." She glanced at Kade.

Kade found himself looking into the eyes of the woman whom his life had revolved around for so many years. She had her blond hair pulled back into a business-appropriate ponytail, and she wore a black blazer over a white button shirt. Her T-GAF name tag read *Rachel Edwards – Event Coordinator.* Rachel Edwards, not Mitchell. Right. Back to her maiden name.

"Kade," she said. "What are you doing here?" She seemed surprised.

"I heard there was a poker run happening today and thought I'd check it out."

Jesse laughed. "You guys are playin', right? You came here together."

"Didn't Kade tell you? We're not married anymore." She pushed a clipboard toward Jesse. "You need to sign in before the deadline expires, or you'll default this leg of the run and you won't get your next card."

"Oh, crap. Sorry, I didn't know." Jesse grabbed a pen from the table. "I mean about the marriage thing, not the signing-in thing."

"Jesse and I ran into each other outside," Kade explained. "We haven't talked much yet."

"Apparently."

Jesse popped off the pen cap. "So, is this meeting a coincidence or what?"

Rachel tilted her head toward her ex-husband. "Is it, Kade?"

"You said I might enjoy the poker run, so I decided to come up and check it out. I had no idea you'd be here." He was getting pretty good at lying about that.

Rachel stared at him, like she was trying to determine how much BS she had just heard, and then shifted her attention back to Jesse. "You've got thirty seconds left to sign in."

Jesse scribbled his name on the clipboard. "This isn't a race. It's a poker run, right?"

"The deadline is in the rulebook." Rachel snatched up the clipboard. "There are a lot of planes and pilots participating in the run, and I have to keep everything and everybody moving to stay on schedule."

"Did you write that rulebook?" Kade asked.

She did not reply.

Kade smiled. "I think you're in your element here."

"At least I know what my element is." She pulled a deck of playing cards labeled with Jesse's flight group number from under the table and slid the top card to him without looking at it. "Congratulations on completing the fourth leg of the poker run, Mr. Granger. T-GAF wishes you luck on the final leg, and we look forward to seeing you at the tables this evening."

"Well, thank you, Mrs. Mitchell." Jesse eyed her name tag. "I mean, Ms. Edwards.

She didn't comment on his blunder.

Jesse glanced at his card and smiled. "Let's go see what Cody found out with my plane," he said to Kade. "I got a good feeling about this poker run." Jesse headed for the exit.

Kade did not follow. It was now or never. *You need to decide whether you want to keep living in the past or move forward.*

"Hey, Rachel," he said with a touch of hesitation. "When you wrap up here, can we sit down for a drink somewhere, you know, and try to have an actual conversation?"

"I can't today," she said.

Kade smiled through his disappointment. "That's okay. Just a crazy thought."

She made eye contact with him. "It's a nice thought, but I have to leave soon for the final leg. Planes start touching down on deck this evening, and I have to be there ready for them."

Kade noted her choice of words. Touching down on deck. Rachel had served aboard an aircraft carrier in the Navy a while back, and the terminology had apparently stuck in her head. "No problem. I understand."

She slid the clipboard to the next pilot in line. "Maybe later this week."

Kade lifted his chin. "Just let me know when you have time."

An awkward bit of silence played out between them. "Hey," she said, "anything to report on your friends' visit yesterday?"

Kade thought about Nystrom and Rifkin. He had not figured them out yet, and that bothered him. "No. Nothing new on my end."

"Nothing on my end either. I'll let you know, though."

Kade nodded and turned to leave. "Take care. Hope the rest of the run goes well for you."

"Kade," she said.

He faced her.

"It was good to see you."

He smiled. She seemed to mean it. "It was good to see you too."

The pilot at the table signed in and handed the clipboard back to her. She nodded goodbye to Kade and started into her congratulation speech.

Kade caught up with Jesse at the exit. "Hold that door."

Jesse propped it open with his foot and waited. "You didn't tell me you were divorced."

"I didn't have the chance. Besides, I didn't know she'd be here."

"Do ya really expect me to believe that horseshit?"

"I don't expect you to believe anything. Hey, show me your card."

Jesse handed it to him. It was a jack of hearts.

"Now you've got two pairs," Kade said. "Jacks and aces. You're looking at a possible full house. Your chances of winning this thing are better than average."

"Yeah, if my plane can fly the final leg," Jesse said.

They returned to the Cessna. Cody still had his head inside the engine compartment.

Kade tapped him on the shoulder. "Did you find anything?"

Cody turned around with a frown on his face. "Fuel pump."

"Fuel pump?" Jesse scrutinized the engine compartment. "Can you fix it?"

"When a fuel pump goes bad, you don't fix it," Cody said. "You replace it."

"I don't have time to order a new fuel pump, amigo. The final leg starts in a couple hours." Jesse paced in front of the plane. "And I got a damn good poker hand too. Batshit!"

Cody scratched his whiskers. "Maintenance hangar here, at the airport, might have a spare parts crib. It's a longshot, but they might stock the model pump you need."

"And there are aviation companies based here too," Kade said. "We can call them to see if any operate a Cessna like yours. If they do, they might have a spare pump."

"Yeah … maybe. I'll talk to the FBO. His office is right inside the terminal."

"Wait," Kade said. "The Fixed Base Operator is probably too busy to help you, with this poker run going on."

"So, I shouldn't even bother to ask?"

"Maybe not." Kade had determined the chances of finding a spare fuel pump at the airport were not good. He had already sprung another idea. Sure, there was a touch of selfish motivation behind it, but first and foremost, he would be helping a friend. "What about the Otter?"

Jesse cocked his head. "The Otter's got a couple of Pratt PT6's under her wings. I have a Conti Oh-470 piston in the Cessna. You don't have the fuel pump I need."

"No," Kade said, "but I have a plane that can fly."

"Sure do." Cody didn't seem to get the gist of the comment.

Jesse picked up on it though. "I registered the Cessna in the run. I can't finish in the Otter."

"This isn't a race. It's a poker run. All you're required to do is get from point to point within a certain timeframe. It shouldn't matter which plane gets you there. The important thing is that you are the one collecting the card and playing your hand. Am I right?"

Jesse thought about it. "I don't know. Switching planes mid-stream?"

"Is it specifically prohibited in the rulebook?" Kade asked.

"Uh, I don't think so."

"Then, what are you worried about?"

Jesse rocked on his heels. "You're right. What have I got to lose? Let's just pile into the Otter and take our chances. I mean, if we don't,

I'm finished already. Right?"

"Right." Kade nudged Cody's shoulder. "Let's prep for takeoff. Jesse, make arrangements to get the Cessna off the ramp."

Jesse nodded. "I'm on it." He spun around to head up to the terminal, but turned back around. "Hey, Kade ..."

"What?"

"Thanks for doing this."

"No problem. Get moving."

Jesse stood there a moment longer, like he wanted to say more.

"What?"

Jesse shook his head. "Never mind. I'll be right back."

Kade slapped Cody's shoulder again. "What are you waiting for? Let's get ready to go."

"Sure, Kade." Cody looked puzzled. "Where are we going?"

"Uh ..." Kade realized he did not know where the final leg ended. "I'm not sure. I must have read it somewhere, but it's escaping me. Jesse will tell us when he gets back. I'm sure we can make it to wherever it is without too much trouble."

He and Cody returned to the Otter at the edge of the ramp and began prepping her for takeoff. After running through all the checks, they waited for Jesse. And waited. After two hours, he came walking down the GA ramp.

"What happened? Did you forget the plan?" Kade said to him.

"No, it just took me a lot longer to get the Cessna moved than I thought. The poker run has got this airport turned upside down."

They all boarded the Otter as the taxi time for Jesse's flight group approached.

Kade settled into the pilot's seat. "Jesse, this is probably a good time to tell me where we're going."

Jesse slipped into the copilot's seat and put on an uneasy smile. "Are you serious, Kade?"

"Yeah, I'm serious. It would be nice if you could tell me before we go wheels up."

Jesse pointed out the cockpit window toward Lake Michigan. "That way."

Kade looked east. "What do you mean? Beaver Island?"

"No, I mean *that* way."

"Not funny, Jesse. I need to know before we get going."

Jesse stared at him and his face fell. "You are serious."

"Yeah, that's what I'm trying to tell you."

"Sorry, amigo. I thought you knew." Jesse licked his lips and strapped into his seat. "We're going back in time."

Kade looked him in the eye. "What the hell is that supposed to mean?"

Jesse laughed. "It means you better be as good a pilot as I think you are, because the runway we're headed for is unforgiving. You'll get just one shot to nail the landing, and if you miss the mark, well, we just might not come back from this adventure."

FOURTEEN

DEA, Detroit Office

Ely met DEA Agent Matthew Jordan outside an interview room. The dark-haired man appeared to be at least ten years younger than Ely, but the crow's feet and touch of gray near his temples indicated he would be advancing to Senior Agent status before too long. The job had a way of doing that to people.

"Agent Edwards," Jordan said.

Ely shook hands with him.

"Thanks for coming so quickly."

"Your detainee requested me," Ely said. "That got my attention."

"No doubt." Jordan gestured to the door. "We were conducting interviews with *Blackbird* survivors, trying to get a feel for how much dirt we might get on Perry, and we get to this guy, and all he says is, 'Get me Agent Edwards.' He won't talk to me, or a government-appointed attorney, or anybody. What's the story between you two?"

"There isn't one. I never heard of Reno Lester until this morning."

Jordan looked at Ely like he did not quite believe him. "Why do you suppose he wants to talk to you?"

"Don't know. When I heard you had a *Blackbird* crewman asking for me, I thought you might have a guy named Cobb in there."

"We don't have a Cobb," Jordan said. "Who's he?"

"He *was* an informant I intended to take into custody after we took the *Blackbird*. He had plenty of dirt that would stick to Perry, but he was killed on the ship. Now, Reno Lester comes out of the blue." Ely chuckled. "Maybe he's the phoenix rising from the *Blackbird*'s ashes."

Jordan smiled. "I wouldn't count on this guy being a phoenix."

Ely nodded toward the door. "Let's talk with him and find out."

Jordan pushed the door open into a small room with beige walls. A thin man with wavy, black hair sat behind a beat-up, pressed-wood table. He wore an oversized Coast Guard sweatshirt and navy-blue pants, probably compliments of the cutter crew after his rescue from the lake. He appeared to be thirty-something, and his eyes looked wired open. Reno Lester wrapped his hands around a coffee cup and appraised Ely. "Who's this?"

Jordan laughed. "You don't know him?"

Lester did not reply.

"Look real hard," Jordan said. "You've been asking for him all morning."

Lester's expression brightened. "Agent Ely Edwards."

Ely recognized his face. "You were rounded up in the cabin section of the *Blackbird*. I remember you from the boarding team's video."

Lester cocked his head like he did not understand the reference, and then tapped his finger on the table. "Show me your creds."

Ely pulled his DHS credentials from an inner jacket pocket and set them down.

Lester inspected the badge and ID like a bouncer at a bar. He nodded to Ely. "You stay." He tossed the credentials back to him, and then he pointed at Agent Jordan. "You go."

Ely gave Jordan a nod, and the DEA agent left the room.

Silence. Ely stood with arms crossed, staring at Reno Lester. Lester stared back but said nothing. Ely rolled his eyes. "Okay, I'll go first. You don't know me, so why did you demand to speak with me?"

"I heard about you," Lester said.

"From who?"

"Daryl Cobb."

"Why would Cobb tell you anything about me?"

"We were kindred spirits, two souls serving time on a ship we didn't want to be on. One day we sparked up a conversation over a bottle of Crown Royal. He told me about you, about things you two discussed, and that he was spilling on Perry."

"So much for Cobb keeping our arrangement confidential."

"Don't be too harsh on him. I pried it out of him. I'm good at that kind of thing."

"Why won't you talk to Agent Jordan?"

"Can't tell you that." Lester added, "Not here."

"Why do you want to talk with me?"

"I don't want to talk with you. I want to give you a message."

Ely sat across the table from him. "A message from who?"

Lester nodded toward a camera in the corner of the room, trying not to be obvious about it. "I can't talk freely. They're recording everything. Can you turn that thing off?"

"No. You're going to have to give me your message with it on."

Lester shook his head. "No can do."

Ely leaned forward. "Look, Reno. I've been up thirty-two hours straight. In that time, I've taken part in a drug interdiction that went really bad, lent a hand in a search-and-rescue operation on open water, and drove two over hundred miles back and forth across the state. I'm in no mood to beat around the bush. You called for me. I'm here. Talk to me."

Lester crossed his arms. "Not with that camera on."

"Why?"

"Because I got a thing about Big Brother and black helicopters."

"But black meth ships don't bother you?"

"You're not taking me seriously." Lester looked disappointed. "Cobb said you were for real."

"Would I be sitting here if I wasn't taking you seriously?"

"Maybe you're setting the hook. You might not be who I think you are."

"This is a waste of time." Ely stood. "Good luck, Reno."

Lester sat up straight. "Where are you going?"

"You're not talking. I'm not staying."

"You can't leave. I've got information you need. You need me."

"You've got that backwards." Ely faced him. "You're the one who was apprehended aboard a floating meth lab. That's a minimum of fifteen years. Your ass is in a sling and you need a way out, so you dreamed up a story about a mysterious message, hoping your connection to Cobb would sell it. I don't know exactly what you had in mind, but you're trying to leverage me to get you out of this pickle somehow. I'm not buying."

Concern crept into Lester's eyes. "You're reading it wrong."

Ely walked to the door. "You had your shot, and you blew it." He reached for the doorknob.

Lester squirmed in his chair. "You think they're being hunted," he blurted out. "You're not the only one."

Ely stopped cold. "What did you say?"

"You heard me." Lester straightened his back.

Ely returned to the table. "Who's being hunted?"

Lester leaned forward and gestured for Ely to come closer. "You know who," he said in a hush. "You told Cobb."

Ely's mind went to the *Discord* document and the chart of the sunken trafficking vessels. "Who else believes this?"

"My boss," Lester whispered. "And he doesn't just believe it, he knows who's doing it."

Ely felt a spike of adrenaline. "Enlighten me."

Lester shook his head. "Not a chance. Too many eyes. Too many ears. Besides, that's all I'm supposed to say. If you want to hear more, you've got to talk to the boss."

"Why can't I talk to you?"

"I'm only a messenger."

"A messenger for who? Ricco Perry?"

"No. The *boss*. Don't you get it?"

"Apparently not. Isn't Perry your boss?"

Lester settled back in his chair. "I didn't even belong on the *Blackbird*—can you believe that? He told me to get aboard, find out what's going on. Now, here I sit, at fed central, looking at fifteen years. I'll tell ya, loyalty doesn't pay."

"Depends on who you're loyal to." Ely regarded Lester, trying to sort through his twisting tale. "If it wasn't Perry, who told you to get aboard that ship?"

"You just don't understand." Lester said quietly. "I was supposed to give you this message on neutral ground. The *Blackbird* sinking wasn't part of the plan. Now, I'm a fed prisoner with my balls in a vice. If the boss is wrong about you, my jewels will be the first to get crushed."

"Wrong about me. What the hell is that supposed to mean?"

"High stakes, that's what it means. If he's right, you two will talk, you'll tell him where I am, and he'll find a way to get me out. That's my only shot."

"Then tell me who he is, so I can contact him."

"Yeah, right." Lester glanced at the camera. "I might as well paint a target on his chest."

"Then don't say anything. Write it down."

"Do I look stupid? That's the only camera I can see, but they got eyes everywhere. Besides, everybody knows you don't write down the important stuff."

"Reno, you're very intriguing, but you're pissing me off."

"Pardon me if my concern over my future is inconveniencing you." Lester scrutinized Ely a long while. "I need a drink."

Ely gestured to the cup on the table. "Fresh coffee?"

"I was thinking whiskey."

"Try again."

"What about bourbon? Do you like bourbon? They say the older the better, right?"

Ely had a sharp retort on his tongue, but Lester made eye contact, indicating he wasn't driving aimlessly with this verbal detour. He had a destination in mind. Ely decided to ride along. "If you age it right, there's nothing better than a tumbler of bourbon."

"I have a bartender friend," Lester said. "He runs his own place on Lake St Clair. Great guy. And he likes to SCUBA dive. One day, he hears a story about how the old bootleggers used to drive their Ford Coupes across the frozen lake to get their booze into the States, and how not all of them made it across. It got my friend to thinking that there's a lot of aging whiskey at the bottom of the lake, so he gets out his SCUBA gear and starts searching."

"Not a bad idea," Ely said. "There's probably enough cars down there to fill a parking lot."

"Yeah, well he found one, and he was right. He brought up a crate of whiskey from 1922. Says the cold water preserved it perfectly. Now he serves shots of ninety-year-old bourbon at his place to VIP customers. If you like bourbon, that's the place to go."

Ely understood. "What's the atmosphere like at his place?"

"The best. Friendly people and interesting conversation." Lester added, "You might even find a new drinking buddy there."

"You convinced me to give it a try. How do I get there?"

Lester cradled his chin as if in deep thought. "I'm not real good at directions. It's on the lake. My friend bought it from a guy who knew the original owners. They opened it right after World War Two. Boy, it's been a while. Last time I was there, I was having a pretty good day. I'd just hit it big at the Motor City Casino, and I was lookin' to celebrate with that bourbon. I felt like a real champion heading over there, but things went south and I ended up in Canada."

"I'll just Google it. What's the name of this place?"

"That's the crazy part. I don't remember the name. Something earthy. I don't know. It's not coming to me." Lester gave Ely a sly look. "You'll just have to find it with what I've told you."

"You haven't told me anything."

"I've told you everything you need."

Ely began parsing every word Lester had said. "It'll be a miracle if I find it. And if I do walk into a bar thinking it's the one, how will I know I've actually found it?"

"Ask for Jimmy. If he's the bartender, you're probably there."

"Jimmy. That's an uncommon name. Wonderful. This bourbon better be worth it."

"Best *you'll* ever have," Lester said. "Oh, and it isn't on the drink menu. You have to ask Jimmy for the Sugar Hill bourbon."

"That's it? Ask Jimmy for the Sugar Hill bourbon?"

"That'll tell him you're a VIP. Introduce yourself, and the rest will take care of itself."

"Reno, if you're jerking me around, I promise you, those meth ship charges will stick. I might even find a few more to tack on. Understand?"

"Sure. But you better understand, the boss isn't screwing around. If he's reaching out to you, there's some serious shit going down."

Ely stood. "I know. Why do you think I'm even entertaining this fairytale?"

"Make sure he knows I stayed loyal and delivered his message."

"If I find him, I'll tell him. Until then, sit tight and cooperate with Agent Jordan."

"Cooperation ends once you leave. After that, I'm a mute again."

"You're only making it harder on yourself."

"Trust me, I know when to talk and I know when to shut up. In this building, I shut up."

Ely stared at him a moment, and then walked into the hallway and closed the door.

Agent Jordan met him there. "What was all that about?"

"Serendipity."

"What?"

"Reno Lester may have just led me to a lot of answers. He might be the phoenix after all."

Jordan chuckled. "All I heard was double-talk and a wild goose chase."

Ely smiled. "Me too."

He left the building and hopped into his Tahoe. Before pulling out of the parking lot, he gazed up at the federal building to the floor where Reno Lester sat in the interview room. Did Lester's boss really know who was targeting the traffickers? With any luck he did, but before Ely could find out, he needed to solve a puzzle.

BOOK II

ECHOES

FIFTEEN

Above Lake Michigan

Kade piloted the Otter in a northerly direction. A series of sandy beaches outlined the shoreline far off the aircraft's starboard wingtip, while a horizon of water and sky played out to port. Kade kept his eyes on the shimmering water ahead. He bled off air speed and lowered altitude a hundred feet. It had to be close now.

Jesse scanned the water from the copilot's seat.

"Are you sure about those numbers?" Kade said.

"Yeah, I'm sure." Jesse flicked a notepad in his lap. "Your wife gave me the coordinates."

"Ex-wife."

Cody squeezed into the cockpit from the passenger cabin and gave a cursory look out the windows. "Finding the runway is only half the problem," he said. "You sure about this, Kade?"

"Yeah, I'm sure about this."

"I'm just asking because, you know, it's ... different."

"Cody, the Otter has the best STOL specs in the industry."

"I'm not worried about the Otter's short takeoff and landing specs. I'm wondering if you can stick a landing on a runway a fraction the length of the one we just came from in Traverse City."

"Yee of little faith."

Kade had plenty of confidence in his piloting skills, but even he had to think twice before taking on this challenge. It *was* a first for him. He had never landed on a moving airstrip just five hundred and fifty feet long—and that is what awaited him.

According to Jesse, the final runway in the poker run was the flight deck of an aircraft carrier named *Wolverine*. Apparently, during World War Two, a steam-powered paddlewheel carrier named *U.S.S Wolverine* sailed the Great Lakes, tasked with a mission to train naval aviators. The ship Kade now searched for, however, was not the original *Wolverine*, but a complete replica, commissioned and built by logistics tycoon Galen Teague, who also happened to be Rachel's boss. A reputed aviation-history buff, Teague apparently had more money than he knew what to do with. Where the idea had come from to build such a unique craft was anybody's guess, but Kade imagined it grew out of Teague's well-known philanthropic partnership with the Blue Water Foundation. Bits and pieces of the replica's construction had made it into media reports along the way, but Kade had not been paying attention, especially during the time when his pilot license was suspended and he was trying to stay away from anything having to do with flight. Well, the blinders were off now. *Wolverine* was the biggest ship in a bottle Kade had ever heard of, and he held the Otter on course to intercept her in the middle of Lake Michigan.

The vessel first appeared as an odd shape on the distant water. She was long and flat, with a structure like a tower rising from her aft quarter, looking like an island in a sea of oak planking. She was under way, but instead of propellers at her stern, a pair of paddlewheels protruded below her flattop amidships, port and starboard, and churned the water to drive her forward. As the distance closed, runway markings became visible on the deck.

Kade felt an excitement in his chest he had not felt since being a kid. Setting the Otter down on what looked like a shoebox from this altitude would test his piloting like never before, and he relished the challenge. "Jesse, tell them we're arriving."

Jesse set the radio to a frequency designated for poker-run communications and spoke into the boom mic on his headset. "*Wolverine. Wolverine.* This is Jesse Granger, flight group number 1-3, requesting clearance to land. Please confirm."

They waited for a response. None came. Jesse repeated the hail. Nothing.

"You got the right frequency, buddy?" Kade said.

"Yeah, I got it right. Why do you keep doubting me?" Jesse checked the setting anyway.

Cody studied the indicators on the console. "Radio seems to be working okay."

Jesse took a breath to call again, but a voice replied through the comm speaker. "Jesse Granger, flight group number 1-3, this is *Wolverine* ATC …"

Aboard *Wolverine*

Rachel Edwards studied the poker-run registration screen on her tablet. "All but three pilots have landed," she said. "We should have everyone aboard within the hour."

Galen Teague, commander of *Wolverine*, and president and CEO of Teague Global Associated Freight, gazed out the bridge windows at the wave crests breaking beyond the flight deck below. "How many turned back when they couldn't manage a landing?"

"Four," Rachel said.

"Were there any near misses?"

"Just one. A pilot came in too fast on final, and the LSO had to wave him off. He barely throttled up in time to avoid a nosedive into the lake."

Teague's smile deepened the lines around his eyes. "It's a shame T-GAF business kept me on shore so long. I wanted to watch the arrivals." He faced Rachel, and the afternoon sun shimmered on the salt in his salt-and-pepper hair. "So, we'll have eight pilots left in the run to play out their hands. Correct?"

"Yes, assuming the last three successfully land on deck."

Teague glanced around at the bridge crew. "And everything is on schedule?"

"Yes, I'm making sure of that." She added, "Weather reports have a storm front tracking this way. Models predict it will reach our position in about four hours. That should give us enough time to play the hands, name the winner, and send the pilots off."

Teague nodded his approval. "Make sure you re-spot the last few planes as soon as they land. Salvio will be arriving early with the Wildcat, and he'll need the deck space."

Rachel gestured through the aft bridge windows to five aircraft parked at the extreme edges of the flight deck. "I've packed them pretty tight already. Salvio shouldn't have a problem."

"Be certain of that," Teague said.

"Sir," the radar operator called out from his station. "I've got an inbound contact that is not squawking a transponder code."

Teague raised an eyebrow. "Is it approaching on a flight path we would expect a poker-run participant to follow?"

"Yes, sir."

Teague looked to Rachel. "You did emphasize to the pilots the importance of properly setting their transponders for the final leg, didn't you?"

"Of course, I did." Rachel approached the radar station. "Mr. Kendrick, hail that aircraft. Tell the pilot to keep a five-mile perimeter from our position unless and until he can confirm he is a poker-run participant."

Kendrick prepared to transmit the hail, but a voice through the comm console interrupted. "*Wolverine. Wolverine.* This is Jesse Granger, flight group number 1-3, requesting clearance to land. Please confirm."

Rachel's ears perked. *Jesse Granger.* Wheels began turning in her head.

Teague noticed. "What is it?"

"I know that pilot." Rachel glanced over the radar operator's shoulder. "Mr. Kendrick, send that aircraft a challenge. Find out if Mr. Granger's transponder is working."

Kendrick checked his transmission frequency and keyed his switch. "Jesse Granger, flight group number 1-3, this is *Wolverine* ATC. You are not transmitting your pre-assigned transponder code. Please engage your transponder now."

* * *

"You didn't tell me about a transponder code," Kade said to Jesse.

"I completely forgot about it. All the excitement back at Cherry Capital had me flustered."

"You're not flustered now," Kade said. "What's the code?"

"Uh … I don't remember."

"You don't remember? Don't you have it documented somewhere in your registration paperwork?"

"I left that stuff in the Cessna, but I do remember setting my transponder."

"You remember setting it to what?"

Jesse closed his eyes and snapped his fingers. "Two-something-something, whatever. Shit, I don't remember. Let's just tell them the transponder is broke."

"Then they'll ask for the code verbally." Kade watched *Wolverine* making way through Lake Michigan far below. "Okay, let's think. The transponder code is just a means for them to verify that a plane coming in for a landing is a registered poker-run aircraft, right? You gave them your name and flight group number, right? Why isn't that enough?"

"Because it's in the rulebook," Jesse said. "Inbound planes must squawk their pre-assigned codes to receive clearance to land."

Cody chuckled. "And we know who wrote the rulebook."

Kade glanced at Jesse. "No exceptions?"

Jesse fumbled through his memory. "Hell, I don't remember. There was a lot of fine print."

"For crying out loud, Jesse. How did you make it this far?"

"Rachel wrote the rulebook," Cody said. "What do you think she put in that fine print?"

"God only knows." Kade gave *Wolverine* another long look. "Okay, forget the rulebook. We're here. One way or another, we're landing on that thing."

"We need clearance," Jesse said.

Kade did not reply.

"What's your plan?" Cody asked.

Kade checked the gauges on the instrument panel. "Rachel said she was going to be at the tables when the poker hands are played out. Maybe she's on the bridge of that ship right now."

"And?" Jesse said.

Kade activated his headset radio and spoke into the boom mic. "*Wolverine* ATC, this is aircraft November-3-2-7-Delta-Bravo, two miles out and approaching your position on heading 2-8-0. On board I have Jesse Granger, flight group 1-3. Mr. Granger's aircraft suffered a mechanical failure at Cherry Capital, and he is completing the final leg of the run in this aircraft. We request clearance to land. Please respond."

* * *

Rachel cursed under her breath. "It's Kade."

Galen Teague faced her. "Your ex-husband?"

"Yes." She tried to spot the Otter through the port windows. "That's his plane's registration number."

"Did you invite him to the ship?"

"No. This is his initiative. I should have known when I saw him at Cherry Capital. He was there with Jesse." She turned from the windows. "Kade wanted to talk with me. I told him I couldn't until after the poker run ended."

"Is he trying to reconcile with you?"

"Who knows?" She cast off the suggestion like it didn't matter.

Teague regarded her. "If we allow him to land, will his presence be a problem?"

She didn't hesitate. "No. We're divorced, but we're civil ... mostly"

"I must admit," Teague said, "I am interested in meeting him."

She did not reply.

"But can we permit him to land?" Teague shrugged. "If I heard him correctly, his friend registered with a different airplane. How does that comport with your rulebook?"

Rachel thought through the regulations she had crafted for the poker run and realized she had failed to address this particular situation. "I think, technically, Jesse is not breaking a rule by flying here in another aircraft."

"You left a loophole." Teague said. "That bothers you, doesn't it?"

"I'll get over it. Besides, letting Jesse finish the run keeps with the spirit of the event."

"Perhaps, but there are other things to consider." Teague gazed into the eastern sky. "Is your ex-husband skilled enough to land safely on deck?"

"I'm sure he thinks he can do it."

"What do you think?"

She pondered the question a moment. "He can do it."

Teague faced her and smiled. "Then let's give him the chance and see how he does. But let me be clear. His business on board will be restricted to poker-run activities. I will not permit personal issues to contaminate the atmosphere on this ship. Understood?"

"Perfectly." Rachel nodded to Kendrick. "Mr. Kendrick, grant that aircraft clearance to land."

* * *

Kade banked the Otter into a wide circle above *Wolverine*. "Maybe you should have tattooed the damned code on the back of your hand," he said to Jesse.

"Maybe you shouldn't whine over every little hiccup," Jesse replied.

"This little hiccup might send us back to Traverse City. I'd say that's whine worthy."

Jesse peeled off his headset. "It's the principle of the thing. You don't offer someone help and then bitch and moan with every bump in the road later."

"The principle," Kade said, "is you should have had your crap together before we left, so we could at least finish this leg. I sure as hell would have."

"Well, forgive me for not being you." Jesse put his headset back on. "Besides, I thought you said we were landing on that carrier no matter what."

Kade raised a finger to retort, but a voice through the radio interrupted him.

"November-3-2-7-Delta-Bravo, this is *Wolverine* ATC. You have clearance to land."

Kade's jaw dropped open and he scrambled to reply. "Copy that, *Wolverine* ATC."

"We are adjusting course to receive you," Kendrick replied. "Wind direction is southeasterly at 2-1 MPH. Ship speed is 1-5 knots. Begin your downwind approach."

"Copy that, *Wolverine* ATC. November-3-2-7-Delta-Bravo beginning downwind approach."

Jesse gave him a look like the issue was a fait accompli. "See. No problem."

"This *is* your lucky day."

"You think Rachel's down there and recognized your registration number?" Cody said.

"That was the plan," Kade laughed. "Could have gone either way though."

Wolverine came about, putting her bow into the wind. Kade glided into the downwind leg of his landing approach. His stomach tightened when Kendrick radioed *Wolverine* was in position.

Jesse poised his hands over the copilot's yoke. "You want me to take her in?"

"Not a chance." Kade banked the Otter into a ninety-degree turn, transitioning to base. He resisted the impulse to look at the carrier's flight deck during the turn, concerned it might distort his sense of height. He waited until he came out of the turn, and then checked the carrier's position. A slight crosswind rocked the Otter. He compensated with rudder and ailerons, and then executed another ninety. The carrier's flight deck came up front and center.

Rachel watched his approach from *Wolverine's* bridge. "He's on final."

Teague walked up next to her. "How is he doing?"

"Coming in a little high," she said.

Teague looked to the radar operator. "Mr. Kendrick?"

Kendrick studied his display. "Yes, sir, about two degrees above nominal approach angle."

"Tell him he's too high," Rachel said. "We've had a good day. I don't want to ruin it by fishing my ex-husband out of Lake Michigan."

Kendrick hit the transmit button.

Aboard the Otter, Kade eased back the throttle levers and watched his air speed decrease on the indicator gauge. He intended to cut it back as far as he could, just short of a stall. He had to minimize landing roll. The carrier's runway was just five hundred and fifty feet long, and the Otter did not have a tail hook. If Kade overshot, he might not have time to power up and climb.

"November-3-2-7-Delta-Bravo," Kendrick called, "reduce approach angle two degrees."

Kade checked his glide path and frowned. "Roger that, *Wolverine*." He glanced at Jesse. "That's Rachel talking right there. Always correcting me."

The distance to *Wolverine* closed, and her flight deck grew larger in the windshield.

In the Otter's passenger cabin, Cody calculated numbers on a clipboard. "Our shortest landing roll is six hundred feet," he said. "Kade, if you reduce speed to sixty knots, and we're flying into a twenty-one MPH wind, and *Wolverine* is steaming at fifteen knots …" He scribbled numbers on the clipboard. "That would reduce our landing roll to about five hundred feet. This could work."

"That's what I'm thinking." Kade nodded to Jesse. "How did you prepare for this landing?"

"I painted a big rectangle on the road into that old quarry by my place and practiced touching down inside it for a week. I'll hand it to ya', Kade-O, you got cojones coming in cold like this."

The yoke shuddered, and Kade adjusted trim to calm it down.

Kendrick's voice. "November-3-2-7-Delta-Bravo, approach looks good. Watch the landing signal officer on deck to bring you home."

"Copy that," Kade replied.

A man holding a pair of red paddles with arms spread apart appeared on the flight deck.

"I'm not a naval aviator," Kade said to Jesse. "What's this guy trying to tell us?"

Jesse snapped his fingers. "Hold on." He dug into his jean pocket and pulled out a folded piece of paper. "I knew I was going to need this." He unfolded the paper and showed Kade a series of diagrams of a man holding paddles at different orientations. "The seven basic signals of an LSO. It was in the poker run rulebook."

"That's great," Kade said. "What's he telling us?"

Jesse studied the diagrams. "Arms spread apart ... it means your approach is okay."

"I know that," Kade chuckled. "Teague must have spent millions building this ship. Why didn't he just throw in an optical landing system into the package?"

"Who knows?" Jesse said. "Maybe he's a tightwad. That's how a lot of rich guys get rich."

The LSO on deck tilted one paddle down and the other up.

Jesse referenced the diagrams. "Shift your glide path to starboard."

"I was just about to do that." Kade adjusted course and glanced at the instrument panel. Air speed: seventy-five knots. Altitude: five hundred feet. He eased back the throttle levers a hair and lowered the landing flaps. A wind gust swept the plane off centerline. He pulled it back with the yoke. The LSO signaled okay, but then waved both paddles in an upward motion.

"Get your nose up," Kendrick said in the headset. "Watch your pitch."

Jesse checked the diagrams. "LSO is telling you to climb slightly."

"I got it." Kade eased back the yoke and raised the nose. Negotiating the wind gust and reducing speed had taken his mind off pitch for a second. Rookie mistake.

The flight deck had suddenly gotten a lot closer. Kade checked air speed; sixty-two knots. He watched for the stall.

Altitude: hundred and fifty feet.

Glide path locked on centerline.

Rachel fixed her eyes on the Otter's descent. "Just relax, Kade."

"Looking good," Kendrick called.

Seconds from touchdown. Kade flared the nose. The Otter glided in hot just inches over *Wolverine*'s flight deck. The LSO slashed the air over his throat with a paddle, and then dashed for safety. Kade chopped both throttle levers to zero. The main landing gear thumped down on oak planks. The Otter rolled left at fifty-three knots and her nose gear dropped onto the deck.

Kade hit the brakes hard and stayed on them.

Jesse howled, "Woo-hoo! Wheels down, nugget."

Cody clenched the clipboard. "Five hundred feet. Five hundred feet."

"Gonna be close," Kade said.

The Otter decelerated to under thirty knots as she rolled past *Wolverine's* island. There wasn't much runway left. Kade pressed harder on the brake pedal and the calipers screeched. "Come on, come on!"

The runway dwindled and the lake loomed large in the cockpit window. Kade held the yoke in a white-knuckle grip. But then, forward momentum eased and the plane heaved to a stop just ten feet from the end of the flight deck.

Kade felt the calm of the Otter at rest, and a smile crept across his face. "Not bad, right?"

Jesse assessed their position on the flight deck. "I would've had a little more runway left."

Kade laughed. "You're dreaming, amigo."

Cody came into the cockpit. "I don't care how much runway is left, we're walking away from this landing instead of swimming away. That's all right in my book." He added, "But I *could* use a beer."

Kade unbuckled from his seat. "No arguments here."

Kendrick radioed in. "Jesse Granger, flight group 1-3, welcome aboard *Wolverine*. Please disembark your aircraft and head to the final check-in station."

Kade slapped Jesse's shoulder. "Go get your last card and win this thing."

They popped the cockpit doors and climbed down to the flight deck amid a balmy wind gust. On the distant horizon, a gray cloud bank encroached on blue sky. A storm front appeared to be building, moving closer. If it grew and intensified, Kade thought, getting off this ship might be more difficult than getting on.

"Why didn't you tell me you were coming here?"

Kade recognized Rachel's voice immediately.

She approached from the island superstructure, walking beside a tall man with salt-and-pepper hair. The man wore aviator sunglasses and a leather flight jacket. He seemed to be studying the Otter and the man who flew her.

"Was this always your plan," Rachel said, "or is this another last-second scheme of yours?"

Yeah, Kade thought, *a storm is coming.*

SIXTEEN

Kade did not quite know how to answer the question. He decided on a stripped-down version of the truth. "Jesse had engine trouble," he said. "I wanted to help him out."

Rachel and Teague met Kade near the Otter's tail.

"That's your story?" she said.

"It's not a story, it's the truth."

"It can be both," Teague said with a subtle smile.

Jesse walked up and joined their circle. "My fuel pump took a shit," he said to Rachel. "Honest truth."

"Jesse, you'd say that even if it didn't. You've covered for him before." She added, "For some reason, you admire Kade."

"Admire?" Jesse made a face.

Kade chuckled. "Rachel, what are you suggesting I came here for then?"

She did not reply.

"Look," Kade said. "I didn't know about Jesse's engine trouble until after we talked in the terminal. I didn't plan this. Believe me, if I knew I was headed for a carrier landing, I would have thought twice before offering to fly Jesse in the last leg."

Teague cocked his head. "You didn't know you were going to have to land on a carrier deck when you took off from Cherry Capital?"

"I found out on taxi before takeoff."

Teague regarded him with a bit of surprise. "So you didn't practice a short-field landing, or prepare in any way to set down on *Wolverine?*"

"No. I'm a bush pilot. I've landed on riverbanks and at the base of narrow canyons. This kind of thing isn't new to me." Kade shrugged. "It's different, but not new."

Teague smiled. "You did well. Welcome aboard." He reached out and they shook hands.

Cody came around the nose of the plane. "Hey, Rachel."

"Cody!" She gave him a hug. "Great to see you. Is Kade keeping you out of trouble, or getting you into it?"

"Mostly out," Cody said. "Like last night. I was drinkin' at the Cellar and got into a brawl."

Kade gestured over Rachel's shoulder for him to stop with the story.

"Uh … it turned out okay, though."

Teague scanned the horizon. "I hate to cut the reunion short, but we have a poker run to conduct, and two more planes to bring in."

Rachel took her boss's cue and slipped into business mode. "Jesse, you have fifteen minutes to check in or you'll forfeit the final leg." She pointed to a watertight door at the base of the island. "Walk through that door and a crewman will guide you where to go." She faced Cody. "The deck crew is coming to re-spot the Otter. I'd appreciate it if you worked with them."

"Yeah, sure," Cody said.

"I better go get checked in." Jesse headed for the island. Teague joined him.

Kade and Rachel followed, but Kade held them back a step and spoke so only she could hear him. "I didn't go to Cherry Capital with a plan to follow you out here. That just happened."

"Then why did you go to Cherry Capital?" she said equally hushed.

"I wanted to talk with you about my visit from the feds."

"Is that all?"

"That's half of it." They walked a few steps. "You've been on my mind, Rach."

She glanced at him. "I hate when you call me that."

"A better response would have been, 'I've been thinking about you too.'"

She let slip a little smile. "It's awkward talking like this here." She put her eyes forward. "But yeah, I've been thinking about you too."

They filed through the bulkhead door into the island superstructure. A crewman directed Jesse to a vertical ladder leading down through a hatchway in the center of the deck. Teague separated from the group and climbed the first step of a steel stairwell leading upward. "I have business to attend to," he said. "Rachel will see you through the remainder of the poker run. Good luck, Mr. Granger." He nodded to Kade. "A pleasure meeting you, Mr. Mitchell. It's good to put a face with the name."

It surprised Kade that Rachel had spoken of him to her boss. "Good meeting you too. I'd like to talk about *Wolverine* later, if you have the time."

Teague smiled. "I would enjoy that."

Rachel prompted Jesse to start down the ladder through the deck.

He did, Rachel followed, and Kade brought up the rear. They landed in a corridor below the island, but it seemed to Kade they were not quite below deck yet. Rachel gestured to an open door roped off at waist level. "On the original *Wolverine*, or as we call it, *Wolverine Prime*, this compartment served as the radio room. Although we installed state-of-the-art comms and radar gear in the bridge on our replica, Teague wanted to keep this room authentic, so we dressed it out like it was back then."

Kade studied the war-era radio gear, headset, and wooden desk. "I like it."

Rachel led them past a closed door to the end of the corridor and disappeared around a corner. Kade and Jesse followed, and found themselves in a much wider open space than one would expect to find on a naval vessel. The spacious compartment evoked an officer's ward room, but leaned more toward a swanky officer's club. It stretched nearly forty feet long, with an overhead reach of at least fifteen feet. A trio of ceiling fans spun in unison among a network of neatly packed duct. Art-nouveau wall sconces made of iron and glass lined the bulkhead on both sides of the compartment and lit the space with white incandescence. A handful of tables arranged like a nightclub were spaced evenly across the deck, and a dozen people milled about in front of a fully stocked bar that stretched the width of the far bulkhead.

Kade took it all in. "You can't tell me this place existed on the original *Wolverine*."

Smiling, Rachel said, "It didn't. This compartment housed the smokestacks for the ship's boilers on *Wolverine Prime*. Our replica is powered by a pair of diesel engines. They're more reliable and easier to maintain than steam engines. No need for smokestacks, so Teague dressed this space for recreation. He calls it 'The Brigg.'"

"So, Teague didn't build an exact replica?"

"Not exact," Rachel said. "This ship has the feel and function of *Wolverine Prime*, but her key systems are updated to allow her to operate without issue in the modern Great Lakes."

"If Teague didn't go all old school, why didn't he put in an optical system to assist pilots with deck landings, instead of using a guy with paddles?"

Rachel laughed. "You'll have to ask him that question."

"I'm going to." Kade observed the poker run pilots in the compartment, checking if he knew any of them. Nope. He tapped Jesse on the shoulder. "Better go get your card."

"I would if I knew where to go," Jesse said.

"Check-in station is at the bar. I'll take you there." Rachel walked with Jesse into The Brigg.

Kade was impressed with *Wolverine*, and he wanted to see more of the ship. Aircraft had always been his primary obsession, but he had a special interest in naval vessels as well. Ely had told him more than once to enlist and become a naval aviator, thinking it a natural, logical, and responsible choice for him, that combined his interests in ships and aircraft. Kade did not agree. He enjoyed his freedom too much. Military structure and hierarchy would grate against his instincts. The only person he wanted to take orders from was himself.

Rachel and Jesse were still at the check-in station, and Kade decided to do some people watching. He scanned through the crowd in The Brigg, stopping at two guys discussing a poker run event called Homecoming. Kade leaned into their space. "What's Homecoming all about?"

"A Grumman F4F Wildcat fighter," one of them said. "It's landing on deck this afternoon."

"Yeah," the other guy said to Kade. "Didn't you read the info packet?"

"I must have missed it."

Kade smiled like he had just experienced an educational moment and stepped away. Rachel and Jesse returned. "Well?" Kade said, trying to read Jesse's expression. "What have you got?"

Jesse showed him what appeared to be a playing card wrapped in brown paper. "We don't get to see it until everyone is seated and ready to play."

"Rules of the run," Rachel said.

Kade chuckled. "Of course."

"It keeps the suspense going until the very end," she added.

"No doubt." Kade gestured to the pilots he had just talked with. "Those guys were discussing Homecoming. What's that all about?"

"You'll like it," Rachel said. "Back in 1943, a rookie pilot put a Wildcat fighter into Lake Michigan during a failed landing attempt on *Wolverine Prime*. A few years ago, that plane was pulled from the lakebed and refurbished. Today it will, in essence, return home to *Wolverine*."

"I could have told you that," Jesse said. "It's one thing I do remember from the literature."

"I'd like to see that plane come in," Kade said.

"Salvio is scheduled to land right before we play the poker hands." Rachel glanced at papers she had picked up at the check-in station. "I just hope he makes it here before the storm moves in. Updated reports show the front moving faster than anticipated."

"Salvio," Kade said. "Who's that?"

"He's the guy flying the Wildcat, one of T-GAF's best pilots."

Something about the mention of this Salvio guy bothered Kade. "I guess we'll see how good he is. Those old warbirds are heavy, and they come in a lot hotter than modern GA aircraft. If he doesn't snag an arresting cable with his tail hook, that plane will have a different kind of homecoming today, one returning it to the bottom of Lake Michigan."

"Don't worry," Rachel said. "He's good."

Kade did not like the way she said that.

A crewman walked into The Brigg from the corridor and approached Rachel. "Ma'am, a pilot is on approach. You're being requested on the bridge."

"Okay, I'll be up in a minute." She touched Kade's arm. "I've got to go. You and Jesse hang here. The poker game should start in an hour, maybe two. I'll be back before then." She left them and headed for the bridge.

Kade and Jesse stood observing the activity in The Brigg a moment. Jesse nudged Kade. "You think that's an open bar or what?"

SEVENTEEN

Sparta Airport, Sparta, Michigan

Danny lit a cigarette and watched a pair of moving guys carry her workbench across the tarmac and onto a steel trailer. It was the last big piece of her welding set-up that she had kept inside Kade's hangar. She did not want to move out, but she had no choice. Kade had unfinished emotional business to address with his ex-wife, and until he did, Danny could not continue with their relationship. As a result of her decision, she now had to find another place to set up her gear. Sometimes she spoke before thinking things through, but nonetheless, she always followed through on her words. Unfortunately, every now and then, that proud personality trait came back to bite her.

"Is that it?" one of the moving guys said.

Danny flicked her spent cigarette onto the ground and crushed the butt under foot. "Did you get the argon tank next to the office?"

"The *what* tank?"

She rolled her eyes and marched into the hangar. "Steel tank. Five feet tall. Right there."

The moving guy followed her in. "Geez, Danny, I'm not a welder. Give me a break."

"I'm giving you two hundred bucks to move my stuff. All of it." She pulled a pack of L&M menthols from her jean pocket and lit another cigarette. The split from Kade was already getting to her. She had the note that he wrote her folded up in her pocket; she took it out and read it again. *I have to get my head together. I promise you I will.* I hope so, sweetheart.

She puffed on the cigarette and contemplated things that could have been, and what might be. Her melancholy thoughts were interrupted by two men in suits approaching the hangar. She didn't recognize them but had a hunch as to who they might be. "He's not here," she said.

One of the men put on a business smile. "Who is not here?"

"Kade," she said. "That's who you're looking for, isn't it?"

"Yes, as a matter of fact, we are." The man regarded her a moment. "And you are …?"

"Morgan," she said, flicking ash to the ground. "Danielle Morgan."

"Do you know where he went, Ms. Morgan?"

The other man stood silent beside his companion, but studied the inside of the hangar, as if expecting to see Kade hiding somewhere. Danny scrutinized them. "How about some identification?"

"Certainly." The man pulled a credentials wallet from an inner suit pocket.

The other did likewise, although a bit reluctantly. "You know who we are," he said.

Danny studied their IDs. "Rifkin and Nystrom. U.S. Customs and Border Protection." She took a drag off the cigarette. "Kade said one of you guys was named Agent Numbnuts."

Nystrom clenched his teeth behind pressed lips.

"I'm guessing that's you," she said.

"Mr. Mitchell was mistaken." Rifkin put his creds back into his pocket. "Now, where is he?"

"Not a clue."

"Are you certain?"

"Yeah, I'm certain. Do you have his cell number?"

"Yes."

"Did you try to call him?"

"Of course, but all my calls go immediately to his voicemail."

Danny chuckled. "Yeah, he's not real good taking calls, or listening to voicemail."

"It's our understanding that you and Mitchell are in a relationship," Nystrom said. "So when you tell us you don't know where he is, we're reluctant to believe it."

Danny glared at him. "Where did you get that understanding?"

"Observation. Deductive reasoning."

"Well, you're wrong, Sherlock. We're not together anymore."

"Be that as it may," Rifkin said, "you still have a better-than-average chance of knowing where Mitchell has gone."

"Sorry to disappoint you, but as of this morning, Kade went his way ..." She gestured to the steel trailer loaded down with her welding equipment. "And I'm going mine."

"Convenient timing," Nystrom said.

"You think I'm lying to you, Agent Numbnuts?"

"Yes, Miss Morgan, I think you are lying to us."

She flicked her cigarette at his feet. "Tough shit."

"Hold on," Rifkin said in a conciliatory tone. "We're not here for a confrontation."

"Then why are you here?"

"We only want to talk with Mr. Mitchell."

"Why? What do you think he's done?"

"We don't know that he's done anything," Rifkin said.

"We just suspect that he has," Nystrom added.

The moving guys came out of the hangar carrying the tall metal tank. One of them dropped his end and it crashed to the tarmac with a metallic *thunk*. Nystrom and Rifkin flinched.

Danny laughed. "That tank is full of inert gas, fellas. It's not going to explode."

Nystrom was not amused. "If it turns out Mitchell is engaged in illegal activity, you can be charged as an accessory to the crime by withholding information."

"I'm not withholding anything." She inspected the tank for damage as the moving guys hoisted it back up. "It's okay, guys. Load it." She faced the feds again. "You two asked your questions, and I answered. Are we through?"

"Not quite," Nystrom said.

"Look, I told you, I don't know where he went, or when he'll be back."

Rifkin regarded her. "We would appreciate your cooperation in this matter." He fished a business card out of his pocket. "If Mr. Mitchell comes back, or contacts you, it is very important that you let us know. It's for his well-being."

"Is that right?" She took the card and glanced at Rifkin's name and cell number, and the Customs and Border Protection Agency logo. She shoved it into her pocket with no intention of ever using it. "If I squeal to you, how is that good for Kade?"

"Trust us," Nystrom said. "Our concerns are in his best interests."

Danny laughed. "Why the hell would I believe that?"

Rifkin opened his mouth to speak, but his cell phone rang and distracted him. He checked caller ID, and then turned around for privacy.

"So, tell me," Nystrom said to Danny. "Did you dump Mitchell, or did he dump you?"

"That's none of your damned business."

Nystrom smirked. "My guess is you dumped him."

"Spoken like a man with a lot of experience being dumped." Danny fumed, but Rifkin's private conversation drew her attention.

"Are you serious?" he said. "When did this happen?" Rifkin glanced at Nystrom. Listened some more. "Okay, contain the situation. I'll get back to you with instructions." He disconnected and tapped Nystrom on the shoulder. "It's escalated. We have to go."

Nystrom nodded. "We're done here," he said to Danny. "For now."

She did not reply. Their shift in focus confused her.

"We apologize for taking up your time this afternoon," Rifkin said. They left in a brisk walk.

"Apology accepted." She laughed.

They kept walking.

"Hey!" she called after them. "What happened? Is somebody trying to sneak a bunch of cigarettes past Customs?"

Danny watched them leave, wondering what they were after. Kade had mentioned that the feds thought he was involved with the smugglers on that cargo ship, like Ely Edwards had the other day, but these guys never mentioned it. They just wanted to know where he had gone, and were intent on finding out—until the phone call sidetracked them. She pulled another cigarette from the pack and stepped into the hangar. She looked at the empty space where the Otter was normally parked and at the door to the little office in back. Where did Kade go? He wasn't at the airport like he said he would be. She tried to call his cell phone again but got thrown into voicemail. Did he stumble into trouble that he didn't tell her about?

She considered the unlit cigarette in her hand. Kade had never liked that she smoked, told her he didn't want her to get cancer or emphysema. He cared about her, more than anyone she had been with. She realized right then just how much she cared for him. The breakup started feeling like a mistake. If Kade was in trouble, she needed to be by his side and help him any way she could. But what could she do? She didn't even know where to begin.

She put the cigarette pack away.

One of the moving guys lifted the trailer's tailgate and pinned it in place. "Hey, Danny, where are we going with this stuff?"

"I don't know," she said. "I don't know where I'm going yet."

EIGHTEEN

Okemos, Michigan

What a difference five hours of sleep made. When Ely stumbled into his apartment after returning from Detroit, Reno Lester's fragmented clues collided like pinballs in his head, bouncing everywhere and leading nowhere. Now, lying in bed staring at the ceiling after his extended power nap, he knew where to start. He picked up his phone and searched for bars on Lake St. Clair. Thirty-nine hits. He considered Lester's comment that the name of the place was earthy. Did he mean crude-sounding or dirt-related, or perhaps a tone? Covering all bases, Ely selected the River Rat, Shores Inn, Blue Goose, Double D, Dirty Dog, Brownies, and Browns as possible bar names. He studied their websites and dropped four places from the list for having been established either long before or long after 1945. That left just Shores Inn, Double D, and Browns.

Ely jumped in the shower and pondered Lester's remaining clues. Lester said he had won big at the Motor City Casino the last time he had gone to his friend's bar, and that he felt like a champion going there, but things went south and he ended up in Canada. Right. Ely toweled off, got dressed, and went back to his internet research. In ten minutes he knew which bar to visit.

Two hours later, he pulled his Tahoe onto a small auto ferry docked in Algonac, Michigan … Champion's Auto Ferry. Its destination: Harsens Island, home to Brown's Bar. The small ferry could carry six vehicles but, on this 7:00 p.m. trip, only three cars besides Ely's were parked on deck. The ferry captain guided the craft on a ten-minute trip across Lake St. Clair, and into a slip on the shores of Harsens Island. The bow ramp lowered, and a dockhand secured the ferry. Ely drove down the ramp and onto North Channel Drive, wondering if Reno Lester's boss really knew who was targeting the traffickers.

An overcast sky made early evening darker than it should have been this time of year. Sparse traffic and marshy terrain surrounded the road and gave the island a desolate feel. Ely checked the navigation app on his phone and watched for the upcoming turn onto Cottage Lane. Driving in silence, he pondered rum-running cars at the bottom of Lake St. Clair. If nothing else, Reno's tale was accurate in one respect. During Prohibition, the Great Lakes played a major role in circumventing the Volstead Act. Harsens Island's proximity to Canada made it a virtual waystation for bootleggers transporting their casks and kegs into the States. In that moment, it struck Ely that this tiny clump of American soil was one of only two places in the country where Canada was located south of the United States, the other being Detroit. *Things went south and I ended up in Canada.* Ely was even more confident he had picked the right bar.

He turned onto Middle Channel Drive and before too long a gravel entry drive came up on the right side of the road. A rustic sign near a pine tree informed Ely he had arrived at Browns, a landmark on Harsens Island since 1946. There were not many cars in the parking lot, and he found a spot close to the building. The old one-story, clapped in dark-varnished weatherboard, sat at the edge of the island's North Channel. A dock ran alongside the parking lot. The mini marina stretched from the road to the back of the building, and had a couple dozen slips, but only a few boats were tied up this evening. Ely hopped out of the Tahoe and walked around to the front door. An inverted bow of a small boat served as an awning over the entry. It reminded him of a summer camp he once attended as a kid. Ely walked in.

The place had a tall peaked ceiling with exposed timber trusses, and a mix of plywood and pine boards lined the walls. The crowd was thin, and deep-fried food flavored the air. In Ely's estimate, Brown's fell somewhere between cozy rustic and flat out dive. He found the bar across the room. Only three guys were seated there. Ely claimed a spot near the center and observed the bartender drawing beer from a tap. The guy was nearly six feet tall, with a brown wave of hair over his forehead and hands like a bricklayer. He seemed to sense Ely watching, and gave him a nod. "Welcome to Browns. Can I get you something?"

"That depends," Ely said. "Are you Jimmy?"

The bartender smiled and set down the glass he had just drawn in front of one of the patrons. "Here's our selections." He gestured to a shelf filled with a dozen different beer bottles.

Ely glanced at the shelf. "Should I take that as no?"

"Sitting at this bar ain't free, buddy."

Ely studied his options. "Oberon."

The guy who might be Jimmy reached into a cooler behind the bar and snatched out a bottle. He popped its cap and set it down on a napkin in front of Ely. "You want to start a tab?"

"Sure." Ely lifted the bottle and took a swig. Yes, he was on duty, but technically it was after hours. Back in the day, a beer or two during a long shift did not raise an eyebrow, but somewhere along the way the world had gotten uptight. What a shame.

A guy at the end of the bar raised a hand. "Can I get another one down here?"

"You certainly can, sir." Could-be-Jimmy grabbed another beer and headed that way.

Ely took in the details around him. A set of louvered windows behind the bar were cranked half open. A chalkboard on the adjacent wall advertised a cheeseburger-basket dinner special. Beneath a Bud Light Lime poster, a little red flag with a white diagonal stripe was thumbtacked into pine board. Ely dwelled on it. SCUBA divers used such flags to signal to boaters that they were diving in a particular area. Diver down. Jimmy was a SCUBA diver.

When the bartender returned, Ely pointed to the flag. "Do you dive?"

The bartender's eyes brightened. "Yeah, I love it. Got five hundred hours of bottom time."

"I used to dive." Ely took another pull of the Oberon. "Back when I was in the Navy."

"No kidding. You've must have seen some things."

"The underside of a submarine mostly. I served a tour aboard the *USS Texas*. My duties included sweeping the hull for sabotage while we were in port."

"No shit. I just get to dive on freshwater shipwrecks."

Ely smiled. "Shipwrecks aren't the only things to dive on in the lakes."

"I know. I've seen steam engines, barges, airplanes …"

"Cars?"

The bartender did not reply.

Ely set down his beer. "Is your name Jimmy?"

The bartender wiped up water droplets with a rag. "Do you think you know me from someplace, buddy? Because I don't know you."

"My name is Ely. Ely Edwards."

"Well, Mr. Edwards, I still don't know you. Am I supposed to?"

"No, but I heard you have the best bourbon this side of the border."

"Who did you hear that from?"

Ely hesitated. "Reno Lester told me."

The name seemed to register with Jimmy. "Reno?" he laughed. "I haven't seen Reno in a long time. When did you talk to him?"

A couple in the dining area seated near an exit got up from their table and left the restaurant. Ely took note, and then took a swig of beer and considered how to answer the question. If Jimmy knew that Reno had been sent aboard the *Blackbird*, this conversation might get sticky. Ely rolled the dice. "I talked to him yesterday."

Jimmy nodded and made a face. "You don't say. How's he doin'?"

"He's had better days," Ely said. "But all things considered, he's doing okay."

"That don't surprise me. Reno's got a knack for steppin' in it." Jimmy walked to a shelf full of whiskey bottles. "Bourbon, you say?"

"I did. But not just any bourbon. I want the Sugar Hill bottle."

Jimmy stopped short of grabbing a fifth of Jim Beam. "Sugar Hill, you say?"

The atmosphere inside Brown's shifted to something dark and uneasy. The guy at the end of the bar stared at Ely. Jimmy turned around and stared as well. Ely rested a hand on the 9mm holstered under his jacket. "None of those bottles look like they spent ninety years in a trunk at the bottom of the lake. I hope Reno didn't steer me wrong."

Jimmy smiled. "Are you sure you want some of that stuff? It's dynamite in a glass."

"I didn't come all this way for run-of-the mill bourbon."

Jimmy wiped his large hands with the rag. "The vintage stuff is served in the cigar parlor." He walked to the end of the bar and motioned to Ely. "Follow me."

Ely stood. A guy to his left tossed some cash next to an empty glass and headed for the exit. These people knew something was going down. Ely just wished he knew exactly what. Jimmy waited near the back wall beside a door with a sign that read "Employees Only." Ely's instincts ignited. Things waiting behind doors to backrooms tended to be unpleasant.

Maybe Reno's boss only wants to meet a nosy federal agent to shut him up. The thought made sense. Lure the fed to Harsens Island. Find out what he knows. Boom. *Pull it together, Edwards. The guy wants something from you. He doesn't want you dead.*

Ely kept a hand close to his 9mm and walked a tightrope toward that door.

Jimmy waved him onward. "Come on, Ely Edwards. Aren't you thirsty?"

Ely's phone buzzed with a call. It was a number he did not recognize. He ignored it.

Jimmy opened the door. "You like your bourbon neat or straight up?"

"Neat," Ely said, pocketing his phone.

Jimmy went into the room.

Ely drew a deep breath and followed. He fully expected to see a fat crime boss in a cloud of cigar smoke flanked by thug bodyguards, but instead he found Jimmy pouring a glass of bourbon from an old brown bottle behind an oak bar. The room's walls were dark burgundy, recessed lights lit a pair of plush leather chairs, and the residual scent of cigar tobacco lingered in the air.

"You look surprised," Jimmy said. "Were you expecting a moose head and a picnic table?"

Ely studied the empty room a bit longer. "Not quite."

"We're not all backwoods hicks around here."

"That's not what I meant."

Jimmy handed him the glass. "You might want to take it slow. This stuff packs a punch."

"I'll bet." Ely took the glass, disappointed that Reno's boss was not there. He started to wonder if the trip had been a waste of time. "I expected to see at least one other person in here that I could spark up a conversation with."

Jimmy shrugged. "Not tonight."

Ely's phone vibrated with another call. Same number. He ignored it, and then sniffed the dark-amber liquor in the glass. It had a burnt-sugar aroma with a mix of spice. He sipped it. Sweet and strong, with a bite on the backside. It was very good.

Jimmy smiled with arms crossed. "What do you think?"

"I have to admit," Ely said, "best bourbon I've ever had."

"I thought so." Jimmy rubbed his hands together. "One more thing."

Ely set the glass on the bar. "What's that?"

"The boss wants me to tell you, welcome to Harsens Island."

The sound of rushing footsteps entered the room. The bourbon glass reflected something approaching from behind. Ely reached for his 9mm and spun around. A tall man in a dark suit was nearly on top of him, swinging a slender black object toward his head. It struck Ely hard at the base of his skull. His vision went into a tunnel, his knees buckled, and the world went black and silent.

NINETEEN

Aboard *Wolverine*

The Grumman F4F Wildcat came in fast and bounced heavy on *Wolverine*'s wooden flight deck. Her powerful engine throttled back and she rolled down the centerline of the runway, snagging an arresting cable with her tail hook and jerking to a stop just past the island. Watching from the sidelines, poker run pilots and *Wolverine* crewmen applauded the return of the resurrected aircraft to her reincarnated home carrier.

Kade imagined himself at the controls of the old fighter, wondering how different it felt in comparison to the Otter. "Hey, Cody, how'd you like to get under the hood of that thing?"

"I'd love it," Cody said. "Those old warbirds were all horsepower and armor."

"What did you think of Salvio's landing?" Rachel said above the crosswind on deck.

Kade cracked a sarcastic smile. "I think he came in too heavy."

"I think he did great." She walked onto the runway toward the fighter.

Kade glanced at Cody. "She's got a thing for him, doesn't she?"

"Maybe," Cody said. "How much does that bother you?"

"Who said it bothers me?" Kade watched Rachel greet the Salvio guy as he came out of the cockpit. He gave her a high five, and she gave him a hug. A bit too friendly for Kade's liking. "Why did she do that? Rachel's not a huggy person."

"You two haven't been married for a couple of years," Cody said. "People change."

"No, they don't." Kade searched through the pilots admiring the Wildcat. "Where's Jesse?"

"He's sitting in The Brigg, staring at his last card."

"It's wrapped in brown paper. What good will staring at it do?"

"He's trying to make it an ace through willpower."

"If that works, I need to talk to him," Kade said, watching Rachel and Salvio converse on the flight deck. "I haven't had much success with the power of positive thinking."

Galen Teague emerged from the cluster of crewmen near the island and greeted Salvio with a handshake. Then he turned to the poker run pilots and set a stance like a true Navy captain addressing his men before a mission. The guy seemed to be getting into his role. He projected his voice so they could all hear him. "Now that our lost warbird has come home, let's get on with the business of playing cards. Poker run pilots, please return to The Brigg. You must play your hands as quickly as possible so we can find our winner. A storm front is approaching, and I want you all to get home safely this evening."

"Game time," Kade said.

The group of poker run pilots migrated toward the island. Rachel, Salvio, and Teague trailed behind them. Beyond the island, a deck crew prepared to move the Wildcat off the runway, but Kade focused on the Otter, which sat parked on the edge of the flight deck. He thought back to when he and Rachel were together, starting up the air charter business. Things sure had changed.

"Hey, Kade," Cody said. "You think Jesse's going to win?"

"If he gets that ace he's thinking about, he's got a pretty good shot."

They filed in through the island door with the flow of the others.

"Hey, Kade," Cody said.

"What?" Kade knew what was coming.

"Think we can up the limit from one beer to two tonight?"

"We're flying out right after the game. I think we should keep it to one." Kade added, "Besides, you drank a month's worth last night, remember?"

Cody snapped his fingers. "Oh, yeah."

They climbed down the ladder and followed the corridor into The Brigg. Rachel was already there. She divided the eight remaining pilots into two groups of four and seated each group at a designated table staffed with a bona fide Las Vegas card dealer. Kade and Cody spotted Jesse at the table nearest the bar.

Rachel finished some organizing business with Teague and the card dealers, and then joined Kade and Cody. "After a year of planning this thing, it's all in the cards now," she said.

"You two seem friendly," Kade said without looking at her.

"Who two?"

"You and Sylvester."

"It's Salvio."

"Whatever."

"We work together," she said. "We're friends."

Kade gave her a look like she had fed him a line of crap. "I don't remember you being so touchy-feely when we were together."

"People change," she said.

Cody prodded Kade. "Told you."

Kade crossed his arms and stared at Jesse's poker table.

"Why are you bent out of shape?" she said.

"I'm not bent out of shape." Kade shifted from foot to foot, listening to the dealers going over the rules of the poker game with the pilots. "When do they start playing?"

"As soon as Teague gives the word."

Kade faced her. "Are you pissed that I'm here?"

She exhaled. "A little."

"Why? Did I misread you back at Cherry Capital?"

"You didn't misread me." She got a little flustered. "This ship, the poker run, it's my job. I told you when the run was over we could get together." She noticed Teague looking in their direction. "We can't do this here."

"Do what?"

She rolled her eyes and blew a frustrated breath.

Galen Teague approached the poker tables. "Gentlemen, as sponsor of the Bluewater Foundation Aerial Poker Run and the commander of this vessel, I order you to reveal your final card." He glanced over at Kade and Rachel. "Let the game begin."

The players peeled off the brown wrapping paper from their last card. Kade and Cody craned their necks to see over Jesse's shoulder. "Jack of spades," Kade said into Cody's ear. "That gives him a full house, jacks over aces. Pretty good hand."

Most of the pilots did a passable job of concealing the strength of their hands. Jesse's poker face, however, needed some work. He grinned from ear to ear. The dealer, an attractive woman with a nametag reading "Brenda," called all players to show. One by one they complied.

Kade quickly scanned the cards on the table. "Three of a kind. Two pair. A straight." He nudged Cody with his elbow. "Jesse won his table."

Brenda agreed with Kade's assessment and announced Jesse the winner. The losing pilots cursed and laughed. Jesse whooped and pushed away from the table. "Mr. Teague, make that check out to Jesse W. Granger."

Rachel stepped forward. "Jesse, you won your table, not the game."

"I what?" Jesse suddenly realized the second table also had a winner. "Camel shit."

"Now what?" Kade asked.

"Jesse and the winner from the other table face off in a final hand of five-card stud, dealt from a fresh deck." Rachel walked to the second poker table and regarded the other winner, who had not left his chair. He was a heavyset man with a shaved head and a long goatee. "Congratulations, Mr. ...?"

"Kehoe," the man said through a smile. "Manny Kehoe."

"Congratulations, Mr. Kehoe." Rachel gestured to Jesse. "Mr. Granger, please take a seat at this table." She then started into a soliloquy on the rules and guidelines for the final round.

Kade tuned out her dissertation, focusing instead on Salvio and Teague, who were having a private conversation beyond the poker tables. Teague had a hand on Salvio's shoulder, speaking to him as a coach might speak to a player, or a boss to an underling. The Wildcat pilot had dark hair and olive skin; it seemed to Kade the guy might have relatives still living in Sicily. Salvio nodded to his coach, or his boss, and headed out of The Brigg.

"I don't like that guy," Kade said to Cody.

"You don't know him," Cody said. "How can you not like him?"

"I get a sense for people."

Cody chuckled. "You're jealous."

"Jealous of what?"

"You think he and Rachel are, you know, together."

Kade looked at him crosswise. "We're not married anymore. She can do whatever she wants. I'm okay with it."

"You're not fooling anyone."

Kade noticed his mechanic had a beer in his hand. "Hey, where did you get that?"

"Duh," Cody said. "The bar."

"How many have you had?"

"Just this one." He added, "I don't drink 'em that fast."

"Good one." Kade put his attention back on the poker table.

Brenda had taken over as dealer for the final round. She dealt new cards to Jesse and Manny. Rachel studied a screen on her tablet, swiping pages back and forth.

"Are you going to steal her away from me?"

Galen Teague's voice. The shipping tycoon had edged in beside Kade unnoticed. "I'm not stealing anyone from anybody," Kade said. "I'm just here helping out my friend."

"That's good," Teague said, "because I'm not inclined to lose her just yet."

Kade faced him. "What is her position with T-GAF anyway?"

"She's my VP of North American Import Operations. She also chairs T-GAF's Public Relations department."

"Do you need a PR department? I mean, it's pretty well known that your donations help keep Great Lakes' beaches clean and support the fight against the Asian carp invasion."

Teague smiled. "How do you think those efforts have become well known?"

"I see."

"The world is a hostile place toward corporate America these days, Mr. Mitchell. Unless you prove you are a good corporate neighbor and steward of the environment, you will be targeted."

"Are you saying your philanthropy is just a tactic to keep the attack dogs off your back?"

Teague smiled. "You're a very direct man. I like that." He gestured to the poker table. "They're about to play."

Kade leaned in to see Jesse's cards. Two pair: queens over deuces, with a seven of hearts as a side card. Not spectacular.

Rachel approached the table with her tablet. "Gentlemen, according to poker run regulations, each player that has committed no rule infractions throughout all legs of the run will be permitted to discard and draw two new cards in this final round."

Jesse smiled and laid his seven of hearts face down on the table.

Rachel glanced at the tablet screen. "Mr. Kehoe, my records show you have successfully completed all five legs of the run without incident. Congratulations, you may draw two cards."

Jesse cocked his head. "And, what about Mr. Granger?"

"Mr. Granger." Rachel swiped the tablet screen. "I'm afraid you have an infraction."

Kade rubbed a hand over his eyes. *Here it comes.*

Jesse sat up straight. "What did I do?"

Rachel read from the tablet. "Rules Section 3, Paragraph 1: Final Leg. For safety and security reasons, each pilot shall set his/her aircraft transponder to the unique ID code assigned during Poker Run registration. Failure of any aircraft to squawk its assigned ID code will be considered a breach of communication protocol and may result in denial of clearance to land, or disqualification. Penalty for this infraction will be adjudicated by run officials."

Jesse stared blankly at her. "Um ... you gave us clearance to land."

"It's still an infraction."

"You're not lettin' me draw my cards because of that?"

"Jesse, I'm sorry, but it's right here in black and white."

"Can't you make an extraordinary circumstance exception?" Kade said. "His plane died."

"I did. I gave you clearance to land instead of disqualifying him."

Jesse grumbled. "Hell, let's just play it out."

Manny Kehoe agreed and laid two cards face down in front of Brenda. She dealt him two fresh ones from the deck. He picked them up and put them in his hand. Kade had played poker with a lot of people, and he had gotten pretty good at reading faces. Judging from Manny's veiled expression, Jesse was in trouble.

A crewman walked up and spoke into Teague's ear. Teague nodded, and then addressed the crowd in The Brigg. "Attention, please. The latest weather update has the storm reaching our position within the hour. She's bringing gale-force winds, so I want flights off deck to commence immediately. Gentlemen, check your schedules and proceed to your aircraft. The deck crew is waiting to assist your departure. Thank you all for participating. It's been a fantastic run."

Pilots and support crew herded toward the Brigg's exit. Kade tapped Cody on the shoulder. "Go preflight the Otter."

"Hey, I want to see who wins the game," Cody said.

"I'll tell you later. Right now, you have to make sure we're ready to go when our slot comes up. I have no intention of flying home in a thunderhead."

Cody frowned. "I guess you're right. It's going to be a madhouse on deck with all these planes trying to leave. I'll see ya topside." He joined the exodus of pilots.

Kade watched Jesse and Manny stare each other down across the poker table.

"Gentlemen," Brenda said, "please show your hands."

Both men laid their cards on the table. Kade knew what Jesse had, so he focused on Manny's hand. It was a powerful queen-high straight. That beat Jesse's two pair. Game over.

Manny belted a hearty laugh and shook hands with Teague.

Jesse dropped his head to the table. "Defeated by a transponder infraction."

Kade put an arm over his shoulder. "Cheer up. You took second place. Not too shabby."

Jesse gave him the stink eye. "Second place is the first loser." He stared at Manny's cards. "That queen could have been mine. I could have had another full house and won."

"I hate to say it, Jess, but winning just wasn't in the cards for you."

"Very funny, amigo. Let's get the hell out of here."

"My feelings exactly." Kade and Jesse started for the exit corridor.

Rachel touched Kade's arm. "Be careful. Doppler shows seventy-mile-per-hour wind gusts in that storm. Stay ahead of it."

"No problem," Kade said, "if I make my time slot."

"You will." She closed her tablet. "We'll talk later this week. Okay?"

"Sounds good. Take care, Rach."

She flashed an irritated look at him. "I hate when you call me that."

Kade smiled at her, and then hurried Jesse into the corridor and up the ladder to the island.

"I really needed that grand prize money," Jesse said.

"Do you get anything for second place?"

"Just a refund of my registration fee, which wasn't cheap."

They stepped onto the flight deck through the island's bulkhead doorway. A Cessna roared past them on the runway and lifted into the sky off the carrier's bow. Far aft on the ship, the deck crew positioned the next aircraft for takeoff. Pilots and crewmen scurried about the fringe of the flight deck, rifling through preflight checks and shuffling planes into position for their scheduled departure slots. In the southeastern sky, an ominous black cloud closed in, churning and bellowing with flashes of lightning in its belly.

Kade headed for the Otter. "We're cutting this close."

Jesse stayed with him. "What number are we?"

"We're slot five." Kade pointed at the Cessna that had just taken off. "One." He gestured to the plane revving its engine on the aft section of the flight deck. "Two."

A Cirrus 22 on the far side of the Otter fired up its turboprop. "Three," Jesse said.

"Come on." Kade broke into a jog.

They darted and dodged their way around crewmen and climbed into the Otter through the open door in the main cabin. Kade worked his way to the cockpit and found Cody in the copilot seat. "How are we lookin'?"

Cody didn't answer. He scanned the instrument panel and flicked a couple of switches up and down. "Not good."

"What's the matter?"

"I'm not getting light-off."

Kade dropped into the pilot's seat. "Bus voltage okay?"

Cody tapped the gauge. "We have power. Battery's at twenty-three volts. I'm spinning the props, I just can't get light-off."

Kade checked that the port engine was clear, and then hit the start switch. The propeller wound up on battery power. He scanned the instrument panel. "Rotor speed in green zone. Injecting fuel." He toggled the fuel switch and watched the engine gauges. They did not climb as expected. The fuel-air mix in the chamber was not igniting. "Turbine temp is flat line." He flicked the fuel switch off. "What the hell?"

"I told you, we're not getting light-off. Something's fouled up in the ignition circuit. I have to trace the problem back through electrical."

"That takes time."

"You bet."

Kade glanced through the cockpit window at the black cloud filling the horizon. "We don't have that kind of time."

The radio crackled. "November-3-2-7 Delta-Bravo, this is *Wolverine* ATC. Deck crew is ready to position you in standby zone for takeoff. Are you good to go?"

Kade looked to Cody. "We're not getting this fixed in five minutes, are we?"

Cody laughed. "It'll take me five minutes just to get my hands near the engine."

Kade dropped his head and lifted the mic from the instrument panel cradle. He keyed the switch. "*Wolverine* ATC, this is November-

3-2-7-Delta-Bravo. We are negative for standby zone. Repeat. Negative for standby zone. We are experiencing engine malfunction."

"Copy that," the controller replied. "Can you correct the problem in time to depart in your slot?"

"Negative," Kade said. "We're not going anywhere."

TWENTY

Harsens Island

Consciousness came to Ely with the sound of a door clapping shut. He opened his eyes and only saw a red blur. Cigarette smoke stung his nostrils and his skull throbbed. He righted himself in what felt like a cushioned armchair. He blinked to sharpen his focus. The blur clarified into a tumbled red-brick wall lit by soft light from wall sconces of another era. Ely guessed that era to be the 20s or 30s, but it was the guy sitting in front of him that commanded his attention.

Leaning slightly to the left, with his chin thoughtfully nestled in the palm of his hand, the man studied Ely from a lacquered dining chair. He was a dark-haired fifty-something, with a shock of gray overhanging his forehead and inquisitive brown eyes. The man lowered his arms and straightened the wrinkles in his dark suit, and then loosened the black tie around his neck and pulled open the collar of his maroon shirt. Something about him seemed familiar.

"I'm glad Reno got my message to you," the man said. "When I heard what happened to the *Blackbird,* I was concerned."

Ely readjusted his focus. "Concerned about Reno or your message being lost?"

"Both." The man sat silent a moment. "So, you're with Homeland Security?"

Ely felt inside his jacket for his creds. Gone. He noticed the Glock 9mm was missing from its holster too. At least he had not been bound and gagged. "Yes, I'm with DHS."

The man smiled. "That's good."

Ely remembered where he had seen that smiling face: FBI surveillance photos. Specifically, photos of crime boss Aldo Dinapoli; suspected trafficker of drugs and other contraband. As happens too often, however, solid evidence to charge him with a crime had not been compiled yet, but the Bureau considered him a big fish in the organized-crime pond. At the moment, Ely just considered him a man of unknown intent who had him at an uncomfortable disadvantage.

"I thought you wanted to talk, not kidnap me." Ely rubbed the bump on his head.

"We are talking. And, if you'll notice, you're not stuffed into a trunk."

"Right." Ely repositioned himself in the chair. "By the way, the DEA has Reno in the Detroit office."

"I'll send a lawyer in the morning." Dinapoli stood. "I think we need a drink before we start."

"I was having a drink before you brought me … here." Ely studied the room. It appeared to be a small but upscale tavern. A mahogany bar sat in the corner, with a darkened flat-screen television mounted above it. Half a dozen tables-for-two draped in white linen were arranged in a half circle in front of a brick arch on the far wall, over what looked to be a small, elevated stage. Half-finished drinks on the tables and cigarette smoke in the air gave the place an eerie feel, like people had been there enjoying the night moments before—but had left suddenly.

"Where am I?" Ely said.

Dinapoli grinned. "I don't want you to know where here is. Why do you think I had Anthony deliver you the way that he did?"

"I would imagine you don't want me to come back with a bunch of friends someday."

"A return visit does become more difficult if you don't know where you are now."

"It's not good to begin a relationship with a lack of trust."

"A relationship?" Dinapoli chuckled. "Let's not get ahead of ourselves."

Ely adjusted to a more comfortable position. "We've got to start somewhere."

"You're right." Dinapoli spread his arms as if presenting the tavern-like room to an audience. "You like my place? I call it my man cave. It used to be a speakeasy during Prohibition." He chuckled. "Prohibition, what a stupid law—but it made a lot of people money. Like my Nonno."

"Nonno," Ely said. "That means 'grandfather' in Italian, right?" He managed a slight smile. "Let me go out on a limb and ask, is your grandfather the legendary Rocco Dinapoli?"

Dinapoli did not reply.

"If he is, that would make you Aldo, his grandson, wouldn't it?"

Dinapoli regarded Ely a long while. "You know my name," he finally said. "I'm flattered." He walked to the mahogany bar. "You want that drink?"

"I'd rather get to the point of this meeting."

Aldo Dinapoli lifted a bottle of Bushmills from a liquor shelf. "I apologize for having Anthony crack your melon like I did, but you *are* a fed after all."

"I've been called worse things."

"Yeah, I bet you have." Aldo poured whiskey into two glasses and lifted one of them up. "It's funny. Ninety years ago, having this stuff would've put me in jail. Today, not only is the country drinking more than ever, but weed is legal in nine states."

Ely feigned concern. "That must really be cutting in on your profit margin."

Dinapoli raised an eyebrow. "What's that supposed to mean?"

"Come on, Aldo. I know who you are. If I wanted to nail you for trafficking, I would have ridden that ferry across with five other cars filled with DEA agents. Let's stop pretending and get to the issue at hand. You've got a problem and, for some reason, you think I can help."

Dinapoli slapped the glass down on the bar top. "You're damn right I've got a problem, but the part about you helping?" He watched the whiskey slosh around in the glass. "That all depends on if I'm right about you or not."

"Right about me? Reno said that too. What does that mean?"

Dinapoli picked up the glass again. "You ever see a fox hunt in an old movie, Agent Edwards? There's a pack of dogs and a bunch of limeys on horses, with guns and bugles and crazy stuff like that, and they're chasing a fox through the woods. The little rodent doesn't have a chance, does he?" Dinapoli downed the whiskey. "That's what's happening to me … to us."

"Reno told me you think you're being hunted."

"I don't think it. I know it."

"He also said you know who's doing it."

Dinapoli fixed Ely with an accusing eye. "Yeah, I know. That's why you're here."

Ely considered his theory about terrorists targeting traffickers. "Who did you rub the wrong way, Aldo? What organization did you piss off?"

"I didn't piss off anyone. I just woke up one day with crosshairs on my back." He poured another drink and lifted it to his lips. "Guess I didn't fill the right coffers."

"Don't you know if you cozy up to a scorpion, you're going to get stung?"

Dinapoli stared at him over the rim of the glass. "I've never heard a politician called a scorpion before. A snake, yes, but a scorpion, that's too kind."

Ely looked at him funny. "I'm not talking about politicians."

"Then what the hell are you talking about? We're on different channels here."

Ely leaned forward. "Let me dial it in nice and clear. You and your counterparts got into business with Al Qaeda, or ISIS, or some goddamned fascist militant group to make a lot of money off narcotics, but the deal went south and they declared a jihad against the whole North American drug trafficking network."

Dinapoli stared at Ely, dumbfounded. "Where the hell did you get that story?"

"Don't play ignorant. I've been watching what's going on out there. Trafficking vessels with direct or tangential ties to Al Qaeda and the Taliban are being sunk."

"Oh, really?" Dinapoli said. "I haven't joined a single deal in the sandlot, but I've lost three ships just the same. If you think that, I got the wrong guy in here."

Ely considered Dinapoli's rebuttal. "Then your counterparts struck the deal, and when it soured, it tainted the water for every one of you."

Dinapoli shook his head. "You're way off base, Elias J. Edwards."

"Then enlighten me."

"Mohammed isn't hunting us," Dinapoli said, "it's Uncle Sam."

"That's absurd."

"It's a fact. No one else could carry out the scope of what I've seen."

"Really? That's like finding a broken window in your house and blaming the police, when the most likely person to have thrown the rock is your neighbor."

"My neighbor?"

"Your counterparts," Ely said. "Your competition, Perry and Firth, and all the others. You swear you've got no ties to a terrorist organization. Fine, then this all starts to look like a standard turf war, not a government hit job."

"You think I wouldn't know a turf war if I was in one? This isn't a fight for territory."

"Why can't it be Firth or Perry doing this to you, and to each other?"

"Those meatballs couldn't pull off the hits I've seen. It's bigger." Ely scoffed. "The government would never engage in a literal war on drug traffickers. We have laws in this country, and rules, and something called due process. You know all about that, Aldo, you've benefitted from it. We don't make battlefield decisions to take out a perceived criminal. Our whole legal system is based on innocence until proven guilty, and fairness before the court. I've seen men I know are guilty go free for lack of evidence."

"And I've seen innocent men get thrown in the joint. It goes both ways."

"We don't shoot suspected criminals dead in the street without a fair trial."

Dinapoli wagged a finger at him. "Depends which city you happen to be in."

"Not funny."

"Not trying to be."

Ely regarded Dinapoli a long while. The man believed what he was saying. "Okay," Ely said. "Do you have any evidence to support this insane accusation?"

"I got my instincts. They've never let me down."

"That's inadmissible." Ely rose from the armchair and stood, glancing around to see if some thug would come out of the shadows to push him back down.

"We're alone in here," Dinapoli said. "This is a private conversation. If anyone knew I was talking to a fed, I might have problems on my end."

Ely walked over to the bar. Dinapoli did not react or try to restrict his movement in any way. "You have anything besides instincts?"

"Yeah, an epiphany."

"That's also inadmissible." Ely eyed the glass of Bushmills on the bar.

"Let me explain." Dinapoli sat on a stool. "So, I'm losing ships, and I admit, my first thought was someone is making a move to grab a bigger part of the Lakes' territory. I start wracking my brain one day, trying to figure out how Firth, or Perry, or whoever, is getting the upper hand on me." Dinapoli jabbed a thumb at the flat-screen overhead. "This TV is tuned to a news channel, and a story comes on about the War on Terror, and they're talkin' about the military checking off names on their ISIS kill list with drone strikes. Then they show this video of a raghead in a Jeep getting whacked by a Hellfire missile. And I'm like, holy shit, that's it, that's it."

"What's it?"

"That's what's happening to my innocent merchant vessels."

"Drone strikes?" Ely laughed. "You can't be serious."

"As a heart attack."

"That's impossible."

"Nothing's impossible."

Ely bristled. "The United States military does not conduct combat operations inside US borders, and definitely not against US citizens, criminals or not."

"Kent State."

"That was the National Guard in a case of civil unrest."

"The Civil War."

"Preserving the Union and abolishing slavery were kind of extenuating circumstances."

"Waco."

"The FBI. And I'm not going to argue with you all night about this."

"My point is the government does carry out battlefield executions when it suits them."

"Those examples can't be defined as executions. And what you're suggesting here is different. Killing drug traffickers without due process in an unprovoked attack goes against everything this country was founded on."

Dinapoli laughed. "Oh, sweet Jesus, Elias J. Wake up from dreamland. The world is an ugly place, and ugly things happen."

"Ugly things like drug smuggling and human trafficking?"

"Things like invading small countries to win an election and selling weapons to dictators to fill a politician's bank account."

"Let's just stick to the accusation at hand. Do you have anything besides imagination to back up your claim?"

"I got a video."

Ely stumbled on that one. "A video of what?"

Dinapoli framed his hands as if focusing his story. "Okay, so I hit on this idea about the drones, and I tell my guys to watch the skies, like those old sci-fi movies. Keep watching the skies. And of all people, my son sees it." Dinapoli pulled a smartphone from his jacket pocket. "My kid's twenty-four, and he always has his damned phone in his hand. One day, he's aboard one of my merchant ships and he's taking this selfie video to send to his girlfriend, which I tell him to never do … for obvious reasons, right? But he does, and he catches something on camera."

Dinapoli leaned the phone against the bottle of whiskey so Ely could see the screen, and then rolled a video clip. A man resembling a much younger Aldo appeared, holding his phone to record a video of himself. He stood near a gunwale at what appeared to be the stern quarter of a ship. Over his shoulder, the deck of the vessel scrolled out toward the bow. An overcast sky painted a drab background, and white-capped swells gently pitched the ship fore and aft. Wind noise muddled the audio, but the man spoke into the camera, saying something about missing his girlfriend. And then, in the sky behind him, a dark blur with a flare of light on its tail streaked down. It crossed the screen in half a second, and the bow of the ship burst open atop a ball of fire. A boom like thunder sounded, and the man dropped into a panicked crouch. The picture spun into a blurry image, and then it went black.

Ely stood, speechless. He had seen plenty of drone-strike videos throughout his career. In most of them, an unsuspecting target sits under a pair of crosshairs in the middle of a grainy video until a Hellfire missile streaks in and blows it to pieces. Not much warning, just a blurry streak prior to impact. What he had just watched looked a hell of a lot like that. Ely's mouth felt dry and he tried to swallow. "Is your son okay?"

"Yeah," Dinapoli said. "He made it off the ship all right. He got lucky. Not everyone aboard got lucky."

Ely thought about the *Blackbird* and the flash of light he saw just before the meth ship erupted into flames. He lifted the glass from the bar and downed his whiskey.

Dinapoli studied Ely's face. "That video surprised you."

Damned right it surprised me, Ely thought. "It intrigues me," he said.

"Good. That makes me feel like I'm right about you and your boys."

"My boys?"

"It's like this." Dinapoli said. "I look at the government and all its little fed agencies like it's a family. You know? A big family."

"A dysfunctional family."

"Yeah, but aren't they all? Now, I come from a big family, and not all of us get along. Me and my youngest brother, Nikko, we're close. He works for me, and I take care of him. My oldest brother, Sal, not so much. We butt heads. We've given each other stitches before, probably will again. I love him, we have dinner sometimes, but we do our own thing. Capisce?"

"Not really." Ely sat on a bar stool. "Where are you going with this story?"

"All those fed agencies," Dinapoli said, "they're like brothers. Right? Some get along. Some don't. Some of them do things without telling the others. You follow?"

"I think I do." Ely set the empty glass down. "When Reno told you a guy from Homeland Security was taking one of Perry's men into protective custody to question him about trafficking ships sinking, you thought, why would this guy be sniffing around the issue if his department was behind what's going on?"

"Exactly." Dinapoli swiveled his stool to face Ely. "I don't know which fed agency is on the hunt, but I'm rollin' the dice that Homeland Security isn't part of it."

"It's not Homeland," Ely said, "at least not to my knowledge."

Dinapoli crinkled his brow. "You seem so certain. Why don't I feel warm and fuzzy?"

"DHS is a big department. It oversees a lot of agencies. All I can tell you is I'm not part of some hunting party, and neither are the people I work with."

"Fantastic. So, all I have to do is convince you I'm being targeted by some agency, and then you go back to your Homeland boys and butt heads with big brother." Dinapoli laughed.

Ely considered Dinapoli's suspicion, and his logic, and his video clip. "If you believe the government is doing this to you, then why did you send Reno to infiltrate the *Blackbird*?"

"I was conducting an investigation, just like you feds do."

"To find out what?"

"To find out if Perry is helping the government with their hunt."

"Isn't Perry losing ships too?"

"That could be a smokescreen."

"I see."

"Listen, the government isn't doing this on its own. Sure, they have the hardware to pull it off, but they don't have the brains to know where and when to hit. That kind of insight only comes from somebody with inside knowledge of how the ... import industry ... works."

"You thought Perry was trading his knowledge of trafficking methods and players to Uncle Sam in exchange for immunity to charges, or a payoff, or something?"

"I did, until you and your Coast Guard buddies blew up his ghost ship. Now, I'm not so sure."

"We didn't blow up the *Blackbird*." Ely thought about that flash of light again. The timing of the explosion that took out the meth ship seemed more and more suspicious. "All I can say for certain is it wasn't me, and it wasn't the Coast Guard crew I was with."

Dinapoli gave him a long, contemplative look. "For the record, Agent Edwards, I deal strictly in South American weed. I don't get involved with what Perry was cooking on the *Blackbird*. That garbage is poison. I know that means something to you. Capisce?"

Ely did not reply. Memories of his daughter Leah, and how she had died from a meth addiction, flooded his thoughts. Aldo Dinapoli had done his homework on Elias J. Edwards.

"I do background checks too. I like to know who I'm dealing with."

"We're not dealing," Ely said. "You're simply trying to convince me something is happening that I've spent my whole life believing could never happen."

"Time to face the truth. All you good guys aren't so good."

"And all you bad guys aren't so bad?"

"Hey, who said I was a bad guy?"

Ely frowned. "Aldo, I have a real hard time believing the government would do what you're suggesting, and partner with a drug trafficker to do it."

"For real?" Dinapoli chuckled. "The US government is like a whore. It doesn't care who it gets into the sack with to handle a dirty job. Remember the ragheads we armed in Afghanistan to beat up on the Russians? One of them was named Bin Laden, so the track record is not so good."

"Good point," Ely said. "Still, the political fallout from a government-sanctioned hunt-and-kill operation on US soil getting out to the public would be doomsday for any official involved. And an operation like that would definitely need Congressional or Cabinet approval. I just don't see it happening."

"You forget one thing. In addition to being a natural-born liar, a politician is an illusionist. He can hide a mountain of evidence behind a single seed of doubt. Remember how Reagan convinced the whole country that he didn't know he was trading arms for hostages?"

Ely really wanted Dinapoli to stop making good points.

"So, have I convinced you to go back and raise holy hell at fed headquarters?"

"Aldo, if any of what you suspect is true, I have to tread very carefully. Anyone involved in a rogue operation to exterminate drug traffickers will not want that secret getting out, capisce?"

Dinapoli smirked. "Capisco."

"But, I will start treading. You've got me considering things I never would have an hour ago."

"That's great. And if I can help you to help me, just let me know." Dinapoli smiled. "As a gesture of good faith, I won't make you wear a hood on the way out." He laughed.

"I don't want another goose egg on my head either."

"We're past that."

"That's comforting." Ely glanced around the room. "Where are my personal effects?"

Dinapoli whistled, and a tall man in a dark suit came into the old speakeasy through a door across the room. Ely recognized him as the man who had clobbered him in the cigar parlor.

"Anthony," Dinapoli said, "give back Agent Edwards his creds, his phone, and his piece ... after you return him to his car."

Ely frowned. "There's that trust thing again."

Dinapoli shrugged. "Think of it as prudence."

Anthony motioned toward the door. Ely started for it, but Dinapoli stopped him with a hand on the shoulder. "You showed guts coming here alone. That means something to me. Capisce?"

Ely smiled. "You took a chance bringing me here. That wasn't lost on me either."

Ely and Anthony climbed a flight of stairs out of the speakeasy and exited the building through a heavy wooden door into a dark parking lot. They got into a black Cadillac CTS. Raindrops spotted the windshield as Anthony drove down a desolate road. Ely began to recognize the surroundings. Before long, he was sitting behind the wheel of his Tahoe, holstering his 9mm. He turned on his phone and got a voicemail notification as soon as it powered up. It was from that unfamiliar number that had called him earlier. He listened to the message.

"Mr. Edwards, this is Danielle Morgan. We met when you came to talk to Kade at the hangar the other day. You might delete this message after you hear it, but I didn't know who else to call ... I think Kade is in trouble, and you might be the only person who can help."

TWENTY-ONE

Aboard *Wolverine*

Kade worked the lever on a ratchet strap, securing the Otter's nose gear to a tie-down ring in the flight deck. Sideways rain blurred his vision and stung his cheeks, but he kept working the lever until the nylon band firmed up nice and tight. He wiped his eyes and called to the other side of the plane. "Cody, you all set?"

With rain-soaked clothes hanging off him like wet rags, Cody gave a thumbs up.

Kade leaned into the wind and walked to the tail section. "Jesse?"

"All locked down, amigo," Jesse shouted. "A hurricane couldn't sweep her off the deck."

"If this isn't a hurricane, it's pretty damn close." Kade waved to a pair of crewmen who had helped re-spot and secure the Otter. "Okay," he said to Cody and Jesse. "Let's get below."

They headed for the island, fighting the rain and gusting wind with every step. It seemed the storm didn't want them to get inside. Kade let his companions rush through the bulkhead door first, taking the moment to check on his airplane banded to the flight deck. That Otter was his baby. She had never let him down, until today.

A fork of lightning split the sky fifty yards off *Wolverine*'s port quarter, peeling off a blast of thunder like a stick of dynamite. Kade took the hint and stepped through the bulkhead doorway into the island's superstructure, and then dogged the door down tight.

"Kade, this way." Cody motioned him to the ladder leading down to The Brigg.

Kade followed after him, shaking off the rain. They descended to the corridor and walked into the compartment where the poker run had been played out. Jesse was already wringing out his clothes in the light of the wall sconces. Teague and Rachel were sitting at a table near the bar.

"Come in and dry off," Teague said. "Get a drink, and we'll ride this storm out together."

"Not a bad idea." Kade gave Rachel a glance, wondering if she suspected his engine trouble was a ruse to say aboard the ship longer. *The answer, sweetheart, is no.*

Wolverine pitched and the lights flickered in The Brigg. Kade maintained his balance and ordered a Corona from the crewman on bartender duty. He pushed a slice of lime inside the neck of the bottle and then joined Teague and Rachel at their table. Over the years, Kade had come to the conclusion that he could tell a lot about people by the drinks they chose. He noted Teague had an Imperial Stout in front of him. Something in that seemed appropriate. Rachel, on the other hand, appeared to have chosen mineral water with a twist of lime. Of course, it could have been vodka on the rocks. She still liked to keep him guessing.

Kade sat down and smiled at her. "Looks like you're stuck with me a little longer."

She returned the smile. "It would seem so."

"Fortunately, all the other pilots made it off the ship before the storm hit," Teague said. "What happened with your plane, Mr. Mitchell?"

"Good question. Something blew out in electrical, took down my ignition system." Kade added, "You can call me Kade, by the way."

"Well, Kade, I have a rather good aviation mechanic on board today to support the poker run. I'll have him take a look, if you'd like."

"That's okay. I have a good mechanic. He'll tear into it when the storm lets up."

As if on cue, Cody walked over and eyed Kade's beer. "Hey, Kade . . ."

"Yeah, go ahead," Kade said. "Just try to keep it under control, okay? You need to be sharp in the morning to figure out what's wrong with the Otter."

"No problem." Cody headed for the bar.

Jesse joined him on the way. "Hey, hold up."

Kade gave The Brigg a long, impressed look. "Mr. Teague—"

"Call me Galen," Teague said with a wink.

"Galen," Kade said. "This ship must have cost a fortune. What possessed you to build it?"

Teague thought about that a moment. "The short answer is, I absolutely love naval aviation history, and *Wolverine* represents a unique and ingenious part of it."

Kade smiled. "You spare no expense on your passions, do you?"

"I think you understand putting everything you've got into a dream," Rachel interrupted dryly. "Like, for instance, an air charter company."

Kade made a face. "Apples and oranges."

"The long answer," Teague said, glancing between the two, "is more complex."

"In what way?" Kade asked.

"First, it's never been done. Tall-ship replicas are a dime a dozen, but no one has built a replica vessel of this magnitude, from this era, before. I relish a challenge like that."

Kade nodded. "I can appreciate that."

"Second," Teague said, "*Wolverine*'s story is unique to this region, and my company has a strong presence here. Working with the Blue Water Foundation and investing in a maritime monument, such as this ship, demonstrates my commitment to preserving the heritage of the Great Lakes."

"Like we discussed earlier, a little good PR goes a long way," Kade said.

Teague smiled. "Third, *Wolverine* is a forgotten piece of history. She played a significant role in the war effort, and I believe people should be reminded of her story."

"The best way to learn it is to live it," Kade said.

"It's important to know what came before us, so we can better shape the days ahead."

"Wow, Galen, that's pretty philosophical for a twenty-first-century capitalist."

"Some of us capitalists have more than one dimension."

"I'd be careful just how many dimensions I had if I were you. I've known people with one too many, and it's usually not a good thing."

Teague laughed. "I know what you mean. I've met a few people like that myself."

Wolverine pitched to starboard, and the drinks slid across the table.

"So, tell me," Teague said to Kade. "How much do you know about the original *Wolverine*?"

Kade paused to recall his conversation with Jesse in the Otter. "Not a whole lot. She was built to train carrier pilots during the war, right?"

"Yes, and there's a story behind that." Teague sat forward. "See, the admiralty at the time didn't put a strong naval-aviation program high on the priority list. They were still thinking in terms of battleship tactics. But when Pearl Harbor was attacked, they realized how effective naval air power could be, and they changed their minds."

Kade put on a smirk. "Are you a conspiracy-theory guy?"

Teague paused, as though the comment had derailed him. "Pardon me?"

"There are people who believe FDR knew the Japanese were coming to attack Pearl Harbor, so he put the carrier fleet out to sea to protect them, and then let the attack happen just to stoke the country into entering the war."

"I've never given conspiracy theories much credence," Teague said. "Especially that one."

Kade shrugged and smiled. "I was just curious."

Rachel gave him a look like she might kick him under the table.

"Be that as it may," Teague said. "In the wake of Pearl Harbor, the Navy initiated an ambitious plan to qualify thousands of pilots for carrier duty, but to do that they needed at least one carrier in a protected body of water."

"This country is surrounded by oceans," Kade said. "And we're thousands of miles from the South Pacific and Europe. Setting up that training should have been easy."

"You might think so." Teague took a draw of his stout. "But in 1942, German U-boats had the country in a stranglehold. They were sinking nearly every ship steaming through the Gulf of Mexico and along the Eastern seaboard. The government kept knowledge of this under wraps to prevent a national panic, but the Navy knew, and they weren't about to commit one of their vital aircraft carriers to those waters to train pilots."

"A government cover-up? That sounds like a conspiracy to me," Kade said.

Teague ignored him. "Fear of Japanese subs paralyzed the West Coast, so the Navy decided to station their aviator training in the Great Lakes. The only problem with that was the Saint Lawrence Seaway."

"What about it?" Kade said.

Rachel set down her glass. "It didn't exist in 1942."

"That would make it difficult to get an aircraft carrier down here."

"Quite right," Teague said. "So, they built one."

Kade leaned back with his beer. "How long did it take to build an aircraft carrier back then, a year, a year-and-a-half? That's a long time to wait to begin a critical training program."

"It didn't take them that long," Teague said. "They stripped down an old passenger steamer already in the Lakes, built a flight deck over her keel, and christened her *USS Wolverine.*"

"They commenced qualifying pilots in just five months," Rachel said.

"A passenger steamer?" Kade flashed a genuine smile. "That explains the paddlewheels."

Teague pulled an Arturo Fuente cigar from his shirt pocket and lit up. "The training program was a success. A second steamer was converted to a flat top, the *Sable,* and by the end of the war, nearly eighteen thousand pilots qualified for carrier duty on Lake Michigan."

"What happened to those original training carriers?"

"After the war, they weren't needed anymore and the Navy decommissioned them," Rachel said. "A few years later, they were sold for scrap."

Teague blew a stream of cigar smoke. "That made building my replica more challenging. We had no real-world reference to guide us. No surviving section of keel or superstructure to help with our reproduction. All we had was an incomplete set of blueprints drawn up for the *USS Wolverine.*"

"From what I've seen, you've done a pretty good job. She's a beautiful vessel."

"It wasn't easy. We faced a lot of hurdles getting all the pieces together." Teague appraised The Brigg's interior in a wistful manner. "Now, after all the work, I have to be concerned about losing her."

"Losing her?" Kade sat up straight. "What happened? Did you miss a payment to the bank?"

"Nothing so mundane, I'm afraid." Teague turned a shade serious. "I don't know if you're aware, but there's a dark little secret unfolding on the Great Lakes. Ships are under attack, many are being sunk, and the Coast Guard is unable to stop it."

"You mean, like, a terrorist attack?"

"Possibly. I don't know. All I know is someone is attacking ships, and it stands to reason that *Wolverine* would make a tempting target."

Kade thought about his encounter with the cargo ship in a new light.

"The latest incident occurred last night," Rachel said. "A merchant ship went up in flames and sank while the Coast Guard was conducting a routine boarding operation." She added, "My dad was out there with the Guard when the ship went down."

Kade felt a ripple of concern "Is he okay?"

"Yes, he's fine, but it really shook me up when I found out he was that close to it."

"Ely's stitched together pretty tough. It'll take more than a sinking ship to get him."

Rachel smiled. "Wow. That was almost a compliment you paid my dad."

"Almost."

"You know, he's the one who nearly got blown to pieces, and he tells me to be careful." She wiped a tear from the corner of her eye. "He told me to stay off the Lakes because of what's going on out here ... I didn't tell him about the poker run or my duty on *Wolverine*."

"He's your father," Kade said. "You're all he has left. Of course, he's concerned about you."

"What about you?" she said.

"I don't think Ely is concerned about me."

"No, you had an incident of your own with that cargo ship."

"Yeah, that was an odd thing too. Still don't know what to make of it." Kade didn't bother mentioning that the ship in question, according to Mr. Nystrom and Mr. Rifkin, was owned and operated by Raymond Firth. "Galen, I think you're on to something with the terror-plot theory."

"I hope I'm not," Teague said.

Kade wanted to change the subject. He glanced around The Brigg. "This is a fine ship, but Rachel mentioned you didn't build a completely faithful replica. For instance, this compartment housed smokestacks on the original *Wolverine*."

"She's faithful in style and function," Teague said, "but I did give her modern navigation and communications systems, and an updated powerhouse to keep her in line with current maritime requirements and regulations."

"Well, I approve your use of this space." Kade said. "Speaking of modernization, why the hell didn't you install an optical system to assist pilots with landings? Why are you using a guy with paddles on deck?"

Teague pulled the cigar from his mouth and laughed. "Like I said, I wanted to keep *Wolverine* authentic in style and function. The pilots back then didn't have an optical guidance system to show them the way. They had a guy with paddles. Skill and instincts did the rest."

"I would have appreciated the optics," Kade said. "But I didn't need it."

"No, you didn't." Teague regarded him. "You came into the landing cold, without having practiced, and you still nailed it. Impressive. You're a very talented pilot. If the rigors of running your own business ever get tiresome for you, I think I can find a place for you at T-GAF. We can always use another good pilot."

"I appreciate that, Galen, but I don't think I'll work for anyone else ever again." He lifted his beer. "I'm sure Rachel has told you how attached I am to the charter business."

"She has mentioned it once or twice."

"Is that all? I figure with the number of times we've … discussed the matter—"

"No need to beat a dead horse," Rachel said.

Teague smiled and set the cigar between his teeth. "You two sound like you're married."

Rachel sent a glare in his direction.

Kade chuckled and tried to make eye contact with Rachel, but a boom of thunder rumbled through The Brigg, startling everyone.

"The storm isn't letting up," Teague said. "Looks like you're my guest tonight."

"Seems that way."

"I'll have my ward officer prepare cabins and arrange for dry clothes to be brought to you."

"That would be great," Kade said.

Teague finished off his stout and stood. "I'd offer to give you a tour of the ship, but I think you'd rather have Rachel show you around."

"I'm sure you're a busy man, Galen."

"I do have a couple of things to take care of yet today. There's never enough time."

"That's one of the dangers of being a successful businessman."

"Yes, it is." Teague started away from the table, but then stopped after a few steps and turned. "You know, there's one more reason I built *Wolverine*."

"Oh?" Kade said. "And what's that?"

"I always wanted to be the captain of a warship."

"You're the leader of a very successful corporation. Doesn't that count?"

Teague smiled. "It isn't quite the same thing."

"No, I don't suppose it is."

"Enjoy your evening, Mr. Mitchell." Teague left The Brigg.

Kade and Rachel sat alone at the table, their eyes finally connecting.

But, without warning, Cody plopped down in Teague's vacated chair. "Hey, guys," he said. "What are we talking about?"

TWENTY-TWO

Kade and Rachel disengaged from each other, opening up the conversation space to include Cody. She gave him a smile. "We're talking about history, terrorism, and the difficulty of rebuilding the past," she said.

"Oh." Cody's beer-glazed eyes brightened. "That sounds interesting."

"To say the least," Kade said. "Where's Jesse?"

Cody pointed toward the center of The Brigg. "Blackjack."

Kade followed his finger, and found Jesse seated at a table with a pair of cards lying face down in front of him. Brenda stood behind the table with a deck in her hand, waiting for Jesse's decision to either take a hit or stand pat.

"That dealer lady came to get a drink and Jesse talked her into a game of blackjack. I think he's trying to get lucky." Cody smiled and considered his companions. "When's the last time we were together like this?"

Kade thought about it. "Petoskey, I think. After the Pellston Air Race. Remember?"

"Pellston! Yeah, I do." Cody buried his head in his hands.

"Talk about the blind leading the blind," Rachel said.

"If my copilot could pay attention to course markers," Kade said, "it would've been fine."

Cody lifted his head. "Why is it my fault?"

"You told me that last marker was pylon number five."

"I thought it was pylon number five."

"It wasn't. It was the *outer* pylon, and if we'd pulled our one-eighty around it, we would've placed, maybe even won."

Cody frowned. "Those pylons weren't marked very clearly."

"Clear enough."

"Then why didn't you see it? Were you flying with your eyes closed?"

"For the umpteenth time, lap traffic was insane and that Glasair disappeared under our starboard wing. I had to focus on finding him."

"You aerial Magellans were a mile over Lake Michigan before you realized you'd missed the pylon," Rachel said.

Kade shrugged. "Race officials said it was a first. At least we were original."

"Original doesn't get you prize money," Cody said.

"No, but it does make for a good story." Rachel sipped her drink. "And good memories."

Kade smiled at her. "We had a few of those, didn't we?"

"We had a lot of those."

Cody searched his memory. "What was the name of that place we went to after the race?"

"City Park Grill," Rachel said. "The race organizers had an after-event party there."

"That place was a blast. I think. It's kind of a blur."

"It should all be a blur," Kade said. "You drowned your sorrows pretty deep that night."

"You weren't too happy either," Cody said.

"I'll admit I was pissed at the time, but looking back, it was a pretty good day."

Rachel looked at him with a warmth that had been absent for years. "It really was."

Kade smiled. "The creditors hadn't started hounding us yet."

"And it was before Leah died," Rachel said quietly.

"And Travis," Cody added.

Kade raised his beer bottle. "To the good days."

Rachel and Cody touched their bottles together with Kade's, and they all took a drink.

"Ma'am?" A man in an authentic-looking Navy uniform approached the table.

Rachel faced him. "Yes, Mr. White."

"The captain has asked me to show our guests to their quarters for the night."

"Where are we putting them?" she asked.

"Aft cabins," White said. "Port row."

"Not bad." She said to Kade, "Port row cabins have nicer amenities."

Cody finished his beer. "I *am* getting tired. A comfy cot sounds good."

"Jesse," Kade called across the deck. "We're getting quarters, let's go."

Jesse finished his hand of blackjack, said a few words to Brenda, and headed over.

Mr. White gestured to The Brigg's exit. "Gentlemen, please follow me to your quarters."

"Catch up with you later?" Kade said to Rachel.

"Yes," she replied. "I just need to wrap up some poker run business."

Kade fell in line with Cody and Jesse, and followed Mr. White out of The Brigg, past the old radio room and up the ladder. They entered a little compartment at the base of the island and started down a ladder well to the main deck. Mr. White continued through a boxy corridor with light-gray bulkheads that smelled of diesel oil. Kade noted runs of large diameter pipe, ventilation duct, and electrical conduit that ran through the overhead space. They walked past a trio of diesel generators, a bank of gauges, and entered an open space with a stainless-steel counter and half a dozen picnic-type steel tables. Kade figured it to be the crew mess. Mr. White pressed on through a narrow corridor that opened into another open space, this one with an arrangement of small square tables and chairs, a ladder well leading down through the center of the deck, and a series of doors along both the port and starboard bulkheads.

"This is the ward room," Mr. White said, "and those doors open to your cabins."

"Were these the officers' quarters on *Wolverine Prime?*" Kade said.

"Yes, but we've upgraded them to accommodate VIP guests," Mr. White explained. "Each cabin has a bunk fitted with a custom Amerisleep mattress, individual climate controls, a private head, and ... oh yes, cable television." He smiled like he had just made a pretty funny joke.

"Tell Mr. Teague we appreciate the hospitality," Kade said.

Mr. White nodded. "You will find a dry set of clothes on your bunks."

"Thank you, Mr. White." Kade pushed open the door to the nearest cabin. "Guys," he said to Cody and Jesse. "I'll see you in the morning."

He walked in and found a somewhat spartan cabin, but with a touch of Marriot, as Mr. White had explained. Overhead track lighting lit flat-gray walls, A sturdy bunk, made up smart with clean linen, sat on the outer bulkhead, with a folded set of clothing lying at the foot.

Wood trim dressed out a single porthole window above the bunk, and a flat-screen television hung in the corner. A narrow doorway to his right opened to a compact shower stall and toilet. Kade closed the door. It was cool inside, and he felt a chill. His wet clothing wasn't helping matters. He bumped the temperature up on the thermostat control mounted next to an intercom box on the bulkhead. He peeled off his shirt and pants and hung them over the shower stall, and then pulled on the khaki pants and blue Polo shirt with T-GAF logo that Mr. White had left on the bunk. He realized the ship had not pitched to any great degree in a while, and he had not heard cracks of thunder like earlier. Perhaps the storm was weakening. He retrieved his cell phone from the pocket of his wet pants. Good news. Still working. He considered calling Danny to let her know where he had gone, but realized he had no service in the middle of the lake. He sat on the bunk and pondered the last few days. He had come a long way since dropping off that hunting group in Copper Harbor, all the way to the flight deck of an aircraft carrier in the middle of Lake Michigan, and then on to having drinks with Rachel aboard said carrier. In the realm of his wildest imagination, this would not have shown up on the radar.

He turned on the TV with a remote and flipped through fifty channels of nothing worth watching. Periodically the picture would freeze, like a storm cloud or lightning strike had interfered with the ship's satellite connection. He settled on a cable news network and pondered his situation as he half listened to the news anchor read his report. A knock sounded on the cabin door. Kade rolled off the bunk to answer it.

Rachel waited on the other side. "You ready for your tour?" she said.

Kade noticed she had put her hair down. He always liked when she wore it that way. "Let's go." He stepped out of the cabin and caught the scent of his favorite perfume.

She gave his attire a once over. "Nice outfit. You look like a real company man."

"Compliments of Galen Teague."

"Of course." She motioned for him to follow her through the ward room. "We had photographs of this compartment taken during a Christmas dinner in 1943, so we were able to authentically reproduce it."

Kade nodded and followed her aft into a short corridor.

"Ship's dispensary and sick bay are also faithful reproductions," she continued. "We had detailed drawings and references from other war-era ships to work from."

Kade studied the cabinets, medicine bottles, and medical apparatus on display in the dispensary, and then the exam tables and surgical tools in the sick bay. "For a training ship, they had a pretty sweet medical set-up."

"Training naval aviators is risky business." Rachel motioned with her index finger. "Follow."

She walked back into the ward room and descended the ladder well through the center of the deck. It delivered them to another passageway. She pointed aft. "The yeoman's office and ready room are down there."

"Ready room?" Kade said. "Like where the pilots are briefed on the big mission in *Thirty Seconds Over Tokyo*?"

Rachel looked at him with deadpan eyes. "Yes, just like that." She headed forward.

Kade grinned and stayed with her. "So, where's your friend Favio?"

"Salvio," she said, a little irked. "What is your problem with him?"

"I don't have a problem with him. Not yet, at least."

"Sounds like you do." She turned around. "And why would you?"

Kade thought about his answer. "Maybe I'm jealous."

She laughed and continued walking the corridor.

He kept on her heels. "Hey, you're the one who filed for divorce. I didn't ask for it."

"Ha!" She spun around. "You asked for it. Maybe not with words, but you asked for it."

"How does that even work?"

"Oh!" She took off in a snit again. "You're infuriating."

"I don't try to be. It just happens."

"We're not doing this now." She marched into another compartment and motioned to a long bank of ovens and industrial mixing bowls. "Ship's galley."

"We keep putting it off," Kade said, glancing at the nautical kitchen. "We have to do it sooner or later. This whole unresolved thing between us has been hanging out there too long."

"We both signed the papers. I call that resolution." She started up a stairwell.

"You know what I mean." He stood at the bottom of the stairs. "Why are you running away?"

"I'm not running away." She faced him. "I'm giving you a tour of *Wolverine*."

"I know what it is," he said, "what it's always been."

She turned her back and finished climbing the stairs.

Kade followed her up and recognized the compartment at the top. "Crew mess," he said. "Mr. White took us through here earlier."

"Very good." She led him through the battery corridor, into the generator room, and down another steep set of stairs. It landed them in a large compartment in the belly of the ship where fuel-oil fumes hung heavy in the air. Two massive diesel engines sat side by side, filling the space with a loud rumble. A maintenance catwalk ran alongside and between them, and a ceiling of pipe and conduit filled the overhead. A mechanic in oil-stained clothes walked the catwalk, monitoring the ship's powerhouse.

"Diesel engines," Kade said above the mechanical wall of sound. "A break from the past?"

"*Wolverine Prime* had a big steam engine down here, but Teague felt operating and maintaining a steam engine would be more trouble than it was worth. He didn't believe having it was essential to fulfill this vessel's mission."

"Not to mention steam engines are hard to come by these days," Kade said. "He'd have to have it built from scratch. Being a business-man, I'm sure he kept cost in mind."

Rachel pointed to a great spinning driveshaft that ran from a link-age assembly near the closest engine to a coupling through the starboard bulkhead. "Each engine drives a paddlewheel. They're mechanically synchronized. Our *Wolverine* tops out around twenty-eight knots, faster than the original."

"And that kept in line with Teague's goal of preserving authentic style and function?"

"Apparently so." Rachel walked into the engine room between the rumbling diesels, and then circled around the stairs to a door in the aft bulkhead. "Another benefit of employing diesel engines instead of a steam engine is behind this door."

Kade stood beside her. "What is it?"

Rachel unlatched the dogging lever and pushed open the door, revealing the Wildcat fighter that Salvio had arrived in earlier. It sat on the far side of a large, open bay that spanned the beam of the ship. Bright lights on bulkhead fixtures shined down, illuminating the plane and the surrounding deck. Beyond the old fighter, a tall folding wall, like an industrial curtain, stretched across the bay, bisecting the space.

Rachel stepped through the door. "This section of the ship housed the boilers and coal bunkers that fed the steam engine on *Wolverine Prime*. The decision to go with diesel opened up this space to repurposing. Teague utilized half of it to build The Brigg, just forward of our location. The other half, here, he decided to use for below-deck storage of refurbished aircraft. The Wildcat is the first of three planes he hopes to have on board."

Kade was about to ask how the hell they got the fighter below deck, but then noticed cables and guide tracks running up the port and starboard bulkheads. "An elevator to the flight deck," he said. "Another replica enhancement."

"Teague likes to think of it as behind-the-curtain magic."

"He's a regular Wizard of Oz." Kade caught the lingering scent of cigar smoke in the air, and remembered Teague lighting up in The Brigg. "This ship is a great big toy to him, isn't it?"

Rachel smiled. "In a way, it is. He spends every moment he can aboard, but it's not just a toy. Like he explained, it represents something far more important to him."

Kade noticed an undercurrent of sentiment in her voice as she spoke. "Do you have a soft spot in your heart for this ship too?"

She gave a look like she had not considered that before. "I think I do. I've been on the *Wolverine* Committee from the beginning. I've watched her go from blueprints to steel, and I was there when we dedicated her at Navy Pier. Now that she's sailing ..." Her voice trailed off and she glanced around the bay. "Now that she's sailing, I'm fully invested in her mission."

Kade heard movement behind the Wildcat and startled a bit when a man came walking around the tail. He was a big guy, tall and musclebound, with a shiny bald head. He wore one of Teague's authentic-looking Navy uniforms. "Can I help you with something, Miss Edwards?"

"No, Cam. I'm just showing a guest around the ship."

That seemed to make Cam a little uptight.

"It's okay," she said. "Mr. Teague approved the tour."

He settled back on his heels.

Kade noticed Cam had a pistol holstered on his waist.

Rachel walked over to a pushbutton control box on the bulkhead. "We're going up, Cam. How's the weather up there?"

"Storm's blown over for the most part," he said. "Just some wind and drizzle left."

Rachel hit a button on the box, and a large section of the overhead structure began to slide down along the guide tracks. "Stand back, the sky is falling."

Kade stepped away to clear deck space for the elevator to land. A balmy breeze and a spray of rain blew in through the opening above. The moving section of flight deck settled into its lower position with a clunk, and Kade and Rachel stepped into the center of it. Kade estimated it was just large enough to accommodate the Wildcat's wingspan.

Cam hit another button on the control box, and the elevator started up.

Kade waited until they were out of earshot. "Cam is carrying."

"He's part of Teague's security detail," Rachel said. "Galen is a rather outspoken CEO. At times he says things that aren't politically correct." She added, "There've been threats."

"Isn't all that philanthropic crap he does supposed to be a firewall against that kind of thing?"

"No firewall is a hundred percent effective. Add into the mix the attacks on shipping in the Lakes lately, and Teague decided beefing up security was a prudent idea."

Kade shrugged. "If you ask me, it makes him look a little para-noid."

The elevator continued upward, finally locking into position at the flight-deck level. The hum of the motors stopped and the rumble of the guide tracks subsided. They walked off the platform toward the edge of the deck. Far off in the distant sky, the storm front that had battered *Wolverine* rolled eastward, peeling off flashes of lightning and echoes of thunder.

Rachel gazed at the light show on the horizon. "It looks pretty from this vantage point."

Kade admired the lines of her face in the dim lighting on deck. "I agree."

She faced him. "Why did you come here, Kade?"

"I told you, we never really talked about what happened between us. I thought it was time."

She did not reply.

"I know why you gave up on our marriage," he said quietly.

"I'm not the one who gave up," she said. "You left me, only it wasn't for another woman, it was for a Viking Twin Otter turboprop."

Kade shook his head. "No, you were just as invested in making the business succeed as I. Yes, we worked long hours, the work was hard, and we sacrificed some things in our marriage, but you were hanging in there." He made eye contact with her. "Right up until Leah died."

Rachel's expression turned sour. "Leah didn't die. She was killed."

"She died from a drug addiction."

"People die from disease, or old age, or car accidents. When it's drug addiction, it's murder."

Kade studied the grooves between the wooden planks under his feet. "As hard as it is to accept, Leah made each decision that led to her death."

"That dealer killed her," Rachel said, "the same as if he pulled the trigger on a gun."

"There's truth in that, but the police never conclusively identified who sold to her."

"Kish," Rachel spat. "Rolle Kish is his name. I told them."

"And they pulled him in, and they questioned him, and they searched for any shred of evidence to tie him to Leah's death, but they couldn't find anything more than circumstantial threads, so he walked." Kade softened his tone. "I understand how that angered you."

"I don't think you do."

"There was no justice. No closure. Nobody was punished, so you punished yourself."

Rachel's eyes turned glassy. "Her last call was to me, Kade. She wanted me to take her to see Dad. I don't know why, and I never found out. By the time I got to her, she was gone. I found her in that filth. I can't believe how bad life had gotten for her." Rachel wiped a stream of tears from her cheek. "I was angry at her for being weak, for turning to drugs. I didn't help her. I condemned her. What the hell kind of sister was I?"

"It wasn't your fault. I know it's hard to accept. Guilt is a soul-sucking bastard, trust me. It tricks you, makes you obsess on what you could have done, what you should have done. Don't let it control you anymore."

"But if I only—"

"Rach, there is no path you could have taken that would have saved Leah's life."

"There's always another way," she said defiantly. "I just didn't look hard enough."

"Believing that lie fuels the guilt. It's burning you up like a fire, destroying everything inside. That's what happened to us. Guilt over Leah's death hollowed you out, and grief filled in the void. There wasn't room for anything else, not even our marriage."

"You don't know what you're talking about."

"I know better than anyone how powerful that kind of guilt can be."

She brought her gaze back to his face. "How can you preach to me about letting go of guilt when you still blame yourself for what happened to Travis?"

"Not like I used to. I turned a corner. I had to. Two years of drowning in self-pity and alcohol nearly killed me. I finally realized that blaming myself wouldn't bring him back."

"What were you drinking? I could use one right now."

Kade smiled. "Listen, I didn't get through the darkest times on my own. Travis gave me a message in his last words. He told me I did the right thing, tipping off the law on that shipment and informing on Firth. He used his last breath to tell me it was worth it to him, the chance to take down a powerful drug trafficker. It took me so long to realize that. I heard his words but not his message. Guilt kept it hidden from me."

"I don't have a message like that from Leah, to help me through this."

"Now, hold on. You said Leah made her last call to you, and she asked you to take her to see Ely. If she was angry with you, if she thought you had abandoned her, she wouldn't have reached out to you like she did. She loved you, Rach, and she didn't blame you for her situation."

Rachel didn't reply.

"And there's one more thing," he said. "I owe you an apology for taking that job with Firth, and for all the fallout that came after."

"You don't have to apologize to me for that. You were trying to save the business. Creditors were surrounding the hangar with torches and pitchforks. You were backed into a corner and did the only thing you thought you could do."

"I wasn't just trying to save the business. I was trying to save us. I thought if I could get the bank off our backs it would be one less thing tearing us apart; then maybe we could stop the bleeding, and start fixing things between us." Kade put his gaze on the dark water mixing in the wake of the ship. "Looking back, it was an insane decision. I took a job smuggling narcotics for a drug runner right on the heels of Leah dying from a meth overdose. Swallowing that irony nearly choked me to death. I'm so sorry, Rachel."

She listened quietly, and after a long while, she reached for his hand. "Let me ask you something." She took a breath. "When you were flying for Firth, trying to save us, did you ever feel you were doing the absolute wrong thing and the absolute right thing at the same time?"

Kade looked at her funny. "I guess, in a way, I did. I walked that tightrope for a while, until one day it stopped feeling like the right thing. That's the day I called Travis. I had to end it." He thought on the question a moment longer. "You know, I used to think I had pretty solid morals. It's funny how flexible they become when you're desperate."

"I don't think you're the only one to ever realize that."

"No, I suppose not." Kade looked aft and checked on the Otter. She had made it through the storm in one piece, strapped down just as they had left her. That aircraft had been the source of his greatest joy, and his most profound tragedy. It amazed him how much an airframe, a couple of engines, and a sheet-metal skin had come to mean to him. He recalled the day he found her in that yard of decommissioned government aircraft.

"Hey, Rach, do you remember—"

He turned around to talk to her, but she was right there, leaning in to give him a kiss. Their lips pressed together and he put his arms around her. The scent of her perfume clouded his thoughts. They embraced near the edge of the flight deck, storm clouds flickering and rumbling along the dark horizon miles away. Kade lost himself in the moment, forgetting all about the day he bought the Otter, and Firth's sunken cargo ship, and the uneasy questions raised by federal agents Nystrom and Rifkin.

TWENTY-THREE

Michigan Intelligence Operational Center (MIOC)
Lansing, Michigan

Ely stared at the lake chart with the broken-ship icons on his computer screen. He had opened the *Discord* file earlier that morning and had been parsing through the information ever since. His meeting with Aldo Dinapoli the previous day had his mind rushing down an unexpected path, and he hoped to find something new in the names, dates, coordinates, and enrollment data that he had not noticed before. So far, nothing.

Dinapoli's video of the missile strike had shaken him. Could the government really be hunting and killing drug traffickers without due process, practicing annihilation instead of prosecution? Or had terrorists gotten their hands on a drone? Either way, Ely could not let it continue. As much as he loathed the criminal-drug industry, and despite the pain it had caused him personally, he could not condone its demise through blatant murder and destruction. He wanted to see the kingpins burned down more than anybody, but it had to be done the right way.

Ely decided his first step had to be finding out if it was being done the wrong way. He started with Dinapoli's assertion that the US government was hunting the drug smugglers. Assuming that to be true, solely for the sake of argument, he pondered which agencies' involvement would make the most sense. Obviously, the Drug Enforcement Agency came first to mind, but the Coast Guard, and even Customs and Border Protection might have interests in such an operation too. Terminating the drug problem would certainly make attaining their stated mission goals easier. Shoot first, don't bother asking questions. Ely saw the appeal some might have for this operation.

"Are you expecting a visitor?" Lieutenant Walker said, standing in the cubicle entrance.

Ely glanced up from his computer. "Yes. Why do you ask?"

"I met her downstairs in the lobby, on my way in just now. She said her name is Danielle Morgan and she has an appointment with you. She tried to call but you didn't answer."

Ely took his phone out of his pocket. The battery had died. He had been so busy the last couple of days he had forgotten to charge it. "I'll go get her. Thanks, Gabriel."

"She's a looker," Walker said, "but she's got a problem with authority figures."

"Why do you say that?"

"Because she asked if I was a fed, like that would make me some kind of asshole."

Ely laughed. "I met her once before. I picked that up too."

"Geez, Ely, why do you have to go around giving people that impression of feds?"

"I don't think she got that impression from me."

"If you're the only one she's met, I wouldn't be so sure." Walker smiled.

"Nice." Ely said. "Hey, Gabriel, you're a law-and-order kind of guy, right?"

"I'm not a crime-and-chaos kind of guy, or else I wouldn't have joined the Coast Guard."

"Which one do you put more emphasis on, law or order?"

Walker stared at him a second. "I hold each in equally high esteem. Why ask?"

"Just curious. I'm taking a poll."

Walker laughed. "I'd like to see what goes on in your head sometimes."

"You don't want to know." Ely shut down the *Discord* document and pocketed his phone. "Better go meet my visitor before she offends someone else coming in to work."

He left his cubicle and hopped in the elevator outside the MIOC offices. On the way to ground level, he wondered what type of trouble Kade had gotten into. Danielle Morgan intended to fill him in on that, but Ely figured he could make an educated guess. Kade had a history of poor judgment. The elevator doors opened, and Ely found Danielle Morgan pacing the floor in the sparse lobby. He walked over to her. "Good morning, Miss Morgan."

She shook his hand. "Call me Danny."

"Nice grip, Danny."

"I work for a living," she said. "Thanks for meeting with me."

"Would you like to talk over coffee? There's a decent shop not far from here."

"Don't you have an office upstairs?"

"I think the coffee shop would be a better atmosphere for our discussion."

She nodded. "I get it. Let's go."

Ely walked her to his Tahoe. The streets and sidewalks were still wet from the storm that had rolled through overnight. They drove off the lot onto Cedar Street. At the first light, he plugged his phone into the car charger. "Sorry I didn't get your call when you arrived."

"That's okay." She took a cigarette from the pack in her purse. "Do you mind?"

"Not too much."

She cracked open her window and lit up. "I'll keep the smoke outside."

"That works." Ely stopped at another light.

"I suppose you're wondering why I called you to help Kade after I saw your conversation with him the other day."

"The thought had crossed my mind."

She took a drag off her cigarette. "You two argued, but I picked up that you weren't really angry with him."

"Most people wouldn't have seen it that way. What did you perceive?"

"You were disappointed in him, and that means, on some level, you care about him, maybe even like him."

The light turned green and Ely continued down Cedar. "That's quite an assumption."

"I'm good at reading people's emotions. You're easy."

Ely laughed. "What emotion am I feeling now?"

"Look, Mr. Edwards, my dad was a leather-necked asshole too—"

"Too?"

"But I could tell when he was being a jerk because he cared."

"And you somehow determined that I care for Kade?"

"He was married to your daughter. There's a connection. You may have decided that he wasn't right for her, but that doesn't mean you can't like him. That's why you're disappointed."

"Are we getting to the part about how Kade is in trouble?"

"My point is you're different than those other guys who came to talk to him."

Ely glanced at her. "What other guys?"

"Two feds from a border patrol agency or something showed up a day after you did. Kade said they were real pricks. I believe it, because they came back looking for him yesterday and talked to me instead." She flicked ash out the window. "Couple of real dickheads."

"What did they want with Kade?"

"The same thing you did. He said they asked about the cargo ship he tried to help, wanted to know if he had any connection with the smugglers on board."

"What did he say about that?"

"He said he didn't have anything to do with them … He said he told you the same thing, but you didn't believe him. Why not?"

"You should ask *him* that." Ely turned onto Michigan Avenue. "What did the feds ask you?"

"They asked where Kade had gone. I guess they were expecting him to be at the hangar. I told them that I didn't know."

"Do you know?"

She gave him a crosswise look and blew a steam of smoke inside the cab. "No, I have no idea where he went. He left early that morning. That's all I know. I told those guys the same thing, and they didn't believe me. Said I was lying to them."

"Why?"

"They think I'm involved with Kade."

"Are you?"

"Not after yesterday morning." She tapped another bit of ash out the window. "Or rather, not so much anymore … it's complicated."

"What's complicated about it?"

"Your daughter."

Ely took his eyes off the road and stared at her. "What do you mean?"

"Kade's still in love with her." She considered the spent cigarette in her hand, and then flicked it out the window. "How do you feel about that, Mr. Edwards?"

"That's littering. I could have a lieutenant at the office write you a ticket."

She smiled. "No, I mean about Kade still loving Rachel."

"Seems like I should be asking how *you* feel about it."

"That was the discussion before he left. I told him he needed to figure it out, and to let me know when he did."

Ely drove the Tahoe into the public parking lot across the street from the Strange Matter coffee shop. He put it in park and switched off the engine. "Is that the trouble Kade is in, torn between two lovers? If so, I've got more important things to worry about."

"No, those feds wanted to get their hands on him."

"Maybe they had good reason. Kade has a tendency to create his own problems."

She shook her head. "I've known Kade for six months. We got pretty close. I'm telling you, he isn't doing anything to get the federal government after him."

"I've known him five years, and I'm telling you, it's possible."

Danny stared at him like she couldn't believe what he had just said. "Kade hasn't done a damn thing wrong. He told me he had nothing to do with the smugglers on that cargo ship, and I believe him. He's never lied to me. I trust him. On the other hand, those two agents wouldn't even tell me what they were really after. They never explained why they needed to find Kade so badly. They couldn't even keep their story straight."

"How so?"

"One guy said he didn't think Kade had done anything wrong, but the other guy said he had." Danny pulled out another cigarette and put it between her lips. "If I hear from Kade, I'm supposed to let them know right away. It's for his 'well-being' they said." She let out a sarcastic laugh. "Bullshit."

"Why do you say that?"

"Look, all the men in my life have been losers, liars, and assholes. It's made me kind of an expert on the subject. I know when a guy is feeding me a line of crap, and those feds were feeding it. Big time. They wanted Kade for something, but it wasn't for his own good."

Ely regarded her a long while. "Did they ask you about anything else?"

"No, they just wanted to know where Kade had gone, and then one of them got a phone call, and all of a sudden talking to me wasn't important anymore. They took off like I wasn't even there." She thought it over a few seconds. "Something tells me that phone call was about Kade."

Ely found himself on the fence with this one. Danny really seemed to believe what she was saying, but the fact that a federal agency had Kade in their sights just reinforced his own suspicions that his former son-in-law was up to no good again. "Let's get some coffee and think about all this," he finally said.

They left the Tahoe and walked across the street to the coffee shop. They placed their order with the hipster barista; two nitro cold-brew coffees. Ely studied an abstract painting on the wall while they waited. The barista handed them their coffees, and Ely paid him. There were no empty seats so they headed back to the Tahoe. Once across the street, Ely had made up his mind. "How were you supposed to contact those agents?" he said to Danny.

She pulled the card that Rifkin had given her from her pocket and handed it over. Ely studied it. *Agent Gerald Rifkin, U.S. Customs and Border Protection.* "CBP falls under the direction of Homeland Security," he said. "I'll call this agent, try to get something out of him regarding his investigation into Kade. How does that sound?"

"Sounds great."

They climbed into the Tahoe. Ely set down his coffee and picked up his charging cell phone. He keyed in the number on the card, but then paused before initiating the call. That missile-strike video came to mind, and Dinapoli's suspicions, and how perhaps some federal agencies do things without telling other agencies. Ely cleared the number from the phone. "Better idea."

"Aren't you going to call him?" Danny asked.

"I don't know this Rifkin guy," Ely said, "but I do know his boss. I think I'll get better cooperation from her than him. I've worked with her before, and I know I can trust her."

Ely searched through his contacts and selected Judith Conway, Deputy Commissioner US Customs and Border Protection. He called her, and she answered after a few rings.

"Judith, this is Ely Edwards. Do you have a minute to talk shop?"

"For you, Ely, just a minute."

"They keeping you busy at CBP?"

"Busy is an understatement. The new administration's border-policy changes have us jumping through hoops. Do more with less. You know the drill."

"I'm sure you'll hold it together somehow. This shouldn't take long. I'm investigating suspect activity on the Great Lakes for DHS, and I think a couple of your agents are working on a similar investigation. Maybe we can share information."

"Sure, Ely. What are you investigating?"

"The formation of a new drug-trafficking network operating between Canada and the Upper Midwest. A couple of the people I've interviewed regarding this network have told me they've also talked with CBP agents recently. Do you know anything about that investigation?"

"No, but I'm not appraised of everything our field offices are involved in. Have you tried calling the Detroit office?"

Ely balked. "You're my first call, Judith. I figured I'd go straight to the top and avoid the runaround I'd probably get from the SAC in Detroit."

Deputy Commissioner Conway exhaled. "What are the agents' names? I'll pull up our directory and get you their contact information. You can talk directly with them."

Ely read from the card. "Agent Gerald Rifkin, and agent …" He gestured to Danny for the other name.

"Nystrom," she said in a hush.

"Nystrom," Ely repeated. "Agents Rifkin and Nystrom." He heard typing over the phone.

"Just a second, Ely." Deputy Commissioner Conway made a sound like she was miffed. "Spell those names for me," she said.

Ely did, guessing at how to spell Nystrom. More typing.

"Ely, I think you've got the wrong federal agency."

Ely sat up straight. "What do you mean?"

"We don't have an Agent Rifkin or Nystrom on our roster."

Ely studied the card again, scrutinizing the Customs and Border Protection logo in the corner. "Are you absolutely sure?"

"Absolutely."

"Just for laughs then, run this phone number through your directory." Ely read her the number on the card.

"If you have a phone number, why don't you just call it?"

"Humor me, would you please, Judith?"

She mumbled something and began typing again. "It's not one of our numbers, at least not a phone we've issued to an agent."

Ely's mind started racing a hundred miles an hour. "I'm sorry to bother you, Judith. My interviewees must have given me wrong information."

"No big deal, Ely. Sorry I couldn't help."

"You did help, more than you know. Thanks again." Ely disconnected.

Danny rested her coffee cup in the console holder and stared at him. "What's the matter?"

"Score one for woman's intuition."

"What do you mean?"

Ely flicked Rifkin's contact card with his thumb. "Those men who visited you were not with the Customs and Border Protection Agency."

Danny's eyes opened wide. "I knew they were bullshitting me." She frantically puffed on her cigarette. "If they aren't feds, who are they?"

"I don't know," Ely said, "but your story just got real interesting." She fidgeted in the seat. "Okay, so what's next?"

"Let me think. This is new territory for me."

"I'll give you five minutes."

"Thanks."

Ely's thought process had latched on like a vice to the fact that two guys were posing as federal agents, asking about Kade and the cargo ship. Who were they, and why were they doing it? Was this the first lead in Dinapoli's conspiracy theory? Ely wanted to find out.

"Danny," he said. "How far into this are you willing to go?"

TWENTY-FOUR

Aboard *Wolverine*

Sunlight streamed through the porthole window into Kade's eyes. He stirred awake and pulled a pillow over his head, wondering where he was. Then the memories filtered in. The conversation with Rachel, their kiss on the flight deck, and what happened after. He tossed the pillow aside and looked for her, but she was not with him in the rack, or elsewhere in the cabin. For a moment, he thought he might have dreamt the whole thing, but the scent of her perfume lingered on the pillow, and someone was running water in the restroom basin.

"Rachel?"

She stepped from the restroom, putting in an earring. "Were you expecting someone else?"

"Cute." Kade noticed she was dressed in her black blazer and white buttoned shirt from yesterday, and she had her hair up in a ponytail again. She had fixed herself up like she was headed out. "Going somewhere?"

"Teague wants me to cover a couple corporate meetings for him in Grand Rapids today. A helicopter is on the way to pick me up."

Kade threw off the blanket and rolled out of the rack. Wearing a pair of blue sleeping pants with the T-GAF logo on the front pocket and no shirt, he walked over to her. "I was hoping we could have breakfast together."

"We slept past breakfast. It's getting close to lunch."

"Lunch then," he said. "And we can talk about, you know … last night."

She put in the other earring. "It's not like it was our first time, Kade. We were married two years for crying out loud."

"Yes, but you have to admit it was a little different this time. I mean, I didn't think we'd ever be together like that again. Did you?"

She straightened her blazer. "It was always possible, to me at least. Passion was never our problem." She thought about it. "I guess I never completely closed the door on us."

"You made me sign the papers. It felt like that door slammed in my face."

She smiled. "We were both going through a lot back then. We hurt each other, but I think we've come out of it stronger, more confident in knowing who we are. Yes?"

"Maybe," Kade said. "So, where does that leave us here, today?"

She leaned forward and kissed him. "With more questions than we had yesterday."

"That doesn't help."

"I have to go. The helicopter arrives in five minutes."

"I'll go up with you." Kade rushed around, picking up his clothes and putting them on.

A voice sounded through the inter-ship PA system. "Miss Edwards, the chopper is setting down on the flight deck."

"They got here early. Time to leave." Rachel pushed through the cabin door.

Still tucking in his shirt, Kade followed her. "Hey, Miss Edwards. If you didn't close the door on us, why aren't you still Ms. Mitchell?"

"Professional career considerations."

They climbed the stairs out of the ward room. "Are you coming back to the *Wolverine* today?"

"Depends how the operations meeting goes," she said. "If no big issues pop up, I might be back. I have a few duties on board left to complete." She led them through the generator room and up to the base of the island superstructure. "Will you be here in the afternoon?"

"If Cody finds the gremlin in the system, we'll probably be gone."

They exited the island and a cool breeze washed over Kade's face. Bright sunlight warmed the flight deck, drying the rain from the seams in the planks. Tranquil water surrounded the ship. It seemed the storm had never happened. Kade checked on the Otter and found Cody already there, up on a stepstool with his hands inside an engine-access panel. On the bow deck, a black Bell 206 Long Ranger helicopter sat with rotors whirling at idle, waiting for its sole passenger.

Rachel hugged Kade and kissed his cheek. "I've got to run." She stood there a moment longer. "Last night was nice."

"It was," he said. "I'm glad I got stranded aboard."

"Me too." She smiled and headed for the chopper.

Kade watched her duck under the rotor wash and climb into the passenger cabin. Someone inside the craft slid the door closed for her, and the helicopter lifted off the deck, banking into a turn toward the Michigan shore. Kade watched it go, wondering where this thing with Rachel was headed.

Galen Teague, wearing his aviator sunglasses and flight jacket, approached with a pleasant smile on his face. "Good morning, Kade. How did you sleep on my flagship?"

"Not too bad," Kade said. "The accommodations were very … comfortable."

Teague nodded to the helicopter. "Looks like you two are patching up your differences."

Kade smiled. "Our relationship suffered a lot of structural damage during the divorce," he said. "It would take a public works project to repair it all."

Teague chuckled. "Speaking of repairs, has your mechanic found your plane's problem?"

"I don't know, haven't talked with him yet. He's deep into it though."

"You're a businessman like me," Teague said. "I'm sure you have things to attend to and you're anxious to get going. Let me call my mechanic to help."

"Cody will get it. But if he tells me he can't, I'll take you up on that offer." Kade noticed Cam, the security guard, standing near the island door with a couple of his comrades in arms. "What's with the security detail, Galen? Are you getting death threats or something?"

"I've gotten a few over the years. It goes with the territory."

"All that public support of popular causes isn't getting the job done?"

"There will always be kneejerk reactionaries prepared to be offended at the slightest word."

"You should reach out to them," Kade said as a wise guy. "Change their thinking about you."

"I don't care what they think."

"You might if one of them decides to follow through on a threat."

"That's what the security is for," Teague said, "to keep crazy reactionary bastards at bay."

"Do you really think one of them will try to sneak aboard this ship?"

"You never know where they're going to show up."

Kade smiled. "To be honest, some people have accused me of being reactionary."

Teague returned the smile. "Do I need to call Cam over here to shoot you?"

"That would make you seem paranoid."

"There's a fine line between paranoid and prepared."

At the island door, Cam stepped aside to let someone through; hotshot pilot Salvio emerged. Sporting an authentic bomber jacket and pulling on a worn pair of leather gloves, the tall Italian strode across the flight deck with a cocky swagger. "Mr. Teague," Salvio said with a slight Sicilian accent, "request permission to conduct flight exercises."

"Permission granted," Teague said.

Salvio signaled toward the bridge windows with a circular hand motion. The section of the flight deck that served as the elevator platform began to drop away.

"Kade," Teague said, "have you met Salvio?"

"No, I haven't had the, uh, opportunity."

"Kade Mitchell?" Salvio said.

"The one and only." Kade offered his hand.

Salvio took it and squeezed hard. "I have not heard much about you."

Kade clamped Salvio's hand in response. "Good. There's usually a lot of BS going around."

"Rachel is a joy to work with," Salvio said. "It must be difficult to have lost her."

"You know what they say. It's better to have loved and lost. But then, I'm here now. Right?"

Salvio chuckled. "To what end, Mr. Mitchell?"

Teague stepped in. "Salvio's my best pilot," he said to Kade. "I can use another one like him in the group, so think about our discussion yesterday."

"Do you really want another one like him?" Kade smiled with his wisecrack.

Salvio stared at him. "You are funny."

"I try my best," Kade said. "So, what sort of flight exercises are you conducting?"

"Precisione," Salvio said with exaggerated Italian flare.

"Salvio is showcasing the Wildcat at a number of air shows this summer," Teague explained. "He's going to demonstrate what the old warbird can do."

"Practice," Salvio said, "makes you perfect."

"It helps," Kade said. "But then, some of us are just naturals."

Salvio gave him an artificial smile. "Excuse me, please." He walked to the edge of the elevator shaft and watched for his aircraft to arrive.

"Two skilled pilots digging at each other," Teague said. "Professional rivalry?"

Kade made a face. "No, I just don't like him."

Teague laughed. "Like I said, you're a direct man. That's a breath of fresh air."

Kade pretended like he appreciated the comment.

"In all seriousness," Teague said. "I have a couple business associates visiting me aboard *Wolverine* this afternoon. I think you would be interested in meeting them."

Kade glanced crosswise at him. "Why is that?"

"They have a keen interest in the aviation industry. If you hit it off with them, they might be interested in becoming clients."

"If I'm still here, Galen, maybe I'll meet with them."

The elevator delivered the refurbished Wildcat to flight-deck level and the platform locked in place. Salvio walked around the aircraft, inspecting it prior to his flight.

"Salvio is getting ready to take his joy ride," Kade said. "And I need to get my plane back in the air. Thanks for the hospitality, Galen. I'll let you know what Cody and I find out."

"Remember, I have—"

"I know. You have a good mechanic on board. Thanks again."

Kade shook his hand and headed for the Otter. As he approached, he heard music coming from inside the cabin. Cody had his iPod plugged into the plane's intercom system and was playing "Baker Street" by Gerry Rafferty. The sax solo wailed through the air in a haunting way. Something about it raised goose bumps on Kade's arms.

He found Cody studying the starboard engine, scratching his razor stubble.

"What's the matter?" Kade asked.

"I don't get it. I mean, I really don't get it."

"You don't get what?"

"I don't get what I found." Cody frowned. "Let me run through this with you. Okay?"

"Okay."

Cody reached up and tapped the engine's midsection. "We're not getting light-off. Right?"

"Right."

"Light-off happens here, in the combustion chamber, where a couple of igniter plugs spark the fuel-air mix, causing it to combust. Right?"

"Right."

"If the plugs fail, we don't get a spark. No combustion. No light-off."

"Yeah, I'm with you."

"So, I check the plugs first. They look good. I check the plug connectors. Also, good. I trace the wire harnesses back through the system from the plugs to the exciter module."

Kade felt a longwinded dissertation on troubleshooting a PT6 turboprop engine coming on. "Cliff Notes version, please."

"Okay, okay. I run a continuity test through each harness conductor and guess what?" Cody did not wait for a guess. "I found a broken wire … in both harnesses."

The oddity of a double failure like that sent up red flares in Kade's thoughts. "Both harnesses had a broken wire?"

Cody reached in through the engine-access panel and took hold of a wire harness; one of two that were plugged into a black electric module. "Look."

Kade stepped up on the stool and examined the harness. It caught his eye right away, a broken red wire at the tie-in point to the connector. It was a clean break. A very clean break. "Looks like it was cut. Are you sure you didn't do this when you checked continuity?"

Cody grabbed the second harness and showed it to Kade. "If I did, I made the exact same mistake on the exact same wire on this one."

"That does seem unlikely."

Cody pointed to the engine on other side of the plane. "I found the same thing over there."

"Four harnesses and four cut wires?"

Cody nodded.

"Are you telling me someone sabotaged my plane?"

"I think I am."

Kade stared at him, waiting for the punchline. It didn't come. Instead, the Wildcat's engine coughed and roared to life across the flight deck. Salvio was preparing to take off for his exercises. Kade blocked out the noise and rifled through the implications of intentional sabotage.

"Who would do this?" Cody asked.

"I don't know, but whoever it is, doesn't want us to leave."

"Ya think?"

"Yeah, I think. But here's the real question." Kade stepped off the stool. "Why the hell would someone want to keep us on board this ship?"

- TWENTY-FIVE –

Firekeepers Casino Hotel, Battle Creek, Michigan

Nystrom tucked a rolled-up windbreaker into a small, canvas overnight bag. "I don't like ships."

Rifkin regarded him over the top of his laptop screen. "I know." He reached into his suit pocket and tossed a small pill bottle to his partner across the room.

Nystrom snatched it out of the air. "What's this?"

"Dramamine."

"I don't think so." Nystrom tossed it back. "That stuff makes you drowsy."

"Suit yourself. But if you get sick, don't bitch to me." Rifkin put his gaze back on the laptop screen and finished reading the message he had received. "They're voting today."

"That was fast."

"Legislators can move fast if they want to, they just need an incentive."

Nystrom smirked. "Fear of losing an election is typically their incentive." He shoved a pair of ammunition clips for his Glock into the bag.

"You expecting trouble?" Rifkin said.

"I always expect trouble." He gestured to the laptop. "Especially today."

Rifkin shut down the computer. "Gaetano's sure he has the votes to renew the charter."

"Don't hold your breath," Nystrom said. "Politicians don't have spines. They're like ..." He lifted the bag to his shoulder in thought. "Jellyfish. They're like jellyfish, sloshing around in the political current of the day. Any little riptide can flip a vote to no, and if they terminate the charter, you know what they'll tell us to do."

Rifkin frowned. "The committee likes the results we've shown them so far. No one will flip."

"I have contacts on The Hill," Nystrom said. "Some members are already waffling, talking about conventional approaches to the problem."

"Convention isn't effective."

"Tell that to the jellyfish."

Rifkin slid the laptop into a satchel. "It doesn't matter. It's out of our hands. Besides, we've got other concerns to think about, like containment."

"Agreed," Nystrom said.

Rifkin stood. "We're closing shop here, right?"

Nystrom nodded.

Rifkin pulled a cell phone from his pocket and set it on the desktop. "Then we don't need this anymore." He searched the room for a suitable blunt object to use to smash it to pieces.

The phone rang before he found one. They exchanged a glance.

Rifkin picked it up. "Hello, Agent Rifkin speaking."

"This is Danielle Morgan," the female voice said. "You spoke with me yesterday, at the Sparta Airport. You told me to call if I heard from Kade. Well, I just did."

"You heard from Mr. Mitchell?" Rifkin repositioned the phone on his ear and made eye contact with Nystrom. "Tell me about your conversation with him."

Nystrom cursed under his breath.

"You were right, he got himself into trouble," Danny said. "I don't want to say more over the phone. I'd rather tell you about it face to face."

"Of course, I understand. Are you at the airport? We can meet you there," Rifkin said.

"No, and I don't want to meet at your office either. Cops make me nervous. I pick the place."

Rifkin exhaled. "Where would you like to meet?"

"Grand Ledge, a place called Crossroads Barbecue."

"Crossroads." Rifkin scribbled the name down on a Firekeepers Hotel notepad. "I can be in Grand Ledge in about an hour. Are you there now?"

"I will be when you get there."

"Okay. Try to relax. Agent Nystrom and I will see you shortly, and we'll sort all this out."

"All right. Just hurry." She disconnected.

Rifkin tossed the phone back into his suit pocket. "That was unexpected."

"Really, Einstein?" Nystrom said. "How the hell did Mitchell contact her?"

"I don't know, but containment is getting more complicated."

Nystrom threw his bag onto the bed. "I'll inform the chopper we're going to be late."

Rifkin lifted a satellite phone from a suit pocket. "I'll find out what's going on out there."

TWENTY-SIX

Michigan Intelligence Operations Center (MIOC)
Lansing, Michigan

Danny set her cell phone in her lap. "How was that?"

"Perfect," Ely said. "We waved something shiny in their faces. Now, let's set the hook."

"Gladly. Those guys are trouble. I feel it." She took a cigarette from the pack in her back pocket. "I hope you know what you're doing."

Ely grabbed the cigarette from her hand. "No smoking on federal property," he said. "And you're right, those guys *are* trouble. Impersonating a federal agent is a little more serious than running a stop sign."

Danny laughed. "You feds don't like people pretending to be you?"

"I'm more concerned about *why* someone would pretend to be a fed."

"Why do you think they're doing it?"

"I'd rather not say ... not yet." Ely checked for a message he expected on his phone. Nothing.

Lieutenant Walker stepped into Ely's cubicle. "You want me to pick you up some lunch?"

Ely smiled. "No, I'm good. But thanks."

"I'm not asking again." Walker nodded to Danny, and then walked away.

"Are you clear on the plan?" Ely said to Danny.

She narrowed her eyes at him. "I may be blonde, but I'm not stupid. I know what to do."

"No one said you were stupid." Ely slipped on his jacket over his 9mm holster and pocketed his cell phone. "Let's go."

He led Danny from the MIOC offices to the elevator, and down to the lobby, all the while pondering Dinapoli's theory. If a government conspiracy to execute drug traffickers existed, then who could Ely trust in his investigation to expose it? Nystrom and Rifkin were posing as Customs and Border Protection agents, so logically CBP was not involved. Ely favored a broader conjecture that no agencies or organizations under the Department of Homeland Security were involved. Keeping a big, bloody conspiracy hidden from DHS oversight just seemed too unlikely. That narrowed the possible field of rogue agencies capable of carrying out an operation like Dinapoli had suggested to a select few. Ely had a few top picks, but no evidence to indict any of them. Of course, this was all speculation. Without a smoking gun, he could not know who was in on it, and that was the crux of it. The pool of people Ely could count on to not be involved was a select group indeed.

"You ever do something like this before?" Danny asked as she climbed into the Tahoe.

"Something *like* this? Yes." Ely started the engine. "Exactly like this, no." He pulled out of the parking lot and set course for Grand Ledge. "So, how did you and Kade meet?"

"Through Baldy, I guess," Danny said. "Thad Baldwin is the manager of Sparta Airport. Everyone calls him Baldy. Back in January, he hired me to weld a broken runway plow. I ran into Kade at the airport. Turned out we were both looking for a spot to set up shop. We got along really well and agreed to share hangar space. One thing led to another. You know how it goes."

"Love at first sight?"

Danny laughed. "I don't believe in that. Not anymore. Kade had to earn it, show me his heart." She gazed at the passing storefronts of East Lansing. "And he did."

"But there was a complication," Ely said.

"Yeah, a complication." She fell silent.

Ely glanced over and found her staring at the busy sidewalks. "You don't have to put yourself out there for him like this."

"I know. I want to do it."

Ely drove a while in silence. "When we get there, let me pick out the specific meeting spot."

"Are you going to arrest them?"

"That's my endgame."

"Why aren't we bringing more agents with us?"

"Don't worry. I have a plan."

"Why doesn't it feel that way?"

"Listen," Ely said. "There's more going on than you know. These guys might be part of something very big, and I have to approach the situation a little unorthodox."

She regarded him. "Do you *really* know what you're doing?"

He stopped at a traffic light and looked directly at her. "Yes, I do."

She did not reply.

"You told me I'm easy to read. Read me now. Am I being honest with you?"

"Yes," she said. "But all that means is you *think* you know what you're doing."

The light turned green and Ely drove through. "You want to back out of this?"

"Hell, no. I just want to make sure you're not going to."

Ely chuckled. "Okay, I think we're on the same page."

He drove onto Interstate 496, hooked up with Saginaw Highway, and negotiated traffic into Grand Ledge. He parked in a lot near Russel Street, a block away from Crossroads Barbecue.

"We're a half hour early." Ely popped open the driver's door. "Nystrom and Rifkin didn't have a lot of advance warning to plan for this meeting. That should play to our advantage."

"You think they'll suspect that I'm not alone?" Danny said.

"No, but we can't assume anything. Stay alert. And if I tell you to do something off script, you do it." They started walking up Russel Street. "You okay?"

"Yeah, why do you ask?"

"You're not smoking."

"Very funny."

They turned onto River Street, walked into a parking lot, and headed for the restaurant's back entrance. Ely scanned the cars in the lot, checking for anyone or anything that did not look right. All seemed as expected. They entered the building and walked through a narrow hallway, past the restrooms and into a small dining area filled with lunchtime customers. Table conversations merged into a noisy drone, and a mesquite aroma filled Ely's nose. He found an empty table near the order counter, away from the front windows. "Take a seat," he said to Danny.

She did. Ely grabbed a menu from the counter and tossed it in front of her. The cover of the menu had a drawing of a cleaver and a carving knife crossed like swords. From the wall, a pink cartoon pig face in a framed picture smiled down on her. "Why did you pick this place to meet them?"

"I like the brisket." Ely checked his phone. His message had come in. One word. *Fatto.*

"You sure you don't want me to talk longer with them," Danny said, "get them to admit something?"

"That's my job." Ely spotted a couple leaving a small table nearby. "I'll be sitting right here." He claimed the table as the couple left, and had them leave their empty food baskets and cups. "Remember," he said to Danny, "once agents Ying and Yang take a seat, excuse yourself to the restroom. Tell them you have a nervous bladder or something."

"That should be easy to sell."

Ely set one of the empty cups from his table in front of her. "Even easier now."

He positioned himself so he could watch Danny in his peripheral vision. They both settled in to wait. She started fidgeting after a few minutes and reached for the cigarette pack in her pocket. Ely gave her a cross look. *No smoking in a public place.* She cursed and shoved the pack back into her pocket. "Stupid law." She strummed her fingers on the tabletop.

The front door opened, and a tall man in a suit entered.

"Get ready," Danny said. "Agent Numbnuts just walked in."

Ely kept his eyes on his table. "Which one is that?"

"Nystrom."

"Is Rifkin with him?"

"I don't see him."

"Shit." Ely wanted them together.

Nystrom strode into the restaurant, scanning faces in the crowd. He spotted Danny and headed over. Unsmiling, showing no identifiable emotion at all, he studied the people in the dining area before deciding to sit across from her. "Miss Morgan," he said.

"Agent Nystrom." She glanced at the front door. "Where's your partner?"

"He's parking the car."

"I'd rather talk to him. He's not as big an ass as you."

"Mitchell contacted you," Nystrom said, unfazed. "What did he say?"

"Before I get into that, I have to go to the little girl's room." She lifted the empty cup. "I've been waiting a while."

Nystrom frowned. "You could have done that before I got here."

"Didn't have to." She stood. "Be right back. Don't go anywhere."

He didn't reply but gave her a displeased stare as she headed into the hallway toward the restrooms. Ely made his move, rising from his chair with a smooth, casual motion and sliding into Danny's spot at the table. Nystrom snapped his gaze onto Ely and cocked his head in a what-the-hell-are-you-doing manner. "That seat is taken," he said.

Ely flipped open his credentials wallet and presented his Homeland Security badge. Underneath the table, he trained his 9mm on Nystrom's stomach. "Agent Edwards, DHS," he said, staring into Nystrom's eyes. "Get your hands on the table right now."

Nystrom sat still, assessing the scenario.

"There's one in the chamber," Ely said. "And I can't miss at this range."

"I would hope not." Nystrom studied Ely's face. "Do I know you, Agent Edwards?"

"No, we've never met. Get your damned hands on the table."

Nystrom clenched his teeth and complied. "I underestimated Miss Morgan."

"Yeah, you screwed the pooch on that one."

"You don't know what you're doing," Nystrom said.

"Funny, you're the second person today to suggest that." Ely glanced around the restaurant. "Where's Rifkin?"

"He's standing behind you with a Glock pointed at your head."

Ely frowned. "Give me more credit than that." He stayed focused on Nystrom. "I'd ask to see your ID, but I know you forged whatever you're carrying."

"I'm with Customs and Border Protection."

Ely scoffed. "Whoever you're with, it's not CBP. I know Deputy Commissioner Conway, and she says you're not part of the family."

"Maybe I got the acronym wrong. Either way, I haven't done anything to warrant a government-issued sidearm pointed at my gut."

"Impersonating a federal agent is a felony that carries a three-year prison sentence, which means you're a felon. That's all the reason I need to draw my weapon."

"I'm not *impersonating* a federal agent."

Ely gave him a subtle smile. "Thank you for answering my first question."

Nystrom exhaled slowly, realizing he had just given up something.

"What's your acronym?" Ely said.

Nystrom didn't reply.

"I checked the deconfliction office in Detroit, just to make sure you're not on some secret undercover assignment. Your name does not show up on any list for any agency."

Nystrom remained silent.

"I didn't think you'd answer that," Ely said. "No problem. I'll find out when I bring you in and run your prints." He slid his creds back into his jacket pocket. "Next question. Why are you interested in Kade Mitchell?"

"You don't need to know that."

"That may be true, but I really, really want to know."

"You can't always get what you want." Nystrom smirked.

"You look too young to be a Stones fan."

"I am."

"Give me a real answer."

"You're not important enough for a real answer. All I'll tell you is we're on the same side."

"I'm not so sure we are," Ely said.

Nystrom pressed his palms against the table. "You've stumbled into something high above your pay grade."

"How high?"

"Nosebleed."

"But you're not going to tell me about it?"

"Not a chance."

"Then I'm taking you in and processing you. That'll get me the answers I'm after."

"I wouldn't put money on that," Nystrom said. "All you'll do is waste my time and embarrass yourself."

Ely reached for a pair of handcuffs he had strapped to his belt. "Far be it from me to waste your time, but I do need to find out who you are and what you want from Mitchell."

"Think this through, Agent Edwards. If you push this issue, someone is going to push back, and push back ... hard ..." Nystrom let his words trail off, and he regarded Ely as if recognizing an old acquaintance.

"What's the matter?"

Nystrom grinned like he had just eaten a couple canaries. "Nothing."

"You're full of things you don't want to say." Ely set the handcuffs on the table, concealing them under a sandwich wrapper. "Put them on. Let's go."

Nystrom eyed the cuffs. "We're not doing this."

"Yes, we are. Put those on, right wrist first."

Nystrom did not budge. "I've got someplace I need to be soon. Getting arrested would set me back a couple hours. Not happening."

Ely leaned forward. "Do you know what a 9mm at close range will do to a lower intestine?"

"You won't shoot me. I'm not a threat to you."

"Who said you're not a threat."

"I know your type. You're a law-and-order man. You'd never pull the trigger. Not like this."

"Try me."

Nystrom smirked.

"I'll give you the count of three," Ely said. "At which point, I'll deem you a threat to the people in this restaurant and take you down. You have a weapon holstered under your jacket, so I think I can make my reasoning stick with my superiors." Ely smiled. "One."

Nystrom did not blink.

"Two."

A cell phone rang. Nystrom glanced down at his suit pocket. "Can I take this call?"

"Depends who it is."

Nystrom cautiously retrieved the phone and checked the ID of the incoming call. "It's my partner, Agent Rifkin."

Ely gestured to the phone. "Slide it over here."

TWENTY-SEVEN

Danny reached the end of the hallway and put her hand on the exit door. Ely had told her to leave the building as soon as he had engaged Nystrom and Rifkin, but she did not feel right about leaving him alone in there. He had listened to her, and he was trying to help, and in Danny's world that earned him a little loyalty in return. She did not want to abandon him. She had been in her share of domestic disputes and barroom brawls, and never once had she shrunk away from a fight. Watching Ely's back did not frighten her either. She decided she had to go back inside.

The door suddenly swung open and startled her.

Sunlight silhouetted a man standing in the frame. "Come on, time to go."

She recognized the voice, and her eyes adjusted to the light. "Nice timing, Lieutenant Walker. You scared the hell out of me."

"You should've been out here five minutes ago. What's happening?"

"Ely's in there talking to one of the agents."

"I thought there were two agents."

"There are. Only one showed up."

Walker searched the hallway. "That could be bad for Ely."

"That's why I'm going back in."

"No way, Miss Morgan. My job is to take you back to MIOC."

"And leave Ely to get ambushed by Rifkin?"

"That's not going to happen." Walker sucked in his bottom lip and glanced down the hallway again. "You sure Rifkin's not in there?"

"I'm sure. He's not."

"He might be waiting out front for Ely and the other guy to come out. Let's go around and check, just to be sure."

"He might be standing behind you." A third voice had entered the conversation.

Danny recognized it. She and Walker turned around, and found Rifkin standing there with a pistol pointing at them from five feet away. "Seems I just overheard a conspiracy to impede and quite possibly assault a federal agent."

"You're not a federal agent," Danny said.

"Oh, you'd be surprised, Miss Morgan."

Walker opened his hands to show no threat. "I'm Lieutenant Gabriel Walker, United States Coast Guard. Creds in my pocket. I'm a federal officer. If you really are one too, then we've got one hell of a misunderstanding here."

Rifkin made no effort to produce his credentials. "Miss Morgan knows who I am."

"You're a liar," Danny said. "You're not with Customs and Border Protection."

Rifkin motioned with the pistol. "Come over here, please, away from the door. We'll straighten this out right now." He walked them to a dumpster at the corner of the building. "Lieutenant Walker, are you carrying a weapon?"

"No."

Rifkin gave him a once over. "Miss Morgan, pull up his pant legs so I can see his ankles."

"Do it yourself," she said.

Rifkin walked closer and pointed the gun at her. "If you make an aggressive move," he said to Walker, "she takes the bullet." He frisked Walker and found him clean.

"What do you guys want with Kade?" Danny said with a bit of brass in her voice.

"Very brazen, Miss Morgan. Has someone pointed a gun at you before?"

"Yeah, my first ex-husband did. Do all you little guys need guns to feel big?"

Rifkin ignored the taunt and lifted a phone from his suit pocket. He speed-dialed a number, keeping the pistol trained on Walker and Danny. It rang several times; just when it seemed the call would go to voicemail, the line clicked.

"Hello?"

"What's going on in there?" Rifkin said.

"A pulled pork special to die for."

"Who is this?"

"A fly in the ointment," Ely said. "A real, live fed, not the Cracker Jack kind you and your buddy are pretending to be. By the way, I've got Nystrom at the business end of a 9mm."

Rifkin paused. "You must be Ely."

Ely did not reply.

"I suppose you're wondering how I knew that." Rifkin grinned at his captives. "Perhaps I met an acquaintance of yours in the restaurant parking lot. Perhaps she told me a lot about you."

"Perhaps you and I should meet and keep innocent bystanders out of this."

"Nobody's innocent," Rifkin said. "Let me talk to Nystrom."

"I'll bring him to you. I assume you're in the back lot?"

"I am. Put Nystrom on the phone."

Ely disconnected.

Rifkin grit his teeth. "Your friend Ely is making this difficult."

"That's what he does best," Walker replied.

* * *

Ely dropped the phone into his pocket. "Put on those handcuffs," he said to Nystrom. "We're going to meet your partner."

"I'll walk back there with you," Nystrom said coolly, "but I'm not wearing the cuffs. If you press me, everybody in here will know we have a problem. I might even get some of these people involved. You hear what I'm saying?"

"Loud and clear." Ely swiped the handcuffs off the table. "Stand up."

Nystrom stood, and his right hand drifted toward his waist.

Ely concealed his 9mm under a crumpled carry-out bag and rose to his feet. "Keep clear of that holster," he warned.

Nystrom held his hand steady, no closer, but no farther from the holster.

Ely scanned the crowd in the dining area, checking if anyone had picked up on what was happening. "Head into this hallway."

Nystrom begrudgingly walked forward, and Ely reached for the gun holstered under his jacket as he passed. Nystrom whipped his head around. "You touch my sidearm, I will resist. Forcefully."

Ely froze his hand in place. "Don't make this harder than it has to be."

"Lots of opportunity for collateral damage in here," Nystrom said. "That doesn't bother me. How about you?"

Ely considered the crowd, the mothers and their kids, couples on a lunch date. A stray bullet could devastate a lot of lives. "Keep moving," he said. "We'll revisit this issue outside." He added, "And if your hand moves any closer to that weapon, I'll drop you here and now."

"Didn't we cover this already?"

"Don't test me. I only need one of you, and Rifkin is right out back."

They moved into the hallway that led past the restrooms and to the back door. Ely trailed far enough behind to deter any type of maneuver Nystrom might try to disarm him. He decided he would stop Nystrom at the door and confiscate his gun before they went outside. As they walked, Ely grew concerned about Danny and Walker, wondering what Rifkin had done with them. He started to doubt his strategy to apprehend the faux agents, but second-guessing things took his eye off the ball one second too long.

The men's restroom door suddenly shot open like a wedge between Ely and Nystrom, and a teen with a nose ring and spiked hair stumbled out. "Whoa, sorry, dude."

Nystrom realized he had a shield and bolted for the exit.

Ely slammed the door shut and shoved the kid aside. He discarded the carry-out bag and aimed the 9mm at his fleeing captive. "Nystrom, stop where you are!"

Nystrom kept going, throwing open the back door and disappearing through it. Ely cursed and raced after him. He reached the door before it had latched closed and kicked it wide open. He stepped through and drew down. Nystrom had gained some distance from the building, and he spun around with the Glock from his holster in hand.

Ely drew a bead on his chest. "Put it down. Goddammit, put it down."

"You put it down," a voice shouted from the corner of the building. "And I mean right now."

Ely kept Nystrom under the gun but checked his flank. A middle-aged guy in a suit had a pistol pointed at Walker and Danny near a dumpster. Ely brought his gaze forward again and found Nystrom aiming at him with the Glock. Nobody moved.

"You know how this works," Nystrom said. "Somebody shoots first, everybody gets trigger happy, and a lot of people die. Are you ready to play that game, Agent Edwards?"

Ely stood firm and kept his 9mm square on Nystrom's chest. "Not really. How about this one? You and your partner lay down your guns, and I take you back with me to find out who you are. If you resist, you get gunned down, and I run prints from your cold, dead hands anyway."

"That's one hell of a hollow threat. I expected more from a seasoned DHS agent."

"Then I won't disappoint you." Ely drew a breath and shouted into the parking lot behind Nystrom, "Anthony!"

A roar of engines swelled from the collection of parked cars and two black Cadillac CTSs surged forward, rolling out of their spaces like tanks emerging from behind a net of camouflage. In seconds they screeched to a stop behind Nystrom, and all the doors flew open. Men in suits and dark clothing piled out, four from each car, all armed with pistols and short-barrel automatic weapons. They encircled the area and trained their firepower on Nystrom and Rifkin.

"How about it?" Ely said to Nystrom. "Everybody gets trigger happy and a lot of people die. You still feel like playing?"

Nystrom kept his aim on Ely. "You'll be the first to go."

"Maybe. Maybe not. But I know one thing for sure. When the smoke clears, you'll be face down on the asphalt."

Nystrom stood there, thinking real hard.

Rifkin calculated things more quickly. He lowered his pistol and set it down on the parking lot. Walker rushed over and picked it up.

Nystrom finally saw the writing on the wall and dangled his Glock from the trigger guard.

Ely cautiously walked up and took the weapon. "First smart thing you've done all day."

"Interesting group of friends you have," Nystrom said.

"I know. Believe it or not, I felt I could trust them more than someone like, well, like you."

The men from the Cadillacs closed in and pulled Nystrom's and Rifkin's arms behind them, binding their wrists with zip ties. Ely nodded to a man he recognized as Anthony, the guy who drove him back to his car from Dinapoli's place the night before. "Tell Aldo I owe him one."

"Don't worry," Anthony said. "Mr. Dinapoli keeps a tally of things like this. If he needs a favor from you, he won't be shy to ask for it."

"I kind of figured that," Ely said.

"You want us to do something with these two?"

Ely regarded Nystrom. "Give me a minute to think about that."

Danny walked up to Ely. "So, you really did have a plan."

"Up to this point, yes. Now I'm winging it."

"I told you what will happen if you arrest us," Nystrom said.

"I know. That's why I changed my mind about that. You and I are going to hang with my new friends for a while instead of going back to my office. I'm willing to bet you don't have connections inside their organization."

Nystrom looked like this prospect bothered him. "That doesn't work for me. I've got someplace I need to be soon. Remember?"

"I don't care about your schedule. I care about the truth, and what's at the center of this mess with you, and Mitchell, and everything going down on the Lakes."

"You don't see what's right in front of you," Nystrom said. "You'd better pull your head out of the sand, or you're going to regret it."

Something in Nystrom's voice gave Ely pause. "What do you mean by that?"

"This op we're running, it isn't about Mitchell," Nystrom said. "It's about your daughter."

TWENTY-EIGHT

Aboard *Wolverine*

Kade worked his way through the Otter's main cabin, entered the cockpit, climbed into the pilot's seat, and picked up the radio mic from its cradle on the instrument panel. Cody followed him in and took the copilot's seat. Kade switched on the radio and spun the frequency knob to emergency channel 16. He keyed the mic. "Mayday! Mayday! Mayday, this is aircraft November-3-2-7-Delta-Bravo requesting assistance. Over." He repeated the hail two more times, and then waited for a response. A blast of static answered. He transmitted again. Static again. "I don't think we're getting a signal out."

Cody scrutinized the radio. "Let me take a look." He stuck his head under the instrument panel and inspected the wiring. He sat back up with an anxious, pale cast on his face.

"What's the matter?" Kade said.

"The coax cable to the antenna is cut. About a foot of it is missing."

"Are you serious?"

"Dead serious." Cody stroked his razor stubble. "Didn't we use the radio to talk with *Wolverine's* ATC after the engines wouldn't start?"

"We did, but the guy who cut the ignition wires probably came back and cut the cable while we were riding out the storm in The Brigg, or sometime during the night." Kade keyed the mic several times out of frustration. "I didn't think we needed to keep watch over the plane here."

"Guess we should start locking the doors."

"I don't think that would have helped." Kade pulled his cell phone from his pocket and checked for service. Still none. Too far out in the lake.

Cody settled back into the copilot's seat. "So, we're not allowed to leave and we're not allowed to call for help. This is kind of freaking me out."

"It's kind of pissing me off." Kade slapped the mic back onto its cradle. "Nobody tells me what to do or when to do it. If I wanted that kind of bullshit, I would've joined the Navy."

"So now what?"

"We figure out who and why."

The Wildcat soared off the bow and climbed into the sky. Kade watched it through the Otter's cockpit window, more than a little suspicious of the man piloting her.

"Could have been Rachel," Cody said. "Maybe she wanted you to stay but was afraid to ask."

"I doubt that. She wasn't real pleased when we landed. I don't believe keeping me around longer was on her mind then."

"But you two did hang out together, and you were getting along pretty well."

"Exactly," Kade said. "She was in The Brigg during the poker game, and she was with us during the storm. She didn't have the opportunity to go topside and slice up my plane."

Cody thought on it. "After Mr. White brought us to our cabins, she could have come out here and done the radio though."

"I can tell you with great confidence that she didn't come back out here last night."

"How can you be so sure?"

Kade did not reply.

Cody deciphered his silence. "No way. Really? You two? Together?"

"Anyway," Kade said. "If I had to put money on it, I'd say Salvio is the culprit. That jackass left The Brigg during the poker game after talking with Teague."

"You really don't like that guy, do you?"

"No, and this just gives me more reason."

"But you don't know for sure if he did this."

"Doesn't matter. I don't care for him either way. But if Salvio did sabotage my plane, he's only a cog in the machine. Teague is the driver."

"Why would Teague want to keep us here?"

"Who knows? Maybe those two Customs and Border Protection agents asked him to hold me here so they could entrap me with something. He enjoys pretending to be a captain, he'd probably jump at the chance to work with real agents."

"Wait a minute, what agents are you talking about?"

"That's right, you weren't there when they came by the hangar. They showed up with attitudes and questioned me about our encounter with those smugglers, and asked if I'd been in touch with Rachel."

Cody screwed up his face. "Why'd they ask you about Rachel?"

"It had something to do with my past, and Rachel's job at T-GAF, and a suspicion that we'd gotten together to break trafficking laws or something. It was all BS."

Cody thought on it. "Wouldn't that mean they think T-GAF is into something illegal too?"

"I suppose that was their general implication."

"So, if that's true, and Rachel works for T-GAF, doesn't that kind of make her involved?"

"Cody, she's not involved in anything. It was a screwball theory the feds dreamed up because they think I'm still flying for drug smugglers. They're out to get me, plain and simple."

"But even if they are," Cody said, "how did the feds know we were coming to the *Wolverine?* We didn't even know that until we left Cherry Capital."

Kade did not reply, because the same notion had occurred to him. "I don't have all the answers." He nodded to the starboard engine through the copilot's window. "Can you fix us?"

Cody frowned. "Are you *trying* to insult me?"

"Sorry. How long will it take you to fix us?"

Cody calculated things in his head, humming quietly to himself. "Give me two hours. That includes patching the coax for the radio. Then we can try to call for help again."

"We're not going to call for help again," Kade said.

"Why not?"

"Whoever cut that coax might be monitoring radio transmissions, just in case we discovered the sabotage, like we did. We're going keep quiet and fly off this ship without saying a word."

"Okay, if you think that's the best way to go."

"Cody, I don't know the best way to go. All I know is someone is trying to manipulate us, and I don't play that game."

"I'm good with whatever you decide," Cody said. "I trust you."

Kade smiled. "Hey, have you seen Jesse this morning?"

"Not yet." Cody pondered a moment. "I thought he might have hooked up with Brenda, but when I came out here to work on the plane, I saw a helicopter picking up staff people from the poker run. I think I saw her with that group."

"Then I won't be interrupting anything if I go to his cabin and roust him awake."

"Nothing but a hangover probably."

Kade climbed out of the pilot's seat. "I need to tell him what you found with the Otter."

"Okay. I'll get to work on the wire harnesses."

"Work quietly," Kade said, "and keep the sabotage stuff to yourself. I want everyone on this ship to think we're still blind to what's going on."

"Got it."

Kade crawled into the main cabin. "And don't let anyone near this plane. Teague's been pushing me to let his mechanic help fix our problem. I think I know why now."

"What should I do if someone comes out here? Scare 'em off with the Scoutmaster?"

Kade glanced back at him. "If you feel you have to, yeah."

Cody paused at the grave tone in Kade's voice. "For real?"

Kade tried to lighten up. "Just keep it in reach, as a security blanket."

"Yeah, okay, I'll do that."

Kade exited the cabin and climbed down to the flight deck, second guessing the advice he had just given Cody. Maybe he was overreacting. Maybe Rachel did have the ignition wires cut in an innocent ploy to keep him there. She had been far more amicable toward him than he imagined she would. He kept rolling it over in his mind as he headed for the island.

High in the sky, south of the ship, Salvio maneuvered the Wildcat through a barrel roll. Kade gave the fighter a passing glance before pulling open the door at the base of the island. He had not stepped through yet when a staccato burst of noise turned his head. Salvio had put the Wildcat into a steep dive, wing guns blazing, kicking up the surface of the lake with .50 caliber ammunition in a textbook strafing run. Kade watched as the fighter pulled up and out of the dive. That little maneuver would not be performed at any airshow.

Things just kept sinking deeper into the surreal.

Kade entered the island.

"Can I help you, Mr. Mitchell?"

Big, bald Cam approached from the stairwell leading down from the bridge. Kade noted his hand was poised closer than necessary to his holstered sidearm. Yesterday Kade would not have thought twice about it, but today? Different story.

"No," Kade said. "I'm just heading to my cabin for a quick shower."

"Do you need an escort back there?"

Kade put on a lighthearted smile. "You sure know how to make a guy feel awkward."

Cam's posture changed from menacing to uneasy. "I meant that if the ship's passageways were still unfamiliar to you, I would show you to the crew quarters."

"I know what you meant. I'm just messing with you, Cam. I can find the cabin on my own. But thanks anyway."

Cam gave him an irritated nod and reversed course back toward the bridge.

Kade took the ladder well down to main deck and walked past the generators and the crew mess into the ward room. He went to Jesse's cabin door and knocked. No answer. Knocked again. No sounds of movement inside. He tried the latch. It wasn't locked. He pushed it open. The sight sucked the air out of his chest.

Jesse lay crumpled next to a cabinet near the aft bulkhead, blood pooling around his head. Kade rushed in and knelt by his side. "Jesse!"

Jesse did not move. A long gash across his forehead bled deep red.

"Jess, what happened?" Kade looked frantically for something to dress the wound and found a T-GAF polo shirt lying on the cabinet amongst a litter of snack wrappers, glasses, and an empty whiskey bottle. He snatched up the shirt and knocked over the bottle.

He pressed the fabric into the wound. "Jesse, can you hear me?"

Jesse moaned and mumbled, but did not move.

"Hold on, buddy." Kade rose and punched the transmit button on the cabin's intercom box. "Hey, I need help down here. There's a man with a serious head injury. Aft quarters. Port row." He let off the button and waited.

"This is Lieutenant Paulus," a voice replied. "Please identify yourself."

"This is Mitchell, Kade Mitchell."

"Mr. Mitchell," Paulus said, "repeat your location."

Kade did.

"A med tech is on the way. He will be there shortly."

Kade went back to Jesse's side and wrapped the shirt to cushion Jesse's head on the steel deck. "Help's coming. Hold on."

Jesse's eyelids fluttered. "Hell ... of a hangover."

"You've got more than a hangover," Kade said. "What happened?"

Jesse rolled to his back and his confused eyes searched the room. He reached for his head and touched the bloodied shirt. "Don't remember."

"What *do* you remember?"

"Drinking. Cards." Jesse smiled. "Brenda."

"She's not here. Did she do this to you?"

Jesse chuckled. "No, I didn't let a girl bash my head in." He tried to sit up but failed. "She left after a few drinks." He reached for his head again. "Wish this cabin would stop spinning. And would you get my head out of this vice. Hurts like hell."

Kade lifted the whiskey bottle. "Let me guess. Brenda left, you drank yourself silly, and you cracked your head open as you passed out and fell down."

"I don't remember that." Jesse blinked. "Weird dream though."

"Tell me about it," Kade said, to keep him talking and engaged.

Jesse closed his eyes. "I was walkin' through a loud hallway. I mean, the walls were roaring at me. Pipes and gauges. Air was thick. And then there was this skinny Corsair in a hangar, only it didn't have cockpit windows. And I said to someone, 'Hell, I can fly it anyway.' And then my head explodes, and I see you hovering over me."

"Weird is right."

A voice called from the ward room. "Mr. Mitchell?"

"In here," Kade said.

Mr. White rushed into the cabin.

Kade regarded him. "Paulus told me he was sending a med tech."

"I am a med tech." Mr. White knelt beside Jesse and inspected the wound. He checked Jesse's pupils, and then asked him a few simple questions to determine awareness and cognizance. "We need to close that wound," he said to Kade. "Help me get him to the sick bay."

They each took one of Jesse's arms and lifted him off the deck, and then draped his arms over their shoulders and carried him out through the ward room and into the sick bay. Jesse tried to take a few steps, but it was a feeble attempt. They laid him on one of the examination tables. Mr. White grabbed a bottle of iodine and a package of gauze from a cabinet and handed it to Kade. "Clean the wound. I need to prep for stitches."

Kade nodded and opened the iodine bottle. He soaked a handful of gauze and began wiping the blood and clotting from the laceration.

Jesse flinched and gritted his teeth. "Easy, amigo."

Kade tried to hold his head steady as he wiped the gauze over the wound. "You're not making this easy, Jess. Hold still."

Mr. White turned around with a syringe in his hand, flicking the barrel with his finger and clearing an air bubble with a squirt. "I'm going to numb the area, Jesse. This will burn for a second, and then you won't feel a thing."

"I don't like needles." Jesse tensed. Kade held his head in place with both hands. Mr. White sank the needle in near the edge of the gash and pushed a portion of anesthetic into the area. Jesse screeched. Mr. White jabbed him again and pushed the syringe. Jesse fought against Kade's grip, and then slowly relaxed.

Movement drew Kade's attention to the dispensary corridor. More people were coming. It was Teague, and he had two men dressed in security uniforms with him, one with the name Gaddis stenciled over his blue shirt pocket, the other Flynn. Both had pistols in hand. Kade glared at Teague. "You don't need the guns. This isn't a mutiny down here."

Teague seemed to notice just then that his guards had their weapons out. He gestured for them to holster the sidearms. They complied. He approached the exam table. "What happened?"

"I don't know," Kade said. "I'm trying to figure it out."

"How bad is Mr. Granger's injury?"

"He's got a nasty split across his forehead. He's disoriented. Lost a lot of blood. Mr. White is going to stitch him up, but I think he needs better treatment than that."

Mr. White pierced a needle through the tattered, gray edges of Jesse's laceration, and pulled the flesh together with a thread. Kade left the sick bay and walked into the ward room.

Teague followed him. "Your plane is disabled. I'll radio for a medevac chopper."

Kade considered the offer in light of the cut wires Cody had discovered in the Otter. "Right."

"What's that supposed to mean?"

"Nothing." Kade entered Jesse's cabin and stood over the pool of blood. "This is where I found him."

Teague scrutinized the glasses and empty whiskey bottle. "It doesn't take a detective to figure out what happened. Mr. Granger drank too much and cracked his head open in a fall."

Kade studied the cabinet, which was the closest thing Jesse could have hit his head on. He did not see a bloodstain or any mark indicating an impact had occurred. "I guess that makes the most sense, doesn't it?"

"It does to me. If you have a different theory, I'd like to hear it."

"I don't have one," Kade said. "Not yet."

Teague regarded him. "Do you make everything more complicated than it has to be?"

"Rachel thinks so."

"She's right. Sometimes a cigar is just a cigar."

"Yeah, I've heard that one, but I usually hear it right before the cigar turns into something else." Kade set the whiskey bottle upright. "Have your business associates arrived?"

"Not yet. They've been delayed." Teague added, "I still think you should meet them."

"Cody hasn't fixed the problem with the Otter yet, so I just might cross paths with them."

Teague showed just the slightest hint of a grin. "Very good."

"Do you get a finder's fee or something if I talk with these guys?"

"No. I simply get the satisfaction of knowing I've given two parties the opportunity to discuss business with each other."

"Somehow you don't strike me as the kind of guy to put out an effort if you don't benefit."

"Perhaps this twenty-first-century capitalist is showing yet another dimension."

"I'm starting to think you have a whole lot of dimensions going on."

"That's not a good thing, isn't that what you said?"

"It is."

"Well," Teague said, "for now, let's just focus on getting help out here for your friend."

"Agreed," Kade said. But the cut wires kept filling his thoughts.

Teague nodded, as if setting aside unfinished business, and then moved to leave the cabin. He stopped at the door and rested his hand on the bulkhead. "My offer yesterday, to bring you on as a pilot at T-GAF, was genuine."

Kade stood impassive. "Why would I think different?"

"I don't know. Why would you?"

Teague exited the cabin and called for Gaddis and Flynn to fall in behind him. They climbed the stairs out of the ward room. Kade gave the blood on the cabin deck one more look, and then returned to the sick bay. Mr. White had just finished stitching up Jesse's wound. Jesse appeared to be sleeping.

"The anesthetic dulled the pain and allowed him to fall asleep," Mr. White said, "but he needs better care than I can give him here."

"Don't worry. He'll get it."

Mr. White left the sick bay. Kade stayed by Jesse's side a while longer, making sure he was okay and resting comfortably. After a short vigil, Kade climbed to the flight deck and stepped out into the open air. The sky had become overcast. The Wildcat was on deck again, parked aft of the Otter. Just back from his flight, Salvio walked toward Kade. They eyed each other, unsmiling, passing so close their shoulders nearly touched. Kade tensed and curled his hand into a fist. Events had wound him tight, like a heavy-gauge spring. He was ready to snap.

Salvio kept walking.

Kade relaxed his fist and hurried toward the Otter, giving the Wildcat's wing guns a quick look before climbing into the Otter's main cabin. He found Cody in the cockpit.

Cody eyed the blood on Kade's hands. "Did you cut yourself on something?"

"No. I found Jesse. He's hurt."

"What happened?"

"Don't know. He split his head open. It may have been a drunken accident, but with all that's going down, it's just as likely Teague's security guards attacked him for some reason. Teague said he's calling for a medevac chopper, but I don't trust him." Kade glanced through the cockpit window at the starboard engine. "How long until you're finished with repairs, another hour?"

"I'm done."

Kade stared at him. "You told me two hours."

"I know," Cody said. "I got it done in one, like I figured I would."

"Nice work, Scotty."

"Scotty?" Cody looked puzzled. "Oh, Scotty. *Star Trek*. The *Enterprise*. Hey, I like that."

Kade smiled, but it didn't last long. He gazed into the darkening sky. "Now we can take Jesse out of here ourselves."

"The paramedics on board a medevac chopper would be able to help Jesse a lot sooner than if we take him to a hospital."

"I don't think that chopper is coming, Cody. Remember, somebody doesn't want us to leave this ship. I think that someone is Teague. Why would he call in a medevac chopper? If we wait, Jesse might not get any medical attention. We need to move now, before Teague or whoever sabotaged our plane decides to be more forceful about keeping us here."

Cody's face fell into a nervous frown. "Okay. I'm with you."

"I'm going back to the sick bay to get Jesse," Kade said. "Prep the Otter for takeoff while I'm gone, but be sneaky about it. Double check everything, because once we roll, we're not turning back."

- TWENTY-NINE –

Grand Ledge, Michigan

The backroom of Shindig's Landscape Supply warehouse smelled like a TruGreen factory. Bags of chemical fertilizer were stacked against the wall and the aroma of ammonium nitrate permeated the air. Ely paced a dirty concrete floor in front of Nystrom and Rifkin, who sat tie-wrapped to a pair of wooden chairs. A fluorescent fixture cast light down over the area, and a stand-up rotary fan buzzed in the corner. The scene was set for an engaging conversation about secrets, and lies. And Rachel. Somehow this all went back to Rachel.

Dinapoli's henchman Anthony approached from across the room, carrying a Glock .40 pistol in each hand. He held the weapons by the barrel and offered them to Ely. "You want these?"

"Yeah, I'll be needing them soon." Ely reached for the guns and noticed a red blister on Anthony's finger. "You burn yourself?"

Anthony nodded. "Workin' too fast. Hazard of the job."

"You'll survive." Ely set the pistols on a table behind him.

"I'll be over there, if you need me." Anthony walked off to confer with one of his men.

The rest of Aldo Dinapoli's crew were outside the warehouse, presumably on guard duty.

Fifteen minutes earlier, when Ely and Dinapoli's men had rolled into Shindig's parking lot, Ely got the feeling they had been here plenty of times before. They seemed quite familiar with the layout of the place, and Anthony had keys to every lock they encountered. Located in a wooded area just south of Grand Ledge, Shindig's had a large pond beside the warehouse, and a row of concrete stalls east of the main building, each filled with mulch, or gravel, or fieldstones. Ely wondered how often in his business dealings Dinapoli availed himself of these amenities. But he did not spend much time dwelling on the thought. Instead, he focused on the task at hand. He studied the collection of items on the tabletop: two .40 semi-auto pistols, two sets of forged Customs and Border Protection Agency credentials, two satellite phones, and one burner phone.

Ely gestured to the fake CBP badges. "I know you two are not the guys in those creds, so why don't you start by telling me who you are?"

Rifkin scowled. "Why are we tied up like criminals?"

"Because you are criminals. You're impersonating federal officers, and you drew weapons on me and my colleagues."

"You drew first," Nystrom said.

"Let's not get bogged down debating who drew on whom. I'd rather discuss why you're pretending to be CBP agents."

"You're not important enough to know that." Nystrom said.

"So you've told me." Ely lifted one of the Glocks from the table and chambered a round. "I know the game you're playing. You didn't want me to take you in, so you spit out something about my daughter to change my mind about arresting you. Congratulations, it worked. You've got my undivided attention. Make it count."

Rifkin flexed against his restraints. "Untie us and we can have a civil discussion. We're professional peers for crying out loud."

Ely smiled. "Right." He set the pistol down and picked up one of the forged credential wallets. He flipped it open. "Agent Nystrom ... I imagine that's not your real name, but let's stick with it for the sake of conversation. Okay?"

"Suit yourself," Nystrom said.

"How is my daughter involved in your shenanigans?"

"Very deeply."

"Elaborate."

"Not before we come to an agreement about the nature of our discussion," Rifkin said.

"I set the rules here."

"Then get ready for a really long day," Nystrom said.

Ely faced him. "You told me this scheme of yours isn't about Mitchell, but a couple of days ago you questioned him, and later you made clear to Miss Morgan that finding his whereabouts was very important to you. Why?"

"We need to make sure he isn't sticking his nose in where it doesn't belong."

"And, where is that?"

"Up my ass," Nystrom said. "That gets awkward for both of us."

"More content and a little less color in your answers, please."

Nystrom regarded him. "You know, your daughter doesn't look much like you. That's why I didn't put it together right away, the name Edwards, I mean."

"She takes after her mother on that front. Good for her, right?"

"She can be a bitch, though," Nystrom said. "I suppose that comes from you."

Ely kicked him sharp in the shin. "That's my little girl you're talking about. If she was a bitch to you, you had it coming."

Nystrom flinched but kept his cool. "They don't teach torture very well at Homeland."

"That wasn't torture. I was just reminding you to be polite and respectful during our conversation." He added, "But, if we get around to cutting off fingers and breaking bones, I'll leave that to Anthony. Torture is against the rules for me."

"Bringing us here instead of an FBI field office is against the rules," Rifkin said.

"Yes, Agent Edwards, this is a bit rogue for a man like you," Nystrom added.

Ely sat on the table. "You told me you'd disappear into the system if I took you in, and I believed you. I can't have that. You two are just too damned interesting for me to let slip through my fingers. And that bit you teased about my daughter, let's just say I tear out certain pages of the rule book where my family is concerned. Now, tell me how Rachel is involved with you."

Rifkin gave a half smile. "You're an agent with the Department of Homeland Security. I'm sure you understand that in certain matters, information can't be shared cross-department."

"Did I mention I set the rules here?" Ely said. "All limits come off today."

Nystrom laughed. "You talk like you hold all the cards. That's cute."

Ely stood. "You're involved in the criminal execution of American citizens, including three Coast Guard officers killed aboard the *Blackbird* two days ago, and you're illegally using a piece of military hardware to do it. I know what's happening. I've seen the evidence. I hold all the cards I need."

Nystrom's lip twitched into a sneer. "I have no idea what you're talking about." He kept his cool, but a subtle fault line cracked his stone façade.

Ely noticed. "You know exactly what I'm talking about."

Nystrom remained silent.

"What's your acronym, Agent Nystrom?" Ely said.

Nystrom twisted his hand around and flipped up his middle finger.

Ely shifted his gaze to Rifkin. "You seem to be the reasonable one. Tell me, are you CIA?"

Rifkin stared into the middle distance. "I'm not authorized to confirm or deny that question."

"You do realize a non-answer to that question is actually an answer."

"How you interpret it is up to you," Rifkin said.

Ely's pulse pounded in his head. "I'm sick and tired of running in circles with you two. Give me something solid in thirty seconds or this conversation is going to take a sharp turn south."

Rifkin drew in a long, deliberate breath. "Rachel Edwards is supporting a vital national security interest in a sanctioned operation for which she is uniquely qualified."

"Did you recruit her or did she volunteer?"

"That's more than you need to know," Nystrom said.

"I'm her father. I need to know everything."

"Bloodlines are irrelevant in the intelligence service," Rifkin said. "But now that we've shared something with you, it's your turn. Tell me, what evidence have you seen to support that unfounded claim you made?"

"In case you haven't noticed, I'm leading this discussion."

"Then it seems we've reached an impasse," Rifkin said.

Ely picked up the pistol again. "Have we?"

Nystrom chuckled. "You and I both know you're not going to use that on us."

Ely considered jamming the pistol into his kneecap and pulling the trigger, but thought better of it. "You're right." He worked the action and ejected the round from the chamber, catching it in the air and pocketing it. "If you are CIA, torture probably won't get anything useful out of you."

Nystrom smirked. "First smart thing *you've* said all day."

"Maybe I can do worse than torture." Ely pulled out his phone and snapped a nice close-up picture of their faces. He sent the pictures to Walker in a text. "You two yahoos just entered the facial-recognition lottery. Think I'll get any hits?" He gestured to the phones and pistols on the table. "Once I run your prints through the federal database, and I file a report stating you two have turned into whistleblowers, how much you want to bet a big red flag goes up on a mahogany desk somewhere?"

Rifkin's cheeks turned red. "If you start a brushfire, you better be prepared for the blowback."

"The only blowback will be on you two. Turncoat spooks have a short life expectancy."

"You're making yourself a target for sanction," Nystrom said.

"Doubt it. I'm too high profile to get rid of. DHS knows what I'm investigating. If I turn up dead, it'll be obvious why. On the other hand, your boss, whoever he is, can just erase you two." Ely smiled. "That would deprive me of my informants and cripple my case, and it would silence the traitors in his midst. Two birds. One stone. Simple math."

"You're overplaying your hand," Nystrom warned.

"At least I have a hand to play. What sort of future do you think you'll have if I pull the trigger on Operation Screw You?" Ely crossed his arms and stared at them.

Rifkin and Nystrom stared back.

Another stand-off.

Then the satellite phones buzzed on the tabletop. Ely glanced at the incoming messages. "Someone is trying to tell you something."

Nystrom and Rifkin snapped to attention.

"You both got the same text." Ely lifted one of the phones and read from the screen. "'End of days.' What does that mean?"

Rifkin looked to Nystrom. "They shut it down."

"I told you they would."

"This complicates everything."

Ely sensed they were genuinely concerned. "What happened?"

"You need to release us," Rifkin said. "Now."

"The hell I do."

"If we don't acknowledge that message and execute orders, they'll send someone else, a backup team, and you don't want that," Nystrom said.

"This thing that just happened, does it put Rachel in danger?"

"Yes, unless you release us," Rifkin said.

"Tell me what the hell is going on."

"Let us do our job and we'll act in your daughter's best interest. I promise you that," Rifkin said. "I can't say the same for a backup team."

Ely considered them a long while. "You're jerking me around." He threw the phone on the table and walked off.

"You're not being a very good father right now," Nystrom said.

"You stonewall me this whole time," Ely said. "Now you expect me to believe a cryptic text message has instilled you with a sense of urgency and compassion for my daughter's plight?"

"You have to trust us, Edwards," Nystrom said.

"No. No trust. I need facts. Details. What game are you playing? What's Rachel's role?"

"Information this sensitive must be compartmentalized," Nystrom said. "No exceptions."

"I've been involved in my share of covert operations. I have a pretty damned high security clearance. If you're CIA like I suspect, and this is a spook operation, it's safe to brief me on it."

Neither of them replied, and something inside Ely snapped. Leah's casket, and Rachel's breakdown, and the devastation he felt on that gray funeral day surged from memory and filled his head. These two men had admitted Rachel was in danger, yet they were preventing him from doing anything about it. Ely had lost one daughter by failing to engage, and he would not let that happen again. He returned to the table and drew his 9mm. "Enough of the cloak-and-dagger bullshit!" He chambered a round and stuck the barrel into Nystrom's forehead. "Are you with the CIA?"

Nystrom clenched his teeth and did not reply.

Rifkin answered for him. "For Christ's sake, Edwards. Yes, we're with the CIA."

"Tell me how Rachel's in danger. Now."

"She's only in danger if you don't release us," Nystrom said.

"Give me clarity on the situation or I'll keep you rotting in those chairs until hell freezes over, and I swear to God if anything happens to my daughter as a result of your silence, you two will be found in that pond outside with a bullet in your head."

"You're not the type," Nystrom said, bravado strained but still intact.

Ely withered him with a cold, dark stare. "Have you ever buried one of your children, Nystrom? I have, and let me tell you, I will do *anything* to prevent that from happening again."

Rifkin measured Ely's resolve. "This is pointless," he said. "We're on the same side."

Ely set his jaw. "Then let's *be* on the same side."

Nystrom glanced at his partner, a bead of sweat trickling around the barrel of the gun. Rifkin cleared his throat. "They named it Operation Reprimand," he said. "Its objective is to stop North American drug money from reaching terrorist organizations by any means necessary. Since its commencement in the Great Lakes over a year ago, Reprimand has been a political minefield. And your daughter, Agent Edwards, is at the center of it all. "

THIRTY

Aboard *Wolverine*

Kade checked the Scoutmaster's loading gate and found it filled to capacity. The customized-Marlin lever-action rifle could hold four .45 caliber cartridges. Cody had apparently loaded the weapon earlier, when Kade suggested he keep it close. Good. They were on the same page. Kade grabbed a handful of shells from the ammo box in the rifle's foam-lined case and shoved them into his jacket pocket.

Cody watched him from across the aisle in the Otter's main cabin. "You really think you're going to need that to get Jesse out?"

"I don't know, but it doesn't hurt to be prepared."

Cody put on an uneasy smile. "Guess you're right."

Kade clicked on the rifle's safety. "Look, I don't know how much trouble we're in. All I know is ever since we landed next to that cargo ship my life has gone down the rabbit hole. It's like a big joke is playing out, and I'm the only one not in on it."

"I'm not in on it either."

"You know what I mean." Kade threaded his arm through the rifle's leather strap.

"You're making me nervous."

"Cody, I'm just being cautious. Do I think I'll need the Scoutmaster? Probably not. But I'm taking it with me as an insurance policy, because there's a bunch of other guys carrying guns on this ship, and they all work for Galen Teague."

"But we don't even know if Teague's the one who cut the wires."

"Either he did it, or he had one of his crew do it. It doesn't matter. Teague made the decision. He's the man in charge, the captain. He's made that very clear."

Cody nodded. "I know."

Kade presented the rifle to Cody. "Would you feel safer if I left it with you?"

"No. I'm not comfortable with it. I don't even know if I'd be able to use it if I had to."

"Okay." Kade positioned the weapon tight across his chest, barrel down, and adjusted the strap. Perfect location. Easy access. He picked up an oversized windbreaker from a passenger seat and slipped it on, folding it closed over the rifle's stock and its thirteen-inch barrel. "See? Invisible. No one will know I have it."

Cody did not look convinced.

"It'll be all right." Kade moved toward the cabin door. "I'll be back in ten minutes. Give or take. Be ready to spool up the engines."

Cody nodded.

Kade climbed down from the Otter's cabin to the flight deck. He kept the windbreaker tight around him, hiding the rifle beneath. He walked past a deck crewman without incident and entered the island superstructure through the bulkhead door he had become very familiar with. The ladder well leading down to the main deck was just ahead. He cautiously started down, descending through a layer of diesel fumes, into the generator room. Nobody there. He kept walking through the narrow battery corridor and into the crew mess. Again, empty. He began to think he had overreacted to the situation. But then, through the bulkhead door ahead, he spotted a man wearing a security guard uniform in the ward room. Kade's heart jumped and he sidestepped out of sight. He backed against a bulkhead and felt for the Scoutmaster. *Calm down. They're not looking for you ... not yet.*

He peered into the ward room. Two guards stood vigil near the cabins. Kade recognized them as Gaddis and Flynn, the men who were with Teague earlier. If *Wolverine* was just a museum ship, and the security detail was just for Teague's protection, why were they posted here? Answer: those guards had more in their job description than personal protection.

Kade considered walking directly past them into the sick bay. A guy visiting an injured friend would not seem suspicious. Then again, he did not know if the guards had orders to observe or engage. In any event, extracting Jesse without being seen would be problematic. He had to find another way. Kade tried to remember the layout of the sick bay from his tour with Rachel. There was a cage ladder, in the aft quarter, leading up from the lower deck. That's it. He could double back, drop down one deck, and come into the sick bay from there. Maybe Teague did not think to post a guard on that approach. Kade recalled the path he and Rachel had taken to the engine room, down a ladder well near the generator compartment.

He stole another look into the ward room, made sure he had cover, and headed back into the battery corridor. He rushed through the generator compartment, checked for guards, and then started down the ladder well into the belly of the ship. The mechanical rhythm of the diesel engines intensified, and something latched in his memory. That sound reminded him of something. But what? No time to figure it out. He shook it off and continued down, crouching at the bottom of the ladder well. Diesel fumes were heavier down here, and the two massive engines that drove the ship's paddlewheels rumbled in a synchronized clamor. The *Wolverine's* chief mechanic strolled the deck between the diesels, listening to their sound and checking a bank of gauges to make sure all was in order. He had his back turned, and Kade slipped from the stairs to a space behind a large tool enclosure.

Waiting for his next opening, Kade gazed at the piping in the overhead. That bit in his memory latched on again. *Pipes and gauges … walking through a loud hallway … the walls were roaring at me.* Jesse's dream. These were images from Jesse's dream. Except, it wasn't a dream. He must have been in the engine room and he recalled it through a hazy, drunken stupor. What else did he say he saw? Something about a Corsair. Without windows. What the hell did that mean?

The ship's mechanic wheeled around and walked toward the ladder well. Kade crouched low behind the enclosure and rested a hand on the rifle stock beneath the windbreaker. The mechanic climbed the stairs out of the engine room without looking back. Kade took a breath. Time to go. He located a door in the aft bulkhead on the other side of the compartment and took a step toward it. Stopped. Over his left shoulder was another door, one that he had gone through with Rachel the night before, the one leading into the ship's bay. If Jesse had seen something that Teague didn't want him to see, it was probably in that bay. Kade wondered what he had missed in his tour through there with Rachel. He had to find out.

He turned and unlatched the dogging lever on the door, easing it open just enough to see around the frame. There, in the center of the bay, a handful of crewmen scurried around a peculiar aircraft. It was nearly thirty feet long and it stood on a tripod landing-gear assembly that put the top line of its fuselage above all the crewmen's heads. It had a single aft propeller and an inverted V-shape tailfin. The windowless nose resembled a Boeing jetliner, but with a dome-like projection on the underside. Long, narrow wings protruded mid-frame, and were folded up so as to fit the width of the bay. Folded wings, like a war-era Corsair fighter. *A skinny Corsair without cockpit windows.* That fit, but what it looked like to Kade was a military drone.

The crewmen were loading what appeared to be a missile into the aircraft's ordinance rack. Kade could not believe his eyes. Suddenly, Rachel's tour of duty on the *U.S.S Theodore Roosevelt* came to mind, and her job piloting carrier-based drones. Kade stood transfixed until an alarm bell went off in his head. *Warning: You've been here too long. Get away from this thing. Get to the sick bay and get Jesse out of here.*

He pulled the door closed and spun on his heel to make a break for the bulkhead across the room. A .40 caliber semi-automatic pistol pointed at his head stopped him cold. It was in the hands of a security guard with the name Zeke stenciled on his shirt.

"What are you doing?" Zeke said.

Kade took a breath and sharpened his focus. "Just looking around. What's with the gun?"

"You shouldn't be down here unescorted, Mr. Mitchell."

"You know my name?"

"It's my job to know who you are, and everything that goes on aboard this ship."

"Really?" Kade jabbed a thumb at the bulkhead door behind him. "You know what's going on in there?"

"I think we need to go talk with Mr. Teague."

"Don't you mean Captain Teague?"

"I meant what I said, smart ass. Put your hands behind your head."

"You going to shoot me if I don't, Zeke?"

"Most likely."

"For sightseeing?"

"I have my orders."

Kade wasn't about to let this guy take him anywhere. "How about I give you fifty bucks, you holster that Smith & Wesson, and we go our separate ways?"

"Get your hands behind your head."

One distraction. That's all Kade needed. One moment to take Zeke's eye off the prize.

"I'm not screwing around, Mitchell."

Kade raised his hands, wary, watching for an opening. And then the metal ladder well next to them rattled, and the ship's mechanic came scrambling down the steps. He stopped near the bottom, took in the scene a suspended moment. "What the …?"

Zeke cocked his head toward him. "Get out of here, Ian. I've got a situation."

The pistol barrel drifted. Kade lunged. He hit Zeke full force in the chest with his shoulder, driving him back, grappling close to keep the pistol out of play. Momentum slammed them into a catwalk support leg. Steel rang against Zeke's head, dazing him and jarring the gun from his hand. The weapon clanged on the metal deck. Kade stepped back and swept open the windbreaker. He grabbed the rifle stock and swung upward, connecting solid with Zeke's jaw. The security guard's knees buckled.

Ian fled up the stairs. Kade went after him, catching him by the shirt collar in two strides. He yanked him backward, and Ian went airborne, crashing down on his tailbone at the base of the steps. Kade worked the Scoutmaster's lever action and aimed at Ian's chest. "Not a word."

Ian sat, petrified.

Kade glanced at Zeke, who had collapsed a couple feet away. He hoped the guy wasn't hurt too bad. He picked up the pistol from the deck, set the thumb safety, and stuck it under his belt in back. He gestured to Ian with the rifle barrel. "Grab you friend. Drag him over there."

Ian hesitated.

"Now." Kade glanced around the engine room, across the catwalk, to the bulkhead door behind him. Nobody else to worry about. Good. "Take him that way."

Ian got to his feet, obviously sore from the fall, and lifted Zeke under the arms. He dragged the unconscious security guard over the deck plates between the noisy diesel engines as ordered.

"Faster, Ian, I don't have all day." Kade raced around him and opened the aft bulkhead door, peering through to make sure no one waited on the other side. "Okay. Pull him through here."

Ian stepped through the doorway, struggling with Zeke in tow.

Kade oversaw the effort. "Watch his foot."

Ian twisted Zeke's body to keep his boot from getting caught on the door hinge.

Kade kicked it clear. "Keep moving." He followed through and closed the door, dogging it down with the screw. They were in a tight space at the base of a steel ladder. A compact fluorescent bulb burned overhead. A door to starboard had a placard that read Supply Department Storeroom. Kade unlatched the door and pushed it open into a moderate-sized compartment. Steel shelves full of engine components lined the walls, and a large pump motor protruded through the deck plate near the forward bulkhead.

"That should do," Kade said.

"What are you going to do with me?" Ian said with a nervous tremor in his voice.

Kade nodded into the room. "Drag your buddy in there."

Ian heaved Zeke into the storeroom and laid him down near the pump motor. Kade noticed Zeke had a radio earpiece on his right ear, and he pulled the device off the security guard's head. A throat mic came with it, along with a compact Motorola radio, which had been stuffed in Zeke's pocket. Kade took the whole assembly and exited the room.

Ian stood confused. "Now what?"

"Sit tight. Be quiet. I'll be back in five minutes." Kade swung the door closed, then pulled it open again. "If I hear you shout or trying to get out of this room, I'm going to be pissed—and you don't want that." He nodded to the unconscious security guard. "Zeke pissed me off, and look what happened to him." Kade latched the door shut and shouldered the rifle. He put on the earpiece and throat mic, making sure he did not hit the push-to-talk button on the cable. He pocketed the radio and climbed the ladder out of the space. He had no intention of coming back.

At the top of the ladder, he poked his head through a hatchway and found the ship's galley. Kade recalled walking through there with Rachel. The coast seemed clear, and he climbed into the compartment. He pulled the rifle from his shoulder and oriented himself, identifying which way led aft. He followed his instincts to a door and pressed his back against a bulkhead beside it. The door was cracked open. Kade listened but heard nothing but the low rumble of the distant engines. He rolled into the corridor in a crouch, aiming the rifle down range. A narrow passageway lit by a series of overhead fixtures stretched all the way to the aft quarter of the ship. Kade could make out a closed door at the far end. He started toward it, slow at first, and then quickening his pace. The light fixtures were spaced about six strides apart, and he swore he could feel the warmth of their incandescent bulbs as he passed beneath them. With no clear place to duck and hide in that long corridor, he felt exposed. Halfway there.

He clenched the rifle and kept moving.

"Hutchins. Hutchins."

A voice crackled in Kade's ear. His heart pounded and he jumped to a bulkhead between cones of light, landing beneath a stairwell that led up. He searched the passage behind him. Nobody there. Where the hell had that voice come from?

"Go for Hutchins."

The earpiece. The voice was a transmission. Kade closed his eyes and cursed himself for forgetting about the damned thing. His breathing had quickened to near hyperventilation; so he forced himself to draw slow, measured breaths.

"Report to Sports Center," the voice in his ear said. "They're prepping a mission launch, and you're up in rotation to cover." It sounded like Cam.

Kade listened intently.

"Copy that. En route to Sports Center. Hutchins out."

Mission launch. The drone. Mission to do what?

It did not matter to Kade, he wanted no part of it. He just wanted to get Jesse and Cody off the ship. He continued down the passageway, clicking off the Scoutmaster's safety as he reached the door at the end of the line. A placard on the door read Ready Room. Rachel had mentioned it on the tour. Kade smiled despite his circumstance. *Thirty Seconds Over Tokyo.* Right. He pressed his ear to the door and heard nothing. Not helpful. He gently unlatched the dogging lever. A metal screech sounded in the passageway. He clenched his teeth and pushed open the door.

It was a moderate-sized compartment. Several rows of padded chairs faced the port bulkhead. The chairs were arrayed around a duty roster board and a good, old-fashioned blackboard. Light fixtures dimly burned in the overhead, illuminating a security guard seated in one of the chairs. Kade was startled and swung out the rifle. The guard did not move.

Kade stepped into the room. The guard was facing the blackboard, reclined with his head back. Snoring. Kade did not buy it. It had to be a ruse. He moved through the ready room as quickly and silently as he could, keeping the rifle trained on the guard. The closer he got, the more authentic it appeared. The guy's arm dangled over the side of the armrest, and his radio earpiece had fallen out of his ear. Kade circled around. The guy's eyes were plastered shut, and his breaths were slow and relaxed. The stencil on his shirt read Moss.

Kade wasn't sure what to do. The thought of pummeling him as he slept seemed cruel and unusual, but he could not just leave him here dozing. Good old Moss might wake up at the wrong moment and become a problem.

"Zeke, Zeke." A voice exploded in Kade's ear, interrupting his indecision. It sounded like Cam again, calling for Zeke, who was not going to answer. It would not take the big, bald guy long to figure out what had happened to his man. The clock had started running.

"Shit!" The word escaped Kade's mouth before he could stop it. Moss stirred and his eyes fluttered open.

"Sorry, buddy." Kade brought the rifle stock down on Moss's head, dropping him back into unconsciousness. Kade rushed through a door on the aft bulkhead and found a ladder leading straight up on the other side. He shouldered the rifle and climbed, coming up through a hatchway into the extreme aft section of the sick bay. The ladder kept going, and Kade traced the rungs to a closed hatch in the overhead. The only thing up there could be the flight deck. The way out.

"Zeke," Cam said through the earpiece, "report your status."

Kade ran to the exam tables in the sick bay and found Jesse where he had left him, resting with a gauze bandage wrapped around his head. Kade shook him. "Jesse, wake up. We've got to go."

Jesse groaned.

Kade shushed him, worried that Gaddis and Flynn would hear from the ward room just outside. "Jesse, you need to be quiet, and you need to get on your feet."

Jesse laid there in a groggy, half-conscious state.

Cam called for Zeke again on the radio. Things were about to get hot. Kade needed Jesse on his feet. He could not carry him the whole way. He went to the cabinet where Mr. White had gotten the anesthetic earlier and searched through the bottles for something to help the situation. Something like … adrenaline. Got it. He snatched it up, dislodging every other bottle on the shelf. The clinking glass rattled like a bag of marbles. *Slow down, they're going to hear.*

"Patrick," Cam said in the earpiece, "get down to the engine room. Zeke's not responding on the radio, and Ian isn't answering the intercom."

Kade rifled the drawers below the cabinet until he found syringes. He grabbed one, tore off the plastic wrap, and stuck the needle into the adrenaline bottle. He drew out several CCs, made sure there were no air bubbles, and stuck Jesse in the arm.

Jesse's eyes opened wide and he drew a wheezy breath. "What the hell, amigo?"

Kade clamped a hand over his mouth. "Keep it down, Jess. We need to sneak out of here."

"Sneak?" Jesse tried to get his bearings. "What are you talking about?"

"The guys who cracked your head open are out in the ward room."

"Why'd they crack my head open?"

"Later." Kade helped Jesse sit up. "Can you walk?"

"Yeah, I can walk." Jesse looked at him funny. "Why are you carrying a gun?"

"Later! Come on." Kade pulled him off the table.

Jesse stumbled and steadied himself on an exam table. "Whoa, this place is spinnin'."

"Find your legs. Make it quick. We've got to go."

"Where are we going?"

"To the Otter. I'm getting you to a hospital, but we've got to go, now. Now or never."

Jesse seemed ready to argue the point but stopped short when he saw Kade's dower expression. "You're serious."

"As a heart attack, amigo."

Jesse grabbed the ladder and started to climb.

Kade concealed the Scoutmaster under the windbreaker and started after him.

Jesse reached the top, where the ladder ended at the closed hatch. He grabbed the wheel and tried to turn the screw but could not budge it. "Dead end."

Kade climbed to the same rung as Jesse and took hold of the wheel as well. "On three."

They counted down and wrenched the wheel. The screw spun free and Kade pushed the hatch open. Gray daylight and a wind gust rushed in. He climbed out and stood on the flight deck. The hatch had placed them far aft, just beyond the Wildcat, and several yards from the Otter. Perfect.

Kade helped Jesse through the hatch and they skirted around the Wildcat's tailfin. Jesse stumbled, but Kade kept him on his feet. They pushed on toward the Otter's open cabin door. Kade noticed the ratchet straps had been unhooked from the plane's landing gear and the engine access panels had been buttoned up. *All right, Cody.*

Jesse pulled himself through the cabin door. Kade glanced up at the bridge windows atop the island and realized that the Otter was in full sight of anyone watching from there. With any luck, they weren't paying close attention. Kade climbed into the plane and closed the hatch. He made his way forward, patting Jesse on the shoulder in passing. "Take a seat and buckle up."

"Don't you want me in the copilot chair?"

"You can barely walk. I don't want you anywhere near the cockpit."

Jesse dropped into a seat. "That's just mean, Kade-O."

"Stop calling me Kato."

An excited voice called through Kade's earpiece. "I found Zeke and Ian in the engine storeroom. Zeke's out cold. Ian says Mitchell did it."

Cam responded. "Find him! All units, get off your dead asses and find him!"

Kade rushed into the cockpit and threaded into the pilot's seat. Cody was already there, sitting in the copilot seat. "That was more than ten minutes."

"Took a detour," Kade said. "Saw more than I planned."

"What'd you see?"

"Tell you later." Kade checked the port and starboard props. "Clear." He hit the port engine start switch and the propeller began to turn on battery power. "Here we go." He flicked the fuel switch. The port engine popped and a puff of smoke belched out. Gauges across the instrument panel jumped. The turbine roared to life and the propeller wound up on its spindle. Kade checked the gauges. "Chamber temp in green zone. RPMs climbing. Good work, Cody."

Another voice in the earpiece. "Cam, Gaddis. The guy is gone from the sick bay!"

Cam responded, "You idiots let Mitchell get past you … Holy crap, that plane is starting up. Get topside, now! Cut 'em off at the island."

Cody took note of how intently Kade listened to the voices in his ear. "What's wrong?"

"They're coming."

"Who's coming?"

"Teague's security grunts." Kade flicked the starboard engine start switch and the propeller began turning. "I saw what Jesse saw. It's some type of military drone below deck. I don't know what they're doing with it—but they sure don't want us to leave knowing about it."

"They didn't want us to leave *before* you saw it."

Kade injected fuel to the starboard engine. It engaged. "I don't have it all figured out yet."

Across the flight deck, the bulkhead door at the base of the island flew open. Gaddis and Flynn charged through, searching left and right, then zeroing in on the Otter. They drew their pistols and gestured for Kade to shut down the engines.

Cam's voice came through the earpiece. "Don't let that plane leave. You are authorized to shoot if it moves one inch off its mark."

Kade looked to Cody. "Do you think you can fly the Otter off this carrier?"

Cody stammered. "I— I— think so. Maybe. Why?"

Kade climbed out of the pilot's seat. "They're going to try to stop us from taking off. I'm not going to let them."

"What are you going to do?"

"I'm going to have a talk with them. You just get Jesse out of here." Kade left the cockpit, snatching the Scoutmaster from a passenger seat and concealing it under his windbreaker. He snapped the bottom snap to hold the jacket closed, and then shoved his hand in the pocket and verified he still had the handful of bullets.

"I'm not going to leave you here," Cody said.

"You have to, or none of us are going to make it out."

Jesse eyed him nervously. "What the hell are you doing, Kade?"

Kade marched past him to the cabin door. "Jesse, I changed my mind. Get in the copilot seat and give Cody a hand. Get out of here— and send back help."

"We go together, or we don't go at all," Jesse said.

"That won't work. Someone's got to distract these guys. You two get to safety and then send someone to save my ass." Kade unlatched the cabin door. "Now, get into the goddamned cockpit. As soon as I clear the plane, turn her around and go full throttle off the bow."

He kicked open the door on its faulty hydraulic assist and hopped down to the flight deck. He walked as casually as he could toward Gaddis and Flynn, who were waving their pistols and shouting at him to shut down the Otter's engines. Kade held his hands at waist height in a nonthreatening manner. "What's the problem?" he shouted. "We're just testing our engine repairs."

"Mitchell," Gaddis said. "Tell your friends to shut down those props and get them off that plane right now."

"Why are you so excited?" Kade estimated he had just cleared the Otter's turn radius. He kept walking, unhurried, wearing a disarming smile and closing in on Gaddis and Flynn.

Flynn targeted him. "You took down Zeke. Stay back."

The Otter's engines suddenly throttled up, and Kade sensed the aircraft beginning to move behind him. Gaddis aimed toward the plane and shouted for the pilot to stop. Kade did not know exactly where he was aiming, but guessed it was the cockpit. He hoped to God Cody had his head down. The Otter's engines throttled up another notch, and Gaddis opened fire. Flynn wanted in on the action too, and swung his pistol away from Kade to shoot at the airplane.

Kade made his move. He reached under the windbreaker and grabbed the rife. Flynn was close. Easy target. Kade squeezed the trigger, blasting a .45 caliber slug through the guard's thigh and dropping him down. Gaddis saw his partner fall and spun on his heel to counter the threat on his flank. Kade worked the Scoutmaster's lever action and chambered another round. Gaddis stood at midrange, a more difficult shot, and a more frantic shot, because the guy was aiming back at him with a pistol. Kade went for his legs and fired again. A loud blast, and the Scoutmaster jumped. Miss.

Gaddis returned fire in a harried panic, triggering the pistol too soon and sending a volley of bullets clear to the left. The Otter rolled past them toward the centerline of the flight deck. Gaddis did not pay it any attention. He was too concerned about getting shot full of holes.

Kade broke right, cocking the rifle and firing on the run. The slug imbedded in the wooden deck at Gaddis's feet.

Gaddis panicked and returned another volley. Closer to the mark, but still no hits. He dropped to one knee and steadied his aim. The gun popped once and the slide action stuck open. Empty. He reached for a spare magazine on his belt.

Kade worked the lever and chambered his last round. "Hold it right there!"

The earpiece crackled, and Cam's calm voice said, "Patrick, take him alive."

Kade processed that. Who's Patrick? And where is he? Kade scanned the flight deck in his forward field of vision. All he saw was the Otter speeding down the runway.

A voice came from behind. "Drop it, Mitchell."

Kade lowered his head and cautiously turned. A guard named Patrick had a submachine gun pointed at him at close range. The guy had probably come up through the same hatch that he and Jesse had come through. Kade set the Scoutmaster on the deck and, from the corner of his eye, watched the Otter drop off the bow, catch the wind, and then climb into the sky.

At least Cody and Jesse had gotten away.

BOOK III

WILD CARD

Galen Teague climbed the steps to the bridge in a huff. Salvio followed a safe distance behind. They had just come from the drone control room on main deck, forward section, or as the security team had come to call it, the Sports Center.

"They weren't ready," Teague said. "Pathetic."

"It's an unscheduled launch," Salvio replied. "And Rachel is not here to organize them."

"That's no excuse. We've been operating a long time. The crew shouldn't need their shepherd to assemble, fuel, and arm the drone anymore. And that control room should have been lit up and primed to go before I got there."

"Why the urgency?"

Teague stopped climbing and faced him. "This morning I received information detailing a beta. I intend to hit it before Nystrom and Rifkin get here."

"Rachel will be back soon. Wait for her, and she'll take care of it."

"No time. The window of opportunity to hit this target is narrow." He added, "Besides, even I'd have trouble pulling off the hypocrisy of hitting a beta with our handlers aboard."

Salvio smiled. "Somehow, I believe you could manage it."

"Perhaps, but there's a larger point to make. I need this crew mission capable at all times, because the day may come when we don't have our shepherd to rely on anymore."

Salvio cocked his head. "That sounds like you expect Rachel to leave the team."

"I didn't say that."

"What did you say?"

Teague regarded him. "We've known each other a long time, Salvio, before any of this Reprimand business started, even back when you worked with your brother, so I can be candid with you." He paused. "You know that Nystrom and Rifkin are coming to question Mitchell?"

"Yes."

"He's not the only one they're interested in. They're going to question Rachel too."

Salvio nearly gasped. "Why?"

"They suspect she's become a security risk."

"Not possible."

"A week ago, I would've agreed with you. But since Mitchell has appeared, I'm not so sure."

Salvio shook his head. "I don't believe it."

"The feds think Rachel is sharing operational information with him, which is a serious breach of protocol. Some would call it treasonous."

"Why would she put Reprimand at risk? The operation is important to her."

"I don't know. It doesn't fit, does it?"

"Do you believe they're wrong?"

"It doesn't matter what I believe. All that matters is what Nystrom and Rifkin believe. If they determine she's a security risk, they'll strike her from the team, maybe even prosecute her."

"And the crew will lose their shepherd."

"Exactly. That's why I need the men mission-capable without her."

"If they remove Rachel, it will poison the whole mission, and the CIA will end it."

"I doubt it. Important people are invested in Reprimand, and we've been delivering results."

"You are optimistic."

"No, it's just that Reprimand is an effective business tool, and I won't give it up that easily."

"You may not have a choice."

"You underestimate me."

Salvio thought for a moment. "There is a danger in all this."

"How do you mean?"

"If Nystrom and Rifkin press Rachel too hard, she might tell them about the beta targets."

Teague scoffed. "She would never divulge the betas. It's like you said, the operation is important to her. She'd rather face prosecution than see Reprimand end. Trust me on this."

"I hope you're right. If the CIA learns about the betas, we are all in very big trouble."

Teague's phone buzzed. Although cell service did not reach this far into the lake, the ship's Wi-Fi network kept instant messaging up and running. Cam had sent him a troubling text.

Mitchell saw the drone. He's trying to escape.

Teague flushed with anger and texted back a response. **Stop him. Alive.**

"What's wrong?" Salvio asked.

"Mitchell," Teague said. "He's trying to escape the ship."

Salvio's expression soured. "How? His plane is malfunctioned."

"Maybe his mechanic found your handywork and repaired the wires."

"I hid the damage as best I could, but what you say is possible."

Teague began thinking through the scenario, but the sound of distant gunfire interrupted. He bounded up the remaining steps to the bridge and burst through the bulkhead doorway into the ship's nerve center. Cam was there, among the command crew, looking down on the flight deck. He had the PTT button for his headset in his hand. "Patrick, take him alive."

Teague marched over to the windows in time to witness Mitchell's twin-engine airplane soar off the bow and climb into the air. He glared at Cam. "You told me he was *trying* to escape. You didn't say he was succeeding."

"He didn't succeed, sir. We have him down on the deck."

"Then who just took off in the Otter?"

"Most likely his mechanic and that Jesse guy. He's gone from the sick bay."

Teague watched the plane grow distant in the sky. "Get Mitchell up here right now."

Salvio entered the bridge and calmly took in the activity.

Teague faced him. "Is the Wildcat fueled up?"

"She has enough in her tank."

"And ammunition in her wings?"

Salvio nodded.

"Then get in the cockpit," Teague said. "And wait for my word."

THIRTY-TWO

Grand Ledge, Michigan

"Operation Reprimand?" Ely holstered the 9mm, still not believing what he had heard. "You mean to tell me the federal government sanctions what's happening out there?"

"The President himself issued an executive order to get the ball rolling," Rifkin said.

"I doubt he intended you to come up with a domestic seek-and-destroy program."

Rifkin leveled his expression. "Conventional law enforcement has been waging a war on drugs for fifty years. It's as bad now as it has ever been, and when you consider that much of the revenue generated by the illegal drug trade goes to support global-terrorist organizations, it becomes apparent that something new needs to be tried."

"Drug money is the lifeblood of ISIS and Al Qaeda," Nystrom said.

"Afghanistan opium fields net sixty billion dollars in sales a year," Rifkin added. "A large percentage of that money buys guns and equipment for jihadist organizations. Operation Reprimand was designed to stop that flow of cash."

Ely scoffed. "The best way to stop the flow of Afghani drug money is to send in the Air Force and napalm their opium fields. We've got guys over there who can do it right now."

"That may be so, but there's no political will to do that," Rifkin said.

"Politicians are pussies," Nystrom added.

Ely frowned. "So instead, some wizard CIA analyst decided that indiscriminately blowing up drug-smuggling vessels in the Great Lakes would be the next best thing? That's not brilliant."

"There's actually a great deal of discrimination involved," Rifkin said. "Only vessels carrying drugs formulated from Afghani opium are targeted. We're sending a clear message to the traffickers and dealers. Find another business partner or face the consequences."

"I see," Ely said. "You don't care if they're trafficking drugs, they just better not be trafficking Afghani drugs."

"We're restricting the flow of narcotics into North America," Nystrom said. "That should make you happy."

"You're blowing up the rule of law. I'm not too keen on that."

"I prefer to think of it as law enforcement with extreme prejudice."

"Have you ever heard of the concept of due process? And, how do you know these ships are carrying drugs formulated with Afghani opium?"

"Trust me, we know," Rifkin said.

Ely thought a moment. "Drug smuggling may be surging in the Great Lakes, but a lot more of it is going on in the Caribbean and on the southern border. How effective can this op be?"

"Phase one of Reprimand has been active in the Coast Guard's seventh district for two years," Rifkin said. "It's been so effective that most of the top drug traffickers have dropped out of the game, and many of the ones still involved have migrated their operations north to the Great Lakes' region. That's why we're here now."

Ely sat on the table. "The CIA is not permitted to operate domestically. How do you square that?"

Nystrom smirked. "We don't operate on US soil."

"Geography isn't your strong suit, is it?"

"All our planning and mission-related tasks are conducted in the sovereign territories of Native-American reservations," Rifkin said. "Federal law does not apply in those areas."

"You guys really know how to thread the needle, don't you?"

"CIA personnel do not participate in Reprimand's field operations either," Nystrom said.

"That's where your daughter comes in," Rifkin added.

Ely narrowed his eyes. "What's Rachel's role?"

Nystrom seemed disappointed in the question. "Really, Agent Edwards? Put it all together."

Ely considered Rachel, her personality, her heartache, her skills, and her time in the Navy. And then he thought about Dinapoli's missile-strike video. A Hellfire. A Predator. "Oh, my God. Rachel's piloting the drone that's attacking those ships."

"She had the perfect profile for the job," Rifkin said.

"She doesn't mind incinerating drug traffickers," Nystrom said. "I'm sure you understand."

Ely thought about his daughter Leah. "Keep away from that topic."

"She's not in this alone," Rifkin said. "Galen Teague provides logistical support and operational cover. His replica of the carrier *Wolverine* was the ideal platform to base the operation. We couldn't have asked for better mission synergy."

Rachel's employment with T-GAF and her quick rise up the corporate ladder took on a different hue. "What does Galen Teague get out of this?"

"He's a patriotic American. All he's asked is to serve his country."

Ely chewed on that a bit. "What about Mitchell? What's his role?"

"He doesn't play a role," Rifkin said.

"Then why all the interest in him?"

"Mitchell once worked for drug lord Raymond Firth," Rifkin said. "Firth is a sanctioned target under Reprimand's charter. He's a big buyer of Afghani opium. A few days ago, we hit one of his vessels, and literally out of the blue, Mitchell showed up at the site of the sinking."

"It seemed like more than a coincidence to us, given Mitchell's history with Firth and his past relationship with your daughter," Nystrom said.

"You think Mitchell somehow got tangled up in Reprimand?"

"We do," Rifkin said.

"We suspect your daughter is the one who tangled him," Nystrom added.

"She wouldn't do that, especially with Kade. They're not on good terms these days."

"Curious," Rifkin said. "Because Mitchell's on board the *Wolverine* right now, and he's spent a great deal of time with her."

"That's where we were headed when you had Miss Morgan call us," Nystrom said, "to interview Mitchell."

"And if Mitchell knows or is somehow involved in Reprimand, what will you do?"

"Whatever is necessary to achieve containment and keep the op secret."

"But we have a new priority now," Rifkin interjected.

Ely raised an eyebrow. "End of days?"

"Yes," Nystrom said.

Ely frowned. "I figure it's a coded message, but what does it mean?"

Rifkin pondered a bit. "It means the Senate Anti-Terrorism Committee has decided that the political risk of continuing Operation Reprimand has finally exceeded its strategic benefit."

"They're pulling the plug before it goes public and puts a stink on them," Nystrom said.

Ely felt a measure of unease. "What does shutting down Operation Reprimand entail?"

Rifkin shifted position in the chair. "We'll inform the participants that the mission's objectives have been met and their services are no longer required. We'll reclaim or destroy all assets used to carry out the operation, and we'll remind all of the involved team members that their knowledge of and participation in this affair must remain secret for the rest of their natural lives."

"That sounds simple," Ely said.

"Yes, it does, doesn't it?" Rifkin replied.

"Then, why did you make it seem like a bad thing if the backup shuts it down?"

Nystrom huffed. "Just cut us loose and let us take care of it."

"We've been involved with Reprimand since inception," Rifkin said. "We know the players. It will be far more efficient for us to wrap it up."

"And less of a chance for things to go sideways," Nystrom added.

Ely considered all they had said. Their story sounded authentic, it felt real, and it filled in several missing pieces of DNA his own theory lacked, but it didn't explain everything, and Ely needed it all to know for sure how to help Rachel get out. He stood and pulled a multi-tool from his pocket, flicking open a knife with a serrated edge. He reached for one of the zip ties binding Rifkin's wrist to the armrest but paused and gestured with the blade. "There's a hole in your story that's gnawing at me."

Rifkin seemed annoyed. "And what's that, Agent Edwards?"

"The *Blackbird* was a meth lab. She didn't have a single poppy from Afghanistan on board, but a Hellfire missile took her out. I saw it." Ely let Rifkin ponder that a moment. "And then there's Aldo Dinapoli. You know the name?"

"He has some notoriety, yes."

"He swears he only deals in South American marijuana, yet he's lost ships in the same way. How can that be if Reprimand only targets traffickers that deal with Afghanistan suppliers?"

"The answer is simple," Rifkin said. "There's a rogue element at work within the team."

"You don't seem surprised by this."

"We don't have concrete evidence to prove it, but we've suspected it for a while."

"And did nothing? What the hell kind of handlers are you?"

Nystrom sat straighter in his chair. "I remind you, Agent Edwards, company personnel are not integrated with the field operatives, for reasons you mentioned earlier. Believe me, if I was on site running the op, things would be playing out differently."

"But you're not running the op. You're tied to a chair in a land-scape-supply warehouse."

Nystrom did not reply.

"This rogue element is the main reason the committee voted to shut down Reprimand," Rifkin said. "Imagine if these unsanctioned hits became public. It would look like an out-of-control intelligence agency."

"It is out of control."

"Listen," Rifkin said in a calm tone. "It's clear that shutting down this op will not be textbook. There are unknowns involved. That's why it's so important that Nystrom and I do it."

"Not to mention a backup team would find out how badly you screwed things up."

"That's not what I'm saying."

"I know it's not." Ely set the edge of the blade against the restraint around Rifkin's wrist. "Here's the deal. I'll let you go shut down this bullshit operation and clean up your mess on two conditions."

Rifkin frowned. "What are they?"

"First, you give me one solid piece of evidence to validate what you've just told me. A contact name I can check on. A phone call to my boss. Something."

Rifkin nodded. "That can be arranged. What's the second condition?"

Ely gave him a half smile. "I go with you to shut it down."

THIRTY-THREE

Aboard *Wolverine*

Kade laced his fingers behind his head as instructed. Patrick walked up and patted him down, searching for concealed weapons. He found Zeke's pistol tucked in Kade's belt and yanked it out. He also found the Scoutmaster's bullets in Kade's pocket and scattered them across the deck.

"Start walking," Patrick said. "We're going to the bridge."

Kade headed for the island structure, his thoughts racing over what might happen next. His single-minded goal had been to get Cody and Jesse safely off the ship—and he had accomplished that goal—but in the process, he ended up a prisoner. Not quite what he had expected. He would need to take each second as it came and improvise on the fly. Something in that felt right.

A mechanical thumping sound drew his attention to a dark shape in the eastern sky. A helicopter was approaching. It appeared to be the Bell 206 that Rachel had flown out on earlier. Good. He really needed to have a talk with her.

Ahead, Gaddis tended to the bloody hole in Flynn's leg; he glared red-hot at Kade. Kade ignored it. He had bigger problems to deal with.

Patrick prodded him through the open doorway at the base of the island, and up the steps toward the bridge. Salvio happened to be making his way down. As they passed, the cocky Italian grinned. The gesture made Kade uneasy and he glanced back at Salvio, but Patrick ordered Kade to keep his eyes forward. Kade stepped onto the bridge and found himself face to face with Galen Teague. The twenty-first-century capitalist had a stern look on his face. Actually, he looked pissed. *Join the club, buddy.* A tense silence strained the space between them.

"Why do you have it?" Kade finally said.

Teague regarded Kade coolly. "What are you talking about?"

"I'm talking about that drone you've got in the bay. You had Rachel pilot it to blow Firth's cargo ship to hell, didn't you?"

"Did she tell you that?"

"She didn't tell me anything. But I know why she would do it."

Teague contemplated that a moment.

Through the bridge windows, Kade saw the Bell 206 set down on the flight deck. Its side door slid open and Rachel stepped out. As soon as she was clear, it took off again. Touch and go.

Seeing her sparked in Kade a faint sense of relief. Sure, they had their problems, but they had history together, and had forged a deep connection that he trusted. If there was a bright spot to be found in the situation, it had just stepped off that Bell 206.

Teague noted her arrival with a casual glance.

"The feds questioned me the other day," Kade said. "I thought they were trying to pin a bullshit trafficking wrap on me, but it was really about you and that drone, wasn't it?"

Teague grinned. "You shouldn't try to solve a puzzle with so few pieces in hand."

"Then why don't you fill in the picture for me?"

"Do you really think you're in a position to make demands?"

"Hey, I've got a right—"

Patrick swung the butt of the submachine gun into the back of Kade's head. Kade staggered and whirled around with a clenched fist. The gun barrel gave him pause.

"Now," Teague said with authoritative timber, "tell me what you did below deck. A little sabotage, perhaps?"

Kade faced him. "Sabotage is your game, not mine."

Teague addressed Cam. "Get down there. Make sure everything is good to go."

Cam nodded. "Yes, sir." He headed out of the narrow bridge, bumping Kade aside in passing.

Kade kept his eye on Teague. "What's going on here, Galen? A guy like you … an elaborate setup like this. It must be high-stakes."

"It's not what you're thinking."

"Oh, good, because I'm coming up with some pretty crazy shit."

"You saw something you don't understand, and now we have a bad situation to deal with."

"I see a megalomaniac with a military weapon, and he's not afraid to use it," Kade said. "Tell me what I'm missing."

"I assure you, nothing criminal or illegal has occurred aboard the *Wolverine*. There is a rational explanation for everything you've seen, but cooler heads must prevail. If we all sit down and discuss the situation, I'm confident you will come to understand and agree with me."

"Somehow, I doubt that, but I'm all ears. Start explaining."

Teague picked up a mic from the nearby comm station and offered it to Kade. "First things first. Call your friend in the Otter. Tell him to come back to *Wolverine* immediately."

"Don't think so," Kade said.

Teague's nostrils flared. "The things happening aboard this ship must remain secret. Cody and your friend Jesse must return, and they need to do so now."

"I didn't find out about that drone until after you sabotaged my plane, Galen. If keeping this secret is so critical, why the hell did you cut my ignition wires? I would have been gone hours ago if you hadn't, and I never would've even seen the damn thing."

"Sabotaging your plane wasn't my decision."

"Then whose decision was it, Captain?"

Teague held out the mic again. "Call them, Kade. I'm certain you repaired the radio just like you repaired the ignition wires. Call them back, and we'll all sit down together and sort this out."

Kade sensed Teague was dead serious. "And if I refuse?"

"You won't like the alternative."

"What will you do, send the drone after them?"

"Don't be absurd. The drone isn't fast enough." Teague gave a devious little smile. "But the Wildcat is." He walked to a door on the aft bulkhead and shoved it back on its hinges. It opened to a service platform for the faux smokestacks that overlooked the flight deck. The roar of a powerful engine rose up from below. "Do you hear that, Kade? It's a Pratt & Whitney twelve-hundred horsepower, double-row radial engine. Grumman put it in the Wildcat fighter to make sure she had enough power to go toe-to-toe with the Japanese Zero. She tops out at three hundred and twenty miles per hour. What's the Otter's max speed, one eighty, one ninety?"

Kade did not reply.

"Do the math," Teague said. "Salvio will catch up to them in no time." He added, "And his wing guns are fully operational. Is that a clear enough picture for you?"

An icy dread entered Kade's body. He got the picture, all right. Cody was in the crosshairs, all because of him. It felt like Travis all over again.

"Time is running out," Teague said.

Kade glanced around at the bridge crew. They were doing their best to ignore the drama unfolding in front of them. He wondered how many knew exactly what Teague had going on, and how many were fully on board with it? Apparently, all of them. Kade was on his own.

Rachel cautiously entered the bridge. "What's happening?"

Kade faced her. "That's just what I want to ask you, sweetheart."

She studied the faces in the room, observed Teague and Kade's body language, and noted the weapon in Patrick's hands. "Galen, what the hell is going on?"

"Kade made a discovery," Teague said, "and now we have to explain it to him."

She looked to Kade. "Why isn't the Otter on the flight deck?"

"I got Cody out of here before anything could happen to him."

"I'm coming in on this cold," she said, "but that sounds over-the-top, even for you."

"Really? Your boss sabotaged my plane. The security Gestapo bashed in Jesse's head. I saw the drone in the bay, and every goon aboard this ship went after me. I think I'm acting pretty rationally." He glanced at Teague. "By the way, whatever happened to that medevac helicopter?"

Teague gestured with the mic again. "Call your friends. Now."

Kade jabbed a finger at him. "This lunatic is threatening to shoot down the Otter if I don't tell Cody to come back. He's got Salvio on deck, warming up the Wildcat's engine."

Rachel shifted her eyes between the two of them. "Don't be ridiculous. Nobody's going to shoot down the Otter."

"What the hell do you think Salvio's plan is once he catches up, drag it back by the tail?"

"Listen," she said. "Talking this out is not such a bad idea. Galen and I do need to come clean with you on what we've been up to, but it must stay secret. We need the assurance that Cody and Jesse are in agreement with that too."

Kade just stared at her. She did not see the seriousness of Teague's threat—but Kade could think of nothing else. A salvo of .50-caliber rounds belching from the Wildcat's wing guns would shred the Otter to pieces, along with his two friends. He could not let that happen; yet telling Cody to return to the *Wolverine* would be just as dangerous. He and Jesse would be walking into the lion's den. *What the hell am I going to do?*

"Call them," Teague said again.

Rachel gave Kade a reassuring nod. "It will be okay"

"You have thirty seconds to decide," Teague warned.

Kade's pulse pounded in his temples. Time was running out. There had to be something he could do. He focused his thoughts, and then took Teague's advice. He did the math.

From the *Wolverine's* position, the Otter could make it to Sparta Airport in thirty minutes. Cody had been airborne seven or eight minutes. If Salvio left immediately, given the Wildcat's speed advantage, he would overtake Cody in about ten. That meant Kade had to delay Salvio's take-off just twelve minutes for Cody to reach safety. Kade stepped forward and reached for the mic. "I'll do it."

Teague handed it to him. "Reason, at last."

Kade keyed the mic, hoping like crazy his plan would work. "November-3-2-7-Delta-Bravo, this is *Wolverine* ATC, please respond. Over." He hailed two more times, and then said, "Cody, this is Kade. Talk to me."

Cody responded in a hesitant, nervous cadence. "Kade, are you okay?"

"Yeah, I'm fine. Just talking on the bridge with Galen and Rachel. Interesting topic. Matter of fact, they really want you and Jesse to be part of it."

"Yeah, sure. Just relay what they say to me on the radio."

"That's not what they want," Kade said. "They want a face-to-face conference with all of us. They want you to come back."

Long pause. "Kade, are you sure? I mean … I … I don't know if that's such a good idea. That gash on Jesse's head started bleeding again."

Teague frowned. "I suggest you convince him to turn around now. Salvio is eager to go."

Rachel remained silent. Kade cradled the mic and made eye contact with her, trying desperately to read her thoughts. *Are you with me?*

She did not blink.

Kade had to make his play. He keyed the switch. "Cody, listen up. I need you to pull a one eighty and come back here, just like we did around the outer pylon at Pellston Regional. Turn around and come back. You understand?"

Kade counted three heartbeats of silence, and then Cody said, "I got it … just like Pellston. Guess I'll see you in about fifteen minutes."

"Roger that." Kade released the mic switch and wondered how long it would take for them to realize Cody was not turning around. The Otter had flown outside the range of the *Wolverine*'s radar, so it would not be an immediate discovery. Kade watched Teague, searching for signs of suspicion.

Teague wore a wary expression, and his eyebrow raised like a little antenna that had picked up a trace of a signal. He shifted his gaze to Rachel. "Well?"

Rachel threw an irritated look at Kade. "He used a code," she said to Teague. "He told Cody to keep flying away."

Her words hit Kade like a bolt of lightning and his heart turned cold and heavy.

Rachel had betrayed him.

Teague snatched the mic from Kade and switched the radio frequency. "Salvio, take off now. Kendrick will guide you to the Otter's outbound trajectory."

Rachel scowled at Kade. "Why did you do that? Everything was going to be fine."

Kade did not hear her. A ringing filled his ears and an image of a bullet-riddled Cody lying next to his dead brother, Travis, on that rain-soaked runway filled his thoughts. He could not let that happen. Not to both of them. Kade's body went into action before his mind could think it through. He spun around and caught Patrick flat-footed, seizing the barrel of the submachine gun with both hands and driving his head hard into the security guard's nose. The cartilage cracked and bled. Kade kicked his knee into Patrick's groin. Shock and pain crippled Patrick's grip and Kade won control of the weapon. He pointed the barrel at Patrick's foot and fired a round through his boot.

Rachel shouted, "Kade, stop!"

Kade ran headlong for the bulkhead door that Teague had cracked open earlier. The bridge crew seemed frozen, trying to make sense of what was happening. A young man with an ensign's rank stood from his station and moved to intercept, but Kade lowered his shoulder like a linebacker and hit him low, knocking the kid on his ass near the helm console.

Mic still in hand, Teague watched the man he had under his thumb five seconds ago barrel through the cramped bridge like a bull. His eyes narrowed and he reached for the holster under his bomber jacket.

Kade lifted the submachine gun and fired a short, wild burst. Teague ducked for cover near the helm console beside the ensign as the rounds flew over their heads, shattering a monitor on the navigation station. Kade rushed through the bulkhead door and slammed it closed behind him. The dogging lever was on the inside, so he wedged his foot at the base of the door to hold it closed. He scanned the flight deck. Salvio had the Wildcat accelerating for takeoff. In three seconds it would pass within spitting distance of the island. Kade lifted the submachine gun and set its sight on the nose of the fighter. He squeezed the trigger. The muzzle flashed and the weapon vibrated like a jackhammer in his hands. Holes popped into the Wildcat's skin just behind the propeller. Black tendrils of smoke spewed from the punctures. Cracks cobwebbed the cockpit canopy and the plane veered toward the edge of the runway.

A plate of steel slammed against Kade's calf. He glanced behind him. The ensign had tried to force open the door and his straining face filled the tiny porthole window. Kade leveraged more weight against the door. The ensign moved aside and Patrick, his nose bloodied, stepped into view. He raised his pistol and fired through the porthole at Kade's head. Glass chipped and small cracks scarred the surface, but the window held. Bullet resistant. Good choice, Galen.

Kade checked the submachine gun and found it empty. Time to get the hell out of there. He shouldered the weapon and made a break for it, dashing around the first smokestack to a set of stairs leading down the backside of the island structure. He bound down them three at a time, hit the landing, and raced forward. He found himself on a narrow walkway with a waist-high steel wall that circled the exterior of the island. The vantage point gave him an excellent view of the Wildcat careening off the side of the deck and nosing into the lake.

Cody was safe, but there was no time to celebrate.

Kade estimated the elevation of the walkway above the flight deck to be about twelve feet. Close enough. He hopped over the half wall, hung from its cold steel lip, and then dropped to the wooden planks below. His feet hit solid, and he cushioned the impact by lowering to a crouch. Men were shouting across the flight deck. Kade could not tell if they were yelling about him or the fighter that had gone into the lake. He did not intend to stick around to find out. Two steps away, a steel ladder hung off the edge of the deck. He slid down its uprights and landed on a gallery deck catwalk. With the structural cross members of the flight deck overhead and the lake below him, Kade weighed his options. Into the water or into the ship?

In a split second he calculated his odds of survival would be better playing cat-and-mouse inside the ship than they would be with him cutting free a life raft and paddling through open water fifty miles from shore. A recovery crew would likely try to rescue Salvio from the plane, and with all that attention on the water, they would surely see Kade. He ran the short length of catwalk to a set of steel stairs leading down to an exterior section of the main deck. He glanced at the Wildcat wallowing in the lake. No sign of Salvio trying to escape the cockpit yet. The cocky Italian might be dead. Kade felt no joy in the thought, but he did not grieve it either. Salvio should not have gone after Cody. Simple as that.

Kade put his hand on the stairway rail and thought about Rachel's betrayal. How could she have done that, after everything they had together? He closed his eyes and buried the foolish feeling of heartbreak. Naïve son of a bitch. All the signs were there. Even Cody saw it.

Focus, Mitchell. You can't dwell on it now.

Cody would be contacting the Coast Guard, or the FBI, or somebody who would send help. Kade just needed to hold out until they arrived. He slid down the handrails to the main deck, pulled open the nearest access door and went into the ship.

THIRTY-FOUR

The ensign shoved open the bulkhead door and ducked for cover. Patrick hobbled through it, sweeping his pistol left and right as he scanned the service platform around the smokestacks. He returned to the bridge with sweat dripping from his face and leaned on a console to keep weight off his bleeding foot. "Mitchell's gone."

Teague assessed his security guard's condition. "You think you can limp after him?"

"We'll get him, sir."

Rachel approached. "Patrick, if that porthole hadn't been made with bulletproof glass, I would've taken the Glock from Mr. Teague's holster and shot you myself."

"Mitchell put a bullet in my foot and broke my nose," Patrick said. "I sure as hell wasn't going to let him just waltz out of here."

"You weren't authorized to use lethal force."

Patrick rolled his eyes at Teague. *WTF is her problem?*

"Radio the team," Teague said. "Tell them to search for Mitchell deck by deck." He glanced at Rachel, and added, "I suggest you take him alive."

Patrick cursed under his breath. "Yes, sir."

At the comm station, Kendrick listened to an incoming transmission. "Sir, engines are at all stop and the rescue team is in the water."

Teague looked down on the Wildcat as it slowly sank off *Wolverine*'s starboard side wheel. A small motorized raft with three crewmen in it cut through the waves to get to the scene. "We have real trouble coming our way now," he said to Rachel.

She went to the starboard windows and searched for a sign that Salvio had survived the crash. "How do you mean that?"

"Kade's friend is going to tell someone what happened here, and a law enforcement agency is going to pay us a visit very soon. Count on it."

She regarded him. "Aren't you concerned about Salvio, at all?"

"I'm concerned about everyone aboard this ship." Teague noticed the monitor on the radar station had two bullet holes through it, and he snapped his fingers at Kendrick. "Fix that."

"You have a peculiar way of showing it," she said.

Teague put on a nonplused demeanor. "Your husband has caused a lot of damage. He gives a whole new meaning to the term *domestic violence.*"

"He's not my husband."

"No, and you made that clear to him, didn't you?"

Rachel's stomach knotted. "We're doing something important here. Lives are at stake."

"Yes, and you understand that better than anyone."

Rachel did not reply. Instead, she watched the rescue team in the water. They had just reached the Wildcat and were prying open the cockpit. Salvio's arms helped them push back the canopy from the inside. "I need to know something," she said, still facing the windows.

"What's that?"

"Did you really give Salvio an order to shoot down the Otter?"

"It's a little late to be asking me that now, isn't it?"

"Regardless, I'm asking."

Teague paused. "This operation must be kept secret."

She faced him. "Did you order it?"

"It was a bluff."

"Did Salvio know that?"

"Of course, he did."

Rachel considered the fidelity of his answer. Deep down, she didn't believe him, but deeper down, she wanted to. "I suppose it's fitting that the man who just sponsored a prestigious poker run knows how to bluff. You had Kade convinced you were going to shoot down his friend."

"Apparently I convinced you too."

"You didn't consult me about this tactic before you used it. That pisses me off, Galen."

"Forgive me, Miss Edwards, but it was a crucial, time-sensitive situation, and you were not available for consultation. It won't happen again. Is that all?"

"No," she said. "Why did you sabotage Kade's plane?"

A ripple of agitation crossed Teague's face, and he nodded curtly to the bulkhead doorway that exited the bridge. "Out there."

He led her to the stairwell that connected the bridge to the main deck and had her walk with him halfway down. "This is a ship of secrets, and some things even our crew shouldn't know."

Rachel saw no point in his theatrics. "What are you talking about?"

"Nystrom and Rifkin suspect you've compromised Reprimand."
She stared at him blankly.

"They think you told Kade about the operation, and that he is getting involved somehow."

It took her a couple seconds to digest that. "They *what?*"

"When Kade showed up after the strike on Firth's ship, it got them thinking. When he unexpectedly appeared here on *Wolverine*, it convinced them you two were up to something."

"Like what?"

"I don't know, perhaps some scheme to fill your pockets, but what they're really concerned with is Reprimand going public. Rifkin kept talking about containment. He instructed me to keep Kade on board until he and Nystrom could get here to, well, let's be honest, interrogate him. They intend to talk to you as well."

She fumed. "And you didn't tell me about this?"

"Frankly, I wasn't sure what to believe. But you convinced me up there, on the bridge just now, that you're faithful to the cause."

"I haven't breathed a word of this to Kade."

"I believe you, but our CIA handlers are on their way here to determine that for themselves."

"I'll talk with them. I haven't done a damned thing to compromise Reprimand."

"But Kade has caused a problem. The very thing Rifkin was concerned about is unfolding right now. Cody will divulge what Kade has seen. Reprimand is in danger of being exposed, and the CIA is going to rest that square on your shoulders."

Rachel tensed. "I'll fix it. Once security catches up to Kade, I'll talk with him, and Kade will talk with Cody, and we'll get the genie shoved back in the bottle."

"I'm confident you can, but it must be before Nystrom and Rifkin arrive."

"It will be."

"Another thing," Teague said. "We should launch the drone, get it off the ship in case a law enforcement agency pays us a visit. It can stay on station twenty-four hours. We'll have a better idea of how this is all shaking out by then."

Rachel thought things through. "If Cody reports a military drone is on board *Wolverine*, the CIA will catch wind of it and they'll bury the story, citing national security concerns."

"Let's hope that's true. I'd hate to see Reprimand end in a tantrum of public outcry."

"I'd hate to see it end. Period."

"Kade is the lynchpin. You have to assure him we're wearing white hats. If Nystrom and Rifkin determine he's a loose cannon, it puts everything we've worked for in jeopardy."

"I can do it, but it won't be easy. Kade's decided something bad is going on here. Convincing him he is wrong is like telling the wind to change direction."

"If anyone can, it's you. He's still attached, you know."

"I know."

Teague regarded her. "Reprimand is at risk. It could fall to pieces tomorrow."

"We've covered this already. What's your point?"

"This morning I received information detailing a beta target."

Rachel laughed. "Are you serious? After everything we just discussed? Now is not a good time to hit a target outside of mission parameters."

"This could be the last beta we hit. There's no telling how much damage the shockwave from Kade's actions will cause."

She shook her head. "We have to let this one go."

"Why? Do you suddenly feel you've done enough in your crusade?"

"I'll never feel I've done enough, even if I sink a hundred of those bastards' ships, but sometimes you have to retreat from a battle to win the war."

"This beta I'm talking about," Teague said, "Rolle Kish owns it. He may even be on board."

Rachel's thought process froze, and her raw subconscious seized on the name.

"Kish has done well for himself since his street-dealer days. He's climbed the ranks to bona fide drug lord. Does that seem right to you?"

"Of course not. Don't be an ass."

"He never paid for what he did to Leah."

Rachel did not reply.

"I thought you should know. By the way, I left the target dossier for Kish's ship in the Sports Center. Review it after launch."

Rachel's thoughts blurred. "I'll head down there and mobilize the crew."

"Plot a targeting solution at your discretion." Teague climbed one step and paused. "Justice always whirls in equal measure," he said, "but sometimes it needs a helping hand."

THIRTY-FIVE

Grand Ledge, Michigan

Ely liked things that made sense. He liked puzzles that clicked together and formed complete pictures. The Reprimand tale that Nystrom and Rifkin had spun almost fit the bill. Nearly every player's role made sense. For instance, just by watching the world news every night, one could understand why the President would issue a by-any-means-necessary order to restrict cashflow to militant extremists. And it was easy to imagine the President selecting the shadow architects of the CIA to execute such a directive. Rachel's particular mix of professional skills and personal grief plausibly painted her into the picture as well. Nystrom and Rifkin were just following orders.

Which left Galen Teague. He was the odd man out.

Ely could not figure out why a corporate mogul like Teague would get so personally involved in Reprimand. The last business-man/philanthropist to do something similar was Howard Hughes, who had participated in a covert government plan to recover a Soviet nuclear submarine from the ocean floor by providing a ship and a cover story to deflect attention. If that operation had leaked to the public, Hughes would still have been considered a heroic patriot. Teague, on the other hand, was getting his hands dirty in a risky, high-stakes, arguably unconstitutional, operation. If Reprimand went public, he had far more to lose than gain.

Perhaps cynicism had gotten the better of Ely, but he did not buy that Teague was "just serving his country," as Rifkin said. Teague's puzzle piece had blurry edges, and that bothered Ely, so much so that he had Lieutenant Walker check out a few things for him while he paced the grounds near the pond at Shindig's Landscape Supply, waiting for the next shoe to drop.

Danny approached him with a cigarette in her hand. "We're wasting time here."

"Until I get confirmation that Nystrom and Rifkin are telling me the truth, we're in standby mode," Ely said.

"How do you expect to get confirmation?"

"A call from my boss."

"I hate waiting." She puffed on the cigarette. "Who were you on the phone with earlier?"

"Lieutenant Walker. I've got him doing some legwork for me."

"He works for you?"

"He works with me."

She chuckled. "He's okay. Not such the ass I thought when I met him." She flicked ash into the pond. "Do you think Kade's all right?"

"If I take Rifkin at his word, yes, Kade is fine, at least for the moment."

"Where did they find him?"

"He supposedly turned up on a ship in Lake Michigan. Rifkin and Nystrom were on their way there to talk with him when we intercepted them." Ely put a boot imprint in the spongy earth near the water's edge. "He went out there to see Rachel."

Danny did not reply.

"I can't imagine she greeted him with a smile."

"It's like I said. He went there to straighten out his head. He needed to do it."

Ely smiled. "For what it's worth, I hope he U-turns back to you. My daughter has enough trouble on her hands right now."

Danny laughed. "I see right through you, Ely. I know you like him."

"What are you smoking in that cigarette?" Ely's phone buzzed and he swiped it out of his pocket. "Edwards."

"It's Gabriel. Got some info for you."

"Lay it on me."

"Superior Freight."

"It checks all the boxes?"

"Most of them. Superior Freight was incorporated five years ago as a marine transport and logistics company based in the Great Lakes. It operates a small fleet of mid-size cargo vessels that typically transport iron ore, coal, and soybeans between Chicago and the Eastern seaboard. In the last six months, Superior has picked up a handful of contracts to haul sand and limestone through the region on routes that, if you squint and use your imagination, approximate the routes of the ships you've documented in your *Discord* document."

Ely damn near patted himself on the back. "And …"

"Superior Freight is a subsidiary of parent company Teague Global Associated Freight."

"You just made my day."

"It's real thin, Ely."

"It's more than I had a minute ago." Ely's phone beeped with an incoming call. "Is that all you've got, Gabriel?"

"Yeah. What's the matter, that's not enough for me to dig up in a half hour?"

"No, you did great. I've got a call coming in from Gary Anders that I have to take."

"Okay, Ely, talk to the boss. Let me know if you need anything else. Oh, and I didn't tell Gary about our lunch in Grand Ledge, like you asked. Is that still the tact we're taking?"

"It is for now. Keep it under your hat."

"Got it. Talk to you later."

"Thanks, Gabriel." The line clicked off and Ely answered Anders' incoming call. "Gary."

"What the hell have you stumbled into, Ely?"

"I didn't stumble into anything. It took a lot of investigative work to get here."

"I just got off the phone with Warren Lindsey, Director of the CIA."

"Are you sure it was him?"

"Of course, it was him. I know the man. What kind of question is that?"

"A cautious one. What did he tell you?"

"Not much, which I'm not comfortable with. He said your investigation has run tangential with one of theirs, and that it could interfere with an affair of the utmost importance to national security. Is that true?"

"Maybe. I won't know for certain for a couple hours."

"What are you interfering with?"

"I can't tell you. That's part of the deal."

"What deal?"

"I can only divulge what the Director has already told you."

"Don't play games with me, Ely. I just spent a half hour vouching for you, telling Lindsey what an outstanding agent you are, convincing him you're a man of character and integrity, and assuring him your top-secret security clearance was well-earned. Tell me what's going on."

"All I can say is this thing hits close to home. Maybe I can be more candid down the line, off the record, with a scotch in my hand. Right now, I'm still in the dark on the details myself. All I can tell you is I have to do something with the agents I've contacted—but before I do, I need you to confirm that what they've told me is the truth."

"How am I supposed to do that?"

"Did Lindsey say anything about the agents I'm with?"

"Only that if they failed to do their job after requesting your assistance, they would receive a severe reprimand."

Ely parsed his words. "Is that exactly what he said?"

"Yes, I'm sure, he said it twice."

"And you're sure you were talking to Warren Lindsey?"

"Ely, I worked with the man a year at the Department of Justice. I know who I was talking to. Why are you questioning me on this?"

Ely heard the chop of a helicopter rotor in the sky, approaching from the south. "Can't explain, Gary, but I got the message. Have to go now."

"Go where? Damn it, Ely, tell me what's happening. This isn't proper protocol."

Ely disconnected. That helicopter was getting closer.

"Did you get your confirmation?" Danny said.

"Yeah, I think I did. Things are going to start happening fast."

Across the parking lot, the back door to the supply warehouse opened, and Nystrom and Rifkin stepped out. Anthony and his men were in the lot, keeping watch, making sure the feds didn't try anything stupid. The CIA agents made their way to the pond near Ely and Danny.

"I presume you got a call from State Intelligence Officer Anders," Rifkin said.

"I did," Ely replied.

"Are you satisfied we're telling you the truth?"

"Barely. Why couldn't Lindsey just tell Anders the whole story?"

"That's not how we work," Nystrom said. "For obvious reasons."

Danny glanced skyward. "Why do I get the feeling that helicopter is coming here?"

"It is," Rifkin said.

"Where are we going?"

"We're not going anywhere." Ely took his car keys from his pocket and handed them to her. "Take the Tahoe back to MIOC in Lansing and wait there with Walker. I'll contact you when I get back."

"Back from where?"

"Can't tell you."

"Bullshit, Ely. I'm going with you."

"Not happening," Nystrom said.

She glared at him. "Stay out of this, Numbnuts."

"You're the only one staying out of this, Miss Morgan."

Danny turned to Ely.

"Sorry," he said. "You're not coming."

"I asked for your help. Now you're ditching me?"

"I'll get Kade back. Trust me. Now, go to Lansing. Tell Walker to keep his phone in hand. I might need his help."

Danny narrowed her eyes at him and snatched the keys. "Fine."

The helicopter circled Shindig's perimeter, and then set down in the parking lot between the pond and the warehouse. It was a black UH-72 Lakota. Ely guessed it had come from the National Guard's aviation facility in Grand Ledge. Rifkin waved Ely forward. "Let's go."

They ducked under the spinning rotors, shielding their eyes from the dust and debris stirred into a cyclone by the blades. No sooner had they climbed aboard, Nystrom closed the side door and the Lakota lifted into the air. Through a cabin window, Ely watched Danny hop into the Tahoe and gun it out of the lot. Anthony and his boys were craning their necks to watch the helicopter climb away from them. Ely settled into a seat next to Rifkin in the rear of the cabin. Nystrom sat adjacent. They all remained silent for a long while, listening to the drone of the helicopter's twin engines.

Once they were over Lake Michigan, Rifkin leaned in so Ely could hear him. "I told my Deputy Director that bringing you along to shut down Reprimand was a good idea. He agreed that given the unknowns involved, and the potential rogue element at play on board *Wolverine*, you might help stabilize the situation with at least one team member."

"Do you believe that?" Ely said.

"To some degree, yes, but you didn't give me much choice about coming along, did you?"

"Your daughter's a hard dog to keep under the porch," Nystrom added. "She likes to do things her way. For some reason, she thinks it's better than our way."

"Maybe she's right."

Nystrom grinned. "I see the apple didn't fall far from the tree."

Ely regarded him. "Do you really expect trouble when you tell Teague and Rachel that Reprimand has been shut down?"

"I always expect trouble," Nystrom said.

"That's a stressful way to live."

"Teague is a zealot when it comes to Reprimand," Rifkin said, "and he keeps an armed security team on board *Wolverine*."

"They're belligerent, quick to draw, and loyal to a fault," Nystrom added.

Ely gave him a wise-guy grin. "They sound like you."

Rifkin actually smiled at that. "Teague pays them well for that loyalty. Whatever he says, they do."

"You just called Teague a zealot."

"What about it?"

"You called him a patriot earlier. There's a difference."

"How so?" Nystrom said.

"Love of country drives a patriot," Ely explained. "Other things motivate a zealot, like religious dogma or personal interests."

Rifkin chuckled. "I wouldn't call Teague a religious fanatic."

"Then the risk he's taking with Reprimand must be serving personal interest."

"What are you getting at?"

"I met with Aldo Dinapoli," Ely said. "You remember him?"

"I do."

"He's the one who got me thinking about government involvement in this cabal. I thought he had come unhinged, but he turned out to be right, so I started considering other things he said."

"Dinapoli is a criminal," Nystrom said. "He's not a credible source of information."

"And you are?" Ely countered.

Nystrom did not reply.

"Dinapoli believes someone deep inside the drug-trafficking world is helping the government locate and identify smuggling vessels. It would be rather efficient if this informant was also the one carrying out the attacks."

"Are you suggesting Teague is this inside man?" Rifkin said.

"There's reason for me to suspect him. His corporation, T-GAF, has the financial infrastructure to manage and conceal a large-scale trafficking operation. And a paper trail ties him to a small marine-transport company named Superior Freight, which is engaged in suspicious activity."

"What sort of activity?"

"Superior Freight picks up a new route each time Reprimand sinks a trafficking vessel." Ely leaned forward. "Those new routes look a lot like the ones followed by the targeted ships."

Rifkin and Nystrom exchanged a glance.

Ely eyed them both. "Teague is sinking the competition and acquiring their customers."

Rifkin deliberated a moment in silence. "That's a sound bit of reasoning," he finally said.

Ely's jaw dropped open. "Aren't you going to deny it's even possible?"

"Given where we are now, what would be the point?"

"The point?" Ely said. "What the hell is the point of going through the effort to wipe out a slew of drug traffickers, only to let another one fill in the vacuum?"

"I remind you, Agent Edwards, that Reprimand's objective is to eliminate the funding that global terrorist groups receive from the sale of Afghani opium, not to eliminate the drug underworld from North America. That remains the prevue of domestic law enforcement."

"You're aiding and abetting a criminal enterprise."

"We're strengthening national security," Nystrom said.

"This is insane."

"Is it?" Rifkin said. "Teague's connections have helped us track down buyers and dealers of Afghani opium a hell of a lot faster than if we had done it without him. No matter how many phone calls the NSA records or how many satellite photographs they take, they'll never be able to gather the type of reliable intelligence that a man on the inside can provide. And if that man is helping his own cause in the process, he's all the more effective."

"Pay the man off, don't make him the dominant player in an illegal industry."

"You're missing something in all this," Rifkin said. "In the end, it will be better to regulate one drug kingpin than to try and capture ten of them."

"Regulate?"

"Teague has rules he has to follow. Don't believe for a minute that he doesn't."

"Oh, great, he's proven he's good at following rules," Ely said.

"Teague's agreement severely limits the amount of narcotics he is permitted to move annually. As a result, there are far fewer drugs coming into the U.S. through the Great Lakes than prior to Reprimand, and that limit is reduced ten percent each succeeding year."

"That was a key selling point for the senators on the committee to approve the operation," Nystrom added. "Now they can boast that their war on drugs is finally succeeding, and the flow of illegal narcotics coming into the country is dropping year after year. They'll be heroes."

"If it wasn't for the criminal and unconstitutional aspects, it would be a great plan."

Nystrom laughed. "It would've been even better if the committee had approved my suggestion to take a cut from Teague's bottom line and use the money to fund other operations. Brilliant, right? It would've made Iran-Contra look like amateur hour."

"But things didn't go as planned, did they?" Ely said. "Teague got greedy and started hitting targets you didn't tell him to hit."

"Sometimes an op goes off track," Rifkin said. "That's the nature of the business. You take a risk and hope it pays off. If it doesn't, wipe the slate clean and try something else."

"Turn the page," Ely said. "Is it that easy?"

"Not always."

Ely sat quiet a long while. "Rachel doesn't know about Teague, does she?"

"We didn't share it with her," Rifkin said. "If she knows, then Teague told her himself."

"I can't imagine he did. He'd have a problem on his hands." Ely pondered a bit longer. "What about Mitchell?"

"He's still a concern," Rifkin said. "Just because Reprimand is shutting down doesn't mean keeping it a secret is any less critical. If he knows about it, his silence has to be secured."

"Let me talk to him," Ely said, giving Nystrom a glance, "before you make a hasty judgment and decide to do something stupid."

Nystrom smirked. "I've met Mitchell. If anybody is going to do something stupid, it'll be him."

THIRTY-SIX

Aboard *Wolverine*

Kade careened into a bathroom stall, barely catching himself from tumbling into a steel toilet bowl. His jaw throbbed and his vision blurred. He righted himself and shook it off. Heavy footsteps approached from behind. The guy was coming at him again. He turned to set a defensive stance, but the burly security guard with the name Burke stenciled on his shirt seized him by the shoulders and slammed him against the opposite bulkhead. A dozen mirrors over a dozen basins reflected the thrashing. Kade had had enough. He spun around on a burst of adrenaline and slammed an elbow into Burke's temple. The security guard staggered and Kade followed with a quick right. Burke fell back on his heel. Kade jabbed again, but the guy blocked and struck with a jarring left. A few more like that and Kade would be out of the fight.

Burke's pistol lay on the deck near a toilet stall several feet away. Kade eyed it, feigning like he wanted to go after it. Burke followed his intent and rushed toward the weapon. Kade lunged, tackling Burke at the knees. Burke's hand slapped the deck inches from the pistol grip. Kade lifted his legs and pulled him backward, bouncing his head off a toilet stall post and twisting him onto his back. Burke kicked his legs free. Kade set his elbow like a pike and dropped down with all his weight, striking square on Burke's chest and winding him. Kade rolled up onto a knee, drew back, and punched him in the jaw. Burke's eyes rolled back and his body went limp.

Kade swiped the pistol from the deck and scrambled to his feet, training the weapon on Burke, waiting for him to move or speak, or anything. He didn't seem to be pretending, he just lay motionless. Kade approached him. "Burke?" he said, reading the stencil. "How many of you guys are there?"

Kade grabbed Burke's comm radio and listened to the earpiece. No chatter. No sign other guards had been alerted to the scuffle. Good. That was a close one. Kade had ducked into the ship's head to plan his next move after re-entering *Wolverine*. Burke had walked in to take a piss. They had surprised each other.

Kade crouched over Burke, searching his pockets and utility belt. He found two extra clips for the Smith & Wesson, a pair of handcuffs, a butane lighter, and a pack of cigarettes. The cigarettes reminded him of Danny. For a moment he considered that if he had just stayed with her, and had put Rachel behind him, he wouldn't be in this mess. Another would have, could have, should have. His life seemed to be filling up with such things.

Kade took the clips, the cuffs, and the lighter. He checked the magazines and found them loaded with .40 caliber bullets. His empty MP-5 submachine gun took 9mm rounds. So much for that. He pocketed the clips and stripped Burke of his gun belt, and then adjusted the buckle around his own waist and holstered the pistol.

The radio earpiece crackled. "Cam-Gaddis."

"Go for Cam."

"Just got Flynn down to sick bay," Gaddis said. "White's taking care of him. Infirmary is clear. Moving to aft cabins."

"Copy that. I'm sending Zeke to assist. Burke is sweeping bow to amidships. Link up with him in the bay. We'll secure main deck and move to orlop."

"Copy that."

"Report in five minutes. Cam out. Bump channel."

The line went silent. Kade listened a few seconds longer. Nothing. Cam said bump channel. Kade recalled being captured earlier and Patrick finding the radio on him. They must be rotating their frequency to discourage eavesdropping, like he had just done. Now he would have to scan through the channels to find the one they were using to monitor their movements. That could take some time, and he did not have much to spare. Cam had his guys reporting in five-minute intervals, so Burke would be due to report in soon. Kade had to move.

Based on the transmissions he had just heard, the guards were combing through main deck and then moving down. It seemed logical to assume they had already searched the island, the flight deck, and the gallery deck. He thought it best to go somewhere they had already been.

He cracked the door to the central corridor, peered left and right, and then slipped out of the ship's head. He kept in shadows where he could, searching for security cameras as he went. He proceeded on the assumption that Teague did not have enough men to post a guard at every bulkhead, which allowed him, in theory, to move about with relative ease. He just had to make sure he did not get caught in the security guards' dragnet or get seen by a random crewmember.

He travelled as far forward as he could through the empty officers' quarters, and cautiously lifted the dogging lever on a door that led to what he figured had to be an exterior section of main deck. Concerned a guard or a camera waited on the other side, he pushed the door open a fraction of an inch, fighting the resistance of stiff hinges. To his surprise, the door did not open to an exterior deck. It opened to a thirty-foot drop into Lake Michigan. He forced it back a few more inches to get a better look and discovered a way out. Six feet or so above the door, the flight deck's supporting framework ran fore and aft, extending several feet beyond the ship's bow. If he could get up into those cross members and find a nice, dark nook to hide in, he could perhaps evade Cam's search until help arrived. That was it for the good news.

The bad news was he had to find a way to get up there. There were no details on the outer hull to use as handholds to climb up. The door, however, was positioned between a series of large transverse support trusses that tied into the flight deck framework. Their triangular profile extended from the deck to below the door, but the nearest one was about eight feet away. Kade would have to jump to it. If he missed, he would fall into the lake in the path of the starboard paddlewheel, which chopped up the water with 1,200 horsepower of force behind it.

Eight feet began to look a lot like fifty.

Kade pulled back inside the ship and searched the corridor behind him, making sure he had not been discovered. He clicked through several channels on the radio, stopping at each for a second or two to listen for chatter. One came alive.

"Burke's not responding," Cam's voice said. "I'm going forward to check it out."

"Copy that," Gaddis replied. "I've hooked up with Zeke. We're rifling cabins. Out."

No time to think about it anymore. Cam was on the way and he would find Burke, and all his men would converge on the area. Kade had to make the leap to get out of there. He shoved the bulkhead door open wide and considered the distance to the truss. He shook off the thought of being chewed up by the paddlewheel and chose the cross member he would try to reach. He set his angle through the door, took a step back, took a deep breath, said a quick prayer, and ran.

Two massive strides, and he kicked off the lower lip of the door-frame. Free flight. Free fall. Wind in his face. He reached out, extended his fingers. The truss came up fast. Gravity pulled him down. His left hand touched the cross member. He locked his fingers around the lip of the angle iron. His right slapped against steel. Both arms jerked, weight and momentum wrenching hard against them. He frantically pulled himself up, wrapping an arm around the truss frame, his legs dangling thirty feet over the lake. He kicked one foot up over the bottom edge of the frame.

He climbed the structure like a ladder until he felt in a stable position, and then paused to breathe and rest his arms. Savoring his success, he suddenly realized the door remained wide open. If Cam spotted it, he would have a pretty good idea where Kade had gone.

Kade studied the underside of the flight deck and saw that the planking was installed atop evenly spaced I-beams that ran parallel to the ship's centerline. He picked an I-beam near the hull and grabbed its lower flange, clinging with his fingers, and hand walked across it. At the halfway point, between truss frames, his fingers started to ache, but he stopped and kicked at the door with his shoe. He kept kicking against the stiff hinges until the door closed. He could not dog it down, but at least it was not wide open to draw Cam's attention.

Strength drained from Kade's fingers, and he shimmied across to the adjacent truss as quickly as he could. He rested until his hands stopped aching and his fingers recovered some strength; then he worked his way to the next truss. The last one in the series crossed the "T" at the bow and supported the edge of the flight deck. A little too far out there for Kade's liking. He decided to stay put. He squirreled in close to the hull on a cross member suitable for sitting. The perch put him far enough around the curvature of the bow that he could not see the door he had jumped through. It worked both ways. If Cam decided to poke his head out through that door, he would not see Kade either.

Kade leaned against the hull and took in the view of the lake. Eighteen-inch swells rolled eastward under an overcast sky in the waning light of day, and the surface wind carried a bit of a chill. He adjusted the radio earpiece and scanned through the channels. Static, one after the other. He was just about to give it a rest when he heard Cam's voice.

"Found Burke out cold in the head. Mitchell can't be far. Gaddis, Zeke, get up here, forward section, main deck. We'll flush him out. Moss, come forward from orlop deck. Copy?"

His minions acknowledged.

"Bump channel." Static.

Kade closed his eyes and listened to the paddlewheel splashing through the water, wondering if Cam and his boys would figure out where he had gone. He felt for the pistol on his waist, just to make sure he still had it. *Come on, Cody. Where's the cavalry?*

The faint buzz of an engine pricked Kade's ear and opened his eyes. A rumble shook through the deck planks above his head. Something was rolling down the runway. He tracked the sound to the end of the flight deck. The drone soared off the edge, its rear propeller driving the deadly weapon on a graceful path into the sky. Somewhere in the ship, Rachel piloted the craft toward an unknown destination.

He used a code. Her voice echoed in his head. *He told Cody to keep flying away.*

Kade cursed to himself. She had sold him out—and she had put Cody's life in danger. What the hell was she thinking? Kade decided he needed to confront her to find out. He thought about the ship's layout, and his tour with Rachel. He figured he had a pretty good idea of where the drone control room might be located. He just needed to find a way to get there in one piece.

THIRTY-SEVEN

Aboard *Wolverine*

From the smokestack service platform, Galen Teague watched the drone disappear into the distance. A perfect launch. If all went as planned, he would have an obscenely lucrative new deal by morning. But there were loose ends that had to be dealt with first. "Cam and the team are closing in on Mitchell," he said to Patrick, who sat on a stool nearby with an HK416 tactical rifle in his hands and a gauze bandage wrapped around his injured foot. "They might flush him topside. Stay alert."

Patrick nodded. "Is the no-kill order still in effect?"

"For the moment," Teague said. "But that's subject to change."

Kendrick stepped through the bulkhead doorway from the bridge and addressed Teague. "Sir, the chopper is inbound."

"Arrival time?"

"Five minutes."

Teague looked skyward and identified a spec in the eastern grayness coming toward the ship. It was Nystrom and Rifkin. Damn their timing. "Track them in, Mr. Kendrick."

Patrick sighted down the rifle barrel to a random spot on the flight deck. "Should I stand down when they arrive?"

"No. Stay sharp. I got caught with my guard down once today. Not again."

"Yes, sir."

Teague walked onto the bridge. "Mr. Paulus, reduce speed to one-quarter. Adjust course to minimize wind over deck. Give our guests a nice, smooth landing."

Paulus acknowledged.

Teague punched a button on the intercom panel. "Control room-bridge. Status report."

Rachel replied, "Closing on beta. Time to intercept: ten minutes."

Teague glanced at the approaching chopper through the bridge windows. It was close. He pressed the transmit button again. "Mission hold."

A long period of silence played out. "Window on target will close in thirty minutes."

Teague did not want to miss this beta, or the half-million-dollar deal tied to it, but he had to concede Rachel's point. Retreat from battle to win the war. "Company associates are arriving in five," he said. "They have business to discuss." He added, "With both of us."

Another void of silence. "Got it."

"Lock the drone in a standby pattern and report to The Brigg."

"Copy that."

Teague felt energized. Walking the edge gave him a high no drug could match. "Mr. Kendrick," he said, "tie me into the security team."

"Yes, sir." Kendrick consulted a notepad screen and refreshed a channel rotation display. He switched the transmitter frequency to the one currently in use by the team. "All set."

Teague spoke into the station console. "Cam, this is Teague. Where is Mitchell?"

"We've tracked him to main deck, bow section, starboard side," Cam replied.

"I don't hear confidence in your voice."

"We're tightening the noose, sir. We'll have him soon."

"You'd better. I need him in The Brigg in five minutes. If you fail, it's your head."

"Understood. Cam out."

Teague nodded to Kendrick. "You've been monitoring Coast Guard operational channels?"

"Yes, sir. Ever since Mitchell's friend in the Otter called for help."

"Has there been any activity on any channel indicating the Guard is dispatching vessels toward us?"

"No, sir," Kendrick replied. "There's been no crosstalk having anything to do with *Wolverine*." He hedged. "That's not to say the Guard isn't using an unregistered channel to coordinate a response."

"That's possible. I guess we're going to find out if Operation Reprimand is protected by the powerful people that Rifkin says it is. Regardless, we have to be prepared for anything. Inform me immediately if you intercept any communication from a fed agency showing interest in us."

"Yes, sir."

Teague noted the helicopter was very close to the ship. The time had come to receive his associates. He left the bridge and hurried down the stairs.

* * *

Ely spotted *Wolverine* through the Lakota's cockpit window. She seemed out of place, an aircraft carrier underway on Lake Michigan. Back in '43 people probably thought the same thing. "Did the CIA build *Wolverine* for Reprimand?" Ely said to Rifkin.

"No, Teague had started its construction long before Reprimand came about."

"How convenient."

"Very," Rifkin said. "You want to hear something ironic? During the war, the original training carrier *Sable* served as the base for operational testing of the very first pilotless aircraft. They called it a Torpedo Drone."

"History repeats," Nystrom said.

"So it seems." Ely returned to his seat in the Lakota's passenger cabin. Indeed, history did keep coming back around, sometimes as a wave of nostalgia, other times as a flame to burn you with a lesson not learned. From Ely's jaded perspective, it was usually the latter. "Does Rachel attend your meetings with Teague?"

"We don't have many face-to-face meetings," Rifkin said, "but she's typically present."

"Does Teague suspect you're coming to shut him down?"

"He shouldn't, but it never pays to assume. Either way, he won't be happy with the news."

Ely pondered that. "I'll stick by Rachel when you tell him."

"Just remember," Nystrom said, "we take the lead."

"Yes, given the unknowns, it'll be best for us to keep control," Rifkin added.

Ely nodded. "Right. The scenario's unpredictable. Don't worry, I'm just here to make sure my daughter comes out of it okay."

"If you keep that frame of mind," Rifkin said, "this should be a smooth shutdown."

Ely settled back. That passive frame of mind thing wasn't entirely accurate. Intervening in the shutdown wasn't his intention, but if the situation called for it, he wouldn't hesitate, and he had an ace up his sleeve to help the effort.

The helicopter pilot, Corporal Gaines, called into the cabin to inform his passengers they were going in. The Lakota descended, coming about a quarter turn to square up with *Wolverine's* flight deck, and then touched down dead on the marks. Smooth landing. Good pilot. Nystrom threw open the side door. "Let's go, Agent Edwards."

The CIA spooks hopped out of the helicopter. Ely took a moment to check his cell phone. No service. Not good. He followed the agents, stepping down and scanning the flight deck. Nobody was topside on the vessel, save for a man with a rifle up near the smokestacks watching over their arrival like a sentry on a battlement. Ely recalled Nystrom's description of Teague's security team. Belligerent and quick to draw. Nice.

"Do you always get a warm reception like this?" Ely said to Rifkin.

"Not usually," Rifkin replied.

Nystrom assessed the man with the rifle. "Teague would only post a guard like that if he had an active security concern."

"Maybe Teague suspects you're coming to shut him down and he doesn't like it."

Nystrom sneered. "If Teague ever points a rifle at us, it will be the end of him and his whole empire, and he knows it."

"It has to be something else," Rifkin said.

Ely wondered what that would be. For some reason, Kade came to mine.

The door at the base of the island opened and Teague walked out. He gave his handlers an all-business smile. "It's good to see you, gentlemen." He studied Ely. "Who's your colleague?"

"This is Agent Edwards with DHS," Rifkin said. "He's here as an observer."

"I didn't know DHS had an interest in our efforts." Teague scrutinized Ely, almost like he recognized him, although they had never met.

"We don't," Ely said. "I do."

It dawned on Teague right then. "Edwards. You're Rachel's father."

"I am."

Teague scowled at Rifkin. "What's the point of this?"

"I'll explain when we have all the participants together."

Teague did not like that answer. "Follow me. We're meeting in The Brigg."

"Why do you have a man in the guard tower position?" Nystrom asked.

"I'll explain in a moment." He added, "When all participants are together."

They filed through the bulkhead door into the island and down the vertical ladder to the ops corridor. They marched past the roped-off radio room and a closed door farther down the corridor. A security guard with the name Hutchins stenciled on his shirt stood post near a ramp leading down. The group made its way past him in silence and entered the The Brigg. Ely took in the retro forties décor, felt the air on his face from the overhead fans, and saw the only person inside waiting for their arrival.

Rachel stood by the bar across the room, a hint of resolve in her expression and a glass of ice water beside her. When her eyes fell on Ely, resolve gave way to confusion. "Dad?"

"I know about Reprimand," he said without prelude. "And your part in it."

It did not seem to register with her. "How?"

"Long story."

"Everyone who shows up on this ship has a long story."

Ely cracked a half smile. "Must be the only way to get here."

She looked to Teague. "Did you know about this?"

"I'm afraid I'm as in the dark as you are."

"You, in the dark?" Ely said. "That's a joke."

"Is that supposed to mean something to me, Mr. Edwards?"

Nystrom scanned The Brigg. "Where's Mitchell?"

"Main deck, forward section," Teague said.

Rifkin became irritated. "Galen, did you not understand we wanted him here, ready to talk?"

"I got the message. Mitchell didn't. He's been causing trouble aboard all afternoon. My security team is rounding him up as we speak."

"No surprise there," Ely said.

"It isn't his fault." Rachel pointed at Nystrom and Rifkin. "Those two idiots ordered his plane sabotaged to hold him here. Because of that, he saw the drone and went off the deep end over what it meant."

"He never should have been here in the first place," Rifkin said.

"I didn't invite him. I never told him about Reprimand. He came here for a completely different reason, but you jumped to conclusions without talking to me. Now, look what's happened."

"Yes," Nystrom said. "I'm sure you would've come clean about you two, and whatever scheme you've cooked up to undermine the op and jeopardize its secrecy."

"Kade came here because of the poker run, not Reprimand."

"The poker run," Nystrom said. "Another brilliant idea. A public event on a covert vessel."

"Enough," Rifkin said. "The poker run was scheduled and publicized before Reprimand kicked off. We all agreed to let it play out to minimize public scrutiny of *Wolverine*. The risk was acceptable."

"You're right," Nystrom said. "Mitchell would have come here regardless of the run."

"I didn't betray the op," Rachel protested. "Get it through your heads."

"Despite your passionate denial, we still need to talk with Mitchell," Rifkin said.

"Containment is critical," Nystrom added.

"You geniuses created this problem, not me, and not Kade."

Nystrom smirked. "Check that self-righteous attitude, Miss Edwards. Your hands aren't as clean in this as you say."

She did not reply to that. "Dad," she said instead, "why are you here?"

Ely nodded to Nystrom and Rifkin. "Their agenda today doesn't end with grilling you and Kade. They're also delivering a directive. I thought I should be here when they do."

"What directive?" Teague said.

Rifkin glanced at Nystrom, as if checking with him before going forward.

Ely anticipated a speech about shutting down the op. The CIA operatives' body language indicated they were not sure what to expect after giving that order. It made Ely anxious. This could be a more volatile situation than he had thought. He noted everybody's position through a tactical lens: Nystrom, Rifkin, Teague, and Hutchins at the top of the stairs behind them. Ely set his fingertips on the table beside him, positioning his hand to reach for his 9mm.

"The directive he's talking about comes from the Senate Anti-Terrorism Committee," Rifkin said. "The senators have reassessed

Reprimand and, based on escalating risk factors, have unanimously decided to terminate the operation."

"They what?" Teague said.

Nystrom translated. "The spineless jellyfish are shutting you down."

"Why? We've been effective," Rachel said.

"Maybe you've been too effective," Ely offered.

Teague got ruffled. "How can you be too effective?"

"Hitting targets outside mission parameters is one way," Nystrom said bluntly.

Rachel fell back on her heels, like she had just been caught with her hand in the cookie jar.

Teague did a better job maintaining composure. "What are you suggesting?"

"Don't bother denying it," Rifkin said. "We've suspected it for a while. Agent Edwards confirmed our suspicions."

Teague shifted seamlessly from innocence to damage control. "What do the senators know?"

"Nothing specific, but the increased activity has gained the attention of news media, the Coast Guard, and DHS. A ship sinking under mysterious circumstances is interesting. It's like striking a match in the darkness. The senators are afraid that light will shine on them."

Rachel nearly laughed. "They're afraid the public will find out about an operation that's actually working to improve the drug problem and make the country safer?"

"Not everyone agrees with the methods we're employing," Rifkin said.

Teague pondered a short while. "What happens next?"

Rifkin cleared his throat. "Agent Nystrom and I are supposed to immediately terminate all mission activity, confiscate all operational equipment, and debrief all personnel for discharge."

Rachel crossed her arms and turned away.

Ely noted a lack of fireworks. Perhaps this would not be as tricky as expected.

"Will the agreements made in conjunction with Reprimand be honored?" Teague said.

Nystrom scoffed. "Just be happy you're not being prosecuted."

"For what, hitting unsanctioned targets?"

"For everything."

Rachel's eyes narrowed and she glanced at Teague.

Ely noticed.

"At least, that's what's supposed to happen," Rifkin said.

Ely's ears perked.

Rifkin continued, "The Legislative Branch does not have authority over the Executive Branch. As such, the Committee's decision to terminate Reprimand is invalid and the operation will continue solely under Executive prerogative."

Ely came forward. "Hold on. This's not what we discussed."

"It is, Agent Edwards. We just didn't discuss everything."

"Checks and balances," Ely said. "The committee will never roll over and let this happen. They'll demand oversight."

"Oversight?" Nystrom chuckled at the quaint notion. "Over what? As far as the committee knows, this op ends today."

"You need to shut it down, as ordered."

"I answer to the President," Nystrom said, "not a bunch of candy-assed senators."

Rifkin addressed Teague. "*Wolverine* will no longer be our base of operation. You need to launch the drone. I'll provide a set of coordinates to a concealed airstrip near Manistique where you'll land it and await further instructions."

"It's already airborne," Teague said. "Mitchell's friend managed to escape off the ship and send a distress call. I didn't want the drone sitting in the bay if the Coast Guard came to investigate."

"We know about the call. It's being handled," Rifkin said.

Ely mumbled a curse.

"So, we have three problems left to deal with," Nystrom said. "Mitchell, Agent Edwards ..." He nodded to Rachel. "And you."

"I told you, I'm not a problem," she said.

Teague stepped up. "I'll vouch for her. The way she dealt with her husband on the bridge convinced me they're not working together. She's dedicated to the cause. If Reprimand is to continue, she needs to be part of it."

"What about Mitchell?" Nystrom said.

"My men have him surrounded. He'll be in hand very soon. I guarantee it."

"Two down, one to go," Rifkin said. "That leaves us with you, Agent Edwards."

Ely knew how the CIA handled their problems, and he didn't care to become an unsolved mystery. The time had come to play that ace. He repositioned his stance and inched his hand closer to his holstered pistol.

Nystrom read his movements. "Don't do it, Edwards."

"Do what, stop a pair of rogue agents from committing a treasonous act?"

"Treason would be fighting the same losing war against terrorism," Nystrom countered.

"We're all on the same side," Rifkin said. "We all want the same thing. A secure nation. Isn't that what you want, Agent Edwards? Isn't that the treasure you're after too?"

"Same treasure," Ely said, "different maps."

"Who's to say which path is right, and which path is wrong?"

"Today that's gonna be me."

"Dad." Rachel came closer. "Don't make the same mistake Kade did."

"I don't think Kade made a mistake this time."

"You're on the wrong side of this," Nystrom said.

Ely gave him a dry smile. "How about we agree to disagree?"

"How about we don't?" Nystrom drew his Glock in half a breath.

Ely cleared the 9mm from its holster.

Rachel jumped between them. "Stop!"

Rifkin drew his pistol and waved Teague back.

Teague lifted his hands. "This looks like a federal problem to me."

Rachel held her ground. "Both of you, put your guns away."

Ely did not have a clear line of fire with her standing there. "Step aside, baby. I got this."

"You're outnumbered and outgunned. You don't *got* this."

She was jeopardizing his play. Ely bit his lip. "Rachel, let me do my job."

"Your job isn't to stop a counter-terrorist operation ordered by the President of the United States." She walked up close so that he could not aim around her. "We're destroying them, Dad, those monsters that killed Leah. And we're stopping them from funding the fanatics who knocked down the Twin Towers." She reached up and put a hand on the barrel of the pistol. "We're hurting them, and we have to keep hurting them."

It took Ely back, the calm and rational tone she maintained while explaining how two rogue CIA agents and a criminal drug lord were on the side of the angels by subverting Legislative oversight and disobeying a direct order to stand down, all in the name of keeping alive an operation that amounted to the unconstitutional execution of a domestic kill list.

"Rachel, this is wrong."

She angled the barrel of the 9mm toward herself and gently tried to pull the weapon from his hand. "There's nothing wrong about it."

Ely felt his finger contact the trigger. In an instant of panic, he released the pistol grip. "This won't bring Leah back."

"I'm not trying to bring her back. I'm stopping the plague that killed her."

"Three Coast Guard officers were murdered aboard *Blackbird*. Innocent people are dying."

"I didn't know about the boarding team. I didn't know you were on the cutter."

"You don't know a lot of things going on here. You're making a mistake."

"No, Dad. I just stopped you from making one." She worked the action of the 9mm and made the weapon safe.

Ely made eye contact with her. "Those monsters you're destroying, your partner is one of them."

She looked at him like he had just told her a baffling riddle.

"Superior Freight," he said quietly.

Nystrom walked up and forced Ely's arms behind his back. "You wanted to put me in cuffs back in Grand Ledge. Let's see how you feel about it." Nystrom swiped the handcuffs from Ely's belt and flicked open a manacle to slap it on his wrist.

Ely chuckled. "I feel pretty good that a tough guy thirty years my junior is afraid of me."

"Hardly."

Ely held his wrists close together. "Come on, Shelia, before this old man kicks your ass."

Nystrom paused before ratcheting the cuffs closed. He gave Ely a knowing smile and spoke into his ear. "Okay, Edwards, I'm game for round two." He dropped the cuffs into his jacket pocket. "Consider this a professional courtesy."

Ely concealed a subtle smile.

"Step an inch out of line, you'll regret this courtesy." Nystrom took Ely's cell phone and put it in the pocket with the cuffs. He addressed Rifkin. "Now, what do we do with Agent Edwards?"

"Secure him in a cabin," Rifkin said, glancing at Rachel. "Post one of Galen's guards in the ward room and get back up here. We need to hash out the next few steps."

Nystrom slapped Ely hard on the shoulder to prod him along. "Get moving."

Rachel watched her father being led away. "Don't harm him, or Reprimand really will end."

Nystrom and Rifkin stopped and stared at her.

"What do you mean by that?" Teague said.

"The access code for the drone's flight controls. I'm the only one who knows it. If my dad or Kade are hurt, I'll let the damned thing run out of fuel and splash into Lake Michigan."

"Kendrick and I have the access code too," Teague said.

"Per protocol, I changed the code this morning, and I haven't shared it with anyone yet." She walked to the bar and picked up her ice water. Or was it vodka? "Don't worry, as long as they're okay, Reprimand is in business." She took a sip.

"Once again it has to be your way," Nystrom said.

"My way keeps the op running."

"I'm sure we can find an agreeable compromise," Rifkin said.

"There's no compromising my father's safety."

"That's not what I meant. I'm sure we can give you what you want within a framework the CIA can live with as well. Agent Edwards is a reasonable man. I believe he'll come to see how crucial this op is to our country."

Rachel set the glass down. "So do I."

Ely gave her an uncertain smile, hoping she had understood his message to her. "We'll talk later, sweetheart, and you can explain all the things I'm missing in this twisted plan."

She nodded. "I'll do that, Dad."

Nystrom directed him toward a door in The Brigg's starboard bulkhead and pushed him forward. Ely walked, wondering if he could play that ace any longer. It would be a lot more difficult now, but he had to try. According to Rifkin, the CIA was telling the Coast Guard to disregard any incoming reports about *Wolverine*, probably under the guise of a Customs and Border Protection Agency operation. Commander Gerard would have no reason not to believe it. Ely had to get a line of communication off the ship. If he could contact Walker, a fleet of cutters would be steaming over the horizon in no time. All he needed was a way to get that call out.

And then he remembered that Nystrom and Rifkin carried satellite phones.

THIRTY-EIGHT

Ely stepped through the bulkhead doorway onto an exterior section of main deck. The air was cool and the sky was gray, and somewhere a Predator drone stalked, waiting for a command from Rachel to bomb the next name on the hit list. It disturbed Ely a great deal. If she was performing the same duty overseas against enemy combatants, in a clearly designated war zone, it would be a different story. But it was not happening overseas, it was happening here, and the targets were not enemy combatants. Many of them were US citizens. Yes, they were criminals, but they were not subject to summary execution. It had to end.

Nystrom followed five paces behind, training his Glock on Ely's back. They reached a door amidships, underneath four large runs of ductwork that fed into the faux smokestacks topside. Nystrom instructed Ely to open the door. Ely un-dogged it and walked into the ship. The look and feel, and even the smell, of the vessel reminded him of his Navy days. Something in it felt full circle. History coming back around. With teeth.

They were in a corridor that led to what looked like a battery compartment, when Nystrom said, "When are you going to make your move?"

Ely sensed his captor had stopped walking, and he cautiously turned around to face him. "What makes you think I'm going to try something?"

"You practically begged me not to cuff you. Don't think I'm that stupid."

"Then why didn't you do it?"

"I'm curious."

Ely smiled. "The metal irritates my skin, makes me itch. I don't like that."

"And the way you tried to take control of the situation in The Brigg, that's not the action of a man who would give up this easily."

"Maybe I'm just a cocky SOB. Like you."

"There's more to it than that. You came on like you had us by the short hairs. You think you've got some advantage; I just can't figure out what."

Ely nodded to the pistol in Nystrom's hand. "Maybe I had Anthony file down the firing pin on your .40."

Nystrom's eyes shifted to his Glock. "Not buying."

"Are you familiar with the twenty-one-foot rule?"

Nystrom laughed. "Yes, but my weapon isn't holstered, and you don't have a knife."

"No, but we're a lot closer than twenty-one feet apart."

"You don't actually think you can—"

Ely charged. Nystrom eyes popped like he couldn't believe it. He raised his Glock and targeted the crazy DHS agent's body mass. Ely heard two blasts, felt a sharp sting on his chest. He kept rushing forward, hitting Nystrom with as much force as he could muster, lifting his legs and grappling the spook in a brutal bear hug. Nystrom's center of gravity tipped and they crashed onto the deck. A sharp pain shot through Ely's wrist.

Nystrom's body absorbed the impact but it did not faze him. He threw Ely into the corridor bulkhead and tried to get to his feet. Ely shook it off and sprang again, leading with a clenched right that rocked Nystrom's jaw. On his knees, Nystrom took the shot with a jolt and a glare set in his eyes. He swung the Glock like a scythe, glancing the side of Ely's head with the pistol grip. Ely caught himself on the bulkhead. Nystrom was a thicker brick than he figured. He started to think he had miscalculated.

Nystrom scrambled to his feet and aimed the Glock square at Ely's chest. Ely turned to shield himself. Nystrom fired. Ely didn't fall. Ely didn't bleed. Nystrom stared at the pistol. "What the ..."

Another sting burned under Ely's shoulder blade. This time Nystrom was certain to figure out he wasn't shooting live rounds and the tactical advantage would evaporate. The playing field would be level and, in that contest, Nystrom held the edge. Ely clenched his fist and spun around.

Nystrom advanced, wielding the Glock like a hammer this time.

Half a second to react. *Duck under*, Ely thought, *and smash his jewels.* Nystrom drew back to strike.

A gunshot thundered in the corridor. A blood pattern burst on Nystrom's shoulder. He recoiled. The Glock fell from his fingers. He'd been shot.

Ely considered the bullet's trajectory, heard footsteps racing up from behind. He turned.

Kade.

Nystrom staggered, but stayed on his feet. "Mitchell, you son-of-a-bitch."

Kade approached with the Smith & Wesson tight in hand, keeping Nystrom under the gun. "Agent Numbnuts, I figured you'd show up sooner or later."

Nystrom huffed and grimaced from the pain of the gunshot wound. "You just dug a hole so deep you'll never get out."

"I've been deeper." Kade glanced at his ex-father-in-law. "I knew you were a tough guy, Ely, but I didn't know you were bulletproof."

Ely picked up Nystrom's Glock. "Yeah, well I know a Sicilian who can turn a bullet into a blank with a pair of pliers and a glue gun."

"How'd you do that without him knowing?"

"I had Nystrom and his partner in custody earlier, figured a gun filled with blanks would be a useful interrogation tool. Didn't end up using it then. Good thing, I suppose." Ely rubbed the sting on his chest. "Soft glue slugs still hurt."

"*You* apprehended *them*?"

"Things went upside down."

"No kidding. You'll have to tell me the story sometime."

"You'll want to hear it. I wouldn't have gotten this far if it wasn't for Danny."

Kade gave him a puzzled look but said nothing.

Ely stuck the Glock in his empty holster and then retrieved his handcuffs and cell phone from Nystrom's jacket pocket. "I thought you were part of this, Kade. I owe you an apology."

"Forget it. I thought you were with them, until Numbnuts tried to shoot you. This is a crazy."

"You don't know the half of it."

"One thing I do know is Teague has a Predator drone on board and he sank Firth's ship with it. I think Rachel helped him. Do you have any idea what's going on?"

"It's a domestic black op that turned rogue right before my eyes."

"That's classified information," Nystrom said. "You know the penalty for divulging it."

Ely ratcheted one of the handcuff manacles around Nystrom's wrist. "Are you actually lecturing me on treason?"

"It's only treason if you subvert the government. We're protecting it."

"You're betraying it." Ely pulled him to a sturdy-looking pipe along the bulkhead and threaded the cuffs around it. "Give me your other hand."

Nystrom did not comply. "You of all people should be on board with what we're doing."

"Kade, if he doesn't give me that hand in two seconds put another slug in him."

Nystrom reluctantly extended his hand and Ely slapped the cuffs tightly around it.

Kade checked down both directions of the corridor. "Hurry up, Ely. Teague's men are searching for me and we just made a lot of noise."

Ely reached into Nystrom's other pocket and pulled out the satellite phone. "We need this."

"By the way," Kade said. "Your daughter sold me out. Big time. Whatever's going down aboard this ship, she's on the other side."

"I know. She just did something like that to me."

"Nice parenting, Ely. You've raised a stand-up girl."

"She's being played too."

"You can't play a player."

Ely studied the display on the satellite phone. "We need to get away from all this metal to uplink. I have to reach Lieutenant Walker to call in a tactical team."

"Cody escaped in the Otter. I'm sure he's already called for help."

"He did. Nystrom's friends are telling everyone it's a false alarm."

"Who are his friends—and why would the Coast Guard listen to them?"

"They're feds."

"Customs and Border, right?"

"Central Intelligence."

"Why the hell is everyone wearing a mask?"

"The CIA likes masks, especially when they're sneaking around at home."

"You're talking too much," Nystrom said.

Ely faced him. "If I were you, I'd be less concerned about being a good company man, and more concerned about keeping pressure on that shoulder wound. Don't want to bleed out, do you?"

"We're not done, Edwards."

Ely ignored him.

"We need a signal for that phone," Kade said. "I know a way up to the flight deck."

Ely shook his head. "Bad idea. Teague's got a sniper watching from the bridge. We can probably get an uplink outside on main deck, beneath the gallery."

"I just came from port side main," Kade said.

"And I just came from starboard."

"So, which one do we head for?"

"You've got more knowledge about this ship and the security team than I do. Fill me in."

Kade thought before answering. "Teague's men have been sweeping the ship deck-by-deck for me. Had a close call in the bow section of main deck a little while ago, and they rushed in to surround me. I slipped them, though, got up under the flight deck. Found a nice nest to hide in."

"How many men are aboard?"

"Seven or eight security guys that I know of. There's also a dozen or so crewmen, but they haven't been too much trouble. It's the security team I've been bumping heads with."

"Bumping heads how?"

"I knocked out three of them, shot two others, and sent an old fighter into the lake."

Ely stared at him, speechless.

"I've had a busy day."

"I'll say. You shot two men?"

"Three if you count Numbnuts, No, wait. Maybe four. Might have hit the Wildcat pilot. But I didn't kill anyone. I think. And two of the three I knocked out are back on their feet. Heard them on the radio." Kade tapped the earpiece in his ear.

"You're starting to impress me."

"Starting?" Kade frowned. "You're a hard man to impress."

"I know." Ely motioned down the corridor from where he and Nystrom had come. "Let's go to the starboard side. It's closer, and you say the guards are concentrated toward the bow. I think it'll be our best chance at avoiding them."

"Believe it or not, I agree with you."

They took off together. A few steps in Ely said, "That Smith and Wesson you're carrying looks like a .40 cal."

"It is."

"You have an extra magazine?"

Kade pulled one of the clips he got off Burke from his pocket and handed it over.

Ely ejected the Glock's magazine and emptied the remaining blank shells from it. He began loading it with rounds from Kade's spare clip. "If you found a nice hiding place under the flight deck, why did you leave it?"

Kade hesitated. "I was trying to find Rachel."

"I thought you said she sold you out to Teague."

"She did. Cody needed time to get clear of this ship. I tried to trick Teague to buy that time, but Rachel told him what I was doing. She threw me and Cody under the bus."

"Then why go looking for her?"

"I have to find out why she did it."

Ely loaded the magazine into the Glock. "Rachel signed on with Teague and the CIA to destroy drug-smuggling vessels. Think about that."

Kade did. "Leah."

Ely nodded. "Rachel's avenging her sister's death, and she won't let her ex-husband or her father get in the way."

Kade regarded him. "Leah was your daughter. Doesn't some part of you agree with what she's doing?"

Ely stopped at the end of the corridor. "Yes." He pointed to a bulkhead door ahead. "That opens to the exterior. Let's move."

They hurried across the deck and un-dogged the door. Ely cracked it open and peered out. "Clear." He pushed it open.

Kade followed him through and watched their back. "Hurry up and call your buddy. We can't stay in the open too long."

"I've got a signal. Dialing." Ely entered the prefix code and then Walker's number into the satellite phone.

A bulkhead door far forward on the deck swung open.

Kade stepped in front of Ely and drew down on the area. "Dial faster."

THIRTY-NINE

Michigan Intelligence Operations Center (MIOC)
Lansing, Michigan

Danny sat in Lieutenant Walker's cubicle strumming her fingernails on his desktop. Walker lifted his gaze from his computer screen and stared at her. "That sound doesn't make things happen faster."

She considered the teal polish on her nails. "You want me to light a cigarette instead?"

"No. One of the cops in here would come over and arrest you."

She laughed. "Wouldn't be the first time."

Walker sat up straight. "You've been arrested for smoking in a federal building before?"

"No, not for that."

He waited for her to explain.

She didn't.

"Check your phone."

Walker frowned. "Ely didn't call in the last sixty seconds. I have my ringtone on full volume and the notification set on Earthquake. If I get a call, we'll know it."

Danny resumed strumming her fingernails. "Why do you suppose he isn't calling?"

"No news is good news."

She gave him a look like he had said something ridiculous. "Right." She sat back and crossed her arms. "I say he's gotten in deep somewhere. Nystrom and Rifkin are nothing but trouble. I knew it the second I met them."

Walker grabbed a half-filled water bottle from the corner of his deck and slapped it down in front of her. "Is this bottle half empty or half full?"

She raised an eyebrow. "What's in it?"

"That's not the point. The question is—"

Walker's phone chimed and vibrated like it was about to explode. He yanked it from his pocket and checked the screen. "Unknown number."

Danny leaned forward like she might slap him. "Answer it."

He did. "Lieutenant Walker."

A tense, urgent voice responded. "Gabriel, it's Ely. I was right about Teague. I need backup out here now."

Walker gave Danny a nod. "Ely, are you all right?"

"Not quite. Those feds went rogue and their hired guns are trying—" A series of explosive pops crackled through the line, cutting off Ely's voice.

Walker recognized the sound as gunfire. "What's happening?"

No response. More sharp reports. Thuds and scrapes like Ely's phone was being knocked around. Shouts in the audio mud. "Back inside! Back inside!"

Walker pressed the phone tight to his ear. "Ely, what the hell is going on?"

"Need a tac team out here!" Ely shouted. "Tell 'em it's a hot zone."

"Where's here? Give me numbers."

"Aboard *Wolverine*," Ely said. "Teague's ship." Static bled into the chaotic mix.

"I'm losing you. Ely. Where is *Wolverine*?"

A blast of gunfire answered. A background voice yelled, "Get down!"

The line thudded as if the phone had been dropped. "Lake Michigan!" Ely shouted. "Approximate ..." Static surged like a hailstorm.

"Did not copy. Repeat location."

Static overwhelmed Ely's voice. And then a loud click. And then nothing.

"Ely?"

Danny sat frozen, staring hard at Walker. "What happened?"

"Lost him."

"He's in trouble, isn't he?"

"Not just trouble. Serious shit trouble."

"I told you."

Walker jumped out of his chair and marched across the floor to SIO Gary Anders's office.

Danny followed on his heels. "Where are you going?"

Walker knocked on the door but did not wait for an answer. He pushed through. "Gary, Ely's in trouble. We need to send help."

Anders pushed back from his desk, not looking as surprised as Walker thought he might. "What sort of trouble?"

"He's under fire on a ship in Lake Michigan."

"Under fire?" Anders seemed more miffed than shocked. "How?"

"I don't know how. He bumped heads with a couple of guys posing as CBP agents this afternoon, and then he asked me to dig into Galen Teague. Next thing I know he's off on some kind of secret mission."

Anders made a face. "What's Galen Teague got to do with any of this?"

"Ely thinks he's into drug running."

"Whoa, let's walk this back and fill me in from the start."

"Ely put me on a paper chase, and I uncovered a connection between the trafficking vessels he's been investigating and one of Teague's companies. The connection is thin, and the tie to Teague is three banks deep, but it's there."

Anders noticed Danny standing behind Walker. "Who's this?"

Danny stepped into the office. "Danielle Morgan. I told Ely about the phony CBP agents. They were harassing me, trying to find where Kade Mitchell had gone."

Anders looked to Walker for clarity.

"Mitchell was married to Ely's daughter Rachel," Walker said. "He's mixed up in this somehow. Rachel's involved too. That's why Ely jumped in."

"Ely said this thing hit close to home. Now I know what he meant." Anders pondered.

"Mr. Anders, Ely needs help now," Danny said.

"He asked me to send in a tactical team," Walker added.

"Send a tactical team where? You said he was on a ship."

"The *Wolverine*. Galen Teague's museum ship."

"Do we know her location?"

"Lake Michigan is all Ely could tell me before he got cut off."

Anders chewed his bottom lip.

"The *Defiant* is in the Straits of Mackinac," Walker said.

Anders looked through the office doorway to Ely's cubicle. "Ely couldn't tell me where he was headed or what he was going to do. All I know is the CIA is involved at some level."

"Is that a good thing or a bad thing?" Walker said.

"I don't trust Warren Lindsey." Anders punched a button on his desk phone. "Guess that makes it a bad thing."

Walker cocked his head. "Warren Lindsey?"

"Never mind." Anders put the call on speaker, and a grumbly baritone voice answered. "What's up, Gary?"

Anders leaned into the mic. "Commander Gerard, I'm here with Lieutenant Walker. We have an urgent situation that only you can help us with."

"What kind of situation?"

Anders cleared his throat. "Ely Edwards got into trouble aboard a trafficking vessel, and we need HITRON to get him out."

Gerard paused half a second. "Just tell me where and when."

"We need them now," Walker said. "Ely's aboard a ship named *Wolverine* in Lake Michigan. She's that carrier replica that Galen Teague built."

Silence on the line. "Are you serious about this?" Gerard finally said.

Anders gave Walker a glance. "Dead serious, Bob. What's the matter, having trouble associating Mr. Teague with drug trafficking?"

"Not so much that—but the name of the vessel. We received a mayday call concerning *Wolverine* a couple hours ago, some pilot said his friend had been injured by her crew and he just escaped off her flight deck. He claimed he was held captive there. We ran the ship through Ops Center and were prepared to dispatch a cutter to investigate when we got a stand-down order from Customs and Border. Apparently, they're running a sting operation on *Wolverine*, and for the next twenty-four hours we are to disregard all unsecured comms concerning that ship."

Walker recalled the incident with the imposter CBP agents in Grand Ledge. "Commander, I have reason to believe that stand-down order may be bogus."

"It's genuine, Lieutenant. After my call from Customs, we ran the ship through Ops Center again, and now it shows up as a CBP operation. Run it yourself."

Anders loosened his tie. "I agree with Lieutenant Walker. I can't explain why right now but I think we're being manipulated."

"It's in the database, Gary. It's for real."

"I have firsthand knowledge that leads me to believe otherwise."

"For Christ's sake, are you telling me to disregard a by-the-book deconfliction protocol?"

"I'm telling you to trust me when I say a friend and colleague needs our help."

"If we send in HITRON, we could have Guardsmen and CBP agents exchanging fire."

"I don't think that will happen," Walker said.

"Based on what, your gut? A hunch? I need something more concrete before I make a career-ending decision like this."

"Ely's investigation into the drug smugglers led him to a couple of bad actors impersonating CBP agents," Walker said. "That's why I don't think CBP is involved in this at all, and the sting-story someone fed you is BS."

"How the hell did these bad actors get into the Coast Guard Ops Center database?"

"Considering the people Ely is dealing with, anything is possible," Anders said.

"I sure would like you to explain that to me, Gary."

"If we were face-to-face in a secure conference room I would, but right now, on this line, you have to trust me when I say anyone HITRON encounters aboard *Wolverine* will either be a trafficking suspect or someone engaged in federally criminal activity."

Commander Gerard did not reply.

"Bob, you know me. We've worked together five years. You know I wouldn't send you on half-baked debacle. We need to deploy HITRON."

"What's your confidence level this won't blow back in our faces?"

"I can't quantify that," Anders said. "We've crossed into instinct territory."

"I was afraid you'd say that." Gerard went silent. "Okay, I'll go out on that limb with you."

Walker took a relieved breath. "Did you get *Wolverine*'s location from the mayday call?"

"Yeah, but that info is several hours old. It gets us in the ballpark though. Let me off this call and I'll dispatch HITRON now."

"We're doing the right thing, Bob."

"We better be." Gerard disconnected.

Walker turned around. "The tac team is on the way, Danny." She wasn't there. "Danny?"

She had left the office and was already riding the elevator down to ground level, replaying the details of the mayday call in her head. A pilot had escaped that ship. His friend had been injured. That could be Kade and Cody. Which one was hurt and which one was flying the Otter? She needed to find out. Three more floors. She pulled the pack of L&M's from her pocket. The elevator doors opened and she struck her lighter, puffing a cigarette to life. In the parking lot, she tried to call Kade, but still no answer. She climbed into Ely's Tahoe and fired up the engine. She checked the gas level. Three quarters. Plenty.

If Kade and Cody had escaped that ship, they would return to the hangar.

Danny figured she could make it to Sparta Airport in an hour if she pushed it.

She squealed the tires out of the parking lot.

FORTY

Aboard *Wolverine*

Rachel sat at the bar in The Brigg, Ely's 9mm to her left and an ice-filled glass to her right. She kept running her father's words through her head. *Your partner is one of them.* He could only have meant one thing, but how could it be true? Teague's reasons for getting involved in Reprimand had always appeared altruistic. For the greater good. For the country. That's what she believed—but then, she never scrutinized his motives, partly because her own reasons for signing on with the op went far beyond flag-waving loyalty. She had a higher purpose fueling her crusade against the drug lords, a purpose so righteous that she consigned any pesky questions that arose about Teague to the background.

It was Teague who first suggested going outside mission parameters to hit beta targets. She did not question his motivation. Soon thereafter, he restructured Superior Freight, and made it seem on paper to be an autonomous company. Again, she did not ponder why he might want such an entity separate from T-GAF, besides perhaps a tax shelter of some kind. When she overheard bits of hushed conversations between Rifkin and Teague, about operating limits and annual caps, and when Nystrom commented about withheld prosecution, she said nothing. Don't ask questions. Just keep the op going. Keep death raining down on the demons.

She even turned her back on Kade and Cody to preserve the cause.

Rachel swiped a bottle of Stoli from the bar and poured herself a drink. The ice crackled.

Rifkin approached and slid a piece of paper to her. There were handwritten coordinates on it. "This is the location of the airstrip where you'll land the drone."

She glanced at the numbers. "No problem."

"Sooner rather than later," Rifkin said.

She took a sip of vodka. "What about that beta, Galen?"

From a nearby table, Teague glanced awkwardly at Rifkin. "We have to let this one go, just like you said earlier."

"If you're talking about an unsanctioned target, you absolutely will let it go," Rifkin said. "That sort of activity stops immediately. You're both on a very short leash now."

Rachel set her glass down. "Speaking of sanctioned targets, why did we hit the *Blackbird*?"

"Because we told you to," Rifkin said.

"My father told me she was a meth ship. Reprimand is only authorized to target vessels carrying Afghani opium. Why did you tell us to hit the *Blackbird*?"

"You don't need to know that."

"Three Coast Guard officers were killed in the strike. I need to know why."

Rifkin regarded her with an annoyed twitch in his eye. "Containment."

"Containment how?"

"There was a man aboard her who intended to share information with your father that could have exposed Reprimand. We couldn't let that happen. Secrecy had to be maintained."

"So, you assassinated an informant before he could squeal."

"We protected Reprimand's security."

"My father found out about it anyway. Your containment record is not so good." Rachel took another drink. "How did you know this informant was aboard that ship?"

Rifkin nodded toward Teague. "Galen told us."

Rachel swiveled to face Teague. "How did you know, Galen?"

Teague seemed caught off guard, but composed himself and responded. "Salvio heard about the informant through one of his contacts and passed the information on to me."

"How is Salvio connected with anyone who would know about an informant on that ship?"

"His family has ties to the trafficking world."

Rachel found his answer to have all the integrity of rice paper. "So, Salvio goes to a family barbecue or something, and Cousin Vinny just happens to tell him about an informant aboard *Blackbird* who's ready to expose a secret government operation?"

"The Dinapoli family is very active in the Great Lakes trafficking network," Rifkin said. "Although Salvio did not acknowledge it, I suspect his brother Aldo told him about the informant. Your father confirmed Aldo suspects government involvement."

"I didn't know Salvio was a Dinapoli. Sounds like a conflict of interest to me. Why didn't someone mention this before?"

"There was no need," Rifkin said. "Having the last name Dinapoli no more disqualifies Salvio from being on the Reprimand team than having the name Edwards disqualifies you."

"We do not carry the sins of our fathers," Teague said with a smile.

She regarded him. "Did you hire Salvio because of his family connections?"

"I hired Salvio because T-GAF needed a good pilot."

"Miss Edwards," Rifkin said, eyeing the paper with the coordinates on the bar. "We can address all your burning questions *after* you tell the drone to land at those numbers."

Rachel grabbed the sheet of paper. "Yes, sir."

Teague stood. "I'll go with you." He reached for Ely's 9mm.

She picked it up. "It's my father's gun, I'll carry it."

Teague nodded. "Let's go to the Sports Center."

A ringtone chimed, and Rifkin checked his sat phone. "Station Chief is calling for a status report. You two begin reprogramming the drone. I'll be there shortly."

Rachel started across The Brigg with Teague at her side. She bristled at his proximity.

"You seem on edge," he said to her. "What's bothering you?"

She laughed. "You have to ask?"

He looked at her with a measure of sincerity. "I know things seem chaotic right now, but all this will stabilize and we'll be back on track in no time."

He didn't see it yet. Teague had not picked up on her suspicions or the questions whirling inside of her head. It took every bit of self-control she had to hold her tongue and keep it that way. "Nystrom wants to kill my father," she said. "Your men want to do the same to Kade. The CIA questioned my loyalty to the mission. There's a lot putting me on edge."

"Giving up the access code would put the loyalty question to rest."

"Nobody gets that code until my dad and Kade are off this ship."

"You know that will be a hard sell to Rifkin and Nystrom."

"I don't care. Those are my terms. My loyalty to Reprimand has nothing to do with it."

"I know, but they don't understand that."

"You better explain it to them."

They walked up the aft ramp past Hutchins and turned down the corridor. A queasy unease set in her stomach the closer they got to the door to the drone control room. She used to feel exhilarated walking into that compartment. Not today.

A muted bang suddenly bent her ear, like the remnant echo of a gunshot report that had bounced between corridor walls or vibrated through bulkheads. Teague heard it too. Then another. And then a series. Rachel's thoughts went to her father.

Teague's phone chimed with a text. He read it aloud. "Edwards is loose."

A follow up message. "He's with Mitchell now."

Rachel cursed. "They're not making this easy. You'd better go manage the situation. Make sure it doesn't get out of hand any more than it is already."

Teague glanced at the message on his phone. "You may be right. I'll get things under control below deck. You land the drone at those coordinates. Tell Rifkin his partner screwed up." Teague typed a quick reply to Cam. *On my way to main deck.* He turned to Hutchins. "Stay alert. Keep the Sports Center secure. I'll send Gaddis to assist."

Hutchins nodded. "Yes, sir."

Teague rushed past the door to the drone control room and climbed the ladder to the island.

Rachel pushed through the door and secured it behind her. She sat at the drone-piloting station like she had dozens of times before. In front of her the flight stick, two data-display screens, a command-interface keyboard, and a large monitor playing a live-video feed from the drone's onboard camera were all familiar—but today they had a dark feel.

The beta-target dossier that Teague had left for her sat on a table surface between the control station and a computer terminal. She considered the document a moment, and then set the 9mm on top of it. The video monitor was displaying an image of a cargo ship steaming through a body of water. It was taken from altitude as the drone circled in a standby pattern. In the bottom corner of the screen, a timer counted down. Five minutes remained before the ship would sail out of the strike zone, taking her too close to shore or other vessels in the vicinity to safely launch a missile strike against it. According to Teague, that ship carried Rolle Kish's drug shipment. Rachel stared at the vessel, and then at the coordinates that Rifkin had given her.

She could not ignore Ely's warning any longer.

She slid the 9mm aside and picked up the dossier. She scanned through headers on the sheet: Vessel Name, Port of Origin, Destination Port. She skipped over the strike-zone coordinates and timing info, and continued through the headers until she found the Customer Code.

Teague had crafted a coding system to keep the beta paperwork as cryptic as possible. In this dossier, the customer was listed as, BNT1D-MW-475. Translated, it read Buyer of Narcotics, Tier-1 Distributor, Midwest Region-Caldwell, whose name had been assigned the number 475.

She slid over to the computer station and logged into the T-GAF network using her corporate username and password. It took a couple of seconds for the satellite uplink to connect to the network. As VP of North American Import Operations, she had access to a lot of documents and drive locations, perhaps more than Teague realized. She bit her lip and tried to drill through a firewall to an isolated server where all of Superior Freight's operational files were stored. She expected to be blocked, but a dialog box informed her access had been granted. Apparently, the IT department never took away her rights after she had finished her part in setting up the pseudo-autonomous company. Normally she would admonish an employee who failed to follow up in such a way. In this case, she would make an exception.

Having helped structure the server, she knew where to look for what she sought. She accessed Superior Freight's logistical software and searched the company's client database for the customer code from the target dossier. She got a hit.

BNT1D-MW-475: Contract pending.

It took her a second to absorb the meaning of what she had found. Superior Freight sat poised to acquire a contract with one of Rolle Kish's narcotics customers. Pending what? Most likely the impact of a Hellfire missile into Kish's smuggling vessel. Eliminate the competition. The oldest business tactic in the book.

It did not seem real.

She clicked through menus and pulled up a listing of all current Superior Freight customers. More coded numbers popped onto the screen, coded numbers she recognized. They were the codes Teague had used to identify the buyers of the drug shipments they had been targeting, both sanctioned and unsanctioned. Those buyers were now clients of Superior Freight, or more to the point, of Galen Teague.

Rachel stared at the numbers, an avalanche of disbelief burying her. Ely's voice thundered in her head. *Your partner is one of them.* Her hand shook and the mouse buttons clicked, opening a cascade of windows on screen. She clenched her fist. Teague had lied to her from the beginning.

On the video monitor, Rolle Kish's ship drove through the water. But was it really Kish's ship, or did Teague just tell her that so she would agree to strike it now, before the CIA could stop them? It didn't matter. She had learned the truth. Teague had taken her crusade against the demons and used it to strengthen his own hand.

Blinders that vengeance had placed over her eyes peeled away like scales, and she slid her chair in front of the piloting station. Two minutes remained before Kish's ship would exit the strike zone. She watched the vessel and considered her journey from grieving sister, to avenging angel, to pathetic patsy. In that instant, she knew what she had to do.

She entered her access code and took control of the Predator with the flight stick. She broke the drone out of its holding pattern and lined it up on the vector she had calculated in the firing solution earlier, setting a pair of crosshairs over the ship's stern on the monitor. The sensor and flight-data display screens read normal and ready. Without a thought or hint of hesitation, she fired a Hellfire from beneath the aircraft's starboard wing. The missile homed in on its target straight, hot, and true. It intersected the crosshairs on the monitor and the ship's port quarter erupted in a brilliant flash. The vessel heeled over amid a cloud of black smoke and red-hot flames. One less shipment of poison in the world.

She nodded slightly, acknowledging the deed to herself, and then began typing command strings into the interface keyboard. The image on the monitor showed the drone veering away from the sinking vessel, and then it went black.

A sharp knock on the control room door startled her.

She typed in two more lines of code and sent the command.

"Miss Edwards." It was Rifkin.

Rachel gave the control station one more look, checked the time on the display screen, and tucked Ely's 9mm under her belt behind her back. She rose and unlatched the door. Rifkin stood on the other side, fist ready to wrap again.

"Is the drone on its way to Manistique?" he said.

"It's reprogrammed," she replied.

He searched the control room. "Where's Teague?"

"He went to coordinate his security team. Apparently, Nystrom messed up. Now my dad and Kade are both loose on the ship, upsetting the balance of everything."

Rifkin huffed. "We have to get this under control, right now."

"Agreed." Rachel stepped from the control room.

"Your father and husband need to come to heel."

Rachel did not correct him on the 'husband' comment. She walked to the ladder near the radio room and climbed. Once through the overhead hatchway, she waited for Rifkin. "I can diffuse this," she said to him.

Rifkin climbed up to the deck. "How do you figure? Reprimand must be kept secret, but your father is determined to expose it. The irresistible force is clashing with the immovable object."

"Just tell Teague to order his men to stand down. Get everyone to put their guns away and take a breath, then I can talk to my father face-to-face. Give me five minutes to lay it out for him, I guarantee he won't be a problem anymore."

"You're very sure of yourself."

"I'm his only surviving daughter. He'll believe just about anything I tell him."

"And what are you going to tell him?"

"That he owes it to Leah to let our work continue. That hours before she died, she reached out to him and he wasn't there. That for her death to have any meaning, Reprimand must continue, and that I'll make damned sure it's done right."

"What about Mitchell? You've lost sway with him, haven't you?"

Rachel smiled. "Kade's the easy one. Don't worry about him."

Rifkin regarded her. "Do you always manipulate the men in your life like this?"

"You're confusing manipulation with motivation. I'm motivated."

"A rose is a rose."

She glared at him.

"If we permit your father and Mitchell to leave this ship, what guarantee can you possibly give us that they'll keep their mouths shut about Reprimand?"

"Tell them you'll kill me if they talk. That'll be the icing on the cake to keep them quiet."

Rifkin chuckled. "Don't think I haven't considered that already."

"I'm sure you have." She started up the stairs to the bridge. "I'm going to call them topside through 1MC. Contact Teague, tell him my plan."

"You seem to have forgotten that I'm the handler and you're the asset."

"No, I didn't." She stopped climbing and turned around. "I just thought you wanted to keep Reprimand alive as much as I do. Am I wrong?"

"Why do I suddenly feel like just another man in your life?"

"Don't feel that way, Gerald. You're not my type."

Rifkin's expression cooled. He studied her, but it felt more like judgment.

Rachel tensed. "If you have a problem with me or my intentions, then draw your weapon and shoot me, right here, right now." She felt the 9mm on the small of her back and wondered if she could draw it fast enough to defend herself if need be.

Rifkin put on a sarcastic smile. "There's one small problem with that, isn't there?"

Rachel returned the insincere gesture. "After I—manipulate my father and Kade, I want them ferried to shore in the Lakota. I'll give up the drone's access code then."

"We're on the same team," Rifkin said. "Why withhold the code at all?"

She turned her back on him. "Because, Agent Rifkin, I don't trust you."

FORTY-ONE

A caged light fixture near Kade's head shattered, cutting his cheek with errant shards of bulb. He flinched from the plume of glass and pivoted to return fire, but Ely pulled him through the bulkhead doorway for cover. "He's got the drop on you," Ely warned. "Use your head."

"That's Zeke. We don't like each other."

"Nobody on this ship likes you." Ely reached for the watertight door to slam it closed, but a volley of gunfire brushed him back.

"They're not too crazy about you either." Kade gestured down the length of the long compartment they were in toward a door on the other side. "I think that opens near the crew mess."

Ely wedged behind a bundle of conduit on the bulkhead. "Stay there and draw Zeke's fire."

Kade stood, incredulous. "You're using me as a decoy?"

Ely checked the Glock for firing. "Dive for cover behind that duct after he sees you."

Kade eyed the ductwork in question. Sheet metal. Great.

Zeke pounced through the doorway with a submachine gun in hand. Kade locked eyes with him. They both froze a suspended moment. Kade dove for the duct, hitting the deck plate awkward on his shoulder and rolling out as Zeke opened fire. A staccato blast reverberated in the compartment like an echo chamber. Ricochets pinged off steel. Kade thudded into the bulkhead. Gunfire roared for a mad second, and then fell silent. Zeke had remembered he had two targets to worry about. He scanned the compartment, looking for the other guy.

Ely had already drawn a bead and squeezed the Glock's trigger. He had aimed for Zeke's body mass but hit him square in the clavicle. Zeke's arm fell limp and he hollered in pain. The submachine gun dropped from his hands and dangled from the shoulder strap. Ely stepped away from the conduit bundle, took careful aim, and blasted a round into Zeke's leg. The security guard screamed and staggered in retreat through the bulkhead door he had charged through a moment before. Ely rushed over and slammed it closed, dogging it down with the screw.

Kade got back on his feet. His leg burned. A bullet had cut a three-inch tear in his khakis and shaved a couple ounces of flesh off his left thigh. He put all his weight on that leg. It held up. Nothing of import seemed to have been hit. Yeah, it hurt, but he could still walk, and run.

Ely stepped away from the door and noticed the blood on Kade's leg. "You're hit."

"Just a graze." Kade nodded at the duct. "My cover wasn't much cover."

"At least you don't have a hole in your head."

Kade clicked through radio channels, listening to the earpiece. He stopped on a frequency with chatter. Zeke was cursing and calling for help. Moss responded he was on the way. Cam acknowledged he was doubling back. "They're converging on us," Kade said.

"We don't have anything to jam the screw on this door. They can come right through."

"Come on." Kade ran the length of the passageway. The growl of a diesel engine shook through the inner bulkhead to his right, and the rumble of a paddlewheel driveshaft vibrated up through the plates under his feet. He and Ely reached the compartment's far side door and pushed through. Crew mess, just as he thought. A group of cast-aluminum picnic tables and a long stainless-steel counter filled the space. Kade pulled the door closed and dogged it tight. Ely grabbed a metal frame chair from behind the counter and wedged one of its legs between the spokes of the handwheel on the door's screw mechanism.

"That'll slow them down," Ely said.

"From that direction," Kade said. "There are other ways in here. We have to keep moving."

"I know." Ely glanced at Kade's leg wound. "Zeke was trying to kill you."

"Really? You picked up on that?"

"He shouldn't have been. He's under orders not to harm us."

Kade laughed. "Who ordered that?"

"Rachel."

Something in his answer sparked an ember of hope in Kade—but he quickly tamped it out. "Teague's men aren't too concerned with following that order. Guess Rachel's word doesn't carry any weight."

"Maybe not."

"What about your Coast Guard buddy? Did he get the message to send in the troops?"

"He got the message, but he may not know where to send them. We came under fire right when the line connected. It wasn't clear two-way communication."

"So, you don't know?"

"Walker's sharp. He'll know what to do with what little I was able to tell him."

"But you don't know. We may be running around buying time for help that isn't coming."

Ely hedged. "That's possible."

"To hell with it then. We need to change tactics."

"Change tactics?"

Kade paced in a circle. "We have to go on offense. They won't expect it. We fight our way to the engine room, take it over, and find a way to steer east and run aground. We can do it."

"That's insane. Charging through Teague's men to get to the engine room is suicide. And, if we did manage to take it, Teague has six ways from Sunday to take it back, and in every one of those scenarios, we end up dead."

"Teague's little army is too beat up and scattered to stop us."

"You don't know that any more than I know a tac team is on the way."

"Come on, Ely. You always wanted me to join the military. Now that I'm thinking like a soldier, you don't like it?"

"An hour ago, you were hunkered down under the flight deck."

"An hour ago, I didn't have Special Agent Edwards on my side."

"You and I are hardly a strike force."

"Listen, the cavalry isn't coming. Our fate is in our own hands. I say, we take it to them—and if we end up getting killed, at least it'll be facing these guys instead of running from them."

"Classic Kade Mitchell," Ely said. "Get into a tight spot and instead of keeping cool and finding the smart way out, you dream up a wild-assed, over-the-top, impossible plan to fix it."

"It's worked pretty well for me so far."

"Has it?" Ely said. "Did it work for you three years ago?"

"Helluva cheap shot, Ely."

"Is it working today? You're being chased by gunmen through the lower decks of a rogue CIA ship. Exactly how is all this working for you?"

Kade squared up to him. "Cody and Jesse got away, so yeah, it worked today. And in case you haven't noticed, you're stuck here with me. Guess your way sucks too."

"My way doesn't involve a suicide run."

"It's only suicide if you get—"

Movement across the room seized Kade's attention and he swung his pistol that way. Two men rushed in from the battery compartment. Teague and Cam. They had weapons drawn.

"Mitchell!" Teague shouted. "Stand down, now!"

Kade had no such intention. He opened fire. Teague and Cam scattered left and right, taking cover behind a bulkhead. Ely dropped to a crouch and upended the nearest table with a grunt as return fire sounded. He pulled the table over a foot, lining it up along Teague and Cam's line of sight. "Fall back," Ely said, pointing to a door in a rear bulkhead. "Through there."

Kade realized Ely had positioned the table to conceal a path of retreat. Clever, but he said, "I'm not running. The odds are even, and if we take out Teague, it's over."

"It won't be over. The CIA's running the show. Besides, I only have three rounds left."

A bullet punched into the cast-aluminum tabletop, nearly breaking through. Ely eyed the crack in the pock mark. "Our shield isn't going to last long. If they get any closer …"

Kade heard movement across the room. He reached around the table and fired a blind shot. The slide on his pistol locked open. Empty. He ejected the spent magazine and grabbed the last one from the gun belt. "Fine, Ely. You go first."

"I'll check if it's clear. Follow on my signal." Ely raced to the door and turned the screw.

"Kade!" Teague called out. "Rachel will be upset if you get yourself killed."

Kade slapped the clip into the pistol and worked the action. "Then stop shooting at me, asshole."

"Put your guns down, we'll do the same, and let's clear up this misunderstanding."

Ely cracked open the door but he did not signal it was clear.

Kade needed to stall. "Give me one reason to believe I won't get shot the moment I step out."

"Rachel wants you safely off this ship," Teague said.

"Why do you care what she wants? You're the boss."

"She's my partner. If she wants you unharmed, it's my duty to make certain you don't get hurt. Little things like that maintain good working relationships."

Kade cracked a smile. "She's the only one you've got who can fly that drone, isn't she?"

"Assumptions are dangerous things," Teague said.

Ely waved to Kade and then slipped through the open doorway.

"Just give me a minute to think about it," Kade said in response to Teague.

"You have thirty seconds."

Kade rushed to the open doorway. As soon as he stepped through, a hail of gunfire opened up behind him. He rolled for cover behind the bulkhead and got his bearings. He was outside. Exterior main deck, just aft of the starboard paddlewheel casing. Dusk. Dim light fixtures along the bulkhead lit the deck area. Ahead, Ely moved cautiously toward the upturned keel of a twenty-foot lifeboat on its rack. Kade reached out to pull the door closed, but a bullet ricocheted off the steel inches from his hand. The bullet was fired from aft. He dropped to a crouch and made for the whitewashed lifeboat hull. Ely had already claimed a spot there. "Can this wooden boat stop bullets?" Kade said.

"Maybe," Ely replied. "But if Teague comes up from behind it won't be any use."

"Right." Kade whirled about and aimed at the half-opened door he had used to escape the crew mess. Someone inside kicked it open. Kade fired two rounds to ward him back.

A volley of bullets splintered the bow of the lifeboat. "Mitchell, you are in a crossfire."

Kade recognized the slight Italian accent in the voice. "Hey, Salvio, you're still alive."

"Yes, and to my surprise, so are you."

"Crazy, right?"

Ely glanced at Kade. "Is that one of the guys you shot?"

"Maybe. He was the pilot of the plane I told you about." Kade called over the lifeboat. "Salvio, nothing personal about what happened earlier, but you were going after my friend."

"Yes, nothing personal. This is all business." Salvio's voice sounded closer.

"Okay," Kade said quietly to Ely. "What's the cool way out of this one, because my wild-assed plan is to jump up and start shooting?"

Ely set his jaw. "That might be our only play."

"Kade!" Teague shouted through the door. "Let's end this peacefully."

"You said something like that a couple minutes ago, right before you opened fire."

"You needed to understand the seriousness of the situation."

"The Coast Guard is on the way," Ely said. "Step back from this before it's too late."

"Nobody's coming, Edwards. If you want to leave this ship alive, you'll listen to me."

Kade and Ely considered their predicament. "Start talking," Kade said.

"Rachel is proposing a deal to allow you both to leave the ship unharmed, but you must come topside to discuss the details with her. I'll escort you there to insure your safe passage."

"You've been lying to me since we met," Kade said. "Why should I trust you now?"

"Don't trust me," Teague said. "Trust her."

Speakers under the flight deck clicked and Rachel's voice suddenly reverberated throughout the vessel. "Kade, Dad, it's time to end this. Put the guns away and let me help you."

Teague extended a hand through the doorway. He slowly stepped onto the deck with his arms at his side and his pistol in its holster. "Thirty years building a successful business empire has taught me to play straight in negotiations. This is a legitimate offer. You come topside with me now, and you're as good as free."

Kade scrutinized Teague in the light of the doorway. "What do you think, Ely?"

Ely thought on it a second or two. "My daughter would never lead me into a firing squad," he said. "I say, we take the deal."

FORTY-TWO

A westerly wind buffeted Rachel's hair as she watched the familiar collection of faces approach the island. Teague spearheaded the group, with Kade and Ely walking behind and Cam and Salvio bringing up the rear. Everyone had holstered their weapons, save for Cam, who apparently had a hard time with the trust thing. More likely, Teague had told him to make sure everyone else didn't have a problem with the trust thing.

On *Wolverine*'s bow, the Lakota sat on the flight deck with her rotors spinning at low idle. Overhead, Patrick kept an eye on things from the smokestack platform with an HK416 rifle in his hands. Rachel considered them both, and then checked the time on her cell phone.

Rifkin stood beside her, looking as anxious as she felt. "I didn't expect your father to go along with this deal. I don't know whether I should be pleased or concerned."

"Me neither," she said.

Rifkin left her side and met Teague halfway. "Congratulations, you got them both."

"Rachel is the one who convinced them to go along," Teague said. "It's ironic."

"Perhaps." Rifkin glanced at the island structure behind Rachel and lowered his voice. "I put Kendrick in the control room. Once we get the code, he'll confirm its authenticity."

"And then what?"

"That's not for you to worry about."

"Life is a chess game. If you expect to win, you have to plan your moves in advance."

Rifkin corner-eyed him. "Who said I'm not planning?"

Several feet behind them, Ely strained to listen. "I can't hear what they're saying."

"Me neither," Kade said. "We're going to have to wing it."

"That's not how I operate."

"It is tonight. Welcome to my world." Kade glanced behind them. "Salvio's got a bandage on his head. I must've nicked him when I took the plane down. No wonder he's pissed at me."

"You think so?"

Kade nodded to the Lakota. "Twenty bucks says that's our ride out of here."

"Most likely," Ely said. "But ride to where?"

"I don't know. How much do you trust your daughter?"

"Enough to get on board if she says so." Ely paused. "Can you fly that thing?"

"Nope."

Rachel walked past Teague and Rifkin and gave her father a hug. "That was crazy, running around below deck like that. You had me scared."

"You and me both," Ely said.

She turned to Kade and put her arms around him. "I'm sorry."

Kade gently pushed her away. "Am I supposed to just forget you sold me out to Teague?"

"You didn't give me a chance to explain."

"You had plenty of time to explain. You chose to lie to me instead."

"I didn't want anyone to get hurt."

"Throwing me under the bus is one thing, but you put Cody's life on the line."

"It wasn't like that." She looked away. "It's hard to explain. There's a lot going on."

"There is a lot going on," Rifkin said, stepping into the conversation. "And from a national security perspective, the fewer people who know about, it the better. Loose lips sink ships."

Ely did not smile at the quip. "I have a different take on all this."

"I'm aware of that, Agent Edwards, and so here we are with an offer you can't refuse."

Ely looked to Rachel. "Tell me the deal."

"You and Kade are free to leave on the chopper," she replied. "It will take you back to Fort Custer. The only condition is you have to keep quiet about Reprimand."

"I can't keep quiet about an illegal operation."

Rifkin huffed. "Determining Reprimand's legality is not your job."

"No, that was the job of the Oversight Committee, and they shut you down."

"Nor is it your job to interpret the balance of power between the branches of government."

"I sure as hell can interpret that you and Nystrom are disobeying orders."

"Agent Edwards, your only duty here is to maintain the secrecy of Reprimand, as you agreed to back in Grand Ledge. Are you telling me you're incapable of doing that?"

Ely did not reply.

"Accept the terms and get on the chopper," Rachel said. "I need you to leave now. You owe it to Leah to let me finish my work here."

"Leah is not part of this. She never has been."

"You're wrong. She's the only reason I'm here, the only reason I've done the things I did."

"They let you believe that, but they're manipulating you, using you to serve their agenda."

"Get on the chopper, Dad. Forget everything you've learned here. Don't talk about it, don't think about. Lock it away in your head, just like you did when Leah died."

Ely cringed as though she had just slapped him hard. "Is that what you think?"

"That's how I feel."

"It's not true. Leah's death destroyed me."

"Leave now," she said. "Accept the terms." The last vestige of daylight in the sky reflected a glassiness in her eyes. "If you're worried about me, don't."

"You're my little girl. How the hell do you expect me to not worry about you?"

She found a smile to reassure him. "I got this."

Ely stood silent and his shoulders slumped as if a weight had just settled on them.

Kade put a hand on his back. "There's nothing else we can do here, Ely. The cards didn't go our way. Poker run over. Time to fold."

"That doesn't sound like Kade Mitchell to me," Ely said.

"We lost the hand," Kade said quietly. "Doesn't mean we lost the game."

Teague shouted over the sound of the chopper's engine. "Do you accept the deal or not?"

"We will not ask again," Rifkin said.

Ely regarded them. "What's the alternative? We go back to shooting at each other?"

"Most likely," Rifkin said, "and you know how that ends."

"Well then, like you said, it's an offer we can't refuse."

Ely and Kade started walking toward the Lakota.

"Any wild-assed ideas?" Ely said.

"None worth mentioning."

"Gentlemen," Rifkin called after them, "if you decide to renege on our agreement, and you start talking, we will hear about it, so I suggest you keep this in mind. Actions have consequences."

Ely looked back at him. "Meaning what?"

Rifkin smiled. "Meaning, you hurt us, we hurt you."

Ely thought on that, and then continued toward the helicopter. He and Kade ducked under the rotors and silently climbed into the passenger cabin. Before they could slide the door closed, Rachel ran up to them. "Everything that's happened between us," she said to Kade, "it wasn't your fault. You need to know that."

Kade jaw fell open. "What?"

She took hold of the door handle and faced Ely. "Dad, you were right about Teague."

She heaved the door closed and latched it tight, and then slapped the cockpit window to signal the pilot to take off. She hurried away from the chopper, taking a position between Teague and Rifkin. The Lakota's engine wound up and the weight of the aircraft shifted, lifting the landing skids off the flight deck.

"Give us the access code now, Miss Edwards," Rifkin said.

"They're not safely to shore yet."

"That wasn't the agreement. You said once they were airborne you would surrender the code. They're airborne."

"You know that's not what I meant."

Rifkin nodded to Teague.

Teague spoke into the mic of a radio headset he had put on. "Patrick, target the chopper."

On the smokestack platform, Patrick lifted the rifle and aimed at the Lakota's engine panel below the rotor driveshaft. The chopper was still very close, well within range of the weapon.

Rachel panicked. "You son-of-a-bitch."

"Fifteen seconds and he fires," Rifkin said calmly.

Rachel calculated distances, and vectors, and velocities in her head. There might not be enough time. "Access code," she said, "Roger-Echo-Two-Two-Niner-Four-Zero."

"Kendrick," Teague said, "access code: Roger-Echo-Two-Two-Niner-Four-Zero. Confirm."

Rachel stepped away and reached for Ely's 9mm on her back. Teague had his attention on the radio earpiece and did not notice. Nor did Rifkin, who intently watched for Teague's reaction to Kendrick's imminent report. Cam and Salvio seemed unsure what was going down, and split their attention between the chopper, and Patrick, and the group on the flight deck.

Rachel took the pistol grip into her palm and slid it from her belt.

Teague put a hand to his ear to block out the noise. He listened and his expression grew cold and angry. "It didn't work," he said. "That's not the code." He glared at Rachel. Their eyes locked. Teague keyed the transmit button. "Fire on the chopper."

Rachel lifted the 9mm and targeted Patrick. Twenty meters. Short range. She pumped two rounds into his chest. He recoiled backward, falling from the stool. The HK416 belched a wild barrage of fire as it slipped from his hands and tumbled over the handrail.

Rachel leveled her aim at Teague. He had a hand on his pistol and was drawing it from its holster. She fired without hesitation. Two rounds. Hurried and off the mark. The seam over the ball of his shoulder ripped open. He flinched, roared, and returned fire. Wide right.

She sidestepped, kept her arms extended, widened her stance, counted targets. Teague. Cam. Salvio. Where was Rifkin?

Three blasts flashed on her left flank. She pivoted on her heel. Rifkin stood at point blank range, firing rounds at her. She felt a sting over her heart. There had to be a hole through her chest. How long before her body told her mind that she was dead? Make these seconds count. She squeezed the trigger again and again, blasting Rifkin in the chest and knocking him to the deck. She pivoted back, glancing at how bad she had been hit. No blood. Astonished.

Teague watched Rifkin fall, circled right. Fired again. Off target.

Ten yards, twenty degrees, Cam drew a bead on her. Rachel shifted her aim to him.

And then Salvio lunged, trying to knock Cam's arms down. "No!"

Both weapons discharged at once. Cam flinched as a bullet grazed his temple. Rachel felt a fire explode in her abdomen. White-hot pain brought her to her knee. Someone advanced in her periphery. She gasped for air and swung the 9mm around. Teague seized her arm and wrenched the weapon from her fingers. She lashed out with her free hand, trying to gouge his eyes. Her nails ripped strips of skin from his cheek instead. He pistol-whipped her with the 9mm, cracking her jaw and dropping her onto her back. He aimed the gun at her head. "What the hell are you doing? What happened to the mission?"

Rachel seethed. "I'm *on* the mission!"

"I defended you. I took your side."

"You're one of them!" she shouted. "You're a goddamned dealer!"

Teague stared in disbelief, like she had snatched the answer to a million-dollar question from thin air. Anger flooded back. "Give me the code or your father and Kade are as good as dead."

She tried to sit up, but the weight of her wounds kept her down. "Not yet ... Galen," she gasped. "There's one, last, beta ... to hit."

He looked at her funny. "What do you mean?"

"It's coming ... for *Wolverine*." She smiled at him. "Equal measure."

Gears ground behind Teague's eyes. It finally clicked and he understood. "No."

"Galen!" Salvio shouted. "Galen, the chopper!"

* * *

The Lakota's door slammed shut and the pilot throttled up for takeoff.

Ely slapped Kade's arm. "She knows."

"She knows what?"

"She knows Teague is a drug trafficker."

Kade balked. "A what? Wait, she'd never work with him if that was true."

"She just found out. They've been hiding it from her."

"What tipped her off?"

"I did."

Kade replayed Rachel's good-bye in his head. "Did you hear what she said to me? That's the kind of thing you say when you're tying up loose ends in your life."

"She wanted us off that ship in a big hurry." Ely pressed close to the rear cabin window. "She's got something planned."

"Like what?" Kade peered down through an adjacent window.

The Lakota had climbed nearly eight hundred feet, still close enough to identify people on *Wolverine's* flight deck, but far enough away to hide the details of what they were doing.

"Why are they still watching us fly away?" Kade said.

Ely strained to read the situation, saw Rachel step away from the group. The guy in the sniper's nest seemed to be focused on the chopper. And then Rachel shifted into a firing stance. "Oh, my God. Rachel, don't!"

Tracer rounds flew up in a chaotic spray from the smokestack platform, filling the air around the Lakota. "Incoming fire," Ely shouted to the pilot. "Evasive!"

Corporal Gaines throttled up and banked the Lakota hard to starboard.

Kade lost his balance and slid from the window. "They're shooting down there."

"I know," Ely said. "And Rachel's in the middle of it. We have to go back."

"Damned right we have to go back. Now."

Ely fought the roll of the chopper and scrambled forward to the cockpit. "Corporal Gaines, turn around and put us back on that flight deck."

"Can't do that, sir. My orders are to take you to Fort Custer."

"The people who gave you those orders are the ones shooting at us."

"Honestly, sir, I don't know who's shooting at us."

Ely pulled out his creds. "On the authority of the Department of Homeland Security, I order you to turn this aircraft around and land us on that carrier."

"I'm with the National Guard, sir. The DHS does not have authority over our operations."

"Screw authority," Kade said. "People down there are trying to kill us, and they don't give two shits about making you collateral damage. Are you okay with that, Corporal?"

Gaines leveled the helicopter and adjusted course toward the Michigan shoreline.

"My daughter's on board that ship," Ely said. "She's in serious trouble."

Gaines did not reply. He scanned an overhead panel, flicked a couple switches.

"If it was your daughter down there, what would you do?"

Gaines cocked his head to the side and paused, as if in thought. "Understood," he finally said. He put his eyes forward and tightened his grip on the flight stick. "Hang on, sir."

* * *

Teague trained his Glock on Rachel and contemplated the drone closing in on *Wolverine*'s position, trying to conceive a means to get the access code out of her.

"Galen, the chopper!"

Salvio's warning shook him from his thoughts. He searched the sky where he had last seen the helicopter. Not there. It took him two seconds to find it.

The Lakota screamed in from astern, buzzing the carrier at full throttle. Her skids skimmed the flight deck. Salvio dove to get clear. Cam planted himself, blasting rounds from his .40 at the cockpit window. The glass left of center cobwebbed. The chopper kept coming. Cam spun right. The Lakota's port skid struck his chest, cracking three ribs and knocking him ten feet from the point of impact. Teague pulled his Glock away from Rachel and targeted the renegade chopper. He squeezed off two shots before running for safety and dropping to his stomach. Cool deck planks pressed against his cheek as the belly of the aircraft rocketed over his head.

The Lakota zoomed past the island, spun counterclockwise, and lifted into the air. Her forward momentum dropped to zero and she drifted back down, gliding toward the section of deck where Rachel lay wounded.

Flat on his back, Rifkin twitched and breathed in a sharp, short breath. He felt around his chest for an entry wound. Nothing but painful bruises and perhaps a cracked rib. He rolled to his side, and a 9mm slug fell from the weave of his Kevlar vest. He found his pistol lying near his feet and wondered how he had missed Rachel at such a close range. A windstorm from the helicopter blades washed over him. Agent Edwards was returning. Good. One more opportunity to keep him quiet. The HK416 that Patrick had dropped from the smokestack platform lie within reach. Rifkin picked it up and struggled to a knee. He aimed at the Lakota and laid on the trigger, pouring a stream of fire into the engine panel below the rotors until the tracer rounds stopped and the weapon fell silent.

Indicators across the Lakota's instrument panel lit up. "Port engine's hit," Corporal Gaines called out. "It's dead."

The helicopter shuddered and swayed, dropping the last ten feet to the flight deck with a thud, but Gaines had done it. He had managed to put the chopper down between the hostiles and the wounded woman.

"Can we take off on one engine?" Ely said.

"In theory," Gaines replied. "Depends on how heavy we are."

Kade drew the Smith & Wesson. "Come on, Ely, let's go."

Ely joined him near the cabin door. "I'll get Rachel. You cover."

Kade threw open the door and they scrambled out of the cabin. Rachel lay ten yards away. Ely made a beeline for her. Kade tracked with him, staying in the shadow of the Lakota, watching for anyone who might try to rush around the perimeter.

Ely knelt beside Rachel. She had taken a bullet in the abdomen. A pool of blood spread beneath her. "Rachel, I've got to get you out of here."

She focused on her father's face. "You shouldn't have come back ... you have to go."

"I'm going, but I'm taking you with me." He slid his arms under her neck and the crook of her legs. "Ready?"

"No time," she said as Ely lifted her up. She winced in pain but did not cry out. "Drone is coming ... to hit *Wolverine*."

"Oh, no, Rachel. You should have told me." Ely headed for the chopper with his bleeding daughter draped in his arms.

Rifkin appeared near the tail rotor. Kade shifted his stance. Fired. Rifkin crouched and answered with two blasts, and then cursed and disappeared behind the chopper. Movement to the right. Teague rounded the Lakota's nose. Kade swung his arms clockwise, fired before squaring up his aim. Teague recoiled at the incoming rounds, returned fire as he fell back.

Ely reached the chopper with Rachel heavy in his arms. "Kade, we have to get out of here."

"No shit, Sherlock." Kade rushed for the cabin door, checking nose and tail for another blitz.

"Rachel programmed the drone to attack *Wolverine*," Ely said. "It's almost here."

Kade helped lift her into the cabin. "Great idea, sweetheart. What was your escape plan?"

She gave him a grim smile. "Didn't have one."

Near the island, Rifkin ejected the magazine from his Glock. Something was wrong. He wasn't hitting his targets. He checked the remaining rounds. No bullets in the shell casings. *Damn you, Edwards.* He threw the magazine down and grabbed his reserve from his pocket and slapped it in. Behind him, Salvio picked up the empty HK416.

Ely set Rachel down on the cabin floor. "Go, Corporal! Go!"

Gaines throttled up and the Lakota's engine screamed. The chopper lifted, barely coming off the runway. Kade went to the port window and saw Rifkin rush forward into the rotor wash and take careful aim at Corporal Gaines through the cockpit window. But Salvio raced up from behind with the HK416 raised like a club and struck Rifkin in the head with the stock.

Kade watched, wide-eyed, as Rifkin fell. Salvio saw Kade in the window and shouted something. Kade read his lips. *Save her.*

"I don't believe it. Salvio just took out Rifkin."

Ely already had the chopper's trauma kit open, pulling out field dressings and pain meds to treat his daughter. "He must like you more than you thought."

"It's not me he likes."

On deck, Teague shouted at Salvio and then aimed at the Lakota's cockpit window. The chopper continued her slow climb. Teague opened fire. Gaines winced as a bullet pierced the glass, cracking his flight helmet. He shifted the stick and spun the cockpit out of the line of fire. The Lakota crossed over the edge of the flight deck.

A bright shooting star suddenly arced down from the eastern sky. It came in fast, on a precision course, and struck *Wolverine* just aft of her port paddlewheel. Kade barely had time to process what is was before an explosion ripped into the ship's hull and shattered the wheel into fiery quarters, breaking it off the driveshaft. The blast expanded and flickered. Burned a furious moment. Receded. Quiet. Black smoke poured from a dark hull rupture and rose into the carrier's deck lights. Then a secondary explosion blew amidships, vomiting fire and a concussive blast that rippled across the fringe of the flight deck like a wave. Wood and shrapnel spiraled into the air, bombarding the Lakota with a wicked hail.

Gaines fought for control of the chopper as she surged atop the shockwave. He tried to climb above it. Ely and Kade clung to whatever they could find in the cabin, keeping Rachel secure as best they could.

The Lakota pitched. The engine whined. The flight path smoothed. Gaines had reined her in.

Kade pulled up to a window. "The fuel tanks must have blown."

Rachel laughed darkly. "I knew right where ... to hit her."

"Massive hull breach," Ely said. "I give her ten minutes. Nice shooting, baby."

Kade knelt beside Rachel. "You don't do anything halfway, do you?"

"You know I don't."

The Lakota shuddered and a loud bang sounded. The whine of the engine disappeared, taking with it the vibration that normally pulsed through the airframe during powered flight. Silence replaced it. Kade and Ely exchanged a glance in a moment of suspension.

"Shrapnel took out number two," Gaines called back to them. "We're going down."

"We didn't get very far," Kade said.

"No," Ely replied. "This could be a short drop and a quick stop."

The helicopter yawed right. Gaines grabbed the trust lever at his side and lowered the collective pitch, and then adjusted the trim to stay level, working the aircraft into autorotation to cushion the landing. He called a mayday through the boom mic in his flight helmet.

"Life vests," Ely said, pulling one down from a hook. "Once we hit the water we're going under fast."

Kade lifted Rachel to a seated position. Ely threaded her arms through the vest and buckled her in. Kade found two more vests and tossed one to Ely. They put them on and braced themselves on either side of Rachel to shield her from impact. Her calm, unconcerned expression belied the situation they were in, like she didn't know or didn't care what was happening. Kade thought about the black-and-white photograph of her standing beside the Otter so long ago. Happier times. He made eye contact with her. "I always loved you, Rach."

Her lips curved into a little smile. "I hate ... when you call me that."

Kade's stomach dropped as the Lakota fell.

"Hold on." Gaines flared the nose of the chopper.

Kade's pilot mind kicked into gear to decipher the maneuver. Flaring the nose would cut air speed, put the chopper into a vertical drop, and reduce the chance of an end-over-end crash. *Thank God this guy knows what he's doing.*

It almost worked. The Lakota splashed down, but she still carried a hint of forward momentum. The port skid dug into the lake and water seized the aircraft, kicking her up on her nose. The main rotors thrashed into the waves, tearing apart the drive assembly. Inertia tore Kade from his handhold and threw him into the bulkhead. His head struck hard and he blacked out.

"Kade, come on!"

Kade opened his eyes to cold water hitting his face. He startled up from the cabin floor and climbed to a passenger seat. Lake Michigan pooled around his feet. He figured he'd been out only a few seconds, long enough for the helicopter to settle down and begin to sink. Ely stood in the cabin doorway, holding Rachel up under her arm, prodding Kade to consciousness. In the cockpit, Gaines struggled out of the pilot's seat.

Warm and wet, a trickle of liquid touched Kade's lips, and his tongue tasted iron. Blood. He traced the source with his fingers up to a gash in his forehead. It burned at his touch and throbbed with his heartbeat.

"Kade, you're hurt," Ely said. "Can you get up?"

Kade nodded. "Yeah. How'd Rachel do?"

"No worse than before the crash."

Gaines took hold of Kade's arm. "We have to get out of the aircraft, sir."

Kade stood. Water came up to his knees. "Good landing, Corporal."

Ely stepped through the cabin doorway and pushed off into the lake with Rachel at his side, their life vests bobbing them atop the waves. He paddled away from the sinking hulk. Kade and Gaines waded through the doorway after them.

A flourish of dizziness passed through Kade as he swam and his head throbbed, but he fought through it, kept pushing. The cool water kept his senses on edge. He glanced over his shoulder. The Lakota's tail rotor was all that remained above water, and as he watched, that too slipped below the percolating waves.

A half mile off, *Wolverine* burned and listed in her death throws. Kade could make out people moving across her angled flight deck, dodging flames to get lifeboats and rafts into the water. Shouts and calls carried across the distance as eerie whispers of chaos.

A buzzing noise grew from the darkness above. An engine. Kade had heard it before. He craned his neck and searched the sky. The sound of the engine grew louder and passed overhead at perhaps two hundred feet. Pale light from a crescent moon illuminated a thin layer of cloud and revealed the silhouette of the drone on its final flight. It crossed the cloud and disappeared into the darkness again, its engine noise fading. A moment later, *Wolverine's* island structure lit up with a small, fiery explosion as the drone smashed into the bridge, its fuselage collapsing and its wings breaking apart, falling to the flight deck in a heap of debris. The sound of the crash followed, delayed by the distance.

Kade watched the scene, transfixed.

"I hear a chopper," Ely called out. "It's got to be the HITRON team."

"Your buddy must've gotten the message."

Floating nearby, Gaines lifted a pistol into the air and fired. A red flare arced into the sky. The sound of the helicopter drew closer and a searchlight blinked on and scanned the water several hundred yards away.

Rachel's head dipped, and Ely shook her, tried to keep her awake. "Come on, baby. Help is here. Hold on a little longer." He shouted to Gaines. "Corporal, you got your C-SEL on you?"

"Yes, sir."

"Then what are you waiting for? Get it out and contact that Coast Guard chopper. Tell 'em Agent Edwards doesn't need tactical support anymore, he needs a sea rescue. Guide 'em to us with the GPS in that thing."

Kade swam over. "Rachel, you're a Navy Second Class Swimmer. This should be a cakewalk for you."

She lifted her head and narrowed her eyes at him. "I wasn't shot … when I took that test."

Kade smiled. "Hold on to that attitude."

She gazed at the fire consuming *Wolverine's* flight deck in the distance. "It wasn't enough," she said quietly. "I still feel … empty."

Ely found her hand in the water and squeezed it. "Sinking those ships wasn't ever going to make you whole again."

"No," she said, looking back to her father, "but hurting them felt good."

"An eye for an eye only makes the world blind. You need time to do the healing."

The helicopter glided in low and shined its searchlight on them. Ely had guessed right. It was the HITRON chopper from *Defiant*, and the team on board switched their mission from assault to rescue. The side door opened and a rescue swimmer lowered down on a cable to pluck the crash survivors from the lake. He zeroed in on Rachel first. Ely watched the wench line lift her out of the water. "I need to send Choi my personal thanks for this," he said to Kade.

The air crew pulled Rachel into the chopper and sent the line down again. Seeing the gash on Kade's head, the rescue swimmer went to hook him into the harness.

"Hold up," Kade said. "Take Ely first. He needs to be with his daughter."

"You're injured," Ely said. "You go next."

Kade refused.

Ely relented. "Stubborn jackass." He buckled in and started up the line with the swimmer.

As the line came down the third time, Kade saw another silhouette appear against the moonlit cloud. He recognized the shape in an instant. A high-winged, twin-engine airplane with amphibious floats beneath her fuselage. She glided in a graceful banking maneuver. Kade laughed aloud. It was the Otter. Cody had come back for him.

The Coast Guard swimmer arrived on the line and began to hook Kade up a second time.

"Never mind," Kade said.

Corporal Gaines swam over to him. "I won't go until you do."

"I'm not leaving on the chopper."

The swimmer was miffed. "We've got room for four more. We can take you all."

"Go get *Wolverine* crewmen," Kade said. "They weren't all bad guys on board that ship."

"You can't turn down this ride," Gaines said. "What are you going to do, swim home?"

"No. I'm going home on the Otter."

Fifty yards out, the airplane set down on the lake and drifted in on her floats. Her engines throttled down as she approached the rescue site, and a light burst from her passenger cabin when Cody kicked open the hatch. He swept a handheld searchlight across the water. "Anyone out there need help?"

"Cody!" Kade shouted. "Over here." He swam toward the plane.

Cody smiled wide when he recognized his friend. "Kade!" He helped him into the plane.

Kade dropped to his knees and unbuckled the life vest as water drained from his body.

"What happened?" Cody said. "The ship is on fire. It's sinking."

"I'll tell you over a couple of beers." Kade stood and shook himself off. "You understood my message."

"I knew what you were saying." Cody scratched his razor stubble. "I just didn't know why you were saying it."

"Wait for those beers. It's a wild story." Kade felt the cut on his forehead throb. "How's Jesse doing?"

"I think he's going to be okay. I radioed ahead to the airport for paramedics to meet us when we landed at Sparta. They took him to the hospital right away."

"Hey," Kade said a bit puzzled. "What's the story with the floats?"

"You didn't think I was going to try to stick a landing on that carrier, did you?"

"No. But how did you get them installed and turn the Otter around so fast?"

"I had help." Cody gestured up through the plane to the cockpit.

Danny peered into the cabin from the copilot's seat. She climbed out and met Kade in the aisle. He hugged her and she squeezed him tight. She checked out the gash in his forehead. "That looks nasty. I'll bet it hurts."

"Lots."

"Is Ely okay?"

Kade nodded. "Yeah, he's on that Coast Guard chopper out there." He added, "I hear you put him onto Nystrom and Rifkin's trail, and that led him to *Wolverine*. I owe you one."

Danny shook her head. "What about Rachel?"

"She's hurt," Kade said. "Pretty bad."

"Will she be okay?"

"I don't know."

Danny stayed quiet a long while. "Did you find what you were looking for on that ship?"

"No," Kade said. "I found something else, something I didn't expect to find."

She fixed him with a probing stare. "What does that mean?"

He smiled. "That I should have been focusing on what I had, not on what I thought I'd lost."

Cody buttoned up the cabin hatch. "Time to head back, right?"

"Let's see if the Guard could use any help," Kade said.

"Okay, but isn't that what got us into trouble in the first place?"

"That first time I didn't know what I was getting into." Kade grinned. "This time, at least I know I'm getting out."

FORTY-THREE

Washington, D.C., Three weeks later

Kade pushed through the hearing room doors and stormed into the hallway. Getting out of there felt like coming to the surface after a long swim underwater. He pulled loose the knot in his tie and opened the top button of his shirt. He could breathe again.

Ely waited for him on the hallway's polished marble tile. "How did it go?"

"Five hours," Kade said. "Those idiots grilled me for five hours."

"Consider yourself lucky. Yesterday they kept me in there for eight."

"Judging by their questions, half those guys think this fiasco was *my* fault."

"That's politics, Kade. The senators are trying to cover their asses after a covert operation they approved blew up in their faces."

"They're pissed it went public. Senator Crouse actually calculated how many hours cable news has devoted to the Reprimand story since *Wolverine* went down, and lectured me on the damaging effect it could have on national security, not to mention their credibility."

"We did what we had to do," Ely said. "They would have swept everything under the rug if we hadn't gone to the press. Now it's all under the microscope—the CIA, the Anti-Terrorist Committee, even the President's executive order."

Kade studied the polished tile. "They may have turned up the heat on me in there, but I got a feeling they're really going to come down hard on Rachel."

"That's the impression I got too." Ely nodded down the hallway and they started walking. "Teague got released last week from the hospital into federal custody, but he lawyered up like O.J. Simpson and was sleeping at home in his gated-community mansion that night."

"That's bullshit, Ely. He going to get away clean."

"No, he isn't. A friend in the Justice Department tells me they're going to charge him with trafficking, conspiracy, assault, attempted murder, and a bunch of other things."

"Guilty on all counts."

"It's not a slam dunk. Teague's going to play the victim card. His lawyers will argue that the government entrapped him, forced him to do everything he did."

"If his dream team selects the right jurors, that argument might work." Kade shook his head. "Money may not buy happiness, but it can buy a not-guilty verdict."

"This might sound naïve to you, but I still have faith in the justice system."

"What about Nystrom and Rifkin?"

Ely pursed his lips and thought a moment. "They're going to nail Rifkin, or whatever his real name is, with abuse of power, sedition, and a dozen other felonies."

"And Nystrom?"

"Nystrom's gone."

Kade gave Ely a sideways glance. "Gone how? Gone dead?"

"Gone, gone," Ely said. "He wasn't rescued off *Wolverine* that night, and when divers went down on the wreck, they didn't recover his body. At least, that's the way the official report reads."

"You mean to tell me he might have slipped away from all this?"

"He's a spook. I wouldn't be surprised." Ely's phone chimed with a text notification. He read the message. "Walker says all the news feeds at MIOC are going crazy. They're reporting that Warren Lindsey just resigned as Director of the CIA."

"There's blood in the water." Kade said. "The sharks are going to devour as many people as they can for Reprimand, and Rachel's in the middle of it all."

"I'm afraid so," Ely said.

"She doesn't stand much of a chance, does she?"

Ely did not reply. He walked in silence a moment, and then said, "I'm resigning from Homeland Security, taking early retirement. I'm going to help Rachel with her defense. That's my job from this day forward."

Kade regarded him. "She has one hell of a fight ahead of her. She'll be the first to admit she knowingly acted outside mission parameters to sink those other ships, and she won't be shy to tell a jury she did it to avenge Leah's death."

"I know. She's not going to make this easy."

"She never does."

Ely dropped his phone in his jacket pocket. "I've still got Navy connections, and I hooked up with a former JAG lawyer who does private practice now. We met last week. He has an excellent trial record. I like him."

"If anyone can claim an entrapment defense, it's Rachel."

"That's what I'm hoping."

They continued walking.

"We've had a checkered past," Kade said. "You and I. We never saw eye-to-eye on anything, but after what we just went through, I think I'm ready to put that all behind us."

Ely cast his gaze forward, as if seated in a confessional. "I didn't make it easy on you, Kade. I wanted Rachel to end up with someone more respectable, a naval officer on the rise or something. You know, someone more like me." He chuckled. "But I always knew you loved her." He let his smile fade. "Guess that says a lot about me, doesn't it?"

"It says you love your daughter and wanted what's best for her." Kade looked down the hallway to avoid eye contact with Ely. The next thing he had to say was difficult. He remembered Danny's comment about avoiding hard issues. He faced Ely again. "Like I said, I'll help how I can. If you need me to fly your JAG buddy in from Virginia or wherever, just tell me, but I can't dive in. I have to step away from this. I know Leah's death messed with Rachel's head like crazy, but I just can't get past what happened on that ship." He paused. "What does that say about me?"

Ely gave him a resigned smile. "It says you're not a blind fool."

"I still feel responsible for not being there when it could have made a difference. I was too busy fixing chipped china with a bulldozer to work on what was right in front of me."

"Kade, listen. I feel the weight of this too, but Rachel chose this path. She knows that. She's surprised we even came back for her. I appreciate what you're feeling, but I don't expect you to throw away every good thing you've got going now."

"What do you mean?"

"I mean Danny. She's a good woman, and all she cared about through this whole mess was getting you back safely. You can't let that go."

"I know."

"Rachel's facing the possibility of prison for the next thirty years. She's got the battle of her life in front of her, but she's got to climb just one mountain at a time. I'm actually glad you're telling me you have to step away. It'll help get her head focused."

Kade gave him a half smile. "Yeah, I've got a good track record for screwing up people's minds, including my own."

Ely actually chuckled. "It's time to work your magic somewhere else."

"I guess I'm going to find out if Danny can handle me."

"I'm not too concerned about her," Ely said. "I think you're the one who's going to have to keep on his toes."

Kade nodded. "I think you're right."

Other books by J Ryan Fenzel

DESCENDING FROM DUTY

INHERIT ALL THINGS

ALLIED IN IRONS

For more information on *Equal Measure* and J Ryan Fenzel, visit the author's website at www.jryanfenzel.com.

ACKNOWLEDGEMENTS

Writing *Equal Measure* was a challenge on just about every front you could imagine. As such, I received a lot of assistance and support from a lot of people to help me tell the story of pilot Kade Mitchell and the reincarnated USS *Wolverine*. First and foremost, I owe thanks to my lovely wife Melynda, and wonderful daughters Marisa and Keira, for again putting up with me during the research and writing of this book. Breathing life into a novel is a time consuming task, sometimes all consuming, and I appreciate their support through the whole process. I would not have gotten through it if not for them.

Thanks also to Joe Fortman and Jim Norton for sharing their piloting knowledge when I came to them with questions. I worked with Joe a long time before I learned he was a pilot, so it was a pleasure to discuss the critical factors involved in landing a GA aircraft on the deck of a carrier when we probably should have been working on something else. I met Jim after he read my novel *Descending From Duty*, and he introduced himself at an event at the USS Silversides Museum in Muskegon, MI. Jim gave me invaluable insight into basic piloting knowledge from a "been there, done that" perspective, which helped inform writing my protagonist. So, whenever Kade is in the pilot's seat and he does things right, it's due to Joe and Jim. If technical errors exist in the story, however, the fault rests with me.

Once again I thank my friend and brother-in-law Tim Lee for being my law enforcement advisor, often at a moment's notice. Tim's many years with the Michigan State Police and his tenure at MIOC have made him my go-to guy for procedure and protocol questions. As with the piloting scenes, any law enforcement inaccuracies that may have slipped into the story are the fault of me and my poetic license.

Thanks also to Valerie Van Heest, shipwreck hunter extrodinare and determined pursuer of the wreckage of Flight 2501. I met Valerie after writing *Allied In Irons* and we became good friends. She has a great critical eye for all things nautical, and the comments and suggestions she provided for the *Equal Measure* manuscript are greatly appreciated.

Last but not least, thanks to life-long friend Brian Shureb for always being the one who I incessantly pepper with questions regarding story and character while I'm piecing together a new novel. His unique perspective on, well, everything really helps me through the rough spots in my writing process. I truly take his comments to heart. Thanks for hanging with me all these years, Brian.